P9-DMW-395

the Glass Sentence

the Glass Sentence

MAPMAKERS

BOOK ONE

S. E. Grove

VIKING
An imprint of Penguin Group (USA)

VIKING
Published by the Penguin Group
Penguin Group (USA) LLC
375 Hudson Street
New York, New York 10014

USA / Canada / UK / Ireland / Australia / New Zealand / India / South Africa / China

penguin.com
A Penguin Random House Company

First published in the United States of America by Viking,
an imprint of Penguin Young Readers Group, 2014

LIBRARY OF CONGRESS CATALOGING-IN-PUBLICATION DATA
Grove, S. E.
The glass sentence / S. E. Grove.
pages cm. — (Mapmakers ; book 1)
Summary: In 1891, in a world transformed by 1799's Great Disruption—when all of the continents were flung into different time periods—thirteen-year-old Sophia Tims and her friend Theo go in search of Sophia's uncle, Shadrack Elli, Boston's foremost cartologer, who has been kidnapped.
ISBN 978-0-670-78502-5 (hardcover)
[1. Fantasy. 2. Maps—Fiction. 3. Kidnapping—Fiction.] I. Title.
PZ7.G9273Gl 2014
[Fic] —dc23
2013025832

Printed in USA

1 3 5 7 9 10 8 6 4 2

For my parents and my brother

There can be no scholar without the heroic mind. The preamble of thought, the transition through which it passes from the unconscious to the conscious, is action. Only so much do I know, as I have lived. Instantly we know whose words are loaded with life, and whose not.

The world,—this shadow of the soul, or *other me*—lies wide around. Its attractions are the keys which unlock my thoughts and make me acquainted with myself. I run eagerly into this resounding tumult.

—Ralph Waldo Emerson, "The American Scholar," 1837

Contents

Unknown
Unknown
Prehistoric Snows
Papal States
New Occident
The Baldlands
Early Pharaoh
United Indies
Late Patagonia
MAP of the NEW
Unknown

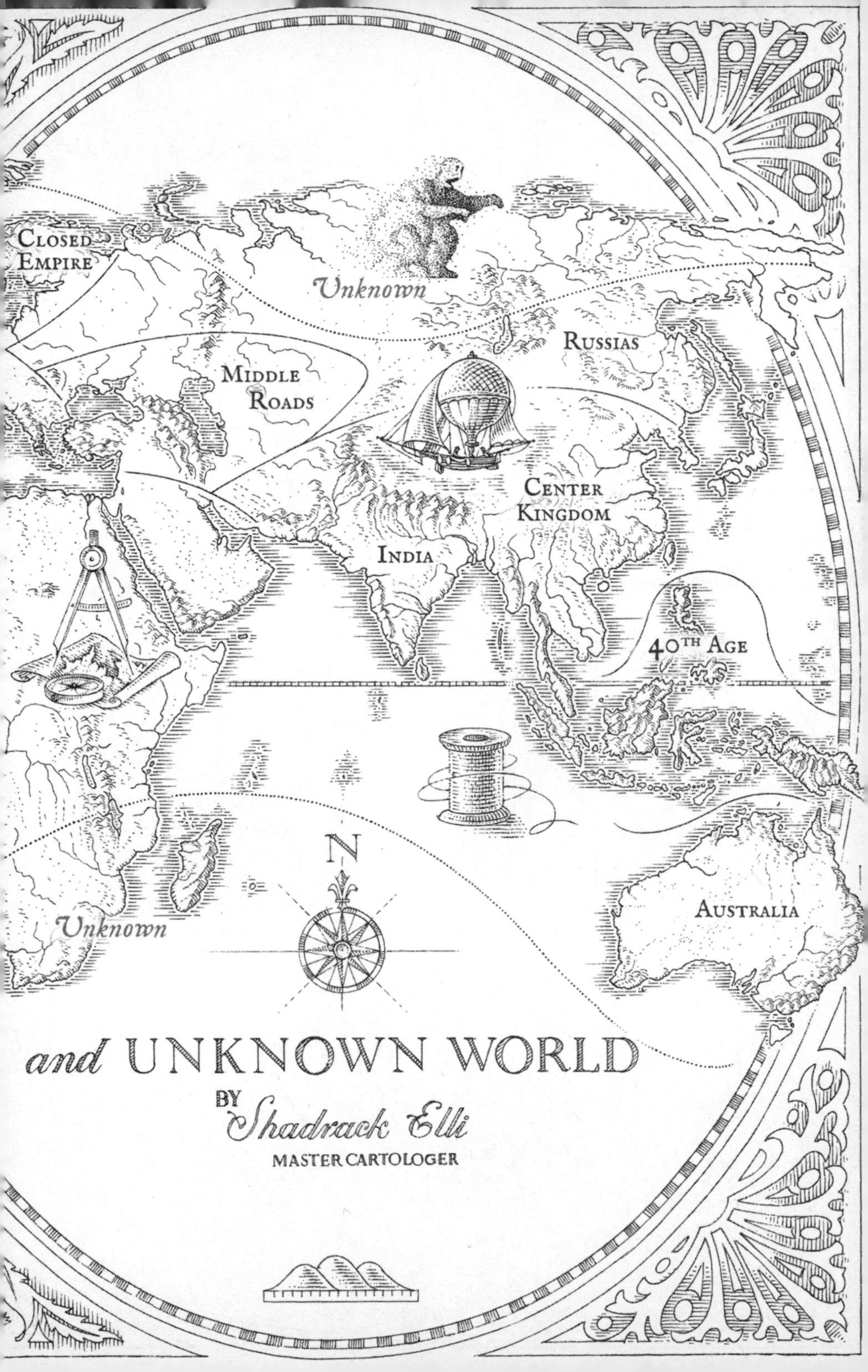

Closed Empire
Unknown
Russias
Middle Roads
Center Kingdom
India
40th Age
Australia
N
Unknown
and UNKNOWN WORLD
BY
Shadrack Elli
MASTER CARTOLOGER

Indian Territories

The Baldlands

N

e

BY Shadrack Elli

MASTER CARTOLOGER

and ITS ADJOINING AGES

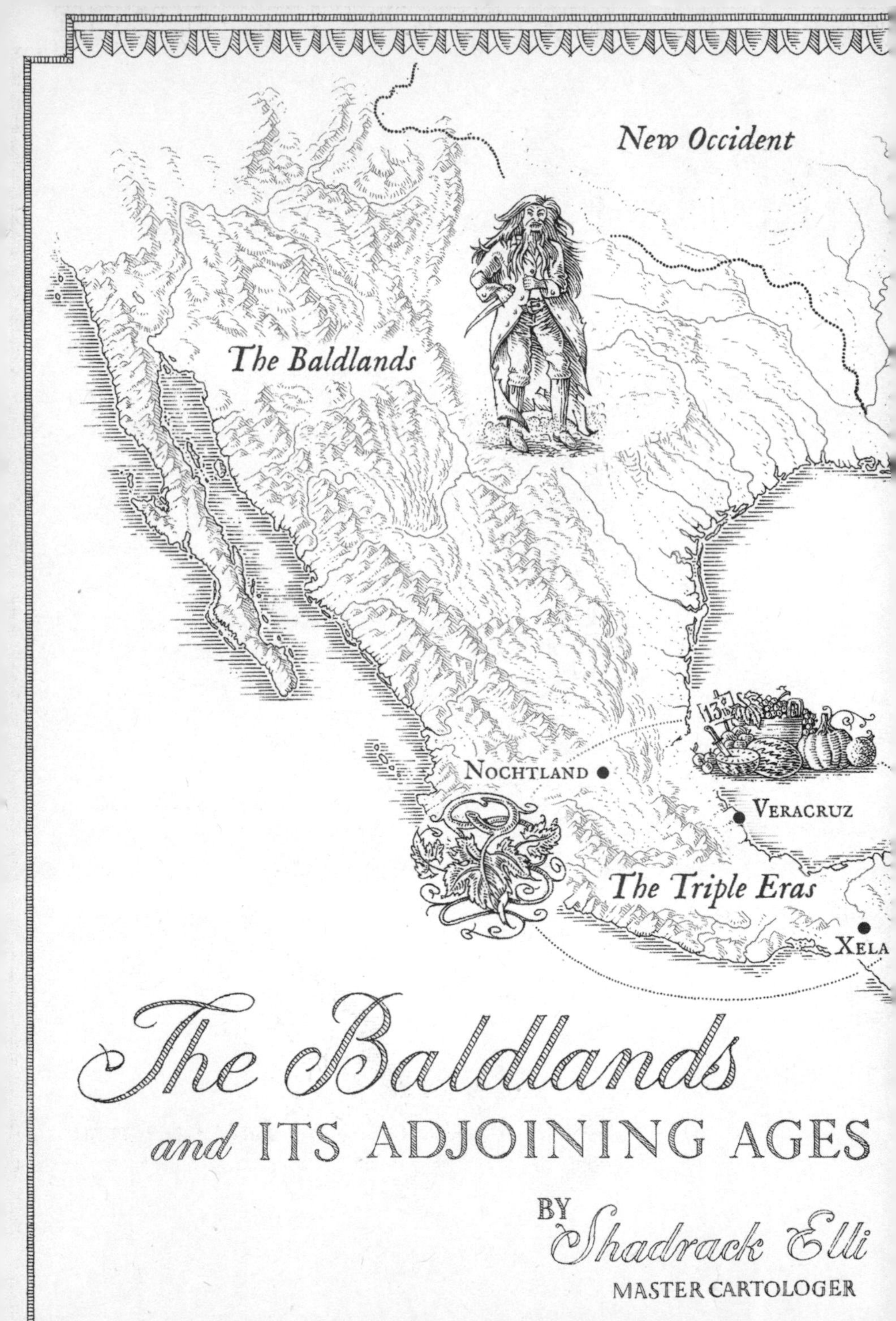
New Occident
The Baldlands
Nochtland
Veracruz
The Triple Eras
Xela
The Baldlands
and ITS ADJOINING AGES
BY
Shadrack Elli
MASTER CARTOLOGER

N
e
United Indies
Late Patagonia

the Glass Sentence

PROLOGUE

IT HAPPENED LONG ago, when I was only a child. Back then, the outskirts of Boston were still farmland, and in the summer I spent the long days out of doors with friends, coming home only when the sun set. We escaped the heat by swimming in Boon's Stream, which had a quick current and a deep pool.

On one especially warm day in the summer of 1799, July 16, all my friends had arrived at the stream before me. I could hear them shouting as I ran toward the bank, and when they saw me standing at the edge of the best diving spot, they called to urge me on. "Jump, Lizzie, jump!" I stripped down to my linen underclothes. Then I took a running start and jumped. I had no way of knowing that when I landed, it would be in a different world.

I found myself suspended over the pool. With my knees curled up and my arms wrapped around them, I hung there, looking at the water and at the bank near it, unable to move. It was like trying to wake while inside a dream. You want to wake, want to move, but you can't; your eyes remain closed, your limbs remain stubbornly still. Only your mind is moving, saying, "Get up, get up!" It was just like that, except the dream that would not let go was the world around me.

Everything had gone quiet. I could not even hear my heart beating. Yet I knew that time was passing, and it was passing too quickly. My friends remained motionless while the water around them rushed past in swirling currents at a frightening speed. And then I saw something happening on the banks of the stream.

The grass began growing before my eyes. It grew steadily, until it reached the height that it normally reached in late summer. Then it began to wilt and brown. The leaves on the trees by the banks of the stream turned yellow and orange and red; before long, they had faded and fluttered to the ground. The light around me shone dully gray, as if stuck between day and night. As the leaves began to fall, the light grew dimmer. The field turned a silvery brown as far as I could see and in the next moment transformed itself into a wide, snow-covered expanse. The stream below me slowed and then froze. The snow rose and fell in waves, as it would through the passage of a long winter, and then it began to recede, pulling away from the naked branches and the soil, leaving muddy earth behind it. The ice on the stream broke into pieces and the water once again rushed through it. Beyond the banks of the stream, the ground turned a pale green, as new shoots sprang up through the soil, and the trees appeared to grow a verdant lace at their edges. Before too long, the leaves took on their darker summer hue and the grass grew higher. It passed in an instant, but I felt as though I had lived an entire year apart from the world while the world moved on.

Suddenly, I dropped. I landed in Boon's Stream and heard, once again, all the sounds of the world around me. The stream gurgled and splashed, and my friends and I looked at one another in shock. We had all seen the same thing, and we had no idea what had happened.

In the days and weeks and months that followed, the people of Boston began to discover the incredible consequences of that moment, even if we could not begin to understand it. The ships from England and France ceased to arrive. When the first sailors who set out from Boston after the change returned, dazed and terrified, they brought back confounding stories of ancient ports and plagues. Traders who headed north described a barren land covered with snow, where all signs of human existence had vanished and incredible beasts known only in myth had suddenly appeared. Travelers who ventured south gave reports so varied—cities of towering glass, and horse raids, and unknown creatures—that no two were the same.

It became apparent that in one terrible moment the various parts of the world had come apart. They were unfastened from time. Spinning freely in different directions, each piece of the world had been flung into a different Age. When the moment passed, the pieces lay scattered, as close to each other in space as they had always been, but hopelessly separated by time. No one knew how old the world truly was, or which Age had caused the catastrophe. The world as we knew it had been broken, and a new world had taken its place.

We called it the Great Disruption.

—Elizabeth Elli to her grandson Shadrack, 1860

PART I
Exploration

1
Closing an Age

1891, June 14: 7-Hour 51

New Occident began its experiment with elected representation full of hope and optimism. But it was soon tainted by corruption and violence, and it became clear that the system had failed. In 1823, a wealthy representative from Boston suggested a radical plan. He proposed that a single parliament govern New Occident and that any person who wished to voice an opinion before it should pay admittance. The plan was hailed—by those who could afford it—as the most democratizing initiative since the Revolution. They had laid the groundwork for the contemporary practice of selling parliament-time by the second.

—From Shadrack Elli's *History of New Occident*

THE DAY NEW OCCIDENT closed its borders, the hottest day of the year, was also the day Sophia Tims changed her life forever by losing track of time.

She had begun the day by keeping a close eye on the hour. In the Boston State House, the grand golden clock with its twenty hours hung ponderously over the speaker's dais. By the time the clock struck eight, the State House was full to capacity. Arranged in a horseshoe around the dais sat the members of parliament: the eighty-eight men and two women rich enough to procure their positions. Facing them sat the visitors who had paid for time to address parliament, and farther back were the members of the public who could afford ground-floor seating. In the cheap seats on the upper balcony, Sophia was surrounded by men and women who had crammed themselves onto the benches. The sun poured in through the tall State House windows, shining off the gilt of the curved balcony rails.

"Brutal, isn't it?" the woman beside Sophia sighed, fanning herself with her periwinkle bonnet. There were beads of sweat on her upper lip, and her poplin dress was wilted and damp. "I would bet it is five degrees cooler on the ground floor."

Sophia smiled at her nervously, shuffling her boots against the wooden floorboards. "My uncle is down there. He's going to speak."

"Is he now? Where?" The woman put her pudgy hand on the rail and peered down.

Sophia pointed out the brown-haired man who sat, straight-backed, his arms folded across his chest. He wore a linen suit and balanced a slim leather book on his knee. His dark eyes calmly assessed the crowded hall. His friend Miles Countryman, the wealthy explorer, sat next to him, red from the heat, his shock of white hair limp with sweat. Miles wiped a handkerchief brusquely across his face. "He's right there—in the front row of speakers."

"Where?" the woman asked, squinting. "Ah, look—the famous Shadrack Elli is here, I see."

Sophia smiled proudly. "That's him. Shadrack is my uncle."

The woman looked at her in surprise, forgetting for a

moment to fan herself. "Imagine that! The niece of the great cartologer." She was clearly impressed. "Tell me your name, dear."

"Sophia."

"Then tell me, Sophia, how it is that your famous uncle can't afford a better seat for you. Did he spend all his money on his time?"

"Oh, Shadrack can't afford time in parliament," Sophia said matter-of-factly. "Miles paid for it—four minutes and thirteen seconds."

As Sophia spoke, the proceedings began. The two timekeepers on either side of the dais, stopwatches in their white-gloved hands, called for the first speaker, a Mr. Rupert Middles. A heavyset man with an elaborate mustache made his way forward. He straightened his mustard-colored cravat, smoothed his mustache with fat fingers, and cleared his throat. Sophia's eyes widened as the timekeeper on the left set the clock to twenty-seven minutes. "Look at that!" the plump woman whispered. "It must have cost him a fortune!"

Sophia nodded. Her stomach tensed as Rupert Middles opened his mouth and his twenty-seven minutes commenced. "I am honored to appear before parliament today," he began thunderously, "this fourteenth of June of the year eighteen ninety-one, to propose a plan for the betterment of our beloved New Occident." He took a deep breath. "The pirates in the United Indies, the hordes of raiders from the Baldlands, the gradual encroachment of our territories from north, west, and south—how long will New Occident go on ignoring the realities of our altered world, while the edges of our territory are eaten away by the greedy mouths of foreigners?" There were boos and cheers from the crowd, but Middles hardly paused. "In the last year alone, fourteen towns in New Akan were overrun by raiders from the Baldlands, paying for none of the privileges that come with living in New Occident but enjoying them all to the full. During the same period, pirates seized thirty-six commercial ships with cargo from the United Indies. I need not remind you that only last week, the *Gusty Nor'easter,* a proud Boston vessel carrying thousands of dollars in payment and merchandise, was seized by the notorious Bluebird, a despicable pirate who," he added, his face red with exertion, "docks not a mile away in Boston harbor!" Growls of angry encouragement surged from the crowd. Middles took a rapid breath and went on. "I am a tolerant man, like the people of Boston." There were faint cheers. "And I am an industrious man, like the people of Boston." The cheers grew louder. "And I am loath to see my tolerance and my industry made a mockery by the greed and cunning of outsiders!" Clapping and cheering erupted from the crowd.

"I am here to propose a detailed plan, which I call the 'Patriot Plan,' and which I am certain will be approved, as it represents the interests of all those who, like me, believe in upholding our tolerance and our industry." He braced himself against the dais. "Effective immediately, the borders must be *closed.*" He paused for the piercing cheers. "Citizens of New Occident may travel freely—*if* they have the proper documentation—to other Ages. Foreigners living in New Occident who do not have citizenship will have several weeks to return to their Ages of origin, and those remaining will be forcibly deported on July fourth of this year, the day on which we celebrate the founding of this great nation." More enthusiastic cries erupted, and a flurry of audience members stood to clap enthusiastically, continuing even as Middles charged ahead.

Sophia felt her stomach sinking as Rupert Middles detailed the penalties for foreigners who remained in New Occident without documents and the citizens who attempted to travel out of the country without permission. He spoke so quickly that she could see a line of foam gathering at the edge of his mustache and his forehead shining with sweat. Gesticulating wildly, without bothering to wipe his brow, he spat across the dais as he enumerated the points of his plan and the crowd around him cheered.

Sophia had heard it all before, of course. Living as she did with the most famous cartologer in Boston, she had met all the great explorers who passed through his study and heard the much-detested arguments championed by those who sought to bring the Age of Exploration to an end. But this did not make the vitriol of Rupert Middles any less appalling or his scheme any less terrible. As Sophia listened to the remaining minutes of the speech, she thought with growing anxiety of what the closing of the borders would mean: New Occident would lose its ties to the other Ages, beloved friends and neighbors would be forced to leave, but she, Sophia, would feel the loss even more acutely. *They won't have the right documents. They won't get in and I will lose them forever,* she thought, her heart pounding.

The woman sitting beside Sophia fanned herself and

shook her head in disapproval. When the twenty-seven minutes finally ran out and the timekeeper rang a loud bell, Middles staggered to his seat—sweating and panting—to wild applause that filled Sophia with dread. She could not imagine how Shadrack stood a chance of swaying his audience with only four minutes.

"Dreadful spitter," Sophia's companion put in with distaste.

"Mr. Augustus Wharton," the first timekeeper called loudly, while his colleague turned the clock to fifteen minutes. The cheering and clapping subsided as a tall, white-haired man with a hooked nose strode confidently forward. He had no notes. He clasped the edges of the dais with long white fingers. "You may begin," the timekeeper said.

"I appear before this assembly," Mr. Wharton began, in a deceptively low tone, "to commend the proposal put forth by Mr. Rupert Middles and persuade the ninety members of this parliament that we should not only put it in place, but we should *carry it further*," he shouted, his voice rising to a crescendo. The audience on the parliament floor clapped ecstatically. Sophia watched, agonized, as Shadrack's expression grew hard and furious.

"Yes, we must close our borders, and yes, we must enact a swift deportation of foreigners who leech this great nation of its strength without giving it anything in return, but we must *also* close our borders to prevent the citizens of New Occident from leaving it and undermining our very foundations. I ask you: why should *anyone* wish to travel to other Ages, which we know to be inferior? Does not the *true* patriot stay home, where he belongs? I have no doubt that our great explorers, of whom we are so proud, have only the best intentions in traveling to distant lands, pursuing that esoteric knowledge which is unfortunately too lofty for many of us to comprehend." He spoke with condescension as he inclined his head toward Shadrack and Miles.

To Sophia's horror, Miles jumped to his feet. The crowd jeered as Shadrack rose quickly, placing a hand on his friend's arm and easing him back into his seat. Miles sat, fuming, while Wharton went on without acknowledging the interruption. "But surely these explorers are on occasion naive," he continued, to loud calls of agreement, "or perhaps we should say idealistic, when they do not realize that the very knowledge they so prize becomes the twisted tool of foreign powers bent on this great nation's destruction!" This was met with roars of approval. "Need I remind you of the great explorer Winston Hedges, whose knowledge of the Gulf Coast was ruthlessly exploited by pirates in the siege of New Orleans." Loud boos indicated that the memory was, indeed, still fresh. "And it may not be lost on anyone," he sneered, "that the masterful creations of a *certain cartologer* gracing us with his presence today make perfect research materials for any pirate, raider, or tyrannical ruler with an eye toward invasion."

The audience, taken aback by this direct attack, clapped somewhat reluctantly. Shadrack sat silently, his eyes furious but his face calm and grim. Sophia swallowed hard. "I'm sorry, dear," the woman murmured. "That was very much uncalled for."

"In sum," Wharton went on, "I wish to add an amendment

that will put into effect a complete closure of the borders not only for foreigners but for citizens as well. Middles has the Patriot Plan, which will protect us from foreigners. I say good—but *not good enough*. I therefore propose here, in addition, a measure to protect us from ourselves. The Protection Amendment: Stay home, stay safe!" The cheers that met this were few but enthusiastic. "I propose that foreign relations be restricted and trade with specified Ages be facilitated, respectively, as follows." Sophia hardly heard the remainder. She was watching Shadrack, wishing desperately that she could be sitting beside him rather than gazing down from the upper balcony, and she was thinking about what would happen if Wharton's plan passed and the Age of Exploration came to an end.

Shadrack had warned her already that this might happen. He had done so again the night before, as he practiced his speech for the fifteenth time, standing at the kitchen table while Sophia made sandwiches. She had found it impossible to imagine that anyone would hold such a close-minded view. And yet it seemed, from the response of the people around her, that it was all too possible.

"Does no one want the borders to remain open?" Sophia whispered at one point.

"Of course they do, my dear," her benchmate said placidly. "Most of us do. But we're not the ones with the money to talk in Parliament, are we? Don't you notice that all the people who clap for the likes of them are on the *ground* floor—in the pricey seats?"

Sophia nodded forlornly.

Finally, the bell rang and Wharton triumphantly left the stage.

The timekeeper called, "Mr. Shadrack Elli." There was a smattering of polite clapping as Shadrack strode to the dais. While the clock was being set to four minutes and thirteen seconds, he glanced up at the balcony and met Sophia's eye. He smiled, tapping the pocket of his jacket. Sophia smiled back.

"What does that mean?" her companion asked excitedly. "A secret sign?"

"I wrote him a note for good luck."

The note was really a drawing, one of the many Shadrack and Sophia left for one another in unexpected places: an ongoing correspondence in images. It showed Clockwork Cora, the heroine they had invented together, standing triumphantly before a cowed Parliament. Clockwork Cora had a clock for a torso, a head full of curls, and rather spindly arms and legs. Fortunately, Shadrack was more dignified. With his dark hair swept back and his strong chin held high, he looked self-assured and ready. "You may begin," the timekeeper said.

"I am here today," Shadrack began quietly, "not as a cartologer or an explorer, but as an inhabitant of our New World." He paused, waiting two precious seconds so that his audience would listen carefully. "There is a great poet," he said softly, "whom we are fortunate to know through his writing. An English poet, born in the sixteenth century, before the Disruption, whose verses every schoolchild learns, whose words have illuminated thousands of minds. But because he was born in the sixteenth century, and to the best of our knowledge England now resides in the Twelfth Age, he has not yet been born. Indeed, as the Fates would have it, he may never be born at all. If he is not, then his surviving books will be all the more precious, and it will fall to us—*to us*—to pass on his words and make certain they do not disappear from this world.

"This great poet," he paused, looking out onto his audience, which had fallen silent, "wrote:

> *No man is an island, entire of itself; Every man is a piece of the continent, a part of the main. If a clod be washed away by the sea, Europe is the less. . . . Any man's death diminishes me, because I am involved in mankind.*

"I need not persuade you of his words. We have learned them to be true. We have seen, after the Great Disruption, the great impoverishment of our world as pieces fell away, washed into the seas of time—the Spanish Empire fragmented, the Northern Territories lost to prehistory, the whole of Europe plunged into a remote century, and many more pieces of our world lost to unknown Ages. It was not so long ago—fewer than one hundred years; we remember that loss still.

"My father's mother Elizabeth Elli—Lizzie, to those who knew her well—lived through the Great Disruption, and she saw that loss firsthand. Yet it was she who inspired me to become a cartologer by telling me the story of that fateful day and reminding me, every time, to think not of what we had lost but what we might gain. It took us years—decades—to realize that this broken world could be mended. That we could reach remote Ages, and overcome the tremendous barriers of time, and be the richer for it. We have perfected our technologies by borrowing from the learning of other Ages. We have discovered new ways of understanding time. We have profited—profited greatly—by our trade and communication with nearby Ages. And we have given.

"My good friend Arthur Whims at the Atlas Press," he said, holding up a slim leather-bound volume, "has reprinted the writings of John Donne, so that his words can be known to others beyond our Age. And this learning across the Ages is not at an end—much of the New World is still unknown to us. Imagine what treasure, be it financial"—he looked keenly at the members of parliament—"scientific, or literary, lies beyond the borders of our Age. Do you truly wish to wash that treasure away into the sea? Would you wish our own wisdom to fall out of this world, imprisoned within our borders? This cannot be, my friends—my fellow Bostonians. We are indeed tolerant, and we are industrious, as Mr. Middles claims, and we are a part of the main. We are not an island. We must not behave like one."

The clock ran out of time just as Shadrack stepped away from the dais, and the timekeeper, caught up by the stirring words, somewhat belatedly rang his bell into the still silence of the State House. Sophia jumped to her feet, clapping loudly. The sound seemed to rouse the audience around her, which broke into applause as Shadrack returned to his seat. Miles pounded him heartily on the back. The other speakers sat stone-faced, but the cheers from the balcony made it clear that Shadrack had been heard.

"That was a good speech, wasn't it?" Sophia asked.

"Marvelous," the woman replied, clapping. "And by so handsome a speaker, my dear," she added somewhat immaterially. "Simply stupendous. I only hope it's enough. Four minutes isn't very much time, and time weighs more than gold."

"I know," Sophia said, looking down at Shadrack, entirely unaware of the heat as the members of parliament withdrew to their chamber to make a decision. She checked her watch, tucked it back into her pocket, and prepared herself to wait.

—9-Hour 27: Parliament in Chambers—

THE HALL WAS stuffy with the smell of damp wool and peanuts, which the audience members bought from the vendors outside. Some people went out to get fresh air but quickly returned. No one wanted to be away when the members of parliament returned and rendered their decision. There were three options: they could take no action at all, or recommend one of the plans for review, or adopt one of them for implementation.

Sophia looked at the clock over the dais and realized that it was ten-hour—midday. As she checked to see if Shadrack had returned, she saw the members of parliament filing into the hall. "They're coming back," she said to her benchmate. Several minutes of rushed scurrying ensued as people tried to find their seats, and then a hush descended over the audience.

The head of parliament walked to the dais, carrying a single sheet of paper. Sophia's stomach seemed to knot of its own accord. If they had voted for no action—as Shadrack recommended—they would not need a sheet of paper to say so.

The man cleared his throat. "The members of parliament," he began slowly, emphasizing that he, for one, did not pay for his time, "have voted on the proposed measures. By a vote of fifty-one to thirty-nine we have approved for immediate implementation"—he coughed—"the Patriot Plan proposed by Mr. Rupert Middles—"

The rest of his words were lost in an uproar. Sophia sat, dazed, trying to comprehend what had happened. She pulled her satchel strap over her shoulder, then stood and peered over the balcony railing, anxious to find Shadrack, but he had been swallowed by the crowd. The audience behind her was expressing its collective disappointment by means of missiles—a crust of bread, a worn shoe, a half-eaten apple, and a rainstorm of peanut shells—hurled down at the members of parliament. Sophia felt herself being pressed up against the lip of the balcony as the enraged crowd pushed forward, and for a terrible moment she clung to the wooden ledge to avoid being pushed over it.

"Down to chambers, down to chambers!" a timekeeper cried in a piercing tone. Sophia caught a glimpse of the members of parliament hurrying past him.

"You'll not get away so easily, cowards!" a man behind her shouted. "Follow them!" To her relief, the crowd suddenly pulled back and began clambering over the benches for the exits. Sophia looked around for the woman who had sat beside her, but she was gone.

She stood for a moment in the thinning crowd, her heart still pounding, wondering what to do. Shadrack had said he would meet her in the balcony, but now he would surely find it impossible. *I promised to wait,* Sophia said to herself firmly. She tried to steady her hands and ignore the shouts from below, which seemed to grow more violent by the second. A minute passed, and then another; Sophia kept her eye on her watch so that she would not lose track of time. Suddenly she heard a distant murmur that became clearer as more people chanted in unison: "Smoke them out, smoke them out, *smoke them out!*" Sophia ran to the stairs.

On the ground floor, a group of men was battering the doors of the parliament chambers with the overturned dais. "Smoke them out!" a woman shrieked, feverishly piling chairs as if preparing for a bonfire. Sophia ran to the front doors, where seemingly the entire audience had congregated, choking off the entrance. "Smoke them out, smoke them out, smoke them *out!*" She hugged the satchel tightly against her chest and elbowed her way through.

"You bigot!" a woman in front of her suddenly shouted, flailing her fists wildly at an older man in a gray suit. Sophia realized with shock that it was Augustus Wharton. As he swung out with his silver-tipped cane, two men with the unmistakable tattoos of the Indies threw themselves against him, one of them wrenching the cane from his hand and the other pulling his arms back behind him. The woman, her blue eyes fierce, her blonde hair clinging to her face, spat at Wharton. Suddenly she crumpled into a pile of her own skirts, revealing a police officer behind her with his club still raised. The officer reached for Wharton protectively, and the two tattooed men melted away.

There was a shout followed by a cascade of screams. Sophia smelled it before seeing it: fire. The crowd parted, and she saw a torch being hurled toward the open doors of the State House. Screams burst out as the torch landed. She pushed her way into the crowd, trying vainly to catch a glimpse of Shadrack as she inched down the steps. The smell of smoke was sharp in her nostrils.

As she neared the bottom, she heard a shrill voice cry out, "*Filthy pirate!*" An unshaven man with more than a few missing teeth suddenly toppled against her, knocking Sophia to the ground. He rose angrily and threw himself back against his assailant. Sophia pushed herself up from hands and knees unsteadily; seeing a clear path down to the street, she hurried down the remaining steps, her knees trembling. There was a trolley stop right by the corner of the State House, and as Sophia ran toward it a car was just arriving. Without stopping to check its destination, she jumped aboard.

2
The Wharf Trolley

1891, June 14: 10-Hour #

To the north lay a prehistoric abyss; to the west and south lay a chaos of jumbled Ages. Most painfully, the temporal chasm between the former United States of America and Europe became undeniably clear in the first few years after the Disruption. The Papal States and the Closed Empire had descended into shadow. It thereby fell to the eastern seaboard on the western edge of the Atlantic to maintain the glorious tradition of the West. The United States became known as New Occident.

—*From Shadrack Elli's* History of New Occident

SOPHIA TOOK A deep breath as the trolley pulled away from the State House to circle Boston Common. She pinned her trembling hands between her knees, but her scraped palms felt hot and began to sting. She could still hear the crowd, and all around her on the trolley the agitated passengers were discussing parliament's shocking decision.

"It won't stand," a portly man with a gleaming pocket watch said, shaking his head. He stamped his patent-leather boot indignantly. "So many in Boston are foreigners; it's entirely impractical. The city will not stand for it."

"But only some of them have papers and watches," objected a young woman beside him. "Not every foreigner does." Her nervous hands crumpled the lap of her flowered skirt.

"Is it true that deportations will begin on July fourth?" an older woman asked, her voice quavering.

Sophia turned away and watched the passing city streets. The great clocks of New Occident with their twenty hours stood on every street corner. They perched on the lampposts; they loomed from every building facade; they gazed over the city from countless monuments. Ponderous bell towers dominated the skyline, and at the city center the chiming could be deafening.

And every New Occident citizen carried a watch that mirrored the movement of these great monuments: a pocket watch inscribed with the moment of its wearer's birth, bearing constant witness to a life unfolding. Sophia often held the smooth metal disc of her lifewatch, taking comfort from its dependable ticking, just as she took pleasure in the reassuring chime and ring of every public clock. Now it seemed that these clocks, which had always been her anchor, were counting down to a disastrous end: July 4, a mere three weeks away. The borders would close and then, without the papers they needed to return, the two people she most wanted to see in the world might be stranded forever.

Sophia could hardly remember her father, Bronson Tims, or her mother, Wilhelmina Elli. They had vanished on an expedition when she was barely three years old. She had one precious memory of them, which she had worn out to a thin, faded, insubstantial thing: they walked on either side of her, each holding one of her hands. Their laughing faces looked down from a distance with great tenderness. "Fly, Sophia, fly!" they called out in unison, and suddenly she was lifted from the ground. She felt her own laugh welling up, joining her mother's trill and her father's deep chuckle. That was all.

Wilhelmina—Minna, for short—and Bronson had been first-class explorers. Before their daughter was born, they had traveled south to the Baldlands, north to the Prehistoric Snows, and even as far east as the Closed Empires; and afterwards they planned to travel with Sophia—once she was old enough. But an urgent message from a fellow explorer, deep in the Papal States, had forced them to leave sooner than expected, and they had struggled terribly with the problem of whether to take their daughter or not.

It was Shadrack who had persuaded his sister Minna and her husband to leave Sophia with him. The message they had received suggested unpredictable dangers for which even he could not prepare them. If Shadrack Elli, Doctor of History and Master Cartologer, could not ensure that the route would be a safe one, surely it posed too many risks for a child of only three years. Who better to understand the potential of those risks? Who better to leave her with than her beloved uncle Shadrack? They had finally departed, anxious but determined, for what they hoped would be only a brief journey.

But they had not returned. As the years passed, the likelihood of their reappearing alive diminished. Shadrack knew it; Sophia sensed it. But she refused to fully believe it. And now the anxiety Sophia felt at the thought of the borders' closing had, in fact, little to do with the grand ambitions of exploration described in Shadrack's speech. It had everything to do with her parents. They had left Boston in a far more lenient age, when traveling without papers was commonplace, even wise, in order to avoid theft or damage on a dangerous voyage. Bronson's and Minna's paper were safely stowed in a little bureau in their bedroom. If New Occident closed itself off to the world, how would they get back in? Lost in somber speculation, Sophia closed her eyes, her head resting against the seat.

With a start she realized that the air around her had grown dark and oddly cold. Her eyes snapped open. *Is it night already?* she thought, panic rising in her chest. She reached for her watch, looked around quickly, and realized the trolley had stopped in a tunnel. Far behind them she could see the bright entryway. So it was still daytime. But when she squinted at the watch, she discovered that it was already fourteen-hour. Sophia gasped. "Four hours!" she exclaimed out loud. "I can't believe it!"

She hurried to the front of the trolley and saw the conductor standing on the tracks a few meters ahead of the car. There was a sharp metallic clang, and then the man lumbered back toward her.

"Still here, are you?" the conductor asked amiably. "You must like this loop to sit through it twenty-three times. That, or you like my driving." He was heavyset, and despite the cool air in the tunnel, sweat poured off his forehead and chin. Smiling, he wiped his face with a red handkerchief as he sat down.

"I lost track of the time," Sophia said anxiously. "Completely."

"Ah, no matter," he replied with a sigh. "On such a bad day—the sooner it ends the better." He released the brake and the trolley began to roll slowly forward.

"Are you going back into the city now?"

He shook his head. "I'm heading out to the yard. You'll have to get off at the wharf and look for a trolley heading back through downtown."

Sophia had not been to this part of Boston in years. "Is it the same stop?"

"I'll point you to it," he assured her. They picked up speed as they made a sudden sharp turn to the left. Then they emerged from the tunnel, the light dazzling Sophia's eyes. The trolley stopped once again almost immediately, and the conductor shouted, "Wharf trolley. Final stop. No passengers." A waiting crowd looked impatiently at the tunnel for the next trolley to emerge. "Walk about fifty paces that way," he said to Sophia, pointing past the crowd. "There's another stop there that says 'inbound.' You can't miss it."

—14-Hour 03: At the Wharf—

NEWS OF THE borders' closure had already reached Boston harbor. People rushed this way and that through a confusion of carts, improvised market stands, and piles of crates, shouting orders, hurriedly unloading cargo, and making hasty arrangements for unexpected journeys. Two men were arguing over a broken crate full of lobsters; claws reached feebly through the cracked wooden slats. Seagulls cried out from every corner, dipping lazily, snapping at the stray pieces of fish and bread. The smell of the harbor—brine, tar, and the faint, enduring scent of something spoiling—wafted by on waves of hot air.

Sophia tried to get out of the way and found herself repeatedly pushed aside. As she struggled to find the trolley stop, she gave in to that familiar sense of defeat that always came with losing track of time. Their housekeeper, Mrs. Clay, would be worried sick. And Shadrack—he might still be looking for her at the State House and fear the worst when she failed to appear. As she stumbled along, Sophia suppressed the tears of frustration that threatened to spill over.

It was a frustration she felt all too frequently. Sophia, to her infinite mortification, had no internal clock. A minute could feel as long as an hour or a day. In the space of a second she might experience a whole month, and a whole month could pass in what felt to her like a second. As a young child, she had fallen daily into difficulties as a consequence. Someone would ask her a question, and Sophia would think for a moment and suddenly find that everyone had been laughing at her for a full five minutes. Once she had waited for six hours on the steps of the Public Library for a friend who never arrived. And it seemed to her that it was always time for bed.

She had learned to compensate for her missing internal clock, and now that she was thirteen she rarely lost track of time during conversations. She observed the people around her to know when it was time to eat or finish school or go to bed. And she had become accustomed to keeping a tight hold on her watch, which she checked constantly. In the drawing notebook that was always in her satchel she kept careful records of her days: maps of past and future that helped guide her through the vast abyss of unmeasured time.

But having no sense of time still troubled her in other ways. Sophia took great pride in her competence: her ability to navigate Boston and even places farther afield, as she grew older and traveled with Shadrack; her carefully disciplined work at school, which made her popular with teachers, if not always with classmates; her capacity to order and make sense of the world, so that all of Shadrack's friends commented that she was wise beyond her years. These mattered deeply to her, and yet they could not compensate for the flaw that made her seem, in her own eyes, as flighty and absentminded as someone who had none of these abilities.

Being from a family famous for its sense of time and direction made it all the more painful. Her parents reputedly had inner compasses and clocks worthy of great explorers. Shadrack could tell the time down to the second without looking at his watch, and no amount of encouragement on his part could persuade Sophia to forget the piece of herself she felt was missing. Their joint creation, Clockwork Cora, made light of a problem that Sophia only pretended to take lightly.

She never spoke of it to her uncle, but she had a dreadful suspicion of how she had come to lose her sense of time. She pictured herself as a very young child, waiting for her parents at a dusty window. The little Sophia's clock had ticked on and on, patiently and then worriedly and finally desperately, counting the seconds as her mother and father failed to come back. And then, when it became clear that the waiting was futile, the little clock had simply broken, leaving her without parents and without any sense of time at all.

However much Shadrack loved his niece, he could not spend every second of every day with her, and the steady stream of graduate students whom he hired to assist with the combined tasks of cartology and child care were prone to the same distractions he was. While her uncle and his assistants pored over maps, the three-year-old Sophia had spent plenty of time alone and had, in fact, sometimes waited for her parents with hands and face pressed up against a window. In her memory—in her imagination—those moments contained long hours of endless waiting. The sun rose and set, and people passed the window in a constant stream, but still she waited expectantly. On occasion, the figure of her imagination blurred, and it seemed that not a near-infant but an older child—one who had waited for many years—stood at the window. And in fact her uncle sometimes found the grown Sophia sitting at her window, lost in thought, her pointed chin tucked into her hand and her brown eyes focused on something far out of sight.

Now she stood on the busy wharf, wiping her eyes angrily and trying hard to compose herself. Then, amidst all the shouts and the bustle, she spotted about a dozen people standing in line. With a monumental effort, she drew her thoughts away from the four hours she had lost. *That must be the line for the inbound trolley,* she thought. As she approached, she heard, over all the other noise, the sound of a man shouting through a megaphone. She tapped the shoulder of the woman ahead of her. "Excuse me, is this the line for the inbound trolley?"

The young woman shook her bonneted head excitedly. She was clutching a flyer, which she pushed into Sophia's hand. "No such thing. They've brought creatures from the other Ages," she said breathlessly. "We're going in to see them while we still can!" Her laced glove pointed to a sign that stood only a few feet away.

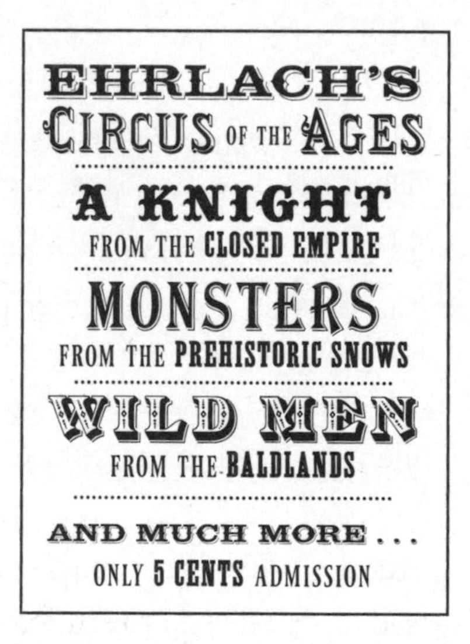

Beside the sign stood the man who was shouting into the megaphone. He was small and sported a small, pointy beard and a tall hat that made his head look tiny. He flourished a silver-topped cane. "Wild men, monsters, creatures that defy your imagination!" he cried, his cheeks red with heat and exertion. He spoke with the accent of the western Baldlands; it made all his vowels sound bow-legged. "Discovered by the intrepid Simon Ehrlach and displayed here for the entertainment and instruction of visitors!" He pointed to a heavy velvet curtain that covered the entryway to the warehouse behind him. A woman even smaller than he was sat to his left, deftly counting money and dispensing and stamping tickets, her small forehead creased with concentration, before ushering each visitor into the curtained warehouse.

"Every man or beast in a continuous exhibition of all the fascinating variety of the Ages!" the little man continued, showering his audience with energetic bursts of spit. "Each enacting constantly the bizarre and indeed mesmerizing habits of its Age, so that the visitor will hardly believe that he stands still in time!" With the tip of his cane, he tapped a large cage that stood to his right. "The wild boy from the Baldlands, in his fierce warrior dress. And inside there are even fiercer creatures from the Baldlands. Centaurs and mermen and children with tails. See them while you still have the chance!"

Sophia stared in fascination at the cage, all other thoughts forgotten. There stood a boy who seemed only a little older than herself, dressed from head to toe in feathers. She could tell at once that he belonged to a different Age. His hair was twisted up around colored plumes that appeared to spring from his skull, and his limbs were covered with multicolored down. A skirt of trailing feathers hung at his waist, while an empty quiver dangled from his shoulder. His costume might once have been impressive, but most of the feathers were broken or crushed. To Sophia he looked like a beautiful bird, trapped in midair and dragged down to earth.

But it was not his beauty that captured her attention. It was his expression. He was imprisoned in a cage, and he was made a spectacle to everyone around him. And yet, for all that, he surveyed the crowd as if *they* and not he were the spectacle. A faint smile tugged at the edges of his mouth. Gazing calmly at them, he made the cage seem like a pedestal; he was serene, unshakable, magnificent. Sophia could not take her eyes off him. She had lost track of time once again, but in a way that seemed entirely new.

"I assure you, ladies and gentlemen," the little man went on, "that you will even see battles enacted among these fierce creatures in Ehrlach's Circus of the Ages. And after today's decision in parliament, your days to view the wonders of the other Ages are numbered! Seize the opportunity now before it's too late!" At this he reached with his cane through the bars of the cage and gave the boy dressed in feathers a careless jab.

The boy looked at the cane and grabbed it easily, as if picking up a stray feather. Then he pushed it back toward the circus master, disinterested, and resumed watching the crowd. As the man continued to advertise Ehrlach's marvels, Sophia realized that the boy was looking directly at her. He raised his hands and placed them on the bars. It seemed to Sophia that he could see her thoughts and that he was about to speak to her. She knew she was blushing, but she could not look away. She could not move; she did not want to move.

"Hey, hey," she heard someone say. The young woman ahead of her in line was shaking her shoulder. "Didn't you want the city trolley, sweetheart? There it is—better run for it."

Sophia tore her eyes away from the boy. Sure enough, a trolley was approaching. If she hurried she would catch it. She looked back once more at the boy, who was still watching her thoughtfully. Then she ran.

3
Shadrack Elli, Cartologer

1891, June 14

And who (in time) knowes whither we may vent
The treasure of our tongue? to what strange shores
This gaine of our best glorie shal be sent,
T'inrich unknowing Nations with our stores?
What worlds in th'yet unformed Occident
May come refin'd with th'accents that are ours?

—*Samuel Daniel,* Musophilus, *1599*

Sophia lived with Shadrack at 34 East Ending Street in the South End of Boston, in the solid brick house her great-grandparents had built. White shutters, an abundance of ivy, and an iron owl perched discreetly over the entryway made it similar to the other brick houses adjoining it on the quiet street. But no other house had the small oval sign, pine-green in color, that hung on the red door, announcing:

In reality, the sign had little use, because anyone who sought out Shadrack knew exactly where to find him; furthermore, they knew that the mere title "cartologer" did not begin to describe his occupation. He was as much historian, geographer, and explorer as he was cartologer. Apart from being a professor at the university, he was a private consultant to explorers and government officials. Anyone who needed expert knowledge of the history and geography of the New World found their way to Shadrack's door.

They came to see Shadrack simply because he was the best. In a time when most of the world was uncharted and no single person knew more than a few Ages, he was the most knowledgeable. Though he was young for a master cartologer, no one could match Shadrack for breadth of knowledge and skill. He had mastered the history of every known continent, he could read the maps of every civilization known to New Occident, and, most importantly, he could draw brilliant maps himself. The great cartologer who had trained him was said to have wept with wonder when Shadrack Elli presented his first complete map of the New World. He had precision and artistic ability on his side, but any draughtsman had that; it was his bottomless knowledge that made Shadrack so extraordinary.

Having grown up surrounded by her uncle's work, Sophia sometimes had difficulty seeing it as exceptional. She thought of mapmaking as a noble, learned, and rather messy profession. The house on East Ending Street was papered from top to bottom with maps. Maps of contemporary, ancient, or imaginary worlds covered every inch of wall space. Books and pens and compasses and rulers and more maps, lying flat or rolled up like scrolls, littered every flat surface. The parlor and the study fairly overflowed with equipment, and even the kitchen had begun to shrink from the edges inward as the countertops and cabinets became receptacles for maps. Sophia moved like a tiny island of tidiness through the house, straightening books, rolling maps, gathering pens, all in the effort to stem the cartologic tide around her. The only two relatively orderly places were her room, which had a few select maps and books, and the third-floor apartment of their housekeeper, Mrs. Clay.

Mrs. Sissal Clay had arrived years earlier, when Sophia was only eight, and after a long consultation with Shadrack had simply moved in to the uninhabited third floor. Shadrack had always frowned upon the custom of keeping servants, believing such arrangements perpetuated a system in which the children of the servant class withdrew early from their schooling. Even when he was entrusted with the care of his three-year-old niece, he refused to hire a nanny, relying instead upon the paid assistance of his graduate students—who, he reasoned, were not abandoning their education to perform domestic duties.

Immense love is almost always enough to sustain a child. But it does not always provide the logistical and practical necessities, including a steady supply of clean clothes and an understanding that toddlers can become bored with certain aspects of adult life, such as two-hour university lectures on the glaciation of the Eerie Sea.

Shadrack's well-meaning but mostly unsuitable assistants had no more command of these necessities than he did, and they were fleeting presences in Sophia's life: brilliant, inventive, memorable, and usually rather incompetent as caretakers. One had built her a magnificent boat out of lacquered paper that she sailed on the Charles River to the everlasting envy of all the neighborhood children. Another had attempted to teach her Latin and had mostly succeeded, so that she could converse quite fluently in that tongue about farmers, sheep, and aqueducts by the time she was seven. All in all they were very lovable, but few understood the usefulness of mealtimes and bedtimes. Sophia had learned early on to see them as friendly companions rather than reliable guardians, and she did what any reasonable person would do: she learned to take care of herself.

Then Mrs. Clay arrived. For reasons he did not explain, Shadrack broke his own rule. Mrs. Clay became the housekeeper at 34 East Ending Street. Had Mrs. Clay been a different sort of woman, Sophia's life might have changed dramatically at this point. Mrs. Clay was a widow, and she had been the housekeeper at the academy of cartology where Shadrack had studied for two years in Nochtland, the Baldlands' capital. The house might have flourished under her guiding hand, so that Shadrack's high-spirited chaos and unbounded affection would have found some complementary order and good sense. But Sophia soon realized, young as she was, that their housekeeper needed more taking care of than she herself did.

A moody, silent woman with sad eyes and a wide face, Mrs.

Clay moved through the rooms of 34 East Ending as she did through the streets of Boston: quietly, almost fearfully, as if the only thing she was looking for was a proper place to hide. She was one part melancholy kindness, two parts mysterious unease; Sophia both liked her and felt that she did not really know her. Over time, Sophia simply accepted Mrs. Clay's presence and went on relying more and more on herself, becoming the independent and peculiarly practical person that she was.

— *15-Hour 19* —

WHEN SOPHIA FINALLY returned home, she found a red-eyed Mrs. Clay and a harried-looking Shadrack at the kitchen table. They both rose to their feet the moment Sophia walked in. Shadrack rushed to embrace her. "Sophia! Finally!"

It was such a comfort to find herself back home, crushed up against the familiar scrape of Shadrack's chin and the familiar smell of Shadrack's pine soap, that she held on tightly for a while before speaking. "I'm sorry," she finally whispered, pulling away. "I lost track of time."

Mrs. Clay placed her hand on Sophia's shoulder, murmuring a fervent thanks to the Fates, and Shadrack shook his head with an affectionate smile that still bore traces of his concern. He tucked her hair behind her ears and held her face in his hands. "I was just about to go back to the State House—for the third time—to look for you," he said. "I thought you were going to wait for me on the balcony."

"I did, but I didn't know how long to wait, and then they started shouting about a fire . . ."

"I know," Shadrack said grimly.

"When I finally got away I took the wrong trolley. And then I lost track of time. I ended up at the wharf," she concluded with embarrassment.

"It's all right," Shadrack said, taking her hand and pulling her over to the kitchen table. "I was worried, but it's all right. I know the fault is not yours." He let out a deep sigh as he sat down.

"What happened to you?" Sophia asked.

"I made my way over to the balcony stairs with Miles, and then he started a fistfight with some hothead in a bow tie. By the time I separated them, the balconies were empty." Shadrack shook his head. "What a day. Mrs. Clay has of course heard the news—the whole of Boston has by now, I'm sure."

"But at least you are home safely, Sophia." Mrs. Clay said. She spoke with the clipped accent of the southern Baldlands, and her manner of dress had never lost its foreign eccentricities. She always tucked a stray flower or clover stem or even an autumn leaf into her buttonhole; today, she wore a wilted violet in her hair. Her face was still blotchy and red, and Sophia understood that the tears had nothing to do with her absence: Mrs. Clay had no lifewatch and no papers.

"Thank you. I'm sorry to have caused you so much worry," Sophia said, sitting down beside them at the table. "Did Miles leave as planned?"

"Yes," Shadrack said, rumpling his hair tiredly. "His ship left at twelve-hour. He hardly expected the day to be so momentous, and now he was more eager to leave than ever."

"He *is* coming back, isn't he?"

"Let us hope so, Soph. For now, the plan is to close the borders and deport people from other Ages unless they have papers. The so-called 'Patriot Plan,'" he said dryly, "is generous enough to permit free travel for citizens of New Occident."

"So we could still travel in and out?" She glanced apologetically at Mrs. Clay. "I mean, anyone with papers can travel in and out?"

Shadrack nodded. "Yes. For now. What you may not have heard over the commotion," he went on, "is that they plan to reconsider Wharton's Protection Amendment at the end of August. They may very well implement it."

"And close the border for all of us? *No one* could go in or out?"

"It would be sheer stupidity, of course, but that has hardly stopped parliament before."

"I just don't understand why this is happening now," Mrs. Clay protested, her voice dangerously wobbly.

"Fear, pure and simple," Shadrack said.

"But my impression has always been—and I know I am still a relative newcomer here—but I had always thought that people in New Occident—in Boston, at least—were rather . . . intrigued," she said carefully, "by the other Ages. They treat foreigners with curiosity, not hostility."

"I know," Sophia agreed. "It makes no sense; people love to see the other Ages. At the wharf, there was this circus with creatures from the other parts of the world. And there was a man selling tickets who had a boy covered with feathers in a cage, and the boy was his prisoner, but he was so calm he hardly seemed to care, even though everyone was staring at him." She found, despite her rush of words, that there was no way she could explain just how remarkable the boy was, or why he had left such an impression upon her.

"Yes," Shadrack said, eyeing her thoughtfully. He ran his hand through his hair and frowned. "I think the majority of the people here *are* intrigued—fascinated, even—by the other Ages. For some that means exploration, for others that means befriending foreigners, for still others it means observing them in cages." His smile had no mirth. "But many others are afraid—not just afraid of people from other Ages who are different, but afraid, however illogically, for their own safety."

"You mean piracy and raiding," Mrs. Clay said.

"I do. No one is denying," Shadrack said, "that the conflicts with the other Ages are real. The pirates in the United Indies are a costly distraction, and it is true that raiding parties from the Baldlands are continually tormenting populations at the edges of New Occident—even more so in the Indian Territories. But," he continued sadly, "it goes the other way, too. Ships sail from Seminole every day under our flag and then, once they're out on the sea, they lower ours and raise a pirate flag. And raiding parties from New Occident go into the Baldlands as often as they come out of them." He paused. "That is why the boy you saw on the wharf, Soph, was a captive."

"You mean he was kidnapped in the Baldlands?"

"Most likely. They would probably claim that they found him in New Occident and that he somehow broke the law, but most certainly he was taken in a raid, and the circus bought him from the raiders as the newest addition to their show." His voice was bitter.

"That's despicable." Sophia was thinking of how calm the boy had seemed and of how he had stepped up to the bars, as if about to speak to her.

"It is." The Elli side of the family, Shadrack and Minna, were all from Boston. But the Timses came from many different places, and Sophia's great-grandparents had been slaves; after the rebellion, they helped to found the new state of New Akan in 1810. Their son, Sophia's grandfather, had moved to Boston to attend the university. "Sophia's great-grandfather was only seventeen when slavery ended," Shadrack explained to Mrs. Clay. Then he turned to Sophia. "It must have shaken you to see a boy behind bars like that."

"This is what I don't understand," the housekeeper said. "Surely people in New Occident see that almost everyone here was once from somewhere else—everyone has a foreigner in their past."

"Yes, but what we have seen today," Shadrack replied, "is what happens when fear overwhelms reason. The decision is illogical. It makes no sense to deport some of our finest laborers, merchants, and tradespeople, not to mention mothers, fathers, and friends. They will live to regret it."

The three sat silently for a while, gazing, each with their own preoccupations, at the empty kitchen table. Sophia sat with her head resting on Shadrack's shoulder. He stirred a moment later, as if something had just occurred to him. "Mrs. Clay, I apologize. You came in an hour ago quite distressed, and I was full of my own concern for Sophia. We should discuss how we will get papers for you, since there is no time to acquire them through the proper channels." Shadrack shook his head. "Naturalization can take months—sometimes years. We will have to find other means."

She looked at him gratefully. "Thank you, Mr. Elli. You are very kind. But it is late, and neither you nor Sophia have eaten. We can speak another time—I do not wish to impose." She rose tentatively to her feet and patted the bun at the nape of her neck, tucking stray hairs into place.

"Nonsense," Shadrack said, gently putting Sophia aside. "You're right, we haven't eaten. And neither have you." He looked at his watch. "I will get in touch with Carlton. Tonight, if possible." Carlton Hopish, fellow cartologer and Shadrack's friend from the university, worked for the Ministry of Relations with Foreign Ages and owed Shadrack more favors than either of them could count. Thanks to his friendship with the most knowledgeable cartologer in New Occident, Carlton always seemed to be the most informed member of government; and Shadrack, in turn, always managed to be conveniently apprised of classified government information. "As a beginning step, I'll write him a note tonight about getting expedited papers for you—may as well try the legal route first. Will you stay to have dinner with us? No one should have to bear such ill news as we heard today alone. Please," he added, when he saw Mrs. Clay hesitate.

"Very well. Thank you for your kindness."

"Soph, can you wait to eat a little while longer while I write to Carlton and discuss things with Mrs. Clay?" Shadrack asked with an apologetic look.

"Yes, of course. I should write to Dorothy, anyhow."

"A good idea." As Shadrack and Mrs. Clay retreated to his study, Sophia made her way upstairs.

—16-Hour 27: Upstairs at East Ending—

SOPHIA SIGHED AS she climbed the stairs. She passed the room that had belonged to her parents, which had remained almost untouched for so many years, and she tapped the door lightly as she did every time she walked by it. When she was very small she would often take refuge there, curling up with the comfort of her parents' belongings all around her. A portrait of her parents drawn by Shadrack sat on the nightstand, and when she was small Sophia had believed it had magical properties. It seemed an ordinary drawing, made with passable skill, since Shadrack was more draughtsman than portrait artist. In the first years after their disappearance, Sophia often picked it up and traced her finger along the inked lines, and somehow she could hear her parents' laughter and sense their presence—as if they were truly in the room beside her. But over time, she visited the room less and less; it came to remind her more of their absence then of their presence. It recalled to her all the times she had gone in and, as always, found the room empty.

There were enough reminders of them elsewhere: the silver star earrings that she always wore, which they had given her on her first birthday; the colorful ribbons her mother often used as bookmarks; her father's pipe, still sitting next to

Shadrack's in the study downstairs. These small objects made tiny anchors all around her, reminding her quietly that Minna and Bronson had, indeed, once existed.

Sophia's bedroom had fewer of these anchors. It was filled instead with the objects that made up *her* life: a potted magnolia that grew in miniature; a watercolor of Salem given to her by an artist friend of Shadrack's; a wardrobe with carefully ordered clothes; a desk with carefully ordered papers; and a bookshelf with carefully ordered books—school books on the bottom shelf and her own on the top shelf. The popular novels of Briony Maverill, the poetry of Prudence Lovelace, and works by Emily Dickinson and Ralph Waldo Emerson all accompanied the picture books that she still cherished and sometimes read.

Sophia unpacked her satchel, taking out her drawing notebook and her pencils. As she did, she found a stray piece of paper, folded in half, and she smiled, knowing already that it would be a drawing Shadrack had somehow sneaked into her satchel that morning. She opened it and laughed at the little sketch of Clockwork Cora, sleeping soundly through a boring speech at parliament, her tiny feet propped up on someone's lap. Unfortunately, Sophia thought, putting the folded paper in a tin box, today it had been anything but boring.

Before sitting down at her desk, she opened the window above her bed to let the air in. She leaned on the sill to look out over the city. From her second-story window, she could see mostly rooftops. She had a narrow view of East Ending Street, where at that moment a boy was slowly pedaling along the cobblestones on a Goodyear. The sun was finally beginning to set, and though the air was no cooler, a breeze had started up.

After unlacing her boots and placing them neatly under her bed, she sat at her desk. She began by writing a letter to her friend Dorothy, who had moved away at the end of the school year. Dorothy's father had an important position in the trade industry, and he had taken a job in New York that inconveniently deprived Sophia of her best—and in many ways her only—friend. Dorothy's easy good humor had a way of tempering Sophia's seriousness, and with her gone, the days of summer vacation had so far been very long and rather lonely. Dorothy had written of her loneliness, too, in the noisy bustle of New York City, so much less civilized than Boston.

But now they both had more pressing concerns. Dorothy's father had been born in the United Indies, and it seemed doubtful they would be able to stay in New Occident. Sophia wrote to express her worry and to say how hard Shadrack had fought to prevent the measure that might now send all of Dorothy's family into exile.

With a sigh, Sophia folded the letter, placed it in an envelope, and took out her drawing book. She always drew at the end of the day; it allowed her to record the hours that would otherwise, all too easily, slip away unnoticed. As images and words those hours became real, tangible, visible.

Years earlier, she had taken a trip with Shadrack to Vermont, and, as they were happening, the days seem to evaporate before her eyes until they lasted no more than minutes.

Upon their return home, Shadrack had given her a notebook with calendar pages as a way of helping her keep track of time. "Memory is a tricky thing, Sophia," he had said to her. "It doesn't just recall the past, it *makes* the past. If you remember our trip as a few minutes, it will *be* a few minutes. If you make it something else, it will be something else." Sophia had found this idea strange, but the more she used the notebook, the more she realized that Shadrack was right. Since Sophia thought most clearly through pictures, she had placed images in the calendar squares to make careful records of her explorations through the year, whether they required leaving Boston or sitting quietly in her room. And incredibly, time became ordered, reliable, constant.

Now she had no need for calendar pages; she had her own method for reining in those slippery hours, minutes, and seconds. She had even devised her own manner of binding the paper, so that her notebook unfolded like an accordion and she was able to see the continuous passage of time in a clear, notched line like a ruler along one side of the page. At the margin she dutifully marked the time and recorded the happenings of the day. She filled the center of the page with the day's images, thoughts, and quotes from people and books. Often she dipped backward or forward to amend how things had happened or speculate how they might happen.

Perhaps due to Shadrack's influence or perhaps due to her own natural inclinations, she had realized that her sketches and recordings were actually maps: maps to guide her through the shapeless time that would otherwise stretch boundlessly into her past and future. Straight lines formed the borders of her observations, and dashed lines linked the borders to memories and wishes. Her thoughts connected to them with hatched lines, marking her mental travels, so that Sophia always knew not only what had happened when, but what she had been thinking at the time.

Using a soft pencil and the tips of her fingers, she began drawing June fourteenth. She found herself sketching the absurd, detestable mustache of Rupert Middles and quickly drew a firm line around him, boxing him off in disgust. *Not that,* she said to herself, trying to put the whole dreadful morning out of her mind. She began again. Soon she realized she was drawing the boy from the circus. It was difficult to capture the expression on his face that had so impressed her: his dark, intent gaze; his careless smile. "He was almost laughing," she murmured. She glanced down at her notebook. *That's not what he looked like,* she thought.

She turned the page to start over and then slowly began turning pages in the opposite direction, back to a drawing she had made on the last day of school.

A woman of middle age with laugh lines and short, wavy hair gazed fondly out at Sophia; a tall man with an impish smile and a bit of a stoop stood protectively behind her. Sophia had drawn her parents many times. She tried to imagine them as they would be now, older and a little heavier; over time the drawings had grown more detailed and vivid. *But I will never really draw them if I never see them again,* she thought. She closed her notebook and put it in the drawer with a sigh of frustration.

Sophia realized as she did so that the room had grown dark. She picked up her watch: it was almost eighteen-hour. *Shadrack has been talking to her for so long,* she thought. As she descended the steps, she could hear his voice—steady, reassuring—coming from the study. But when she reached the open doorway she stopped abruptly, seeing that Mrs. Clay was weeping openly.

"I can't go back, Mr. Elli," she said, with a note of terror in her voice.

"I know, Mrs. Clay. I know. I only say this because I want you to be aware of how difficult it may be. Carlton will hopefully get us the papers, but the government-issued lifewatch is difficult to procure. That's all—"

"I can still hear the Lachrima. I can still hear its cries ringing in my ears. I would rather remain here illegally than go back. *I can't.*"

Sophia took an awkward step forward. "I am sorry to interrupt—"

"And I am sorry we've kept you waiting, Soph. We'll be in the kitchen momentarily," said Shadrack, with a look that was apologetic but firm. Mrs. Clay wiped her nose with her handkerchief and did not look up.

Sophia walked down the hallway, the question in her mind—*What is a Lachrima?*—unasked.

4
Through the Library Door

1891, June 15: 7-Hour 38

This is New Occident's Great Age of Exploration. Travelers head as far as their vessels, mounts, and feet will carry them. But exploration is dangerous work. Many explorers never return, and most of the world remains unknown. Even those places that can be explored prove terribly distant for all but the most elite traveler. Postal routes are fragmentary or nonexistent. Trade routes are painstakingly cultivated, only to crumble. To be connected to the world is a constant, difficult labor.

—*From Shadrack Elli's* History of New Occident

Sophia always told Shadrack everything; usually he knew what she was thinking without having to ask. And Shadrack told Sophia everything. At some point, he had realized that this oddly grown-up child had the maturity and capabilities of someone far older. He had known graduate students less able to keep their lives in order. And so he even shared the complexities of his work with his niece, making her far more knowledgeable about cartology than any other thirteen-year-old in Boston. They did not keep secrets from each other. Or so Sophia thought.

The next morning, Sophia found Shadrack in his study,

writing furiously. The mahogany desk and the ink blotter shook from the pressure of his urgent scribbling. When she came in, he pushed himself back from the table and gave her a tired smile.

"Is Mrs. Clay still here?" Sophia asked.

"She went upstairs around one-hour."

"You haven't slept much."

"No," Shadrack replied shortly. "Apparently everything that could go wrong has. You may as well read it yourself—you'll see the news eventually." He handed Sophia a newspaper that was lying, partially disassembled, on his desk.

The principal story was, of course, the closure of the borders and the adoption of Rupert Middles's Patriot Plan. But the rest of the headlines took Sophia's breath away:

FIRE AT STATE HOUSE TAKES THREE LIVES

PARLIAMENT MEMBER MURDERED LEAVING STATE HOUSE

MINISTER OF FOREIGN RELATIONS SUFFERS "ACCIDENT"

Sophia gasped. "Carlton!" she cried.

MINISTER of Relations with Foreign Ages Doctor Carlton Hopish was discovered this morning in his house on Beacon Hill, suffering from what appears to have been a grievous stroke to his nervous system.

> He was found by his charlady, Samantha Peddlefor, who described her employer's condition when she came upon him as "horrifying."
>
> Dr. Hopish has seemingly lost critical brain function. Doctors at Boston City Hospital say that it is too early to determine whether Dr. Hopish will be able to speak, let alone return to his duties as minister, any time soon.
>
> Considering Dr. Hopish's crucial role in implementing the newly passed Patriot Plan, the connection with parliament's decision at the State House cannot be overlooked. Indeed, certain of Dr. Hopish's colleagues in the ministry, as well as several respected members of parliament, readily assume that the injury was no accident. "I have no doubt," said Mr. Gordon Broadgirdle, MP, "that Hopish has fallen victim to the unrestrained violence of foreigners bent on the vengeful extinction of our nation's leaders."

"How terrible!" she exclaimed.

"It is," Shadrack replied, running a hand through his hair. "As if Carlton's tragedy were not bad enough, all of this will only lead to greater support for the Patriot Plan. They are of course blaming foreigners for all three incidents." He shook his head. "What a disastrous twenty hours."

They were both silent for a moment. "We will be all right, won't we?" Sophia asked quietly.

Shadrack sighed and held out his hand. Sophia took it. Despite her uncle's look of exhaustion, his expression was reassuring. "We will be all right," he said. "But there will be changes."

"What kind of changes?"

"I won't lie to you, Soph. This is a difficult time, and it will remain that way even after the immediate furor subsides. I am most worried about the end of August. As I said yesterday, I would not be surprised if the borders were closed entirely by the ridiculous Protection Amendment—even to us."

"If"—she swallowed hard—"if they did that, then we couldn't leave."

"No," Shadrack agreed.

"And . . . the people from New Occident who are in another age now?"

"I see your point," he said after a moment.

"Their papers are here. If they want to come home now, they won't be able to get in. And, after August, we wouldn't even be able to go out to—to meet them?" She looked down, avoiding Shadrack's gaze.

He stood and put his arm around her shoulders. "You've always held out hope, Soph."

"It is foolish, I know," she muttered.

Shadrack tightened his grasp. "It is not in the least foolish," he said forcefully. "To hold out hope, to be willing to expect the impossible—these are courageous things. You have wonderful resilience."

"I guess."

"All you need, Sophia," he went on, "is something to *do.* You lack the way to apply your exceptional patience, your persistence."

"I don't know what I can possibly *do* about it."

"Yes, Soph, but I know," he said, stepping back and releasing her. "I meant to wait a few more years, but we can't. The time has arrived." He looked her in the eye. "Sophia, you have to make me a promise."

"Okay," she said, surprised.

"Only a handful of people in this Age know what I am about to tell you." Sophia looked at him expectantly. "I won't ask you never to speak of it, because I know you will use your judgment and speak of it only when you must. But," he said, looking down at the floor, "you must promise me something else. You must promise me that you won't . . . You won't decide—you won't even consider," he corrected himself, "going in search of them without me." He met her eyes, his expression earnest. "Can you promise me that?"

Sophia pondered in silence for several seconds, feeling confused, alarmed, and hopeful all at once. "I promise," she whispered.

"Good." He smiled a little sadly. "I hope the long wait will have served its purpose in teaching you caution." He walked to one of the bookshelves and removed a thick leather-bound volume. Reaching behind it, he seemed to turn something. Then the entire bookshelf, which reached from floor to ceiling, swung slowly outward. A wide doorway with a set of steps leading downward stood revealed.

Sophia gaped for a moment, too astonished to speak. Shadrack reached into the open passageway and turned on a series of flame-lamps. He smiled at her expression. "Well? Don't you want to see the map room?"

"This has been here all the time?"

"It has. It's where I do my most important work."

"I thought when you closed the door you were working in your study."

"Sometimes. I am usually downstairs. Follow me." He led her down the steps, which turned twice before opening onto a basement Sophia had never known existed.

The room was fully as large as the entire first floor of the house. Electric flame-lamps dotted the walls and tables. In many ways, it seemed a grander, more orderly version of the library upstairs. Here, too, bookshelves covered the walls and a pair of sturdy wooden tables showed signs of frequent use. The room smelled of old paper, flame-lamp, and polished wood. A thick carpet that muffled Sophia's footsteps covered the floor, and on one side of the room a sofa and two armchairs formed a small sitting area. But in other respects there was a sharp contrast. A long glass display case such as one would see in a museum glinted under the lights by the rear wall, filled with all kinds of strange objects. Nearby was a set of four enormous oak bureaus, each with dozens of shallow drawers. And then there was the most striking difference of all: the room was tidy and well kept. Nothing was out of place.

Sophia stood rooted to the spot, staring around her. She was still having trouble believing that such a room existed. "How long has this been here?" she finally asked, in an awed voice. "And why is it so *clean?*"

Shadrack laughed. "Let me tell you a little family history—some history that you don't know. My father—your grandfather—was, as you know, the curator of the museum at the university. And as a curator, he was also an explorer."

Sophia nodded; this much she knew.

"So Father spent a great deal of time not only curating the museum but also exploring the different Ages and purchasing pieces for it." Again, this was not news. "Well, during his explorations, it was only natural that Father should also acquire things for himself. He was an avid collector, after all. And on his travels to the various Ages, he met people who gave him gifts. The pieces he had purchased for the museum went to the museum, and the pieces that were given to him or purchased for himself were kept here. Father made this space into his own private museum."

"But why was it secret?" she asked.

"It wasn't—not always. At first, he simply wanted a place that was cool and out of the light in order to keep his treasures safe. But then, as word of his private collection got around, Father began getting visitors from all over New Occident—people who wanted to buy his pieces. Needless to say, he wasn't interested. As the attention of other collectors and dealers grew more and more insistent, Father decided he would just cause all of it to disappear. He made it known that he had donated his entire private collection to the museum, and then he built the bookcases to conceal the entrance. It took some time, but after a while the collectors stopped pestering him."

"And everyone forgot the collection existed?"

"Almost everyone. When I started studying cartology," Shadrack went on, "Father suggested I keep my more valuable maps and cartologic instruments here. He had a list of rules that I agreed to observe"—he grimaced—"such as keeping everything tidy. I agreed, and over time I had more maps and tools that needed to be kept hidden. Eventually, after Father passed away, I remade it into a map room, and I've kept it that way ever since. And of course it's still secret, because of the work I do here. Most of it is so sensitive that it must be completely concealed—even from those who live under my own roof," he added apologetically.

"Who else knows about it?"

Something like pain flashed across his face unexpectedly as his dark eyes drew inward, but he recovered himself almost immediately. "Very few living souls know about the map room. My students and colleagues at the university have no idea. Nor does Mrs. Clay. Miles knows. And your parents knew, of course. We spent many hours here together, planning their expeditions."

Her parents had once sat in those very chairs with Shadrack! She could imagine them huddled over the table, poring over maps from all the different Ages and talking animatedly about routes, and supplies, and strange foreign customs.

"We did make a mess of this room before every trip," Shadrack said, smiling. "Here"—he led her to a large, worn map pinned to the wall above the armchairs—"is where we would always begin." It was a map of the world, dotted with pins of different colors. "After they left when you were small," Shadrack said quietly, "I kept track of where they'd gone. This was their planned route." He pointed to a series of blue pins that stretched out across the Atlantic and through the Papal States into the Middle Roads. Sophia had heard why her parents had left many times, but the journey took on a different aspect when accompanied by a map. "The message from our friend Casavetti seemed to suggest he had fallen prisoner while discovering an unknown Age here, in the Papal States." He pointed to a blue pin. "Somehow, though Casavetti knew the region like the back of his hand, he had stumbled upon something new—and clearly dangerous. They planned to arrive, rescue Casavetti, and return.

"But I do not believe they ever arrived at their destination. The green pins show the places where I heard they had been." They were scattered all over the world—the Northern Snows, the Baldlands, the Russias, even Australia. "For years, explorers I knew would bring me news. Very few claimed to have seen them firsthand, but they'd heard a rumor here, a suspicion there. I collected every scrap of information and tried to track their route—make some sense of it. As you can see, there's no sense at all." He gestured at the map. "Then I stopped hearing about them."

They stood in silence for a moment, gazing at the smattering of pinheads. "But you see, Sophia—I did not give up hope either. I wouldn't have dreamed of heading off without you to find them, and taking you with me then was out of the question. While you were little, I learned everything I could about where they had been seen. And I waited. I waited for you to reach an age when I could tell what I knew. An age when it would be possible for us to go in search of them—together."

Sophia took in the far-flung destinations marked by green pins, overwhelmed. "Go in search of them?" she repeated.

"I would have waited another few years, had I been able to," Shadrack went on. "But that is no longer possible. You and I need to start making our plans *now*, so that we can leave in case the borders close for everyone—we have only weeks left. We can't take the map room with us, so we have to take it all up here." He tapped his temple with his forefinger.

Sophia's eyes traveled over the room and settled on the hopeful, determined face of her uncle. She smiled at him elatedly. "How do I start?"

Shadrack smiled back, something like pride in his eyes. "I knew you were ready, Soph." He reached out and placed his large hand gently on her head. "At first, you will have to rely on some of your extraordinary patience, because the first few steps to becoming a cartologer and explorer go slowly."

"I can do it," she said eagerly. "I can be patient."

Shadrack laughed. "Then we'll commence the first lesson. Before that, a brief tour of the map room." He strode to the wooden tables. "Here's where I do the mapmaking." As she walked past them, Sophia noticed that one table had a worn, leather surface, covered with small nicks and scratches. "And these shelves are full of books that are either too valuable or too risky to have upstairs." He indicated a few that were unusual shapes and sizes and then gestured at one of the large wooden bureaus. "I'll show you these later. First—here, in the case, are some really beautiful things. Treasures from the other Ages. Your parents found some of them for me."

Shadrack pointed to a tall metal cylinder studded with tiny gems. "A map reader from Patagonia," he said proudly. Beside it was something that looked like an ordinary seashell, but somehow made her think of warm sunlight and the murmur of underwater voices. "A Finding Shell from the South Seas. And this," he said, indicating a flat, waxy object covered with bright pictures, "is a forest map from the Papal States." As Sophia looked at it, she envisioned it on a lectern in a room filled with incense smoke and faint candlelight. There were many other mysterious objects.

"So these are all actually *maps*?"

"That's the thing, Soph," he said, his eyes gleaming. "We think of maps as drawings on paper—some lines, some words, some symbols. Right?" Sophia nodded. "But in reality, maps come in all shapes and sizes—and in the other Ages, they are nothing like ours. My theory," Shadrack continued, "is that your parents went astray because they could not read the maps *of the Age they were in*. They knew a little bit, but they counted on their paper maps to guide them through everything." He winced. "I counted on their paper maps to guide them. If my theory is correct, there are places you simply cannot navigate without local maps, and that takes an entirely different kind of knowledge. More than skill—it takes a mental adjustment to read and make maps unlike those drawn on paper."

Sophia looked at him in wonder. "Do you mean that *you* make them? You make those other maps?"

"That," he replied, "is what the map room is for. In New Occident we mainly draw maps on paper. But maps can be cast in almost anything—stone, wood, earth, sand, metal, cloth, leather, glass—even made on a piece of soap or a broad leaf. Every mapmaker has specialties, depending on where they are and what Age they belong to. And some people, like me, have tried to learn the cartology of other Ages."

"But not my parents." Sophia's voice was small.

"They knew the rudiments of other cartologic forms. But not enough, I suspect. They may have found themselves somewhere far from the Age of paper maps, with only a sand map before them. What then?" He shook his head. "That won't happen again. You and I will be masters of every manner of map when we go in search of them."

"What other forms do you know?" she asked breathlessly.

Shadrack led her to the large wooden bureaus. "Apart from paper, upon which every cartologer of our Age depends, I've learned mapmaking with four of the essential materials: metal, glass, cloth, and clay." As he spoke, he opened one of the drawers in the nearest bureau and removed a thin rectangle of shining metal, which he held up by the edges. It was no larger than a sheet of paper. In the corner was stamped,

"Boston, February 1831." Beside that was a tiny symbol: a mountain range stacked upon a ruler. The rest of the metal sheet seemed completely blank.

"Let's leave this out for a moment," Shadrack said, placing it on the leather-topped table. He opened a drawer in the next bureau and took out a sheet of glass of about the same size. It, too, was entirely blank except for the place and date, "Boston, February 1831," and the mountain symbol etched into the corner.

"But they are blank," Sophia said.

"Just a little patience!" he said, opening drawers in the third and fourth bureaus. From these he withdrew a thin clay tablet and a rectangle of linen, engraved and embroidered, respectively, with the same information as the other two. He placed them side by side on the table and looked at the array in satisfaction. "There we are. Four maps of the same timeplace."

Sophia frowned. "Timeplace?"

"The meeting of a particular place and time."

"These are maps? They don't even have anything on them. They're just blank rectangles."

Shadrack went to one of the bookcases and ran his hand along the spines of the books. When he found the volume he was looking for, he took it off the shelf and thumbed through its pages. "Here!" he said. He laid the open book on the table. "This is what you're imagining, am I right?"

Sophia saw that the book was open to a map labeled "City of Boston." The familiar shape of the city, with its neighborhoods and waterways and principal roads and rail lines lay before her. "Yes," she said. "That's a map."

"Now, what would you say if I told you that each of these 'blank rectangles,' as you call them, has more information—a hundred times more information—than this paper map? They not only map the place, they map the *time* of Boston in February of 1831."

Sophia furrowed her brow. "Do you mean like how I map things in my sketchbook?"

"Yes, very much like your clever way of recording time through drawings and words. Although in these maps, you won't see pictures and words; you'll see animate impressions of what was happening then and there. It will feel as though you are *actually* there."

She let out a breath of astonishment. "How?"

He smiled. "I can promise you that, with practice, you will not only be able to read every map in those cabinets; you will even be able to make your own." He pulled out a chair. "Have a seat," he said. "And give it a try."

Sophia sat down eagerly and looked expectantly at the four rectangles lying before her.

"What do you think the first step is?"

She looked up at him in astonishment. "You mean you're not going to tell me?"

He smiled. "That would defeat the entire purpose. As I said, it's not skill that's required—it's the ability to think about things differently. If I tell you, you will simply memorize the method. If you have to discover it for yourself, you will understand how to apply the principle you learn. When we are out in another Age, confronted by a map neither of us understands, we'll need as much inventive thinking as both of us can muster. Memorizing won't help."

"But I have no idea how this works!"

"Perhaps not at first," Shadrack said. "But you have imagination, and it will come to you. I'll give you a starting point. And this is at the heart of lesson one—a lesson about paper." He sat down in a chair beside her. "Paper maps are valued all across the Ages for good reason. They're durable, they're unchanging, and they're accessible to anyone who picks them up. That has its uses. But other kinds of maps, while harder to read and in many cases more fragile, are also more dynamic and better at keeping secrets. Those qualities go hand in hand. A paper map is always there, but other maps—well, they sleep most of the time. Something you do has to wake them up so they can be read."

Sophia shook her head, utterly perplexed.

"Trust me, this will be useful," Shadrack said, getting up. He walked toward the stairs. "Now I have to go finish the letters I was writing on behalf of Mrs. Clay so that they go out with the morning post, and I want to enquire about Carlton. I'll be back soon to check on your progress," he said warmly.

After he had gone, Sophia took a deep breath and looked at the objects spread out before her on the table. She ignored the book and concentrated on the four blank rectangles, all with the mysterious words, "Boston, February 1831," in the bottom righthand corner. What did Shadrack mean about "waking up" the maps? And that the maps showed the time as well as the place? How was such a thing possible? She tentatively picked up the metal sheet. It felt cool to the touch and surprisingly light, and she saw herself faintly reflected in the ochre metal. But no matter how much she stared, nothing on its surface changed.

She put it down and picked up the clay tablet. She turned it over; it was just as blank on the back. The glass sheet was more opaque than she had realized at first. She gazed down onto its milky surface and watched her blurry reflection grow larger. Finally, she picked up the piece of linen by the corners and held it up before her face. "What's inside you, little handkerchief?" she murmured. "Why won't you say anything? Wake up, wake up." Nothing happened. She let out a sharp sigh of frustration. The piece of linen fluttered briefly, and as it settled once again something remarkable happened.

The surface started to change. Slowly, lines began to draw themselves across it. Sophia stared, wide-eyed, as the edges filled with scrollwork and a map appeared in the center of the cloth.

5
Learning to Read

1891, June 15: 9-Hour 22

It took decades, after the Disruption, for cartology to assert itself as the most important form of scholarship in New Occident. But as it absorbed the field of history and became essential to the country's efforts at exploration, cartology became the single most important area of scholarly work. What always remained a specialized—even marginal—focus within the broader field, however, was the study of how the other Ages practiced cartology.

—From Shadrack Elli's History of Cartology

Sophia dropped the linen on the table and ran to the base of the stairs. "Shadrack, come look!" she shouted. "Something happened!"

"All right," he called down to her. "Let's see what you've got."

She rushed back to the table to make sure the image was still there; it was. The fine, colored lines on the map looked as though they'd been drawn in ink. On the right-hand side, the legend consisted of two pale blue clocks: the first was numbered from one to twenty-eight, the second was an ordinary twenty-hour clock. A detailed web of brown and green filled the center of the linen, creating the familiar shape of the city of Boston. The borders, drawn in gold, repeated an inscrutable pattern of scrollwork and mysterious symbols.

"So how did you discover it?" Shadrack asked, sitting down next to her. He had brought a glass of water, which he set down at a good distance from the maps.

"I'm not sure. I think I breathed on it."

He smiled, stroking his chin. "All right, good enough. We often discover things by accident. The cloth maps respond to air. A breeze, a gale, a breath—it's all the same. The reason they respond to air is because they're weather maps. You can draw anything on a cloth map, but what they show most clearly are weather patterns. This one shows the weather for Boston in February of 1831."

"But it looks just like an ordinary map. Are those lines the weather?"

"You can't read it because you haven't specified a day and time yet." He pointed to the clocks in the legend.

The clocks had no hands. "These are hours and days?" Sophia asked.

"That's right. Choose one."

"How?"

"Well, the traditional way is to use your fingers. But you can use all kinds of things—beads, pins, things like that. I like these." He went to the closest bureau and removed a small, leather-bound box. Inside it were ordinary pebbles—all of them smooth and smaller than a fingernail.

"Oh, I see!" Sophia said excitedly. She placed a pebble on the day-clock's 8 and another on the hour-clock's 9. Nothing happened.

"Nine in the morning on February 8, 1831," Shadrack murmured. He took a sip of his water.

Sophia squinted at the map. "I still don't see anything."

Shadrack looked at her keenly. "Before you look at the weather for February eighth, let me tell you about an important difference between these maps and the maps you're used to. These are memory maps. They are not just one cartologer's impression of this place and time. They hold the collected memories of real people. They're histories. Some maps hold the memories of one person, others hold the memories of many. This map, for example, holds the memories of hundreds of people who were living in Boston in February of 1831."

"How does it do that?" Sophia breathed.

"That is what you will learn when you start making maps yourself. I can tell you it requires a great deal of research. The important thing to know now is this: when you read the map, it will be like having memories—you'll experience the memories of the people who were there."

Sophia's eyes opened wide. "I want to try it."

Shadrack leaned over the map, carefully keeping his arms on the table. "Try pointing out Boston Common to me. Can you find it on the map?"

"That's easy," Sophia scoffed. She reached out and placed her finger on the five-sided common, drawn in green at the right of the map. And suddenly, as her finger touched the cloth, she had a vivid memory—a memory that seemed her own. She saw the common in the early morning light, with clouds passing overhead. The landscape around her was blurry and dim, but she could recall vividly the cold bite of the wind and the damp in the air. Sophia felt herself shivering, the memory was so clear. She gasped and pulled her finger away from the map. The sensation faded. "Incredible," she said. "It is so real. As if I am remembering it."

Shadrack sat back with a look of gratification. "Yes. That is how it should be. That's what these maps *do*."

"But whose memories are they? Did you put them there?"

"Well, no—and yes. I learned about all the memories I could for this time and place. The map can only contain what the mapmaker finds. It's not an all-seeing eye. The memories come from living people—people who were alive when I made the map—and from written memories."

"I don't understand how they are *there*."

Shadrack paused. "Do you recall the drawing in your parents' room? The one of Minna and Bronson on the day they were married?"

Sophia looked at him. "I didn't know it was drawn the day they were married."

"It was. You may have noticed that the drawing is unlike others. More alive, perhaps."

"I had noticed," she said slowly. "But I thought it was my imagination. When I was younger, I would remember them so clearly whenever I looked at it."

"Whenever you *touched* it," Shadrack corrected. "I used some of the techniques that I use for mapmaking in that drawing. It is not the same, of course—a static portrait is far less powerful than a map. But it is the same principle."

Sophia shook her head in wonder. "But I still don't understand how the memories are *in* the drawing. How did you *make* this?"

"Imagine that when I made this map I traveled around to all the people I knew who remembered this moment, and I asked them to put their memories of it in a box. Then I went home and dove into all the hundreds of memories and used my knowledge about winds and temperature and humidity and sunlight and sorted out all the memories into their correct place and time."

"You actually used a box?"

"No, the 'box' is this cloth itself. Just as you read the map now by touch, it was written by touch. All of the memories were placed there by people who came into contact with this cloth, but then it was my task to give them order and meaning. The cartologer transforms the material into a legible, comprehensible document." He smiled. "It will make more sense when we actually practice it someday. For now, concentrate on reading."

"I'm going to read another time." Sophia moved the pebbles to the 12 on the day-clock and the 20 on the hour-clock. Then she gingerly put her fingertip on Boston Common and immediately recalled something that she had never lived through: standing in Boston Common in the middle of the night while the snowflakes swirled down around her. The sky was silver with clouds, and the air around her tasted cold. The snow moved across the common in gentle currents, as if shaped by an invisible breath. "It's just wonderful," Sophia said drawing her finger away. "I can't believe it."

Shadrack spoke with just the slightest hint of pride. "It's not a bad map, if I say so myself. Took quite a while to pin down the last few days of the month. Very few people remembered the weather." He considered the other maps on the table. "So what about these? Any luck?"

"Not yet."

"Let's look at them then, shall we?" Shadrack collected the pebbles, lifted the linen cloth, and gently turned it over. When he turned it right side up, it was once again blank, save for the inscriptions in the corner. "What about the clay tablet?"

She picked it up dubiously. She tried blowing on it, but nothing happened. "I don't know," she said, frowning.

"Your breath caused the linen to change," Shadrack said. "It was the key to the map—it created a movement, an impetus, a catalyst that unlocked it. What do you think would do that to clay—to a piece of earth?"

Sophia sat silently for a minute, thinking hard. Suddenly something occurred to her. "I know!"

Shadrack raised his eyebrows. "What are you thinking?"

"Hand me your water."

He edged it along the table and she dipped her finger into the cool liquid. Then she held it over the clay tablet and let a single drop fall. Immediately the surface of the clay began to change, and an intricately painted map appeared on the surface.

"I guessed it!"

"Well done. Earth responds to water. So try a date and time."

At the far left of the tablet was a legend like the one on the cloth map. Sophia placed pebbles on the day-clock's 15 and the hour-clock's 10: midday on February the fifteenth. Then she examined the map. The spidery lines on the clay wove their way tightly around the city center and then trailed off as they worked their way outward.

"Clay maps are topographical," Shadrack said. "They show the earth: hills, fields, forests, rivers, and so on. I think for this one it might be a little disorienting to look at the city center. Try an outlying region, out here." Shadrack indicated the western part of Boston, where there was a green expanse of land and almost no lines.

Sophia held her breath with anticipation and touched the map. She was flooded with a memory of rolling hills. In the distance she saw a small pond and farther on an orchard of bare trees. She lifted her finger, pulling herself away from the memories. "What happens if I move?"

"Go ahead—try it."

She carefully edged her finger upward on the map; it was like moving through a cascade of memories. She remembered pine forests and the thick needled carpet that lay underfoot; she remembered a long avenue lined with bare maples; she remembered the edge of a stream that was entirely frozen, dry leaves clumped in bundles at its edges. "It's beautiful," Sophia said quietly. "So many places—and so detailed."

"The clay maps are usually less work-intensive," Shadrack

said. "In this case, the terrain didn't change much over the course of the month, so I was able to spend more time working through the details of the landscape."

"I want to see the others!" Sophia removed the pebbles and then gently turned the clay map face down. She picked up the metal map. "I think I need some matches. Am I right?" She looked at Shadrack inquiringly.

Without speaking, he reached into his pocket and pulled out a box.

Sophia struck one and held it over the metal map. The small orange glow spread from the spot below the match outward, across the coppery surface. As she dropped the match into the glass of water, a clear, silver-lined map appeared in the center of the sheet. It seemed etched, rather than painted, and the lines shone like mercury against the copper surface. Sophia admired the map for only a few seconds before eagerly placing pebbles on the clocks.

"For this one I'd recommend something more precise," Shadrack said, rising from the table. He went to the bureau where he'd retrieved the pebbles and returned holding a long quill. "Should be sharp enough. The maps that contain more detail can sometimes be difficult to see with your fingertip. Try catching a smaller surface with the tip of the quill."

"Can I go back to the common?" she asked hesitantly.

"By all means—try it."

She placed the quill on one corner of Boston Common and at once recalled standing at the intersection of Charles Street and Beacon Street, between the common and the Public

Garden. The landscape around her looked blurry, but the brick houses along Beacon Street stood out sharply. There were fewer buildings in the city center. She had a clear memory of looking up the road and seeing the Park Street Church and then the State House at the top of the hill. She drew the quill along Beacon Street, heading west. The roads unfurled before her, and buildings sprang up as if emerging from a mist. She passed the mansions in the city center, the high churches, and smaller brick row houses, all the way to the small farms at Boston's outskirts. She had a sudden, vivid memory of standing before a red tavern with a low, wooden door. Sophia drew back the quill. "It's beautiful. Just beautiful. I can't believe you made this!"

"Can you find East Ending Street?"

Sophia moved the quill tentatively, hovering over the South End. "There it is!" she suddenly exclaimed. "That's East Ending Street!" She placed the quill on the map. In the memory that flooded her mind, some of the houses she knew were missing and some were unrecognizable, with newly laid bricks and oddly colored doors. But then something stirred in her mind, and she realized she was looking directly at a familiar house—her house. It was almost unchanged—sturdy and dignified, with its white-shuttered windows, its ponderous owl, and its bright red door. Only Shadrack's oval sign and the creeping ivy along the brick walls were missing. "It's our house!" she exclaimed.

Shadrack chuckled.

Sophia lingered over the memory a moment longer and then touched different areas of the map, locating her school and her favorite place by the river. After several minutes of eager exploring, she put the quill down. "So if the cloth map is the weather," she said slowly, "and the clay map is the ground, and the metal map is the buildings—"

"Construction," Shadrack clarified. "That includes roads, railways, bridges, and so on. Everything manmade."

"Everything manmade," Sophia repeated. "That's all there is. What does the glass map show?"

Shadrack raised his eyebrows. "You tell me. What is missing from the memories?"

Sophia stared blankly at the sheet of glass. She picked it up and examined it closely, but all she could see was her cloudy reflection. Suddenly something occurred to her, but the thought was so marvelous that she couldn't quite believe it. "Not . . . *people?*"

"Try it and see."

"But I have no ideas about how to wake it up."

"You're right—this one is the toughest. And it's a little difficult to come up with, in this particular room." He stood. "Normally, you would have a window with daylight, and you would keep the glass covered. Bring it over to the table lamp."

"Oh—light!" Sophia exclaimed. She carried the glass sheet carefully to where her uncle was standing beside the two armchairs. She held the pane under the bright lamp, and immediately the spidery white lines of a finely etched map spread across the surface of the glass like fragile threads of frost on a winter windowpane.

Shadrack took it from her and held it up. "The glass map

recalls human action—human history. It can be disturbing the first time you see one. It is strange to remember people you don't know, saying things you've never heard. You must keep a clear distinction in your mind between the memories that are yours and the memories that come from the map. But you'll learn to do that with time. This map I know for sure has nothing too alarming in it. You can savor all of its memories without concern." He carried the glass back to the main table and gently placed it face up. Then he slid pebbles onto both of the 10s on the two clocks at the left-hand side of the map. "Try the quill," he said encouragingly.

Sophia wrinkled her brow. She felt strangely reluctant to plunge into the memories that she knew were stored before her.

"Go ahead," Shadrack said. "How about here, near the market?"

She held the quill over Quincy Market and set it down. She felt a sudden rush and a powerful wave of recollection. People were talking all around her, laughing and shouting and gossiping in low voices. A woman standing next to her carefully counted her money. A boy walked past with a crate full of flowers, and she had a sudden memory of their powerful, hothouse smell. She could remember seeing the clouds of warm breath in the cold air and the sleepy face of a potato farmer who had driven his cart into the city from far away. It all seemed incredibly vivid—as if she had lived through it herself. The space around them remained blurry. It was as though she had erased all the buildings and streets and the very ground beneath her feet. Beyond the people, her memory was dim.

Sophia lifted the quill and blinked a few times. "It's odd. As though I can remember people, but nothing else. It feels like I could be anywhere."

"I know—it's strange to see ourselves without the world around us, isn't it?" Shadrack gently moved the glass pane aside. "I'll show you what makes it better—what makes them all worthwhile, really." He picked up the cloth, gently blew against, it and placed it face up on the table. With the tip of his finger he drew water onto the clay tablet and placed it on top of the cloth, their corners perfectly aligned. Then he added the metal sheet, with its map still intact. And finally he set the glass pane, with its pebbles on the 10s, on the top of the pile. "Have a go," he said.

Sophia took the quill and hesitantly stared down through the glass. She could see the silver traces of the metal map lying beneath it. Then she took a deep breath and placed the quill at the corner of Beacon and Charles.

All of it—a whole world from February of 1831—came back to her clearly. In Boston Common people were hurrying down the walkways, stamping their feet against the cold. The bare trees nodded gently in the chilly breeze, rattling a little against the gray sky. A small group of skaters whirled over the frozen pond. Along the streets people rushed with their baskets full of purchases or rode past on their Goodyears, the rubber wheels spinning soundlessly. And in all the windows of the houses people moved through their endless routines of eating and talking and working and sleeping.

It was like plunging into another world, but the world was

her own. She knew the memories did not belong to her, and yet they were there—so vivid, so lucid that they seemed to be entirely hers. Sophia lifted the quill with a sigh. "My memories are never that clear," she said. "They are always so patchy. But these are so perfect."

"We are all like that," Shadrack agreed. "That's why it helps to make the maps in layers. We cannot all remember everything at once. In fact, it's surprising how little detail people actually remember. But if you add together what everyone remembers about each piece, it comes together."

Sophia said what had been on her mind since she had first discovered the purpose of the glass map. "Do you think—is there any way . . . Could it be that Mother and Father might have left memories this way, stored in a map somewhere?"

Shadrack ran his hand through his hair. "Perhaps," he said slowly. "They did not know how to make memory maps when they left Boston. But they might have learned."

"Or someone else might have made a map that shows them in it."

"It's a very good thought, Sophia. Even a glimpse could be invaluable. You'll see what I mean if you take a look at East Ending, now that the maps are layered."

Sophia placed the tip of the quill on the map. She remembered a gray sky and a cold, damp breeze. The street was quiet. A few candles shone weakly in the windows, despite the fact that it was midday; the dark sky made them necessary. The bright red door she knew so well was closed. She could see someone through the upstairs window—a boy. He was reading intently at a desk, his chin in his hand. The memory suddenly grew sharper, as if a veil had been lifted from her eyes, and the boy looked up from his reading. He peered straight out at her—at Sophia—and smiled. Sophia gasped and pulled the quill away. "He looked at me." She turned to Shadrack. "The boy in the window. Who was he?"

"You saw him!" Shadrack said, taking the quill. He placed it on East Ending and smiled as the memory came to his mind. "You know who he is—think about it."

"Is it Grandfather?"

"Yes—it's my father; your grandfather."

"But why did he smile at me?"

"Because that is your great-grandmother's memory—Grandmother Lizzie. She was there to see your grandfather smile at her through the window." Shadrack put the quill down a bit wistfully. "Nice one, isn't it?"

Sophia felt a wave of awe: she was seeing the world through the eyes of her great-grandmother, a woman she had never even met. But some part of her felt uneasy, as if she had trespassed on another person's private thoughts. "It's a lovely memory," she said slowly. "But it's not mine. Is it really all right to—to take it like that?"

Shadrack's face was thoughtful. "It's a valuable question, Sophia. It has to do with what I was mentioning before—knowing where your memory stops and the memory of another begins. It may help to know that no one loses their memories in making the map. People share them. But that raises another problem: everyone's memory is imperfect. I tried to learn everything possible about this month in Boston. I put together as many memories as I could find. And I combined them with what I knew—the kinds of clothes people wore, the buildings, the ships, all that. But you must know that memory maps—maps of all kinds, really—are inexact. They are only the best possible approximation. Think of them like books of history: the author will try to be as accurate as possible, but often he or she is relying on slim pieces of evidence, and there is as much art and interpretation as there is factual content. The best maps will show the cartologer's hand at work rather than conceal it, making plain the interpretive work and suggesting, even, other possible interpretations."

"Does that mean that people could create maps that distort what really happened? Maps that are made up?"

"They could indeed," Shadrack said gravely. "It is a serious crime to do so. But all honest mapmakers swear an oath to tell only the truth, and you must look for the mark of that oath when you examine a memory map. Look here," he said, pointing out the small symbol of the mountains atop a ruler that appeared beside the date on each map. "This is the Insignia Rule. It is required on those maps whose truth can only be vouched for by their maker. But even a truthful mapmaker may be inaccurate. For example," he confessed, "there are some streets on this map that no one remembers at two or three in the morning on some day or another. Who is to say that something did not happen that I failed to record? In that way, my map, too, might be a distortion."

“But it is still incredible. It’s the most beautiful thing I’ve ever seen.”

Shadrack shook his head. “My maps are still those of a novice. There are maps that make mine look like mere scribbles. You’ll see some of them, soon enough. I have read memory maps so real one forgets oneself in them. Some so large they fill an entire room. Truly, the maps created by the masters are astonishing.”

Sophia bounced in her chair with excitement. “I want to read them all.”

Shadrack laughed. “Someday you will. But there’s much yet to learn, and we must work quickly. Come, let me show you how to navigate seconds.”

6
A Trail of Feathers

1891, June 15 to 21

The lenient laws of New Occident have long allowed foreigners to enjoy the benefits of residency without requiring their formal application for citizenship. Only foreigners wishing to vote, run for office, or form a corporation have been required to apply. As of July 4, these laws will change. Full naturalization will be necessary for all foreigners. If you are a foreigner and you wish to work or reside in New Occident, you must apply through the attached form for documentation and a foreigner's lifewatch. All those without documentation and watches will be deported on July 4.

—From Application for Citizenship Pursuant to the Patriot Plan

For the remainder of the day Sophia studied the maps of Boston in February 1831, and Shadrack taught her the intricacies of the four map forms. She learned how to use different quills in order to see more or less detail; she learned how to close in on a particular minute or second; and she began to grow more accustomed to the flood of memories that weren't hers.

The glass map still made her uneasy; remembering people she had never met left her feeling disoriented, as if she had woken up in someone else's skin. But she began to find ways of distinguishing between her memories and those she experienced while map-reading: the memories from the maps were far clearer and more vivid than her own. At least one aspect came so naturally that she had nothing to learn: the fact that days, minutes, and hours unfolded at different paces; the sense that time could be short or long, depending on how one chose to read. More than anything, Sophia loved this quality of the memory maps. Though they revealed unknown places, their manner of compressing and expanding time made her feel entirely at home.

In the days that followed, Shadrack began his ambitious plan to teach Sophia about the cartology of the other Ages. She learned that these maps needed particular care; they had to be cleaned and stored carefully to ensure their safety. Mapmaking, Shadrack explained, was a science and an art practiced in every Age, all over the world. The dynamic memory maps had probably been invented in either the Baldlands or the Middle Roads. No one knew for certain, but he believed their invention would only have been possible in one of those regions where the various Ages had been so jumbled that past, present, and future were interwoven.

Shadrack had learned to make memory maps at the academy in Nochtland. The mapmaker's guild was powerful there. The production and circulation of maps was carefully regulated; every Nochtland-created map had to bear the insignia that guaranteed its truthfulness—the tiny mountain range atop a ruler.

His collection of memory maps opened Sophia's eyes even further to the wonders of cartology beyond New Occident. She saw parts of the world she had never imagined she would see. The maps varied in scale: some recalled only a few rooms, others an entire city; some contained memories from only a minute or an hour; others held the memories of a whole year. One map captured twenty-four hours in the Alhambra, in Granada. Another showed the passage of a year in the capitol of the Russias. And another recalled the crucial four months of rebellion that led to the creation of New Akan. It occurred to Sophia, as she studied the maps, that space and skill were the only constraints. On the third day of her studies she turned to Shadrack. "Shadrack, do you think there could be a memory map of the entire world?"

His face had an odd expression. "It would be unimaginably difficult to make such a map," he finally said. "Though there are stories of something called the *carta mayor*, a hidden map that traces the memories of the whole world from the beginning of time to the present."

"That would be incredible."

For a moment, Shadrack's face tensed. "Explorers have spent entire lifetimes pursuing the *carta mayor*. Some have lost themselves searching."

"So it exists?"

"It almost certainly does *not* exist," he said quickly. "I have always argued that it is a Nihilismian myth—one that serves their purposes well but has no basis in fact."

"How is it Nihilismian?" Though there was a large following

of Nihilismians in Boston, Sophia knew little about them beyond what she had learned in school.

Nihilismianism was one of the many religious sects that had sprouted in the wake of the Great Disruption. Many people still followed the old religions of the West, but a growing number believed in the Fates, whose temples depicted over the entryway the three goddesses, each holding the globe on a string. Others practiced Occidental Numism, or Onism, which held that all material and immaterial things were a form of currency to be bought and sold, exchanged and bartered with the higher powers. Sophia had seen an Onist's account book once, when Dorothy—always more intrepid—had stolen a look at the private *Book of Deeds and Debts* that one of their teachers kept on his desk. It was filled with precise and, to Sophia, terrible calculations. One in particular often occurred to her when her mind wandered: "Twenty-one minutes of daydreaming about last year's trip to the seaside with A, to be paid for with twenty-one minutes of housework." It was said that the Onist lifestyle was wonderfully productive, but Sophia found the prospect dreadful.

And there were Nihilismians who believed that the true world had been derailed by the Great Disruption and replaced by a false one. It was unsettling to think that a world no longer in existence was thought by some to be more real than their own.

"The Nihilismians are sure that the *carta mayor* would show the true course of the world—not this one," Shadrack said now. "But I fail to see how such a thing is even possible."

Sophia squinted pensively, considering.

"It is a dangerous myth to believe in," he concluded, with an air of finality.

Every so often during her studies, Sophia would wander over to the wall map, where the blue and green pins marked the voyage her parents never took and the places where they'd appeared. Shadrack told her everything he could. An explorer from Vermont believed he had traded food with them somewhere deep in the Prehistoric Snows. An explorer from Philadelphia had spoken to a street vendor in the Papal States who had sold salt to a pair of young adventurers in Western clothing. A cartologer from the university had spoken to a sailor who might have boarded a ship with them in the United Indies. All of the encounters were brief and vague and inconclusive. Shadrack had noted every one.

Sophia felt a terrible impatience when she contemplated the eventual purpose of her studies. Part of her wanted to leave *at once*, tracing the path of the green pins wherever they led. She had to remind herself that gaining the right store of knowledge for the journey posed a more significant and important challenge than any she might face later. Every moment of learning was essential. "Step by step," Shadrack encouraged her, gesturing towards the wall map. "We have little enough time as it is, Soph. In truth, I wish we could work more slowly."

While Sophia learned to work with the maps, Shadrack shuttled back and forth between the map room and his ground-floor study. He had managed to secure forged papers and a lifewatch for Mrs. Clay, but this task had been only the first of many. Desperate friends from every corner of New Occident began arriving at 34 East Ending Street with requests for maps and route-guides to other Ages. Explorers were leaving the states in droves, panicked by parliament's decision. Shadrack barely had time to answer Sophia's questions.

For her part, she became so engrossed in her studies that she hardly noticed how many days had passed, let alone hours and minutes. Her fascination with map-reading was genuine and all-absorbing; moreover, there were no competing distractions. Yes, it was summer, a time when ordinary schoolchildren spent all day swimming and wasting time and wandering with friends. But with Dorothy gone to New York, there was no one to knock on the door and drag her out into the sunshine.

At the end of the week, Shadrack descended into the map room after a long meeting with an explorer who was leaving for the Russias, and he looked with some concern at his niece, hunched over the leather-topped table. With her dark blonde hair messier than usual, her face pale from lack of sleep, and her light summer clothes uncharacteristically rumpled, she looked more like an overworked office clerk than a child.

Sophia was entirely unaware of Shadrack's scrutiny; she was wrestling with a puzzle that she'd stumbled across while comparing two maps. From the shape and configuration of the islands rendered up them, she could tell that the maps depicted the exact same location. But one was labeled *United Indies* and the other *Terra Incognita,* and they seemed to show two different Ages.

The former held the sound of bells at midday in a quiet stone courtyard; a pair of nuns walked past Sophia in the memory, talking quietly to one another, and the smell of the sea was in the air. The latter showed a cold, stony landscape with no signs of life. The only clue to their difference lay in the fact that the Terra Incognita map had been made more recently: ten years after the United Indies map.

How is this possible? Sophia wondered. *How could the place have changed so much so soon?* She was studying Terra Incognita, scouring the map for signs of what had happened to so alter it, when Shadrack's voice yanked her out of the memory.

"Sophia!"

"Yes?" She looked up, startled.

"You're getting pale from living in this basement. I know we have a lot to do, but you mustn't entomb yourself here. Your limbs will turn to jelly."

"I don't care," Sophia said absently. "Shadrack, did anything happen recently at the eastern edge of the United Indies? I can't figure this out. These two maps show the same place, but one of them shows a convent and the one from ten years after shows . . . well, nothing."

"I determined that the map was mislabeled," Shadrack said peremptorily. "We can look at it later; right now, you need to escape this room for a little while. It will clear your head."

"I don't think it's mislabeled. It's the same spot, but different. And it occurred to me—do you still have the letter Casavetti sent? I think—"

"Sophia!" Shadrack walked over and pulled back her chair. "Your enthusiasm does you credit. But it will not serve our purposes if you can't carry a heavy pack or walk ten paces without collapsing. We'll make a deal. Six days of being an indoor cartologer and one day of being an outdoor explorer."

Sophia grumbled. "It's too hot outside anyway."

"How would you know? You haven't even been outside! I'll tell you what. I have hardly left the house myself, what with all the incoming traffic. When we do leave on our voyage, we'll be utterly unprepared. Let me give you a list so you can begin gathering our supplies."

The prospect of buying supplies made the journey seem suddenly quite real; her pulse quickened. "That's a good idea."

Shadrack chuckled. "I'm glad you approve. All right, I think your best bet will be Harding's Supply out on the wharf. You were near there the other day."

"I know where it is."

"So I have an old pack that will do fine, but you need one. Don't get one that's too big—have them size it for you before you buy it. The other thing we need is a hard roll-tube for paper maps. Mine have all fallen apart, I haven't used them in so long. Get two. And look for a weather-proof case for your lifewatch." He thought for a moment. "That's enough for now. Put it on my credit at the store; I have an account. Sound good?"

"Pack, roll-tubes, watch-case," Sophia repeated. "Sounds good." She climbed the steps to the study, noticing as she walked through the house that the rooms had grown messier and messier during the days she had spent in the map room. Mrs. Clay did her best, but she was really no match for Shadrack's explosive fits of energy. Sophia reached her room and sat down to change her shoes. As she did so, her eye lighted on her sketchbook, and a thought made her rise slowly and turn back the pages to June 14, the day before she'd first gone into the map room—the day she'd gone to parliament. She found herself looking at the drawing she'd made of the caged boy from the circus. *Who knows what will happen to him*, she thought. She stared at the bars she had drawn. *Maybe he's still there. I might see him again.* The prospect gave her a brief flutter, but it was accompanied by a sobering thought. *I wonder if he's ever let out of that horrible cage. I can't believe he might have to eat and sleep in it and everything.* A sudden idea flickered through her mind. *He doesn't belong in that cage*, she said to herself, her thoughts soaring. *He shouldn't spend another minute in that cage.*

With a rising sense of excitement, she finished lacing her boots and ran downstairs. Seeing that it was almost lunchtime, she hastily wrapped a piece of buttered bread in a napkin and tucked it into the apron pocket of her dress. "Bye, Shad," she shouted before heading out the door.

—June 21, 11-Hour 57: Leaving to Buy Supplies—

THE HEAT HAD let up somewhat, dropping into the low nineties. During any other summer, such temperatures would have driven every resident of the city to Cape Cod, but with parliament's deadline hanging over New Occident, Boston bristled with uneasy activity. The accusations against foreigners published in the newspaper had grown more frequent and bitter and had resulted in an unending stream of protests.

As Sophia rode the trolley downtown, she noticed knots of people walking in the direction of the State House. As they passed the building, her eyes widened; it was surrounded by police officers, and hundreds of people were shouting and carrying signs. Shadrack had told her that the police were patrolling around the clock, checking the identity papers of everyone they passed. Anyone without papers found themselves abruptly shuttled to the nearest point of exit from New Occident.

The trolley stopped briefly on the far side of the common, at some distance from the State House, and then veered off, careening into the tunnel that connected to the wharf. Sophia felt nervous at the thought of once again seeing the boy in feathers. *Maybe I should get the supplies first,* she thought. *But I don't want to be carrying the supplies if I try to open the cage. I should go to the circus first.*

The trolley emerged from the tunnel and the conductor called the Wharf stop. Sophia stepped off, edgy with excitement, and looked for the warehouse where she'd seen the circus.

The chaos at the wharf made the protest near the State House pale in comparison. Crowds of people—determined explorers, anxious tradespeople, and exiled foreigners—wove along the cobblestone street and toward the waiting ships. Police officers walked tensely among them, truncheons drawn, checking papers and shepherding people into lines. Every manner of vessel filled the waters beyond the wharf and waited to board passengers, seeking to profit from the sudden exodus. Sophia turned away in dismay as she heard a ship's captain haggling with an explorer over an outrageous fee for passage to the Closed Empire.

Catching sight of a faded warehouse nearby, Sophia pushed past the crowd and hurried toward it. Sure enough, there was the sign for Ehrlach's Circus of the Ages. But something had changed. There was no line for admittance, and the warehouse door was closed. There was no trace of the little man, the ticket vendor, or the boy in the cage.

For a moment she stood hesitantly, watching people pass. Then she approached the door and gave it an experimental push. It seemed to be barred by something on the other side. She pushed a little harder and the door gave way.

"Oh, no," she said out loud. The cavernous warehouse stood completely empty. A pile of hay, a few broken pieces of a set, and some netting lay scattered on the dirt floor. Sophia stood and stared. She recalled once again the boy in feathers—his air of careless grace, the easy way he shoved aside the circus master's cane. Now he was gone. She imagined him traveling to some unknown place, imprisoned forever in his horrible cage, until his lofty expression faded and his eyes lost their animation.

Sophia left the empty warehouse, closing the door behind her. "Excuse me," she said to an old man carrying a heavy traveling case. "Has the circus gone already?"

"It has, miss," he said, taking a moment to rest. "They packed up only this morning."

"I thought they would stay until July fourth."

"They could have, sure, but Ehrlach wanted to spend the last weeks in New York. Seems to think there'll be more business there without the parliament protests to distract them."

"I see. Thank you," Sophia said. "Bad luck, I suppose."

"Bad luck it is—for all of us," the old man replied, shouldering the case again. "I'm sorry, miss."

Sophia stood, staring at the sign and trying to shake off her disappointment. *I should have thought of it sooner,* she said to herself. *I didn't realize how many days had passed.* The familiar sense of frustration washed over her, but she had to admit that in this case her broken internal clock wasn't entirely to blame. She'd been thoughtless in a wholly ordinary way. For an entire week she had forgotten about the boy, and now the chance to help him was gone.

With an abrupt glance at her watch, she realized that she had lost more than an hour and reminded herself sternly of her assigned task. She turned and looked for Harding's Supply with a renewed sense of purpose. It was nearby, its double doors opened wide to allow for the steady stream of customers purchasing last-minute equipment for long overseas journeys. Having lost so much time already, Sophia hurried through the aisles, inspecting waterproof rucksacks, snowshoes, collapsible hats, silk sheets that folded away into a pocket-sized pouch, canteens, and field glasses. She left the store with a small russet-brown pack, two weatherproof roll-tubes for paper maps, and an oiled leather case for her watch.

— *15-Hour 09: Arriving Home* —

IT WAS PAST fifteen-hour when Sophia headed home. The summer sun was still high in the sky, and as she turned onto East Ending Street it occurred to her that she might yet have time to finish solving the puzzle she'd begun that morning. Surely Shadrack wouldn't mind, now that she had dutifully spent the afternoon out of doors.

Sophia neared the house and was surprised to see the side door wide open. When she reached the steps, something odd caught her eye: a long green feather. She picked it up and examined it. "Very strange," she murmured. As soon as she had reached the entryway, she could see that something was very wrong.

The house was a disaster. Something intent on destruction had swept through it. Food and broken dishes lay strewn across the kitchen floor. The rugs in the hallway were twisted and shoved together, while remains of burnt papers and maps littered the stove. Almost all the framed maps that normally hung in every room had been knocked down, leaving the papered walls bare. Even some of the floorboards had been torn up. And lying before her near the entryway was a long red feather. She stood for a moment, her panic mounting, and then she dropped the green feather, threw aside the new pack that hung from her shoulder, and ran toward the study.

"Shadrack!" she shouted. "*Shadrack!*"

He was not there. Maps lay scattered everywhere, many of them torn. The books had been pulled from the shelves and lay on the ground in haphazard piles. With horror, Sophia saw the door to the map room standing open.

"Shadrack?" she called, her voice unsteady, from the top of the stairs. There was no answer. She descended slowly, the wooden treads creaking beneath her feet. When she reached the bottom she stood dazed at the chaos before her.

The glass cases had been shattered, their contents gone. The bureaus lay open, their drawers bare. Here, too, the books had been pulled from the shelves and thrown to the floor. The cabinets that held paper maps stood empty. Sophia took in the destruction, too stunned to call out again. Everything, every single thing in the map room, had been destroyed or stolen. A broken glass map crunched beneath her boot and she looked down blankly at the shards. There was a long, jagged scar across the leather-topped table. She touched it gingerly, as if to make certain that it was real. Then she raised her head and her eye fell on the wall map above the armchairs: the map of her parents' voyage. It had been torn in half, ripped clear through from one end to the other.

Sophia stared numbly at the pins that lay scattered around her on the chairs and carpet, a single thought running through her mind: *Where is he? Where is Shadrack? Where is he?* Then she heard a sound at the other end of the room, and for a moment she was unable to run or scream or even move. Heart pounding in her chest, she forced herself to turn slowly in the direction of the stairs. She saw nothing. It had been only a soft shuffle, but she had heard it, and now she was certain: it had come from the heavy wardrobe below the staircase.

She tiptoed across the carpet, avoiding the glass and picking up the broken leg of a chair. She held it before her with both hands. When she reached the steps, she stopped to listen and heard nothing but the rush of blood in her ears. She reached the wardrobe and paused, standing in front of it silently. Then she reached for the brass handle and in one smooth movement swung open the door.

Feathers, she thought, as the thing that burst from the wardrobe knocked her down flat. She lay there, stunned, staring up at the ceiling, and suddenly a face appeared above hers. The face seemed to have feathers sprouting from it in every direction.

Looking down at Sophia was the boy from Ehrlach's Circus of the Ages.

7
Between Pages

1891, June 21, 15-Hour 52

Consider that we do not even know for certain whether the Great Disruption was caused by mankind and, if so, which Age of mankind caused it. Too many Ages remain unknown, entirely uncharted and beyond communication. Of the Ages we do know, all were thrust into a common confusion and chaos in the first years after the Disruption. All suffered disorientation, or sudden isolation, or unending cycles of violence. What Age would willingly bring this upon itself?

—From Shadrack Elli's History of the New World

"Hey," the boy said. "Are you okay?"

Sophia blinked.

"I'm sorry I knocked you over," he said. "Are you okay? Say something."

She raised herself on her elbow. "Yes," she said. "Yes, I'm all right." She stared at the boy sitting next to her on the carpet. "You were in the wardrobe," she said.

"I was hiding. Where were *you*?"

"I just got here. I was out." Now that the worst was over, the fear began to move in. She felt a cold tremor. The boy reached out a hand to help her, and she recoiled sharply.

"Hey, it's okay. I won't hurt you." He spoke softly, with the truncated words and low twang of the northwest Baldlands. "I didn't do this."

Sophia got to her feet. "What happened? Where's Shadrack?"

The boy looked at her with an odd expression. "Is he your father?"

She shook her head. Her jaw trembled so violently that her teeth had begun to chatter. "He's my uncle. Where is he?" She glanced quickly across the room. "I have to look upstairs."

"No, wait." The boy held up a hand to stop her. "Don't. He's not there," he said quietly.

"Where is he?"

"I don't know—I don't know where he is now."

"But you saw him?"

He nodded slowly. "Yeah, I saw him." He was studying her, trying to decide what to say. "Do you live here? With Shadrack Elli?"

It was strange to hear her uncle's name on the boy's tongue. Sophia nodded impatiently. "Yes. Yes, I live here. I told you—he's my uncle. Please, just tell me what happened!"

The boy paused a moment. "Sorry to have to tell you this. Your uncle is gone."

Sophia felt as though all the air had been squeezed out of her. The words were a shock, but they also struck her as terribly familiar. Some part of her, she realized, always expected those she most loved to vanish.

"I came here looking for him. When I got here, the door was

open. I could hear all kinds of noise inside, but I didn't know what was going on." He paused. "I waited in the bushes outside. After about half an hour, some men took your uncle out of the house." The boy seemed to gauge Sophia's response before continuing. "There were five of them. They put him and some boxes into a coach, and then they left. After they were gone, I went in, and when I heard you upstairs, I hid. I thought they had come back." He looked away. "I'm sorry."

"Who were they—what kind of men were they?"

"I don't know. I mean, they were ordinary. Thugs, I guess." He frowned. "A few of them had some"—he paused, drawing a finger across his face—"scars."

Sophia swallowed hard. "Was he all right?" she asked with an effort. "Was he hurt?"

"He was fine," the boy said firmly. "He was struggling with them—and he was talking back. He was angry, but he wasn't hurt."

Sophia felt her throat tensing, and she realized she wouldn't be able to stop herself from crying. She turned away. "I need to be alone for a while," she whispered.

"I'm really sorry," the boy said. "I, uh . . ." he hesitated. "I'll just be upstairs."

Sophia heard him on the steps, and then the door closed, and then she stopped thinking of him altogether. All her thoughts turned to Shadrack and the fact that he was gone. She sank to the ground. Her sobs came in deep, painful gasps that finally gave way to tears.

None of it made any sense. How could Shadrack be gone—just like that? In the morning, she'd been sitting next to him in this very room, reading a map, and now the room was ruined and Shadrack was gone and she was alone—totally alone. She cried until her head ached, and then when her head hurt too much she sat listlessly on the carpet. Her head throbbed and she needed water and she felt empty, terribly empty.

If I hadn't lost track of time, she thought. *If I hadn't lost track of time at the wharf, I would have been back earlier. I would be wherever he is now. And neither one of us would be alone.*

Only a few minutes had passed, but time expanded around her, filled with a seemingly infinite sense of loss. *He could be anywhere. He could be hurt,* she realized, the thought pounding away at her head insistently.

She heard a sound from the library upstairs and brought herself painfully back to the present. Wiping her eyes, she took a deep breath and got to her feet. She couldn't look around, couldn't bear to see the beautiful map room in its ruined state, so she kept her eyes on the ground and made her way slowly up the stairs. When she reached the library, she closed the map room door behind her.

The boy was crouched on the floor, rummaging through maps on the carpet. He looked up at her and stopped what he was doing. "Hey," he asked again. "Are you okay?"

"Yes. Thank you."

He nodded, then followed her gaze to the strewn papers around him. "I was just looking for a map. Maybe a map of New

Occident. Does he have one? I mean, with all these maps lying around . . ."

"Yes," Sophia said. Her mind moved very slowly. "I can find you one. But I can't—not right now."

"No," he agreed. He stood and tried vainly to arrange some of the broken feathers strung around his waist. He and Sophia stared silently at one another for several seconds. "I'm Theo," the boy finally said.

"Sophia," she replied.

"Sophia, I should have explained that I came to find your uncle so that he could help me. I heard about him at the wharf—the famous cartologer in Boston. I thought he might help me get home. I'm not from here."

"I know," she said softly. "You're a wild boy from the Baldlands."

Theo paused in surprise and then one side of his mouth lifted in a smile. "Yes—I wasn't sure you'd remember."

"Dressed like that? You're very memorable."

"I guess that's true." Theo laughed. He glanced down at himself and then looked at her. "I ran away this morning. When the circus set out."

"You ran away."

"Yes."

Sophia couldn't think of what to say next. Her mind wasn't working properly—she couldn't think why it mattered that he had run away.

"Sophia," Theo said. "You have to figure out what you want

to do, and so do I. Could I—It'd be really nice if I could change out of this."

She blinked. "You mean that's not how you normally dress?"

Theo paused. "Of course not," he finally said. "This was what that idiot Ehrlach put on me for the show."

"Oh."

"I could really use some soap," Theo said. "And maybe some paint thinner. These are stuck on with honey and glue—they're murder to wash off. And some clothes?"

"Of course." Having to think about things like paint thinner and soap was a relief. She could tidy the house and put things in order. The paint thinner was in the washroom next to the kitchen; there were clean rags there, on the rag heap. She moved through the wrecked rooms, through the shattered china, torn paper, and broken furniture. It was as if she had been dropped in a stranger's house. Oddly enough, this thought made it easier to bear. "You can use Shadrack's bathroom," she said, climbing the stairs. Theo followed her, leaving his telltale feathers everywhere.

Surprisingly, the second floor seemed untouched. The men must have found what they were looking for or believed there was nothing of value in the bedrooms. "I think there are some clothes of my uncle's you can wear," she said. "They might be a little big."

"Anything you've got I'd appreciate," Theo said. "So long as I don't have to wear the feathers."

Sophia looked through Shadrack's wardrobe and found a small shirt and some pants and a belt. The shoes would all be too big. She pointed out the bathroom and gave Theo the paint thinner and the clothes. He said, "Thanks," and then paused. "Hey, I—you're not going anywhere, right?" Sophia looked at him blankly. "I was wondering—I'm going to need a place to stay. Just one night."

Sophia realized what he was asking. "You can stay."

"Thanks. I owe you." He snapped his fingers with a practiced air, ending in a gesture like a pointed gun. "It would be good to get that map, too, if that's okay. Tomorrow I'll get out of your hair."

The door shut, and after a moment Sophia heard the sound of running water.

Standing in Shadrack's bedroom, which looked so normal, she was once again overcome. The leather armchair, the books on the end table beside it, and the piles of maps—it was as if her uncle had only left the room for a moment and was about to return. The blue rug was worn in a path from the door to the mahogany secretary, which, for once, stood unlocked and open. Sophia moved toward it, feeling a faint flutter in her stomach. Shadrack never left his desk open.

A splatter of ink on the blotter and the open journal left no doubt in her mind: Shadrack had been surprised while sitting here, writing. Seeing her name on the page, she read the last entry anxiously.

I struggle with how much to tell Sophia. She must understand the dangers, but there is a fine line between useful comprehension and needless alarm. While she left to buy supplies, I visited Carlton in the hospital, and I was shocked by his condition. The article did not mention the horrible mutilation of his limbs and face. I can only assume they mean to withhold this for purposes of the police inquiry. He does not recognize me; he recognizes no one. I doubt if he has preserved any cognitive faculties. He is like a helpless child. He makes inarticulate sounds, occasionally, and seems to feel pain when his injuries are dressed, but he has no other awareness of the world around him. It seems to me impossible that this could be the result of some ordinary assault. . . . Rather, I begin to suspect that someone

The entry ended there. Horrified by the image of Carlton Hopish ruined, Sophia drew back. What had Shadrack suspected? Could he have seen something at the hospital that had placed him in danger? There was no message for her in those pages, as she had hoped—only an ominous riddle that left her even more frightened. She felt the tears welling up in her eyes and took several deep breaths to stop them.

Shadrack's armchair, where he always read for an hour or two before going to bed, still bore the impression of where he had sat the night before. Sophia stumbled over and dropped down into it. It smelled of cedar and pine and paper; Shadrack's smell. What if she had seen him reading in his armchair for the last time? She could already imagine how the room would look in a year, or five, or ten. It would look just like her parents' bedroom down the hall: the walls would discolor in strange patterns; the books would warp from one humid summer after another; the clothes and shoes would seem to shrivel and age. She had been trying to hold the thought at bay, but now that she pictured Shadrack's room slipping into abandonment, she could not avoid it. Again, the moments expanded, and Sophia imagined a long future without him, without her parents—entirely alone. The thought made her curl up in the chair, and she wrapped her arms around her knees.

Sophia felt something sharp against her side. She ignored it. But the more she ignored it the more it jabbed into her ribs, until finally she sat up and shoved the pillow aside. To her surprise, it felt hard. She lifted the pillow. Propped behind it was one of her old drawing notebooks.

What is my old notebook doing in Shadrack's armchair? she wondered dully, picking it up. The notebook felt *heavy*. She untied the two leather laces that held its covers closed, and the book fell open to what looked like a note. She recognized Shadrack's handwriting at once, even though the message was brief. It read:

Sophia—go to Veressa. Take my atlas. Love, SE

Beneath it was a glass map.

Sophia stared at the map and the note in wonder. Shadrack had left her a message after all! And he had found the perfect place for it. Between the heavy pages of her drawing notebook, the thin pane of glass lay well protected. Sophia ran her fingers tenderly over her uncle's writing. The message sounded urgent, but not despairing or afraid. Shadrack hadn't told her to hide or run away. Sophia felt something—not relief, but determination—course through her. She remembered what Shadrack had said before under very different circumstances: "*All you need, Sophia, is something to* do."

And now she *did* have something to do: she had to take Shadrack's atlas and find Veressa, wherever that was. And perhaps when she found Veressa, she would find Shadrack!

Sophia jumped to her feet. First, she decided, she had to read the glass map. The fading sunlight from the window had no effect. She hurriedly lit the flame-lamps and held the map up to one. Once again, nothing happened. The glass had no inscription as to its time or place, and it was completely transparent. *Could this simply be a plain piece of glass?* she wondered. No, impossible. Why would Shadrack leave her a sheet of glass unless it was a map? She examined it carefully, holding it close to the light. Sure enough, in the bottom left corner was the etched mapmaker's sign: a mountain range atop a ruler. But the map would not wake. She bit her lip and carefully placed the glass back between the pages of the notebook. It would have to wait. She had to find Shadrack's atlas.

—17-Hour 45: Searching for the Atlas—

NOTEBOOK IN HAND, Sophia rushed back down to the library. She took a deep breath, placed the book on the sofa, and dropped to her knees. Shadrack's atlas could not be hard to find; it was tall and wide and would stand out from the other volumes. She rummaged through the piles impatiently, searching for the burgundy-colored binding. Then she realized it would be easier if she simply reshelved them.

She began placing the books back on the shelf closest to her. Slowly, the familiar white and slate-blue pattern of the carpet began to emerge. She filled four shelves without spotting the atlas. The books had fallen every which way, and some had torn pages. Sophia tried to be careful while moving quickly. She was filling a fifth shelf when she heard footsteps and looked up to see Theo standing in the doorway.

Sophia hardly recognized him. Without all the feathers, he looked like an ordinary person. He had brown hair that was a little long—just below his ears—and a small dimple in his chin. Wearing Shadrack's clothes, he looked older. Sophia had thought he was about fourteen, but now she wondered whether he wasn't fifteen or sixteen. He even held himself in an older way, with one hand—deeply scarred, as if from years of injuries—resting on the doorframe. But even without the feathers, he was still unlike anyone she had ever met in New Occident.

The boys her age at school were nice or harmless or erratically cruel, depending on their temperaments. None was very interesting. And the older boys, some of whom she had come to know through theater and field sports, seemed to have the same qualities in advanced form: more decidedly nice, harmless, or cruel. Theo seemed none of these. He had the air of calm authority she remembered from the circus. Sophia felt herself blushing when she realized she had no idea how long she had been staring at him.

His brown eyes met hers in amusement. "Are you *cleaning?*"

Sophia blushed a deeper shade of red. "No, I'm not cleaning. I'm looking for something and this is the easiest way." She quickly rose. "You have to see what I found."

Sophia had not yet learned, in her thirteen years, that it is not unusual for strangers in extreme circumstances to find themselves sharing a sudden familiarity. The shock of a shared threat makes the stranger an ally. Then the stranger does not seem strange at all: he, too, is a person in danger attempting to survive. And if the stranger who is no longer a stranger happens to be someone likable, someone who has seemed appealing and intriguing from the very beginning, then he will fit all the more readily into place, almost as if he was always meant to be there.

Having no internal clock exaggerated this effect for Sophia; a brief moment with someone could feel much longer. Theo was a stranger who was no longer a stranger: an intriguing and unexpected ally. If someone had asked her at that very moment whether she had reason to trust Theo, she would have had difficulty answering. The question did not occur to her. She liked him, and so she *wanted* to trust him.

Sophia opened the notebook to show him the glass map and the message. "It is a—"

"Map," Theo said, picking it up carefully with his scarred right hand. "I figured." He held it up to the light, just as Sophia had, while she looked on in surprise.

"How did you know?"

He carefully replaced it, seemingly not hearing her question;

then he frowned thoughtfully over the message. "Is this supposed to be the map to Veressa?"

"I thought it might be. Or Veressa might be in the atlas."

"You've never heard of it before?"

"No. Have you?"

Theo shook his head. He glanced around the room. "What's the atlas look like?"

"Large—about this tall—and fat, and dark red."

"All right, let's hunt it down." He smiled. "And then, when we find it, maybe you can get me a map of New Occident."

He crouched by the closest pile and began shelving books alongside her. They were almost halfway done when Sophia dove toward a pile a few feet away, exclaiming, "There it is!" She hadn't recognized the book because it lay open, pages facing upward.

"This is it," she said excitedly. "This is Shadrack's atlas." She flipped through it quickly. "It's fine—all in one piece." Then she showed Theo the cover, which read, in gold script, *An Annotated and Descriptive Atlas of the New World, Including the Prehistoric Ages and the Unknown Lands, by Shadrack Elli.*

"You mean it's *his*," Theo said, clearly impressed. "He wrote it."

"Oh, yes—it is the best one. The others haven't half the information." Sophia opened the atlas quickly to the index. "Veressa," she murmured. She ran her finger along the *V* column, but *Veressa* wasn't there. "How strange. Every place in the atlas is listed here."

"You're looking at cities and towns," Theo said, pointing

to the page header. "Maybe it's a lake or a desert or a forest or something else."

"Maybe," Sophia murmured. She was going through the index again when a sudden noise made her heart jump. Someone was rattling the side door of the house, the door that Sophia had closed behind her. She and Theo stared at each other, and for a few seconds neither of them spoke; they waited. Then they heard the sound of the door opening.

8
The Exile

1891, June 21, 18-Hour 07

New Occident's northern border with the uninhabited Prehistoric Snows—also called the Northern Snows—remained an unprotected and undefined area. The western and southern borders, however, increasingly became contested zones between the people of the Baldlands and New Occident and its Indian Territories. Though determining an actual border would have been impossible, this did not prevent the inhabitants of the borderlands from going to extreme lengths to defend the boundaries where they imagined them to be.

—*From Shadrack Elli's* History of New Occident

SOPHIA DOVE UNDER Shadrack's heavy oak desk, dragging Theo with her. From the library there was no view of the side door, but as soon as whoever had entered the house came along the passageway they would be visible through the doorway. As it turned out, she didn't have to wait that long.

"Fates protect us!" a woman's voice cried out. "Mr. Elli! Sophia?"

"It's our housekeeper," Sophia told Theo as she scrambled

out from under the desk. "I'm in the library, Mrs. Clay," she called out. "In here."

Mrs. Clay rushed into the library and stopped in the doorway, her eyes wide with fear. "What has happened here? Where is Mr. Elli?"

Sophia saw reflected in Mrs. Clay's horrified expression the full scope of the destruction around her.

"We don't know," Theo replied when Sophia failed to answer. "He's not here."

Mrs. Clay turned to Theo, pausing as she took in his unexpected presence. "What do you mean? Who are *you*?"

"He was taken a few hours ago," Theo said. He gestured at the destruction. "By force." Mrs. Clay stared at him uncomprehendingly. "Theodore Constantine Thackary," he added. "Theo for short."

"Who? Who took him by force?"

"Some men. I couldn't really see them very well. They had a coach. The coach . . ."

Sophia turned to him. "What is it?"

"I just remembered that the coach had something painted on the side—an hourglass."

"That's something to go on, I guess," she said, disappointed.

Mrs. Clay, seeming strangely relieved by the mention of several men and a coach, reached out for Sophia and embraced her. Her frantic terror seemed to have subsided. "I am so sorry, Sophia. So, so sorry. What can I do to help?"

"Well, Shadrack left me a note."

"A note!" exclaimed Mrs. Clay. "Surely that's a good sign. What did it say?"

"He said to take his atlas and go to Veressa." Sophia looked down at the book cradled in her arms. "We were just trying to find it when we heard you come in."

Mrs. Clay had an odd expression. "What? You're sure? He said *Veressa*?"

"Yes."

"Show me," she asked hoarsely.

Sophia put down the atlas and quickly retrieved the note from her drawing notebook. "It says 'Go to Veressa.'" She looked at Mrs. Clay hopefully. "Do you know where that is? Do you think he might be there?"

Mrs. Clay took a deep breath and seemed to collect herself. "Sophia, this is so unexpected. I—I think there are some things I should tell you," she said. She looked around. "Is the whole house this way?"

"No, they didn't go upstairs."

"Let's go to my rooms, then, and get away from this terrible wreck. We will have something to eat, and I can tell you what I know. It might help."

Sophia felt suddenly exhausted. She realized that the last thing she had eaten was the slice of bread on the way to Harding's Supply. She was probably still trembling, in part, from hunger.

"Thank you, Mrs. Clay." It gave her a pang to leave the library in such disorder, but she knew there was nothing else to be done now. She carefully tied her notebook closed and held it tightly along with Shadrack's atlas.

The housekeeper's third-floor apartment always made a striking contrast with the rest of the house; today, it did even more. The rooms were tidy and prettily arranged, with as much light as could be permitted through the open windows. A pale blue sofa dotted with white blossoms, a collection of empty birdcages, and a fragile white coffee table were the principal furnishings of her sitting room. Potted plants, many in bloom, dotted every surface: violets and palms and dozens of ferns. The air was thick with the smell of sun-warmed soil.

What always struck Sophia most was the sound—a light but constant tinkling, as if from hundreds of tiny bells. From every inch of the ceiling hung delicate sculptures: webs of thread strung with crystal, ceramic, and metal. The small globes, bells, mirrors, cylinders, and myriad other shapes turned slowly, colliding gently against one another and emitting a quiet chiming that filled the air. The sculptures almost gave the impression of living things, as if a flock of drowsy butterflies had come to rest in the rafters. Theo craned his neck to stare, fascinated. "I don't like the silence," the housekeeper explained to him. "I hope the noise doesn't bother you." She motioned toward the sitting room. "Why don't you rest? I'll just see about some coffee."

Sophia perched herself on one of the chairs and tried not to think about what was waiting downstairs. The chimes soon began to have the soothing effect that was, no doubt, their intended purpose. She and Theo watched the sculptures turn slowly overhead as Mrs. Clay opened cupboards and set the kettle on the stove. "I'm sorry Shadrack won't be able to help you," Sophia finally said to Theo.

Theo shrugged. "That's how it goes."

"Is Ehrlach going to send someone after you?"

"No. He has no time," Theo said with a half-smile. "He would have before, but now all he wants is to get in one last show in New York. The only good thing about the borders closing is that Ehrlach is out of business. Can't really run a circus when every act in your show is illegal, can you? Although I guess," he added, his smile fading, "he'll just take the show somewhere else. People like the circus everywhere."

Mrs. Clay came in with a tray, which she set on the low wooden coffee table. She'd brought cups and plates, butter and jam, and a loaf of brown bread with raisins. "I'll be right back," she said. When she returned with the coffee pot, she poured them each a cup and then sat back. She traced her temples with her fingertips and patted the bun at the nape of her neck, composing herself. Theo and Sophia ate hungrily. Sophia covered her brown bread with butter and jam and took big bites. As she sipped the warm coffee from its blue porcelain cup, she began to feel better.

"I'm afraid what I have to tell you is unpleasant," Mrs. Clay began, focused on something neither of them could see at the bottom of her cup. "These are very painful memories for me. But Shadrack has told you to find Veressa, and I should explain to you why I can't ever return to the Baldlands."

Theo leaned forward. "You're from the Baldlands?"

Mrs. Clay met his eyes. "Yes."

"So am I."

"I thought you might be. So I'm sure, once you hear my story, you'll understand the difficulty I'm in. But to Sophia it is all new, and it will take some explaining. People here sometimes have trouble believing what it's like outside—in the other Ages."

Sophia drew her legs up underneath her on the velvet chair. Mrs. Clay's voice, high-pitched and fluttery, echoed the quiet tinkling of the chimes overhead. "I don't know how much your uncle has told you," Mrs. Clay began, "about when we knew each other in the Baldlands."

"He told me about the academy. That he studied there—for a couple of years, a long time ago. And that you worked there. Not much else."

"That is correct. Many years ago, he was a student at the Royal Cartological Academy in Nochtland—the capital of the Baldlands and the largest city of the Triple Eras. You've never been to the Baldlands, Sophia, so it's very hard to explain what it's like, but I'm sure you've read about it and heard about it from your uncle."

Sophia nodded.

"It has many regions, and each region contains many former Ages. Nochtland, where I am from, is a beautiful place—sometimes I miss it so much. I miss the gardens. And how, when it rains, it *really* rains. And the pace, so much slower and calmer." She sighed. "But it's also a terrible place. It's a place where anything can happen and everything can change." She shook her head, as if to clear her mind. "Let me tell you the story from the beginning.

"I first met Shadrack more than fifteen years ago. He was a young man in his twenties when he arrived at the academy of cartology in Nochtland. I was the housekeeper. It is a grand old stone building near the center of the city, with lovely courtyards and covered walkways. I had a staff of ten, and I ran everything—the cooking, the cleaning, the laundry. The academy had perhaps fifty students and teachers at any given time. I think it's fair to say that I was good at my job." Mrs. Clay smiled wistfully. Sophia smiled back, but in truth she had difficulty imagining the timid and rather scattered Mrs. Clay overseeing even one employee, let alone ten.

"I'd already been there several years when Shadrack arrived," Mrs. Clay went on. "From the first moment we saw him, we knew he would do well. You see, having students from New Occident is very unusual. The professors, of course, come from almost all over the globe; but the students tend to be from the Baldlands. We were not certain students from New Occident even knew of our existence. Shadrack had somehow learned of the academy and was determined to go there despite—you'll excuse me—the backwardness of his home age.

"During the two years he spent in Nochtland, he grew particularly close to one of the other students in his class, a young woman from the Baldlands—a very gifted cartologer. After the first year, when their degrees were conferred and they began their apprenticeships, they became inseparable. We all were sure they would get married and leave together, heading either north to New Occident or south to her family in Xela.

"But they didn't. Shadrack finished his apprenticeship before she did, and their friendship seemed to cool. No one knew what had happened. And then, instead of waiting a month for her to finish her apprenticeship, Shadrack simply said his good-byes and left. It seemed to me that a part of her had left along with Shadrack. I liked her very much, and I worried about her." Mrs. Clay paused. "Her name was Veressa."

Sophia sat up straight. "What? Veressa is a *person*?"

Mrs. Clay nodded. "She was at one point your uncle's closest friend."

"But he's never mentioned her," Sophia protested.

"Well, as I said, the two of them evidently had a falling out just before Shadrack left. For all I know, they never spoke again. I wouldn't be surprised if Shadrack hasn't mentioned her because the recollection is painful."

Sophia shook her head. "He never told me any of this."

"I'm sure he has good reasons," Mrs. Clay said quietly. "You and Shadrack are as close as two people can be." She furrowed her brow. "Let me tell you the rest." She poured herself more coffee and took several sips. She seemed to be gathering her thoughts—and her strength.

—19-Hour #: Mrs. Clay Tells of the Lachrima—

"AFTER SHADRACK LEFT," Mrs. Clay began, "Veressa was slow to complete her apprenticeship. She was not well during that time; she seemed only a shadow of her former self. I think she must have loved your uncle very much. When she graduated, she came by my room to say good-bye, but I wasn't there. She left me a box of sugared flowers." Mrs. Clay smiled. "Even when she was unhappy, she was always very kind. Well . . . I never saw her again. I heard her name now and then from the professors, but Nochtland is a big city and you can live within its walls a lifetime without ever seeing most of its inhabitants.

"Then we had some quiet years. The students came and went, and the professors continued their teaching and their research. I was very happy. Then, about seven years ago, my troubles began." Mrs. Clay stared into her coffee cup and sighed. "No matter how much you've read, Sophia, there are things you don't know about the Baldlands. There are," she paused, "creatures there that don't exist here. Oh, I know they make a fuss about the raiders at the borders and people with wings or tails or whatever else. But those are, after all, still people. There are other creatures that few have seen and that no one understands. It was my misfortune to meet one.

"I remember that I first heard it on a beautiful Sunday in October. Most of the students spent Sunday resting in the gardens or visiting attractions in the city. I had hung all the bed linens to dry on the back patio, and because the sun was so pleasant I sat at the edge of the courtyard, watching the white sheets flutter in the breeze. My staff took Sunday afternoon off, so I knew I was alone. In those days I wasn't afraid of the silence, the way I am now—on the contrary. I sat there for nearly half an hour, simply soaking in the sun and the silence. And then I heard it. At first I thought it might be coming from the street, but it sounded much too close. It was the quiet, unmistakable sound of someone weeping.

"I sat up, concerned. The sound was quiet but piercing; a stab of grief pulled me to my feet. My thought was that one of my staff had holed up on the back patio to have a cry. I went to look, and as a sheet fluttered in the wind I saw someone hurrying away. Perplexed, I tried to follow, but the person was gone.

"The sound of weeping continued from one of the rooms—I did not know which—and as it did all the sadness of those muffled cries pierced me, so that tears spilled down my cheeks. Suddenly, I was grieving, too. I took all of the bed linens, which had dried, off the laundry lines, and then stood in the middle of the empty patio, trying to control my tears and pinpoint where the sound came from. That's how two of the girls who worked in the kitchen found me—standing there, crying. As soon as they approached me, the weeping stopped and the sense of despair I had felt lifted. 'Did you hear that?' I asked them. They shook their heads, shocked at my appearance. 'Hear what?' they asked.

"The next day, I heard it again—the moment I awoke—and the horrible sensation of grief returned. Before even getting dressed, I knocked on the doors of the rooms to my right and left. No one was weeping; no one could tell me where the sound I heard came from. Still, I believed that there had to be someone who was hiding, sneaking into corners to cry in private. And over the next few days, the weeping grew more constant. I began to hear it everywhere, all the time, even when others were present. And then they began to hear it, too.

"Wherever I went, the sound of weeping followed, and the sadness began to wear on me; though I knew it had no rational cause, as long as the weeping was audible my grief was uncontrollable. The sound was heartbreaking. At times, the thing I heard wept quietly, bitterly. At other times, it moaned and sobbed. And still other times it nearly screamed, as if subjected to some terrible violence. I had no choice, then, but to accept the truth: I was being followed by a Lachrima."

Theo made a noise of surprise. "A real Lachrima?"

Sophia remembered what she had heard Mrs. Clay saying to Shadrack, on the day parliament had closed the borders, and she asked the question she had been unable to ask then. "What's a Lachrima?'

"I've never seen one," Theo said. "They're supposed to be horrible."

The housekeeper nodded sadly. "They are. No one knows what the Lachrima are or where they come from. Some believe they are spirits. Others believe they are creatures from a terrible future Age. There are so many stories about them that it's hard to know which are true. All I know is what I heard—and saw."

"You *saw* it?" Theo asked breathlessly.

"For several weeks, the professors at the academy put up with it very kindly, insisting that the presence of the Lachrima was no fault of mine. But the truth is that everyone—not just me—found it unbearable. Imagine what it is like to hear the sound of weeping all the time—even when you are trying to sleep. Imagine feeling that burden of inexplicable, inconsolable grief. For the sake of the others, I shut myself up in my room, thinking that, if I simply waited, the Lachrima would tire of following me and go on its way.

"One night that week, I finally saw it. The exhaustion of several days without sleep caught up with me, and I fell finally into a heavy slumber. I woke in the middle of the night to a terrible sound—horrible cries, like those made by a frightened animal. I sat up with a start, my heart pounding. And then I saw it. The Lachrima was huddled by my bed."

"What did it look like?" Theo asked eagerly.

"Very much as I'd heard it described, only far more frightening than I'd imagined. It was tall and slender, dressed in thin white robes that trailed down to the floor. Its hair was dark and very long, and its face was buried in its hands. Its whole appearance was worn, as if it had lived for years in some dirty corner and was only now emerging. And then, as it continued to weep, the Lachrima lowered its hands from its face.

"I could never have imagined anything so horrible. I saw that its face—*its face wasn't there*. The Lachrima had only smooth white skin: skin that showed clearly the shape of its eye sockets and mouth and jaw; skin that looked as if someone had smoothed away all its features.

"For a moment I was too terrified to do anything. And then I bolted from my bed and ran. Though I fled to the other side of the house, I could still hear its distant wails. When I returned to my room at dawn it was empty, but the sound was still in my ears, and I knew, then, that I had to leave. That very morning I packed my belongings and told the director of the academy. He didn't try to stop me.

"Part of me had, perhaps, hoped that if I left the academy the Lachrima would remain behind. But of course this didn't happen. For months I tried to outrun it, staying first in Nochtland and then in the smaller towns outside it. Everywhere I went the Lachrima followed, bringing me and everyone near me nothing but terror and despair. After many months of attempting to elude it, I finally made my way north to the border. I no longer cared where I went or what I did, as long as the sound of weeping stopped. The grief wore so heavily upon me that I could not remember what it felt like to live without it. In those days I had yet to discover my faith in the Fates, for the people of the Baldlands follow other religions. But now that I know and believe in those fickle, kind, cruel, and mysterious powers, I believe they were setting me on a deliberate path. They had woven a terrible net around me and were insistently drawing me forward.

"On a day in November, more than a year after the Lachrima first appeared, I found myself in the northern Baldlands, near the border of New Akan. A family of traders was leaving the state, and they took pity on me and took me with them. We entered New Occident at night, and I remember that I fell asleep in the open wagon, listening to the quiet, incessant weeping and watching the stars above me. Then I fell asleep.

"When I awoke, it was midmorning and the young mother sitting next to me in the wagon was quieting her crying baby. The baby began sucking its fingers and a complete silence fell upon us. I could hear the steady *clomp* of the horses' hooves and the creaking of the wagon wheels and the satisfied noises of the drowsy baby. The weeping of the Lachrima had stopped.

"I knew only one person in New Occident—your uncle, Sophia—and I went about trying to find him. Fortunately, he had made quite a name for himself, and it wasn't difficult to learn that he lived in Boston. I took the train, and when I arrived I asked Shadrack to help me. He was kinder than I ever could have expected—as you know, Sophia. You have both been very kind to me. With time, I discovered that though the Lachrima was gone, it had left me changed. Now I cannot bear to be in silence. And I find that I can no longer concentrate as I used to." Mrs. Clay shook her head. "My mind isn't what it was. Still, living with the memory of the Lachrima is better than living with the Lachrima itself. You see now, don't you, why I can never go back?"

9
DEPARTURE

—1891, June 22, 0-Hour 54—

Citizens of New Occident who wish to travel beyond its borders must now carry the identity papers and lifewatch issued at birth, along with an official birth certificate. The serial number engraved on the lifewatch must correspond to the identity number found on the birth certificate. Certified copies by a clerk of court are acceptable in cases where originals have been destroyed.

—Parliamentary decree, June 14, 1891

THEO HAD TO satisfy his curiosity about the appearance of the Lachrima, and Sophia had to learn as much as she could about Veressa. Mrs. Clay told them what she knew, and it was very late when they finally exhausted their questions. She persuaded them to stay the night in her sitting room, in case anyone came to the house, saying that they would all decide what to do in the morning.

The tinkling sound of the chimes above Sophia's head and the anxious thoughts coursing through her brain prevented her from sleeping. The image of Shadrack being led out of the house returned to her, followed by a vision of a faceless creature, wild with grief. Sophia opened her eyes to dispel the image. She could see in the dim light that Theo, bedded down on the carpet, wasn't sleeping either.

"Poor Mrs. Clay," Sophia whispered. "I had no idea she had such a terrible story in her past."

"I wish I'd seen the Lachrima," Theo whispered back.

"Why would you wish *that*? Look what it did to Mrs. Clay!"

"I've heard that if you get close enough you can see through their skin, and that they actually have faces underneath. But hardly anyone gets the chance. If you ask me, the risk is absolutely worth it."

"I suppose. But if I have to go the Baldlands, I would rather not see or even hear one."

She could feel Theo's attention sharpening. "So you're going to the Baldlands?"

"I have to. Shadrack said to find Veressa, and that's probably where she is. I think I have to go to Nochtland and ask at the academy."

Theo lay silently in the darkness for a several seconds. "Tell you what," he said eventually. "Seeing as I don't have papers, it'd be a lot easier for me to get back to the Baldlands if I traveled with you. If you see me to the border, I'll help you get from there to Nochtland."

Sophia knew she could not ask Mrs. Clay to accompany her. Miles and the other explorers Shadrack counted as friends were gone, quick to leave after news of the borders' closing. Traveling by train to New Orleans, the closest point to Nochtland, would be easy, but traveling into the Baldlands by herself would be a significant challenge. Sophia knew she could do it; she had confidence in herself as an explorer. She also knew that she could use help. "Okay," she said. "Thanks," she added, after a moment.

"No problem. Only fair—you help me, I'll help you." She heard him turn over and settle himself for sleep.

Sophia closed her eyes, somewhat relieved now that she had a way forward, a way to follow Shadrack's instructions. But she did not sleep. Her mind turned gratefully from the disturbing images of Shadrack and the Lachrima to train schedules and other preparations. She began listing the items that she would need to pack.

Her thoughts were interrupted by a sound beyond that of the chimes. She lay with her eyes closed as Theo rose from his pallet and left the room. Sophia thought nothing of it until she heard, with surprise, that he was opening the door to the downstairs apartments. Her eyes flew open. She lay motionlessly for a moment longer, listening as he walked down the steps, and then she got to her feet.

She could hear Theo downstairs. He had stopped on the second floor. Sophia could see the pale yellow light of the flame-lamps stretching over the floorboards of the hallway. She frowned, a sense of unease spreading through her. *What is he doing?* she wondered. Very quietly, she began descending the steps to the second floor.

By letting her sense of time relax, Sophia could move so slowly that she made almost no sound. Several minutes later, she stood in the doorway of Shadrack's bedroom, watching as

Theo opened and closed the drawers of her uncle's wardrobe. "What are you doing?" she demanded.

Theo jumped. Then he saw Sophia in the doorway, he shook his head, chuckling. "You're good at that. How'd you walk down so quiet?"

"What are you doing in Shadrack's room?"

"Don't get upset," Theo said placatingly. "I just had an idea."

"What idea?" Sophia asked. For a moment she thought he might have remembered a clue, a sign: something that would lead them to Shadrack.

"I was thinking that, you know, likely your uncle didn't have time to take his papers and lifewatch."

The next moments expanded in her mind to encompass a much longer sense of betrayal. "You were going to *take* them?" she whispered. "You were going to *steal Shadrack's papers*?"

"No!" Theo protested. "No, I wasn't going to . . . steal them."

"Then what?"

"I just thought it would make the trip easier if I had them—you know, if I *borrowed* them."

"You were going to take Shadrack's papers and leave on your own," Sophia said, her tone hardening.

Theo rolled his eyes. "I was *not*. I was going to use the papers so it would be easier along the way and then give them back to you when we got to the Baldlands."

"That doesn't make any sense. Why would you need to travel with me anyway if you had papers? *Stolen* papers," she added bitterly.

"Because I already *said* I would," Theo replied, suddenly

angry as well. "I said I would go with you—we agreed."

"Then you could have just waited until the morning and asked. Don't you think I know where Shadrack keeps his papers?" Sophia's voice was trembling.

"Fine, if you don't want to believe me," Theo shot back. "So what if I was going off on my own? What's that to you?"

"I—"

"Your uncle can get new papers any time." Theo took a deep breath. "I'm used to looking after myself, and that means worrying about myself first. You think I worried what would happen to Ehrlach without his caged pet? No. Where I come from you can't think about other people first. It's every man for himself."

"I see," Sophia said, stung. "So I'm just like Ehrlach then—Shadrack is just like Ehrlach. Every man for himself. Is *that* what you were thinking when you saw them taking Shadrack away?"

Theo paced angrily. "Yes. That's exactly what I was thinking. One kid in feathers and five armed men. Not exactly good odds. I could have run into that mess, and right now I'd be wherever your uncle is. That would have been no help to either of us. Or I could have done what I did: watch what happened, stick around to tell you about it, and be here to help you get into the Baldlands."

"Why should you help me? You don't even care what happened to Shadrack! You just want his papers." Sophia clenched her fists to steady herself.

Theo gave a sharp sigh of frustration. "Look, you've got the wrong idea. Yes—I'd rather do things on my own. That's how I've always been, and I'm not going to apologize for it. But I keep my word. We agreed to help each other, and I'm going to stick to that. You can think what you like; I wasn't going to take your uncle's papers. I was just thinking about what would make getting to Nochtland easier."

Sophia stared at Theo—his brown eyes, narrowed to wary slits, his hands clenched—and she realized that she had no idea who he was. The sense of sudden familiarity, that she could trust him, that he could be a friend, evaporated. "You should go on your own," she said out loud, her cheeks burning. "I'll be fine."

"Don't be ridiculous. Right now it only makes sense for us to help each other. Come on, think about it," Theo said in an appeasing tone. "Do you have any idea how to get to Nochtland from the border?"

Sophia was silent. She felt a surge of panic at the thought. "Fine," she said quietly.

"Good," Theo said. "Our agreement stands, then." He smiled, every trace of anger suddenly gone from his face.

Sophia took in his easy smile with indignation, giving him only a grimace in return. "Shadrack keeps his papers in a leather wallet in his vest," she said softly. "And his lifewatch is on a chain clipped to his pocket. I'm sure he has them both." Without waiting for a reply, she turned, her hair whisking across her shoulder, and stalked up to Mrs. Clay's sitting room.

Soon Theo joined her there, stretching out on the carpet beside the sofa. Sophia was still angry; she could feel the blood pounding in her temples. And she was anxious; she knew she had no better alternative, but the thought of relying on Theo, who now seemed so unpredictable and unknown, filled her with apprehension. She tried to calm herself by staring overhead at the slow rotation of the chimes. They reflected the pale light from the window, casting small glimmers on the wall and ceiling. After several minutes had passed, she heard Theo's heavy breathing and knew that he was asleep. She cast a sharp glance in his direction. *Every man for himself,* Sophia thought bitterly. *What kind of philosophy is that? Not the kind of philosophy that makes you want to rescue someone in a cage, that's for sure. I wish I'd never even thought of helping him.*

— 8-Hour 35: Waking at Mrs. Clay's—

SOPHIA AWOKE WHEN the sun was already high. She checked her watch; it was past eight. Theo still lay fast asleep on the carpet, his face turned toward the wall. Sophia smelled eggs and coffee. In the kitchen, she found Mrs. Clay standing at the stove, quietly humming. With her hair in its usual tidy bun and her dress protected by an embroidered white apron, she seemed calm and well refreshed.

"Good morning, Mrs. Clay," Sophia said.

"Good morning!" the housekeeper replied, turning to her. "Come have some breakfast. I'm feeling optimistic, Sophia." She brought a pan of scrambled eggs from the stove and scooped a large portion onto Sophia's plate. "I feel confident that the Fates will be assisting you."

"Do you think so?" Sophia asked anxiously, taking a seat.

Shadrack thought the Fates were a tolerable convention, at best, and a dangerous delusion, at worst. Sophia wanted to follow Shadrack's example and scoff at such fancies, but part of her worried that the unjust removal of her parents rather verified the existence of those three cruel, arbitrary powers who spun sorrow and misfortune and death as easily as others spun cloth. The more Mrs. Clay had talked about them over the years, the more Sophia became convinced that the Fates were real, and they fashioned all the happenings of the world, weaving them into a pattern only the three of them could comprehend.

"I have taken the liberty," Mrs. Clay went on, pouring Sophia a cup of coffee, "of speaking with the Fates on your behalf." She retrieved her sewing basket from the sideboard. "They really are the most difficult creatures." She shook her head. "Totally heartless. They refused to say anything at all about Shadrack. But they seemed encouraging about your reaching Veressa. They were most insistent that I give you this." She handed Sophia a spool of silver thread. "Who knows what they intend you to do with it," she sighed. "They are fickle, at best—cruel at worst. But I have found that it is generally wise to do as they say when they make such specific recommendations."

"Thank you," Sophia said with sincere gratitude. She tucked the spool into her pocket. "Perhaps they will help me along the way."

"Perhaps so. It's the least I can do, dear, since I can't go with you. Good morning, Theo," she added.

Sophia turned to see a sleepy-looking Theo in the kitchen doorway. She turned back to her plate with annoyance.

"Good morning," Theo replied.

"I hope you slept well."

"Very well. The carpet was extremely comfortable. Were you discussing travel plans?" he asked, sitting down at the table.

"We hadn't begun. Would you like some eggs?" Mrs. Clay asked, going to the stove.

"I'd love some, Mrs. Clay," Theo said in his most courteous tone. Sophia stared into her cup. "We talked it over last night," he went on comfortably, "and we've agreed to travel as far as Nochtland together. Right, Sophia?" He smiled at her.

Sophia looked at him unsmilingly. "That's what we agreed."

"I could travel as far as the border with you," Mrs. Clay said uncertainly, handing Theo a full plate.

"That's kind of you, Mrs. Clay," Sophia told her, "but the trip to New Orleans will be easy. We'll probably just have to change trains once." She did not add that it was the next part of the journey that worried her: where she was most needed, Mrs. Clay could not help. *Maybe we'll get to the border and Theo will just vanish,* she thought.

"They will check for papers on the train," Mrs. Clay said. "I've heard that they're putting foreigners on separate cars."

"Yes, but I'll have my papers, and they won't bother Theo if he's with me," Sophia said flatly. "It isn't July fourth yet."

"Theo, do you need to get word to anyone? The trip to Nochtland will delay you by several weeks."

"My family's not expecting me back for a while," he replied easily.

"And you'll take care of Sophia once you reach the Baldlands?"

"Of course. I've traveled that route dozens of times—no problem."

"It seems a terribly long way for you both to go alone," Mrs. Clay said. She patted her bun and sighed. "If only I knew someone who lived near the border."

"The greatest help," Sophia said, "would be to stay here in case Shadrack returns. Otherwise we'll have no way of knowing."

"Thanks to him I now have papers and a lifewatch, so I can stay without concern. If something should happen in the next twenty hours, I will send letters by express post to the first major station on your route."

With a train schedule from Shadrack's study spread out across the kitchen table, they decided to take the train south through New Occident, all the way to Charleston, South Carolina, and then connect to a train heading west into New Akan. The journey would take several days. The train line ran only as far as New Orleans, and they would have to cross from New Occident into the Baldlands either on horse or on foot.

Sophia looked apprehensively at the blank expanse that bordered New Akan to the west and south. She folded the map slowly. "We should pack," she said. "Maybe we can catch the midday train to Charleston."

—9-Hour 03: Leaving for Charleston—

SOPHIA RETRIEVED HER new pack from where she had left it by the front door. She had never imagined it would be put to use so soon. Pulling a small leather trunk out of the wardrobe in her bedroom, she began stowing her clothes, soap, a hairbrush, and a pair of blankets. Though her everyday boots were comfortable enough, she decided to take the laced leather shoes that she used during the school year for athletic competitions. If nothing else went as planned, at least she would be able to run as fast as her feet could carry her. Theo watched from the doorway. "You can borrow any shirts of Shadrack's that fit," she said, without looking up. "And his socks are in the bottom drawer of the wardrobe. But you probably remember seeing them there yourself."

"Very kind of you," Theo said with a smile, acknowledging the barb. "So you're still mad?"

"I am fine," Sophia said, pushing down on the blankets so that they fit.

"All right, if you say so. I'll be back in a bit—I have to get some shoes."

Sophia closed her trunk and opened her pack. Sewn from durable, waterproof canvas, it had multiple pockets inside and out. She tucked her pencils, erasers, and a ruler into the pockets. She took a spare pillowcase from her wardrobe, wrapped the glass map in it and put it inside her current drawing notebook alongside Shadrack's note. The book and atlas fit nicely.

Steeling herself, she went once more to Shadrack's room and opened the bureau drawer where he kept their currency. After folding the bills into a small leather purse beside her identity papers and her lifewatch, she closed the bureau. She tidied the drawers that Theo had left open and straightened the bed. Then, with one last look around the room, she slung the pack's straps over her shoulders and headed downstairs to find maps for their trip to Nochtland.

When Theo returned, he was wearing a pair of handsome brown boots that looked worn but well cared for. He seemed very pleased with himself. "Where'd you get those?" Sophia asked suspiciously.

"Nice, aren't they? I went around the block until I found a cobbler, and then I just went in and told him that I'd paid for and left a pair of size ten boots there months earlier and had lost the slip. He searched around in the back room and came back with these. He said he'd been on the verge of throwing them away!"

"Well, I hope someone doesn't stop you on the street and ask for them back," she said tersely. She carefully rolled the maps that lay before her on the table and placed them in the new roll-tube. "I have plenty of maps for the rail journey, and I found a map of Nochtland, but there's nothing with enough detail for the border and nothing for the whole piece of the Baldlands between the border and Nochtland."

"I told you—I know that part," Theo said. "No need for a map."

They heard steps on the stairs. "I've packed you some food," said Mrs. Clay as she entered, handing Theo a basket that appeared full to the brim. "I'm sorry I can't do more." Her eyes grew teary. "I'm sorry, Sophia dear, for all of this." She cleared her throat. "Are you packed?"

"We're ready to go," Sophia said.

Mrs. Clay embraced her warmly. "Do be careful, dear. Don't worry about me or the house—we'll be fine. Just take care. I have your schedule, and I'll be here to tell Shadrack what happened should he return."

"Thank you, Mrs. Clay."

The housekeeper shook hands with Theo. "You must take care of each other," she said. "And may the Fates look after you well."

PART II
Pursuit

10
The White Chapel

1891, June 21: Shadrack Missing (Day 1)

Most people believe that The Chronicles of the Great Disruption *were written by a charlatan, a false prophet: a man who called himself Amitto and who, in the early days after the Disruption, decided to take advantage of the widespread fear and panic. They contain little detail and little substance: vague words of war and death and miracles. But in some circles the* Chronicles *have acquired credibility, and Amitto's followers, particularly those of the Nihilismian sect, claim that the* Chronicles *hold not only the true history of the Great Disruption but also true prophecies.*

—From Shadrack Elli's History of the New World

ON A HIGH hill surrounded by pines at the northern edge of New Occident stood a sprawling stone mansion bleached white by the sun. The mansion's windows sparkled in the bright light, and the silver weathervanes on its peaked gables gleamed. A dirt road with a single rail track wove through the pines and up the hill, circling at the entrance. There was no movement along the track. A few crows flapped lazily up through the pines toward a stone cross on the mansion's highest peak. At one end of the mansion, connected by a narrow archway, stood a chapel. The crows wheeled and cawed and then came to rest on its stone cross. As they claimed their perch, the entire scene became one of perfect stillness—even peace. The pine trees, the streaming sunlight, the pale mansion, all formed a serene landscape. But inside the chapel there was no stillness. In the cavernous vault, a purposeful movement was gathering momentum.

Shadrack sat alone, his hands tied behind his back, his ankles bound to the legs of the chair. He was staring up at the ceiling, his head resting against the cool stone wall behind him. The floor had long since been cleared of its pews, so that the chapel appeared more a workroom than a place of worship. Shelves weighed down by thousands of books lined its walls, and the numerous long tables were covered with piles of paper and open books and ink bottles. At the front of the chapel, where the altar would have been, stood a huge, black furnace. The furnace was, at the moment, unlit. It stood quietly in the company of its bellows and tongs and a pair of charred leather gloves. From the tools and materials scattered around it, the furnace appeared to have a single purpose: making glass.

Shadrack watched the furnace's creations circling silently through the chapel vault far above him: hundreds of large glass globes in a gliding constellation, controlled by a single mechanism that rose up from the center of the floor. The metal gears connecting them—not unlike those of a clock, to Shadrack's inexpert eye—must have been well-oiled, because they emitted no sound. He watched the globes' smooth, endless rotations. He had been staring for hours.

The globes' surfaces were not still. Each seemed to shiver

with a perpetual motion that appeared almost lifelike. The light streaming through the stained-glass windows reflected off them onto the stone walls and ceiling. They were too high up for Shadrack to see clearly, but this delicate trembling only added to their beauty. As they dipped closer, the globes seemed at times to reveal subtle shapes or expressions. Shadrack felt certain that if he watched for long enough, the pattern they traced would become clear.

He was also trying with all his might to stay awake. He had not slept since leaving the house on East Ending Street. In part, he had been trying to work out who had taken him captive. The men who had seized him were Nihilismians. It was evident from the amulets that hung from their necks: small or large, metal or wood or carved stone, they all bore the distinctive open-hand symbol. But they were unlike any other followers of Amitto that Shadrack had ever known, and he speculated that they belonged to some obscure, militant sect; for apart from the amulets, they all carried iron grappling hooks. Shadrack could tell by the way they used their weapons in the rooms of his house that they were practiced. Most disturbingly, the silent men all bore the same unusual scars: lines that stretched from the corners of their mouths, across their cheeks, to the tops of their ears. They were gruesome, unchanging, artificial grins, etched onto unsmiling faces.

Once Shadrack had persuaded them that they had found what they were looking for, they had ended their assault on the house and retreated into unresponsive silence. The ride out of Boston in the coach had been a long one, and he had tried—with only partial success—to map the route. It had been difficult once they blindfolded him and placed him in a railway car, but his inner compass told him that they had traveled north several hours, and from the occasional gust of cold wind he suspected that they were no more than an hour or two south of the Prehistoric Snows.

All the anger he had felt when they first captured him had slowly faded during the day-long journey. It had changed to a sharp-edged attentiveness. The night air, as they emerged from the railcar, had felt cool but still summery. He had smelled pine and moss. The scarred Nihilismians had brought him directly from the railway car to the chapel, tied him to a chair, and removed his blindfold. Then they had disappeared. The slow movement of the globes had soothed the remaining sting of his anger, and now he felt only an intense curiosity as to his circumstances and surroundings. His captivity had become another exploration.

As he stared at the globes, he suddenly heard a door open somewhere near the altar. He turned to look. Two of the men entered the chapel, followed by a woman wearing a cream-colored dress with tightly buttoned sleeves. A blond linen veil hid her features entirely. As she approached with a quick, easy step, Shadrack tried to make out what he could from her bearing without being able to see her face.

The woman stopped a few feet away from him. "I have found you at the end of a long search, Shadrack Elli. But not the Tracing Glass that I sought—where is it?"

The moment Shadrack heard the woman speak, the

meaning of her words became indistinct. Her voice was beautiful—and familiar: low, gentle, and even, with a slight accent that he could not place. Though her words betrayed no emotion, their sound threw him into a tempest of inchoate memories. He had heard her voice before; he knew this woman. And she must know him, too; why else hide her face behind the blond veil? But despite the rushing sense of familiarity, he could not remember who she was. Shadrack roused himself, trying to shake off the feeling that had taken hold. He told himself to concentrate and to give nothing away in his reply. "I'm sorry. I gave your men what they asked me for. I don't know what glass you mean."

"You do, Shadrack," the woman said softly. She took a step closer. "You and I are on the same side. Tell me where it is, and I promise I will put everything right."

For a moment, Shadrack believed her. He had to make a monumental effort to hear the meaning of her words and not just their sound. "If you and I are on the same side," he said, "then there is no reason why I should be tied to this chair. In fact," he added, "there is no reason why your Nihilismian thugs should have dragged me from my house in the first place." As he spoke, he found the effect of the woman's voice fading. "Why not let me go, and I promise *I'll* put everything right."

The woman shook her head; her veil quivered. "Before I do anything else, I really must insist that you tell me where it is." She rested her gloved hand lightly on his shoulder. "You fooled my Sandmen, but you won't fool me. Where is the Tracing Glass?" she whispered.

Shadrack stared as hard as he could through the veil, but even this close it revealed nothing. "I have dozens of glass maps. Or at least I did, before your 'Sandmen' broke most of them. Perhaps you should look through the pieces—the glass you want is probably there."

The woman let out a small sigh and stepped away. "I thought it might be this way, Shadrack. Still, I am glad to have you here." The woman's tone was calm and only slightly troubled, as if she were discussing a trifling concern with a friend rather than issuing threats to a bound man. She indicated the swirling glass globes above her. "You may be the greatest known cartologer in New Occident—perhaps in the world," she said. "But you will forgive me for saying that I believe I am the greatest *unknown* cartologer." She gazed up at the globes and spoke to them, rather than to Shadrack. "I would have benefited from your company before now. Years and years of work," she said quietly. "Trial and error—mostly error." She once again looked at her captive. "Do you know how difficult it is to create a spherical glass map? The glass-blowing technique alone took me ages to perfect, and working with a sphere adds a whole new dimension—if you will—to the mapmaking. Still," she said softly, "the effort was well worth it. Don't you think?"

"I'd really have to read them for myself to determine their quality."

The woman turned abruptly. "Yes—why not? I've wanted nothing more for quite some time." She signaled to the two men, who were standing some distance away. "That desk," she said, pointing. Without untying Shadrack, the two men snagged the chair with their grappling hooks and dragged it to a heavy desk that stood several feet away. It held a glass globe on a metal stand.

The woman untied his hands. "Go ahead—please. Look closely."

Shadrack rubbed his wrists and, after a keen glance at his captor, turned his attention to the globe. It was slightly opaque—cloudy—and about the size of a human head. The metal base was intricately wrought—copper, it seemed—and the glass was perfectly smooth. It shimmered with the uneasy movement Shadrack had observed. For several moments he stared at it uncomprehendingly, and then he realized that the play of motion within the globe was created by grains of sand. They moved with some unseen power, circling gently through a kind of dance. They showered down, grazed the bottom of the globe, and arced upward again. Suddenly the sand fell into a pattern, and Shadrack saw an unmistakably human face gazing out at him.

He recoiled. "This is not a map of the world. It's a map of a human mind."

The woman inclined her veiled head toward him, as if conceding a point. "You are very close."

Shadrack had not yet touched the globe. Now, with some trepidation, he placed his fingertips gently on the smooth surface. The memories that surged into his mind were more powerful than any he'd ever experienced. He was assailed by the smell of honeysuckle and he heard the ring of laughter in his ears; he had been tossed into a honeysuckle bush, and he felt the crush of leaves under his hands as he tried to free himself. He recalled getting up and running over a damp lawn and then tripping, falling headlong into the grass. He felt the wet blades against his cheek and the smell of soil in his nose. The memories were those of a child.

Shadrack pulled his fingertips away with a gasp and gazed again at the cloudy globe. He shook his head. "It's remarkable." His voice was frankly admiring. "I've never experienced such powerful smells, sights, sounds. I confess to being curious: how have you mapped such vivid memories?"

The woman leaned forward and touched her gloved fingertip to the globe. "You must know from having made memory maps yourself that no matter how much you try, people always hold something back. The memory is still theirs, after all. As the cartologer you only gather a dim echo."

Shadrack shrugged. "Better a dim memory than none at all. All maps are like that. They only express an outline, a guide, to a far richer world."

"Yes, but I do not want outlines. I want the memories themselves."

Again, he stared intently at the blond veil. "That would be impossible. Besides," he added, with a note of admonishment, "one has one's own memories."

The woman didn't speak. Then she reached out and gently touched the globe again with a gloved finger. She lingered a moment, then pulled away and spoke, ignoring Shadrack's last words. "It is not impossible. I have accomplished it."

"What do you mean?"

"The memories are so vivid because they are *complete*. They are captured whole in those grains of sand." She spoke as if describing something of great beauty.

Shadrack looked at the globe with consternation. "And what of the person they belonged to? The boy—or man—who had these memories?"

"The memories are no longer his."

"You stole them?" The woman shrugged, as if she found the word clumsy but apt. "I don't believe you," Shadrack said. He faced the veil in silence. "How did you do it?" he finally asked.

The woman let out a quick sigh of satisfaction. "I knew you would be interested. I will show you the process sometime. For now, I can tell you that it involves submerging the subject in sand and then using that sand to make a globe. It is a beautiful method. But the results—even more beautiful. You see, the globe you are looking at is not the map. This"—she indicated the constellation of globes circling overhead—"is the map. This is the map that led me to you."

"Then you will have to read it for me," Shadrack said acidly, "because I see no map in that collection of stolen memories."

"Do you not?" the woman asked, sounding faintly surprised. "Look more closely. See how they move—gliding, drifting away, suddenly drawing near. All those memories are connected. Someone passing someone else in the street. One person catching a glimpse of another through a window. Someone finds a lost book here, someone gives it away there. Someone discovers an old crate full of glass panes, and another person sells them in a market. Someone buys one of the panes and makes a cabinet of it. Someone steals the cabinet. Does this sound familiar? It may have occurred before your time. There is a story—a history—circling over your head, and the map it draws has led me to you. I have taken many memories to find the Tracing Glass, and you with it."

Shadrack found it difficult to speak. "Then you have wasted your time."

"No," she said quietly. "I have learned much. Far more than I expected. You see—people's memories are richer than they know. They ignore memories that seem unimportant, but to the careful reader they spring out, full of meaning." She lifted the glass globe and turned it lightly, then replaced it before Shadrack on the desk. "This last one was the key. Read it again."

After a moment's hesitation, Shadrack pressed his fingertips to the globe. Immediately he recalled a study filled with towering piles of books. The musty smell of paper closed in around him, and a dim light shone through the window. At once he knew to whom the room—and the memories—belonged. He gasped in dismay.

As if to dispel any remaining doubt, the memory lingered over an engraved sign on the open door:

CARLTON HOPISH

Cartologer

Minister of Relations with Foreign Ages

A face that seemed simultaneously familiar and oddly distorted appeared suddenly beside the sign. It was his own face.

He wanted to pull away from the globe and the horror it implied, but he could not. He remembered this conversation, now, through the eyes of his friend Carlton, greeting Shadrack Elli and inviting him to sit. Shadrack grimaced; he knew where it was headed, and he suddenly understood with panicked clarity why the veiled woman had abducted him.

"Solebury is leaving next month," Carlton said. "At first he was unwilling to say, but in the end I got it out of him." He leaned forward and slapped Shadrack's knee triumphantly. "He believes he has finally found a definitive indication of the carta mayor's *location."*

Shadrack frowned. "He is chasing an illusion," he said gruffly.

"Don't give me that," Carlton protested. "You, of all people. One of the few who can read and write water maps."

"It is nothing but a fantasy."

"A fantasy? How can you say that? I thought you would want to go with him," Carlton said with an injured air. "It's not like you to pass up a chance for a great discovery—a chance to find the living map of the world, the map containing every moment, past, present, and future, a map that would show when the Disruption occurred—"

"There is nothing to discover."

Carlton remained silent, studying the guarded, reluctant face before him. "You would be a great help. Particularly," he added slyly, "if it's true that you have the Polyglot Tracing Glass."

Shadrack gave him a piercing look. "Where did you hear that?"

"It's true, then!" Carlton exclaimed. "I would give anything to see it."

"I have it." Shadrack turned away. "And there is no pleasure to be had from reading it, believe me."

Carlton's voice dropped to a whisper. "But you could use it to find the carta mayor. *It would be a great service to your country, Shadrack."*

"I said no! I will not discuss it further."

"Come, Shadrack, don't be angry with me," Carlton said, in a conciliatory tone. "I had no idea you felt so strongly about it."

Shadrack yanked his fingers from the globe as though it had stung him. The image of Carlton in his hospital bed, helpless and witless, a mere vacant shell, flooded his mind. "What have you done to him? Are you responsible for leaving him—*ruined?*"

"I treasure his memories," the woman said, with what sounded like a smile. "And I always will. They led me to you."

"You destroyed him for nothing." Shadrack's voice was hard with fury. "If you are seeking the *carta mayor,* you are wasting your time."

"Why are you so vehement in your denial?" Her veil shook slightly. "I wonder. Could it be that you *do* believe it exists? Could it be that the very mention of it touches a sore spot, an old injury that has never quite healed? To think," she said lightly, "that such knowledge might be just on the other side of this fragile wall of skin and bone." She pressed her fingers against Shadrack's forehead.

"You are wasting your time," Shadrack repeated angrily,

shaking her off. And he realized, with shock, that the woman before him could easily leave him as she had left Carlton: empty, helpless, hopelessly damaged. Shadrack made an effort to control his anger.

"Are you familiar with the last section of *The Chronicles of the Great Disruption*?" she asked.

As Shadrack stared at the desk before him, looking anywhere but at the globe, his eye lighted on a pair of scissors. "I am familiar with it, of course, but the Chronicles of Amitto are undoubtedly apocryphal. I consider them a work of manipulative fiction." He rested his arm lightly over the scissors as he spoke.

"Oh no!" she whispered. "They are real. Everything in the Chronicles has come to pass, or will come to pass. Recall the lines toward the end—December twenty-seventh: '*Consider that our time upon the earth is as a living map: a map drawn in water, ever mingling, ever changing, ever flowing.*' "

"I recall it," Shadrack said carefully, easing the scissors into his sleeve. "But it means nothing. It is empty poetry, like the rest of the Chronicles."

She strode around the desk so that she stood across from Shadrack. "What would you say if I told you that I have proof—in the globes overhead—that the *carta mayor* is real: the living map of the world drawn in water exists. What is more, a skilled mapmaker could not only read it," she paused, "but alter it: alter the world by altering the map."

"No one has so much as seen the *carta mayor*," Shadrack said tersely, "so it seems rather presumptuous to begin speculating about its properties."

"You are not listening." She leaned toward him. "I have proof. The *carta mayor* is real. It is not just a map of the world that was and the world that is. It shows all possible worlds. And if a cartologer such as you were to modify the *carta mayor*, he could change the present. He could even change the past—reinvent the past. Rewrite history. Do you understand me? The whole world can be *redrawn*. The Great Disruption can be *undone*."

"It cannot be undone. Every cartologer, scientist, cosmographer will tell you the same thing: there can only be another disruption. The world is what it is now—its course has been set. To change the Ages would mean disrupting the world once again—the costs are unknown, unimaginable. The only manner of making the world whole now is through exploration, communication, alliances, trade. On principle, I object to the kind of change you describe. But my objection is of no matter; the task you have set yourself is impossible." His voice was hard. "You are fooling yourself if you believe otherwise."

"*You* are fooling yourself," she replied, her voice dismissive. "Your faint curiosity in the other Ages. A sea voyage here, a trek across the mountains there. What do you hope to accomplish with such trivial exploration? What is exploration compared with the hope of *synchrony*, harmony? The hope of restoring the *true* world?"

"It can't be done. Believe me, I have worked with water maps. I take it you have not, otherwise I wouldn't be here. It can't be done."

The woman's veil trembled. "But you have not yet seen the *carta mayor.* It will be different."

Shadrack shook his head and hunched farther over the desk. As he did so, he dropped his right hand and felt with the scissors for the rope binding his ankle. The woman was still on the other side of the desk. The two scarred Nihilismians stood by the cold furnace, their grappling hooks hanging by their sides. He glanced quickly toward the other end of the chapel and saw a set of double doors that doubtlessly opened out onto the grounds. Then he leaned in close to the glass globe as if examining it. "Your work is impressive, and I admire your cartologic sensibilities—sincerely. But I can't help you; and even if I could, I wouldn't."

He had cut through the ropes binding his right ankle, and he leaned forward even farther to reach his other ankle under the desk. "I can't help you because I don't believe in the Chronicles or the *carta mayor.* And I won't help you because I have no desire to see the Great Disruption repeated in my lifetime. I want no part of it. My only consolation is that the task you have set yourself is impossible to achieve." Shadrack cut the ropes on his left ankle and quickly slipped the scissors back inside his sleeve and straightened in the chair.

"Ah!" the woman said, circling to Shadrack's side of the desk. "Then shall we put your beliefs to the test? If you truly believe the *carta mayor* does not exist, tell me where the Tracing Glass is. You can prove to me that the Chronicles are nothing but empty poetry." Shadrack sat in silence, his face expressionless.

"I believe if the glass map is not here, there is only one place it can be. With your niece. Sophia."

"I tell you—all my glass maps were broken on the floor of my workroom."

The woman placed her gloved hand on Shadrack's arm—the same arm that concealed the scissors in its sleeve. "I have not told you my name," she said softly. "You may call me Blanca. Like the white of an unmarked page—of a blank map. Or of white sand. Or of fair, unblemished skin."

Shadrack looked at her but said nothing. He glanced at the two Sandmen; they appeared lost in thought, considering the globes overhead.

"Sophia has the map, doesn't she?" Blanca asked. "And all I need is something to persuade her to give it up."

Shadrack suddenly pushed back his chair, flinging off Blanca's arm. The scissors flew into the air and soared in an arc, shattering one of the globes. A shower of glass shards and sand rained down over them, but he had already begun running toward the far end of the chapel, racing for the broad doors at the rear. He heard the footsteps of the men behind him and the furious cry from Blanca at the sight of the broken globe.

The broad double doors ahead of Shadrack suddenly flew open and four Sandmen stepped into the chapel. Shadrack ducked to the left and ran toward one of the windows: he could climb onto one of the desks and leap, hopefully with enough strength to break through the stained glass. Then he felt a sudden, painful snag against his leg.

He was pinned to the floor, his chest crushed painfully

against the stone, and in a moment they were all upon him. He tasted blood in his mouth as the men hauled him to his feet, wrenching his arms behind his back. The grappling hook had ripped his pant leg, leaving two long welts all the way down his thigh. Only chance had prevented the hook's prongs from tearing deep into his muscle.

The Sandmen dragged him, struggling, across the chapel floor and back to the chair by the desk. "Bind his left arm tightly," Blanca said quietly. "Hold his right arm but leave it free." Shadrack's shoulders ached as his chest was pinned back and his left hand tied. "And put the bonnet on him. Just the ribbon—I need his eyes open."

The man standing before him held a small block of wood the size of a bar of soap threaded through with a thin piece of wire. Shadrack clenched his teeth and tucked his chin against his chest. The man standing behind him yanked his head back and hit his windpipe, just hard enough so that Shadrack was forced to cough. Before he could close his mouth, he felt the wooden block between his teeth and the thin wires against his cheeks. Then they were wound together tightly behind his head.

The wire began biting into the corners of his mouth. He knew now how the Nihilismians earned their scars.

"If you don't fight it, the wire won't cut you," Blanca said sweetly. "You are going to write a letter for me." She set paper and pen before him and leaned in. "Now."

Shadrack took the pen unsteadily. Blanca had drawn back, but not soon enough; he had seen the face beneath her veil.

11
On the Tracks

1891, June 22: 11-Hour 36

The rail lines had begun as a government-sponsored venture, but private investors soon began to make their fortune laying tracks across New Occident. The idea of a national railway was abandoned, and by mid-century two or three private companies owned every inch of track and every train car. The millionaires of the rail lines became the most powerful individuals in New Occident.

—*From Shadrack Elli's* History of New Occident

Though Sophia had traveled every summer with Shadrack, she had never been farther south than New York nor farther west than the Berkshires, and poring over maps of train routes had not prepared her for the thrill of riding an electric train over long distances.

She felt light-headed as they sped out of Boston on the Seaboard Limited. She and Theo had a compartment for the entire journey to New Orleans; it had a long leather seat and two bunk beds that folded out of the wall, each with starched white sheets. Theo curled up on the top bunk and slept contentedly. Sophia wished she could sleep as well, but she could not even sit still, and she paced from door to window in the tiny wood-paneled compartment, willing herself to lose track of time. Her hand closed around the spool of silver thread in her skirt pocket and she gripped it hard, as if doing so would call the Fates to her side and make the train go faster. To distract herself, she began reviewing the list of things she had brought, consulting the train schedule, and calculating how long it would take to travel from the border to Nochtland.

As they neared Providence, Rhode Island, she opened the window to look out onto the platform. The city spread out before her like a maze of brickwork dotted here and there with white steeples. Like a dark ribbon, the Blackstone Canal wove its way through the brick buildings. Dusty green trees bordered it on either side and surrounded the nearby train station, providing the only shade on the crowded wooden platform. The air smelled of sawdust and canal water. Police officers and station agents scrutinized tickets and identity papers, herding people into different compartments. Foreign families traveling together, lone exiles weighed down by overstuffed baggage and expressions of despondency—they all waited at the platforms alongside ordinary travelers who looked on curiously, sympathetically, or sometimes indifferently. The scene in Providence was repeated an hour later in the lush green flatlands of Kingston, where cows clustered in the occasional shade; everywhere the sense of disquiet was the same. The train left southern Rhode Island and coursed on into Connecticut.

The windows of the railcar were wide open to let in the

breeze, and Sophia leaned out to cool off. As the train made its way down the coast, she smelled the salt air and stared out at the small white sails skimming the ocean's surface. It seemed to her that time had slowed to an unbearable pace. Sophia sighed. *I have to make the time pass more quickly,* she thought desperately, *or this will feel eternal.* She put aside all thought of East Ending Street, which she was leaving behind, and of Theo, with whom she had hardly exchanged a word since boarding, and she concentrated on the horizon.

As she watched, the landscape changed. The tracks drew away from the coast and headed inland. Slender maples grew close to the rails, and she could smell the dusty scent of leaves that had stood all day in the sun. The train slowed as it approached the final stop in Connecticut, and Sophia watched the trees thin to reveal a low platform and a small station. Only a handful of people stood waiting. Her worries returned as she saw the travelers' anxious faces. What would happen if Shadrack somehow returned home after she had ventured into the Baldlands, where Mrs. Clay would be unable to reach her? She felt a gnawing in her stomach. There was nothing she could do now; if Shadrack returned to Boston, he would have to follow her south.

As Sophia fretted, she noticed two men speaking to the conductor by the station house. She could see only their backs, but it was clear that the conductor was afraid. He had pressed himself uncomfortably against the wall and was leaning as far away from them as his caved chest and the bricks would allow. As he listened, he fiddled with his bristly mustache, then adjusted his hat nervously. Suddenly, one of the men turned, surveying the platform, and his companion did the same. Sophia gasped. They were ordinary men, wearing nondescript clothing. But they had long, crescent-shaped scars across their cheeks. "Theo," she called. "Come look at these two men." As she spoke, the conductor blew the whistle.

Theo, who had apparently been awake for some time, climbed down from his bunk and joined her at the window, but the men were gone. Sophia exhaled with frustration. "They must have boarded the train. There were two men with scars." She traced from the corner of her mouth to her ear. "And you said the ones who came to East Ending had scars."

Theo sat next to her. "Well, if they're on the train, we'll probably see them. Unless they get off in New York. It's probably just a coincidence. No shortage of scars in the world."

"Yes, that's true," she said, not entirely convinced.

She took out her notebook and tried to distract herself by drawing, but this routine, which usually soothed her, made her more anxious: the book was full of Shadrack. The ordinary moments of their shared life—late-night meals after Shadrack's long days, trips to the Boston museums, discussions about their new purchases from the Atlas Book Shop, scraps of paper with Shadrack's rendering of Clockwork Cora—seemed heavy with the weight of things lost and irrecoverable. Quoted passages from his writings were scattered everywhere, speaking in a calm and reassuring voice about the way the world was and should be.

Instead, she took out the atlas and began absently thumbing

through its pages. Sophia had, of course, read most of it many times before, but the atlas seemed to take on new meaning when she thought of it as a guide to places she might actually visit. The long entry on New York described its wharf and parks and the large, indoor marketplaces. The illustrations captured very little of the rumbling coaches and horses and the smell of fish that Sophia remembered.

She turned to the entry on the Baldlands. They were called the Baldlands, she knew, because of how they were described to the early explorers who ventured south and west from New Occident. "*Tierras baldías,*" the inhabitants of those places would say, meaning "fallow lands" or "unfarmed lands" in Spanish. But instead of translating the term completely, explorers translated only half, settling for "the baldlands."

There were three major cities within the Baldlands: Nochtland; the coastal city of Veracruz; and Xela, farther south. Historians posited that all three had emerged from the Disruption as admixtures of three principal Ages: the seventeenth century, as it was known in the old manner of reckoning; an era one thousand years prior to it; and an era one thousand years after it. Small pockets of other Ages existed as well, but the theory of the three eras was well established, and the cities were described collectively as the "Triple Eras." The people of the Triple Eras followed an old religion that understood time as cyclical; the cycles of time were carried like wrapped bundles on the backs of the gods, who trudged tirelessly with their burdens. They were accommodating gods, accepting sacrifice and tribute and granting indulgences where they could.

Beyond the Triple Eras, the Baldlands were far less cohesive. The man who had proclaimed the Baldlands an empire, Emperor Leopoldo Canuto, had cared little for conquest and exploration. Instead, in the early years after the Disruption, he had set about establishing a magnificent court at the heart of Nochtland, sparing no expense in transforming the chaotic city into a sprawling metropolis of splendors. His son, Emperor Julian, had followed in his footsteps, living in isolation with his courtiers and rarely leaving the city boundaries. During their rules, the remainder of the Baldlands had contentedly remained ungoverned. The collision of disparate Ages had unfolded in thousands of different ways, creating in some places peaceful havens and in others lawless expanses. These last had given the Baldlands their reputation for wildness, and it was true that roving bands of marauders had become powerful and greedy, owning entire towns as a farmer would own acres.

Julian's son Sebastian was the opposite of his father. Wholly uninterested in exploration for its own sake, he was undoubtedly a conqueror. When his young wife died, leaving him alone with a daughter, he made it his mission to bring the entire empire of the Baldlands into his fold. For the past twenty years, he had sent his soldiers into every corner of the Baldlands, attempting to weed out those who had for so long ignored the rule of law. But Sebastian had found it more difficult than he had expected. He would stamp out one band of raiders only to have another spring up in its place. Meanwhile his daughter, Justa, remained behind, ruling in his stead. The entry in Shadrack's atlas indicated that the royal family in Nochtland bore the "Mark of the Vine" and not the "Mark of Iron," terms Sophia had never heard before.

"Have you ever seen Princess Justa?" she asked Theo now.

He looked at her with an expression of amusement. "Never. Not many people have."

"What does it mean that she has the 'Mark of the Vine'?"

Theo turned to look out the window. "It's just a thing they say about family lineage."

"Like a family crest?"

"Sort of."

"It says in the atlas that there are more gardens than buildings in Nochtland," Sophia said. "Are there?"

Theo shrugged. "Sounds possible."

"You have *been* to Nochtland, haven't you?" she asked somewhat acidly.

"Of course I've been there. I've just never lived there."

"So if you're not from Nochtland, where *are* you from?"

"I'm from the Northern Baldlands." He folded his hands together. "But I've been all over."

Sophia looked at him intently. "What about your parents? Are they in the northern Baldlands?" She paused. "Don't you think they're worried about you?"

"I'm getting hungry." Theo said abruptly, opening the basket Mrs. Clay had prepared. "Do you want anything?"

Sophia narrowed her eyes. He was ill at ease, which made her more determined to find out why. "Isn't anyone worried you ended up kidnapped in a circus, or does no one know?"

Theo looked like he wanted very much to say, "None of your business," but instead he asked, "Is that the man you saw on the platform?"

Sophia turned in her seat. Standing in the corridor and clearly visible through the window of their compartment was a man with two long scars running from each corner of his mouth. "That's him," she whispered.

He was arguing with a portly man of similar height who stood in his way in the corridor. As Sophia and Theo watched, the argument grew louder, and they could hear it through the compartment's thin door. "I reserved my room weeks ago," the portly man protested, "and I don't give a fig what the conductor promised you. The compartment is mine."

The scarred man's level response was inaudible.

"I certainly will *not* wait in New York for another train. The very idea! Do you think I don't know the value of money? I paid a great deal for that compartment."

The scarred man gave a short, quiet response.

For a moment his antagonist stared at him with growing indignation as his face grew red. "When we get to New York City, sir," he said slowly, "I will summon the first police officer I see and report you. You are a danger to the other passengers on this train." He turned on his heel and stormed off. The scarred man stared after him for a moment. Then he shot a malevolent glance into their compartment, making Sophia recoil against her seat, and walked away.

She sat for a moment in silence. "Definitely him. Was he one of the men from the house?"

Theo shook his head. "I don't think so. Similar kind of scars. But his face is different."

Perhaps it really is only a coincidence, she thought, but she could not entirely convince herself.

A few hours later, the train stopped in New York City. At first, it seemed only a busier version of the other stations. Police officers corralled the waiting passengers and herded them toward the trains; vendors with rolling carts squeezed between them. The platform was littered with loose sheets of newspaper. A tall clock with a broken second hand hung between two parallel rails. And then Sophia caught her breath. "Theo. Come and look."

They watched in dismay as the man they'd seen arguing for his compartment was steered from the train by two men with scarred faces. Sophia gasped as they walked by. "Is that . . ." Her voice trailed off. She had seen the sharp glint of metal near the man's ribs, and there was a look of suppressed terror on his face.

"They've got something on him. A blade or a revolver," Theo said softly. He whistled. "They really wanted that compartment."

Sophia watched in horror as the two led the man directly past a knot of police officers who were guiding passengers onto the train. One of the officers gave them a brief nod. "Did you see that? The police officer let them go by!"

Theo shook his head. "Guess what they say about the police here is true."

"What should we do? Should we tell someone?"

"No way," Theo said emphatically. "If the police wouldn't help that guy, who would? Hey, just be glad they're off the train."

Sophia wrapped her arms around herself. "I am."

—15-Hour 49: On the Train Heading South—

THE *SEABOARD LIMITED* left New York City near sixteen-hour. As night fell, Sophia finally unpacked a sandwich from the basket, forcing herself to swallow the bread and cheese. The porter came by to ensure they had bedding, and Theo climbed up into his bunk, asking Sophia for some of the maps to study. She eventually opened her own bunk and tried to read the atlas, but she could not get the terrified man on the platform out of her mind. Then her thoughts drifted to Shadrack, and her sense of anxiety grew even sharper. The ways of finding him had seemed fragile and uncertain in the daytime; at night, they seemed downright impossible. As she tried to read, she found she could not; her inner mind was trained on imagined horrors. Finally, with a sigh, she closed the atlas and held it tightly against her chest.

She awoke a little while later with her cheek pressed against the book. A nightmare she could not remember had made her heart race, and she stood up to look through the window. Theo leaned over the edge of his bunk. "Thought you'd gone to sleep," he said quietly.

"I had. I'm not sleepy now." She glanced at her watch; it was almost twenty-hour. Then she gazed at the full, pale moon that hung over the trees. "Do you know where we are?"

"No idea. The last few stations have been too dark to read the signs."

Sophia rubbed her eyes. "I'm going to stretch my legs. We've been in here nearly the whole day."

Theo sat up, bumping his head against the roof of the compartment. "Ow. I'll come with you."

"That's fine." Falling asleep full of worry and waking up in a strange place had dispelled her lingering resentment against Theo; she felt too tired, and there were too many other fears crowding the edges of her mind. She placed the atlas in her pack, shouldering it.

They passed the silent compartments on either side as they walked toward the dining car. Cool night air leaked into the passageways from the windows. No one else on the train seemed to be awake, and the dining car was completely deserted but for the faint scent of polished silver and boiled potatoes. The bright moonlight made flame-lamps unnecessary; the entire room, with its white tablecloths and brass-tacked leather seats, was bathed in silver.

"This is the longest I've ever been on a train," Sophia said, taking a seat at one of the tables and looking out at the tracks.

Theo sat down across from her. "Me, too. Actually, it's the first time I've been on a train."

Sophia looked at him in surprise. "Really?"

"I'd seen trains, but never been inside one." He smiled wryly. "First time in New Occident, too. And right when they decide to close the borders."

Sophia smiled back. "You were too much for them. The last straw."

"Must have been. Too hot to handle." He snapped his fingers and pointed the imaginary gun at her, closing the gesture with a wink. For a few minutes both of them sat in silence, staring out at the moon and the dark outline of the trees. Then Theo said, "Nobody's worried."

Sophia looked at him. He was still staring out through the window. "What?" she asked.

"A few people know Ehrlach got me, but they're not worried."

"Why not?"

Theo gave another smile, but his dark eyes, trained on the moon, were serious. "Every man for himself, like I said. I don't have parents—that I know of. I lived with raiders on the western border, and they don't care much if I'm there or in the circus or in the snows. It's all the same to them."

In the pale light it was hard to see Theo's expression, but to Sophia his face looked more thoughtful than sad. "What happened to your parents?"

"I don't know. Never met them. From the earliest I remember, me and the other kids lived with one raider or another."

Sophia could not even imagine it. "So who took care of you?"

"Older kids, mostly. An older girl was the one who found

me. Sue. She found me in an empty barrel behind some watering hole."

"What's a watering hole?"

"A saloon. A tavern." Theo turned and met her eyes. "She got me clothes. Gave me my name. Fed me for years. Then I just took care of myself. It's easier that way. They come and go; so do I. No burdens, no worries."

His brown eyes looked back at her directly, and she had the sense that her whole idea of who he was had suddenly shifted. What was it was like to be alone—truly alone? "Why didn't you say so earlier? Like when Mrs. Clay asked you?"

Theo tossed his head. "People feel sorry for me when I tell them. Older people, especially. You know?"

Sophia did know. "So how did Ehrlach find you?"

"We were trading on the border—selling horses to a man from New Akan. Those border towns are full of people buying and selling everything. Ehrlach seemed like just one more dealer trying to get something cheap. He bought a horse from Aston—that's the raider me and some other guys had been living with—and asked me to bring it into his tent. Aston said, go ahead, deliver it. Moment I got in the tent, he had men standing around me with long knives. I've had my share of one-sided knife fights," he said, holding up his scarred right hand, "and I didn't mind another. I tried to get on the horse and go, but they weren't having it. We were gone before Aston ever missed me." He gave a flat laugh. "Not that he missed me."

He spoke of it all so lightly, with the casual, almost sloppy diction of the Northern Baldlands that made the words seem thrown together every which way. But his easy manner could not entirely muffle the sharp edges of pain that lay underneath: shards of broken glass under a thin rug. Sophia felt something odd in her chest, like a surge of admiration and sadness all at once. His air of being above it all—above every danger, above every indignity—came at a price. "I guess you don't miss Aston, either."

Theo grinned broadly. "Nope."

Now it was Sophia's turn to look away. She kept her eyes on the moon as she said, "I can't remember my parents, but I know a lot about them. I'm lucky. I had Shadrack to tell me. They left when I was little. To go exploring. And they got lost and never came back. Shadrack could have gone to look for them, but he had to take care of me." Sophia didn't know why she had put it that way, except that it had occurred to her for the first time that she had prevented Shadrack from going in search of Minna and Bronson. She had lost her parents, but Shadrack had lost his sister, and yet he had never even suggested that Sophia had stood in the way of finding her.

They sat in silence for a minute, watching the moonlight flicker onto the table as it hit the trees. "Shadrack was teaching me how to read maps," Sophia continued, "so we could go find them together. But the truth is they would be strangers to me. Shadrack was my mother and father."

"You mean he *is*," Theo corrected her. "We'll find him. Have you figured out how to read the glass map yet?"

Sophia reached for her pack. "How did you know this was a map? Most people only know about paper maps."

"They're not so uncommon."

She drew the glass map from the pillowcase and placed it carefully on the table between them. As the two of them peered at it, something remarkable happened. The moon rose above the tree line, and its light fell fully onto the pane of glass. Suddenly an image sprang to life on its surface. The map had awoken.

12
Travel by Moonlight

1891, June 22: 19-Hour #

Among those maps that have made their way into museum collections and university libraries are certain maps of the New World that cartologers of New Occident have not yet learned to read. Either because they were crafted by ancient civilizations or because they reflect some yet undiscovered learning, they are simply illegible to even the most expert Western cartologers.

—*From Shadrack Elli's* History of New Occident

"MOONLIGHT!" SOPHIA BREATHED, leaning in toward the map. "I should have thought of that."

Theo bent forward. "What's it doing?"

"The glass maps respond to light. Usually just lamplight or sunlight. It never occurred to me that there might be some made for moonlight." She kept her eyes on the map, trying to understand the lines that were unfolding on its surface.

It was unlike those she'd seen in Shadrack's map room. Apart from the mapmaker's insignia, there were no clocks and no legend of any kind along the edge. Luminous, silvery writing filled the pane from top to bottom. Most of it was unintelligible. In the middle were five sentences in different languages using the Roman alphabet. The sentence in English read, "You will see it through me." Sophia still remembered enough of the Latin taught to her by the diligent graduate student to realize that the Latin words a few lines down said exactly the same thing.

She shook her head. "I can't even tell if this is a map. I've never seen anything like it. But if it's a memory map we can read it, even if we don't understand the writing."

"It has to mean *something*."

She glanced over the map, unsure of where to place her fingertip. "Try touching part of the surface." They placed their fingertips on different points at the same time.

Sophia had never before experienced such violent emotions from reading a map. Before even seeing anything, she felt awash with an overwhelming sense of desperation and fear. Her heart was pounding; she kept turning her head one way and then another; but nothing was clear and the sense of panic gathered, making every detail around her meaningless, confused, and chaotic.

She felt surrounded by people who were clearly present, but indistinct. They stood to her left, as if lining a long corridor, and they stepped forward to speak with her. Each voice drowned out the next, and she could not make out anything they said. With a sense of mounting alarm she climbed upward, but she could not see the stairs below her feet. She pushed past everyone toward a quiet spot high above. The feeling of desperation mounted. She knew the memory was not hers, but it felt as though she, Sophia, were shoving against some heavy object with all her might. Then she felt it giving way, and then rolling, and then, quite suddenly, falling.

For a few moments she felt herself standing, immobile, as the tension of waiting made every nerve in her body tingle. And then the unseen structure around her began to tremble and shake. She knew without a doubt that soon everything around her would collapse.

She dove back into the corridor lined with people. She ignored them, her heart about to explode in her chest as she ran down along the spiraling passageway. The floor shook beneath her feet and she stumbled and scrambled back up and ran on. People appealed to her as she passed, but their words made no sense; she *would* not hear them—they were unimportant. Her running grew more frantic. A door awaited her—an unseen door that lay somewhere ahead—but she had not yet reached it and the walls around her had begun to fall to pieces. The fear was blinding. All she could see was the blank space in front of her where there had to be a door and there was not. She felt the steps crumbling beneath her.

Then, suddenly, she burst through a doorway—though the door itself was nothing more than a blur. Ahead of her, beyond the opening, there was no one and nothing. The world was empty. There was a faint glimmer in the distance that grew brighter: someone was running toward her. The memory faded.

Sophia pulled back abruptly and saw that Theo had done the same. "What did you remember?" she asked.

"I was in a place filled with people," Theo said haltingly,

clearly shaken. "And I pushed something, and then the place started falling apart and I ran out."

"I saw the same thing." She found that she was breathing hard. They stared at one another. Sophia saw her distress and need for comprehension mirrored in Theo's eyes. "What do you think happened?"

"I don't know," Theo said slowly. "I guess someone destroyed this place—whatever it is. No way to know why."

"I think whoever did it might have been the only person to survive." Sophia said. "And this map is their memory of it."

"But where is it? When did it happen?"

"I don't know. It's hard to tell, because all we can see are the people. We can't see the building or the area around it. We need the other layers of mapping to see those." She shook her head. "There must be some reason why he left it for me. Maybe I'm not supposed to understand it. Maybe I'm just supposed to take care of it."

"It's not much fun to watch," Theo said sourly.

"No, it's horrible." Sophia lifted the pane of glass and gently turned it over. As she slid the blank map back into the pillowcase, a movement in the corner of her eye caught her attention. She looked up across the dining car at the glass porthole in the door that stood closed at the far end. Someone was watching.

Sophia stared back, frozen. The man who'd been arguing outside their compartment was looking straight at her. He held her gaze for a moment, menacingly, and then turned away. "Let's get out of here," Sophia whispered, returning the map to her pack.

"What's wrong?" Theo looked over his shoulder.

"He's there—the man with the scars. He didn't get off in New York." Theo quickly made his way over to the door and peered through the glass. "Don't," Sophia whispered fiercely.

Theo squinted into the corridor beyond. "He's gone."

Sophia shouldered her pack, and they hurried to the opposite end of the car. "He saw us read the map," Sophia whispered anxiously, as they made their way through the train.

"So what? He doesn't know what it is."

She shook her head. "It can't be a coincidence."

They entered their car and Theo opened the compartment door with Sophia on his heels. Then he stopped in his tracks. Sophia bumped into him. A single lamp cast flickering shadows across the walls and upholstery. Scattered across the seat, a pair of revolvers and an assortment of knives glittered in the pale moonlight. A massive grappling hook with sharp points gleamed beside them. Sophia gasped.

Theo turned around and pushed her out through the doorway. They scurried out into the hallway and into their compartment one door down, where they stood in the moonlit room, catching their breath. "It's him—he's right next door," Sophia finally managed. She felt as though it took all the air in her lungs to speak.

"We'll go tell the conductor and get another room."

"No, we can't. He was talking to the conductor before. And I saw how the conductor looked. He was terrified. *That's how he got the room in the first place,*" she whispered desperately.

Theo thought for a moment. "How much longer to Charleston, do you think?"

"I have no idea. I didn't—I can't keep track of time." Her voice trembled.

"It's okay," Theo said reassuringly, misunderstanding her distress. He put his hand out to rest on her shoulder. "Look, he would have already come in here if he wanted to hurt us, right? Just now in the dining room, he could have easily barged in. If he hasn't done anything, it's because he doesn't want to."

Sophia nodded and took a deep breath. "We have to stay in the compartment," she said. "Until we get to Charleston."

—*June 23, 9-Hour 51*—

SOPHIA AWOKE TO find the compartment full of sunlight. She could not believe she had fallen asleep. The thought of their well-armed stalker only one room away had kept them both on edge. They had stayed awake until the early morning, too tense to sleep, talking intermittently and watching the door like hawks. Now Theo was folded up in an uncomfortable position on the bench, fast asleep. Sophia looked at her watch and saw with surprise that it was almost ten-hour. As she stood, Theo awoke. He rubbed his eyes and squinted groggily at the window. "Where are we?"

An overcast sky and a blur of foliage as far as the eye could see told her nothing. "I'm not sure."

Theo groaned and got to his feet, stretching. His borrowed clothes were rumpled and his brown eyes had a foggy look about them. "Well, I'm glad we're not dead." Sophia gave him a stark look. He pulled out the basket and began hunting through it for breakfast. "We'll have to buy food in the dining car after lunch."

"After lunch we can wait until Charleston," Sophia said. "We'll be getting there around dinnertime. If the train is on time."

Theo nodded, chewing thoughtfully on a piece of fruit loaf. Sophia had some as well, swallowing as much as she could and washing it down with water.

He stood up a moment later. "I have to go to the washroom."

"I know; me too. I guess there's no choice. I'll go after you. Be careful."

After he left, Sophia watched the passing trees, waiting for the train to stop at a station so that she would know where they were. She was preoccupied with something that had occurred to her as she was falling asleep; she could not quite remember it. The idea flitted at the edge of her mind, just out of reach. She pulled out her drawing notebook and filled a page aimlessly, hoping the idea would surface. As the train slowed, Sophia checked the sign on the platform. She consulted the train schedule and noted with relief that they were running on time.

The trees beside the tracks nodded in the breeze, and suddenly a sparrow flitted past, swooped back, and perched on the edge of the sill. It turned its head one way and then the other, as if inspecting the compartment. Sophia slowly reached for her sketchbook. She opened it quietly, took a pencil, and began drawing. She lost track of time as her hand moved quickly across the page. The sparrow studied her. Hopping lightly across the sill, it fluttered abruptly onto the seat beside Sophia, seized a crumb in its beak, and flew back to the sill. Then the whistle blew, shattering the quiet, and a moment later the train lurched forward. The sparrow burst out into the air—it was gone. Sophia looked after it wistfully and glanced down at her drawing. And suddenly the idea that had been hovering at the edge of her mind flew directly into view.

She was sitting on the top bunk reading the atlas when Theo returned. He was not alone. His expression furious, he stalked into the room followed by four men: the scarred man they'd seen in the moonlit dining car and three others. Two of the others had identical scars across their faces. As they entered, Sophia noticed the amulets hanging from their necks. Two were wooden on leather laces; one was bronze on a slender bronze chain. They all bore the Nihilismian sign of the open hand. All three scarred men had grappling hooks, which hung from their belts on long, carefully coiled ropes. The fourth man, tall and well-dressed, had no scars, no grappling hook, and no amulet. With a thin mustache above a calm smile and a gray suit that seemed more fitted to a summer wedding than a railway heist, he seemed utterly out of place. His pale blue eyes settled on Sophia.

While Theo and the three scarred men, stone-faced, crowded uncomfortably near the drawn curtains, the tall man sat down and smiled at Sophia with an expression of easy amusement. The space around them seemed impossibly small, as if they had all squeezed into a wardrobe.

"So!" the tall man said, giving her a wide, thin smile. "You keep yourself hidden away, locked up like a princess in a tower."

Sophia stared at him coldly. "I'm not a princess." She was pleased that she sounded calm, although her stomach was churning with fear.

The man laughed, as if he found this a very good joke indeed. "No, you certainly are not, Miss Tims."

"You know who I am. Who are you?"

"Call me Montaigne." He folded his arms comfortably across his chest. "You may not be a princess, Miss Tims, but I hear you have a piece of treasure worthy of one."

"I doubt it," she said evenly.

Montaigne inclined his head to one side. "Come, Miss Tims. You know very well that it is no ordinary sheet of glass. Mortify here"—he waved at the man closest to him—"has seen it work. Moonlight, is it? Very clever." He winked. "I understand how valuable it is, which is why I'm willing to pay for it. Name your price."

Sophia shook her head. "It's not for sale."

"In New Occident," Montaigne said, raising his eyebrows, "everything is for sale." He reached into his jacket and drew out a long leather wallet. "Name the price, Miss Tims."

"No matter what you say, I'm not selling it."

Montaigne's smile shrank at the edges. He stood up and put his hand to his head as if thinking. "Here's the thing, Miss Tims," he said. "Between the four of us, we have six revolvers. That makes three revolvers for each of you. A generous distribution, by any account. Added to which, you're clearly not familiar with the ways of the Sandmen. For your sake, I hope you never have the need to know them better. You see, those fishhooks the Sandmen carry always snag the little fishes, however slippery they may be." He tapped his cheek with a forefinger. "But I've never enjoyed taking things by force. It's cheap. It's distasteful. And," he said, lifting the grappling hook nearest to him with one finger, "it can be so messy." He walked up to the bunk so that his face was just in front of Sophia's knees. Sophia recoiled, shifting farther back. "I would much rather arrange mutually beneficial terms. If you won't take currency, perhaps you'll be interested in an exchange. Does bartering appeal to you?"

"That depends," Sophia said. "What do you have to trade?"

The smile was back on Montaigne's face. "Just about anything. What would you like?"

"Shadrack. You can have the glass if you give me Shadrack."

Montaigne's smile broadened. "How did I know you might say that? What a good thing that I came prepared." He reached into his coat once again for the long leather wallet, and he drew out a small piece of note paper. "I'm afraid Mr. Elli is *ages* away," Montaigne said, "and I wouldn't trade him anyway. But you might be interested in this."

Without letting Sophia see what was on the paper, Montaigne carefully ripped it in half. He handed the top half to Sophia, who snatched it quickly from his hand. It read:

dear sophia,

There was no mistaking Shadrack's handwriting. "Give me the rest of it!" she cried.

"Now, now," Montaigne said. "As I said: I am willing to trade. You can have the rest of the letter when you give me the Tracing Glass."

Sophia sat silently. The train was slowing down. They were doubtlessly nearing a station. The train lurched as it turned the corner, and she glanced down at the torn piece of paper in her hand. She wanted the rest of the letter. More than anything, she wanted to read for herself that Shadrack was safe. "All right," she said.

"Sophia!" Theo burst out. "Don't give it to him. Make him *take* the map if he wants it."

Sophia glanced at him and shook her head. Montaigne nodded, smiling. "Smart girl."

"Give me the letter."

"The glass first, if you please."

Sophia reached for her pack and pulled out the pillowcase. She drew out the sheet of glass that lay inside it and handed it over. Montaigne took it, held it up in his gloved hand, and peered through its clear surface. "Moonlight, eh?" he murmured again. "Very clever." He turned to the other men. "All right, we're done here."

"The letter!" Sophia scrambled to the edge of the bunk.

"Don't fret, Miss Tims—I always keep my word," Montaigne said airily. He dropped the other half of the piece of notepaper on the bed.

Sophia snatched it up, and as the train slowed to a stop and the men began to file out of the compartment, she read Shadrack's message:

T H Ey have said alL i cAn plaCe on tHis papeR Is your naMe.
—shAdrack

"Wait!" Sophia said. "*That's it?*" She jumped down from the bunk. "You made him write it. It doesn't even say anything!"

Montaigne winked once again. "I never said the letter was worth reading. That wasn't part of the deal."

Sophia grabbed his arm. "Where is he?" she asked, her voice near breaking. "Tell me he's all right."

Montaigne calmly freed his arm from Sophia's grasp. "He's not your concern any longer, little girl," he said coldly. Every trace of amusement had vanished from his face. "You should bear that in mind." He shut the door behind him.

13
The Western Line

1891, June 23: 11-Hour 36

New Akan: member of New Occident as of 1810. After the Disruption, the rebellion in Haiti ignited similar rebellions through the slave-holding territories. Uprisings in the former southern colonies of the British empire culminated in a second revolution that, after eight years of intermittent warfare, put an end to slavery and made possible the formation of a large southern state, named by leaders of the rebellion "New Akan."

—From Shadrack Elli's Atlas of the New World

SOPHIA RUSHED TO the window. As she'd expected, Montaigne and the other men were on the platform, walking away. They had gotten what they wanted.

"That's him, Sophia," Theo said. "Montaigne. I saw him outside your house."

Sophia seemed not to hear him. "We should be in Charleston by dinnertime. But will it be dark by the time we leave?"

Theo stared at her as if she had lost her mind.

"I have to check," she said, diving for the folded paper schedule that she'd left on the seat. "The connecting train for New

Akan departs Charleston station at seventeen in the evening. We get in at near sixteen-hour, so we have about an hour before the connection." She sat down with a look of frustration. "That's very close."

"I'd much rather not," Theo said slowly, "but don't you want to follow them? We can still get off. They might lead you to your uncle, and at the very least you can get the map back."

Sophia shook her head. "No. I don't want to be anywhere near them when it gets dark."

The whistle blew and the train lurched forward. "Well, there they go," Theo said. "And there goes your chance to follow them." He looked out through the open window, and then he leaned forward abruptly.

"Hey—!" he said. He closed and opened the small window closest to him. It was set in a metal frame no larger than a sheet of paper and it shut with a small latch. The metal frame of the window was empty; the windowpane had been removed. "Sophia," he said, the truth slowly dawning on him, "you gave them the *windowpane?*"

Sophia nodded. "I thought of it when you went to the washroom. I put the windowpane in the pillowcase. The map is in my sketchbook." She bit her lip. "But once it gets dark and they look at it in the moonlight, they'll know."

Theo raised his eyebrows and dropped down on the seat beside her. "Not bad," he muttered, under his breath.

"Maybe they'll be too far from Charleston by that time," Sophia continued. "Since they got off here. They might stay here or go north. They must not be going to Charleston. So we have a little time—depending on where they are when the moon comes out."

Theo looked at her admiringly. "That's a pretty slick move."

"Yes," she said, without enthusiasm. Now that Montaigne and the Sandmen were gone, she was starting to feel the weight of what she'd done. She clenched her hands tightly; they were trembling. "They will not be happy when they figure it out."

"No doubt," Theo said, leaning back. "Well, there's nothing we can do until we get to Charleston. And at least now we have the train to ourselves."

Sophia nodded. She felt no relief. She was thinking of the hooks that the Sandmen had carried, trying not to imagine how they put them to use. She shivered.

—16-Hour 02: Charleston—

THEY SPENT THE day in dread of the approaching evening. The train reached Charleston late, pulling into the station at almost two past sixteen. They unloaded their trunks and had time to eat a quick dinner of bread and cheese and cold meat in the busy station before the train to New Akan starting boarding. Sophia had written a letter to Mrs. Clay on the train, and she posted it hurriedly. The last rays of sunlight streamed in through the high windows. Pigeons filled the vaulted ceiling of the station, and the sound of train whistles cut shrilly through their low, incessant cooing.

Sophia had seen no sign of Montaigne or the Sandmen.

There were businessmen traveling alone and families traveling in large groups. A small party of nuns waited patiently in the station atrium. The train to New Akan was fully booked, and as they waited on the platform they saw why: a long chain of police officers stood beside a waiting crowd of foreigners, all of whom were departing by train.

Sophia was struck by the defeated look of these unwilling travelers. Some seemed indignant or outraged. But most seemed simply bereft, as did one couple with resigned faces whose child cried quietly and ceaselessly, gripping the skirt of an old woman beside him. In between cries, he pleaded, "Don't go, Grandmother." She placed a trembling hand on the little boy's head and wiped at her own tears. For that moment, as she watched them, Sophia could not think about the approaching darkness and the threat that might come with it.

"All aboard!" the conductor called, and the passengers began to file onto the train. Sophia followed Theo to the last car, dragging her trunk behind her.

Once they had found their compartment and her luggage was stowed, Sophia watched the station platform. *The Gulf Regional* was an older train, with a rather bumpy leather seat and dim lamps. It took several minutes for everyone to board, and then at seventeen-hour the conductor blew the whistle. The train glided out of the station into the falling darkness.

Sophia sighed with relief. "Good thing it's summer and the sun sets so late," she said, eyeing the pale moon.

They settled in and Sophia opened her pack to distract herself. She held the glass map up to the window, but nothing happened; there was still not enough moonlight. As she returned the map to her notebook, she saw the two scraps of paper from Shadrack's letter. There was little satisfaction in having tricked Montaigne, she thought despondently, when Montaigne had managed to trick her as well. They had clearly made Shadrack write the note for the very purpose of deceiving her.

But as Sophia stared at the note, she realized that there was something a little strange about Shadrack's handwriting. His hand was clear and assured, as always, but it was broken in places by strange capitalizations:

dear sophia,
T H Ey have said alL i cAn plaCe on tHis papeR Is your naMe
—shAdrack

She wrote the capitalized letters one by one in her notebook, and as she finished she gasped. "Theo, look!"

After a moment, his face lit up. "The Lachrima," he said softly. "Let me see that." He read it over. "Why would he write that?"

"I don't know."

"He could just be warning you about them," Theo said.

Sophia frowned. "Maybe. It seems strange, though. Why warn me about something that everyone's already afraid of?"

"But he doesn't know you know about them."

"That's true, though I heard Mrs. Clay telling him about what happened to her. It still seems strange." She took back the note. "Theo, tell me what else you know about them."

"I can tell you what I've heard," he said, his voice warming. The Lachrima were clearly a favorite subject. "Like I said before, I've never seen one, but there's a lot of them near the borders. They usually hide—they try to stay away from people."

"Why do you think there are so many near the borders?" Sophia mused.

"I don't know."

"Maybe there's something about the borders—something that draws them there."

"Maybe." But he was clearly unconvinced.

"Have you ever heard one?"

"It's hard to know. Sometimes when you hear someone crying, people say it's a Lachrima, but that's just because they're afraid it might be one. I've heard crying, but supposedly the sound a Lachrima makes is different—much worse. It's a sound you can't get out of your mind."

"Poor Mrs. Clay," Sophia murmured.

"A trader I met once said he'd come across one in his house," Theo went on enthusiastically. "He'd been gone for a week and when he got back, he could hear the Lachrima before he'd even reached the door. He walked in really quietly and just saw this tall person with long, long hair going through the whole house like a whirlwind, pulling things from the walls and wrecking everything. Then it suddenly turned around and looked at him with that faceless face. The trader said he ran right out and never went back."

"Shadrack must know something about them." *The Lachrima, the glass map, Montaigne, and the Nihilismians,* she thought; *what do they have to do with one another?* "Montaigne called the glass map a 'tracing glass.' I wonder what that means."

"Maybe it's just another way to describe a glass map?"

"Maybe," Sophia considered. She tried another tack. "Do you know anything about the people he called 'Sandmen'?"

Theo shook his head. "I've never even heard that name."

"They were all Nihilismians."

"How could you tell?"

"Their amulets," Sophia said, surprised. "The open hand."

Theo shrugged. "I know about Nihilismians, but I've never met one. There aren't many in the Baldlands."

"They're everywhere in New Occident. They think our world isn't real. They use *The Chronicles of the Great Disruption* to prove that the real world was lost at the time of the Disruption and this one—our world—shouldn't exist. The open hand is the sign of the prophet Amitto, who wrote the Chronicles. It means 'to let go.'"

"So you've never heard them called 'Sandmen'?"

"Never. They must be somehow different. But I can't tell how . . ." Her voice dropped off as her mind worked to connect the pieces. What had Shadrack said to her recently about Nihilismians? She could not remember. He had told her something, and it had to do with maps. *Maybe I wrote it in my notebook*, she thought. But it held no clues.

As the train rolled west, the sky darkened and a yellow moon emerged, hanging low behind the trees. Theo climbed up to his bunk to sleep, and Sophia sat watching the passing landscape, feeling anything but sleepy. Hills with crests topped by pines gave way to flatlands dotted with farmhouses. Every time the train pulled into one of the small, rural stations on the westward line, she felt certain that Montaigne and his men would board, but the people who stood under the flame-lamps were invariably sleepy, harried travelers on their way westward. So far, Sophia and Theo were in the clear.

—*June 24: 1-Hour 18*—

IT WAS PAST one in the morning when the train crossed the border between South Carolina and Georgia. Sophia took out her notebook. Men with scars, a cowering faceless creature with long hair, and a small sparrow came to life on the paper. Clockwork Cora sat hunched in the corner, brow furrowed, contemplating the problem. Sophia looked at the page for a long time. There was a riddle there; a riddle she had to solve. She drew a line, making a border around the Lachrima. Her mind whirled wearily over the sketched images like the wheels of the railcar.

Turning the page, she moved on to a more solvable riddle. She wrote, *"Where did T learn to read? He has traveled where else in the Baldlands?"* She glanced up at the bunk overhead where Theo was sleeping silently. *"And why no longer cared for by Sue?"* However much more commonplace, the riddle that was Theo eluded her also, and Sophia closed her notebook with a sigh.

They moved steadily across Georgia. At each stop, the whistle blew into the still night. At five, the train passed into New Akan. The sun had begun to lighten the edges of the horizon, but the sky above was still filled with stars. The flat fields spread out like calm waters on either side of the tracks. As they pulled into the first station in New Akan, Sophia leaned out the window. The humid air smelled of earth. Only a woman with two small children stood next to the station agent on the platform. The three passengers climbed aboard and the train sat idly for several minutes. Two of the ticket collectors walked onto the platform to stretch their legs. They shook hands with the station agent.

"Bill. Surprised to see you here. Thought the mosquitoes would have eaten you alive."

"They come near me, they're liable to drown in sweat," the station agent said, mopping his brow. "Most humid June I can remember."

"My clean shirt feels like I've been wearing it two days," one of the ticket collectors said, fanning the flaps of his uniform jacket.

Then the whistle sounded and the ticket collectors went aboard. As the train pulled out, Sophia saw the pink light of dawn rising behind the platform.

They traveled another half hour into New Akan. The sky was beginning to lighten in earnest when the train suddenly lurched to a stop—but there was no platform. As far as Sophia could tell, they were in the middle of nowhere. Toward the front of the train, she saw what appeared to be a cluster of horses. She leaned farther out to get a better look, her belly pressed against the sill, and in the gray light of dawn she saw that the knot of horses was, in fact, a coach. A number of people were emerging from it right there, beside the tracks, and boarding at the front of the train. Two, three, four men.

The Sandmen had caught up with them.

SOPHIA DUCKED BACK into the compartment. "Theo! They're here. They're boarding the train. *Get up!*"

"What?" he mumbled from the top bunk.

"*Wake up!*" Sophia was almost shouting. "We have to get off, now!" She stuffed the notebook into her pack, shouldered her pack, and tied the lower straps securely around her waist. As she pulled on her shoes, the train began moving once again. "Oh, no! We're too late."

Theo, rumpled but alert, was already tying his boots. "Where are we?"

"Somewhere in New Akan. Four men just got on the train. We weren't even at a station." Sophia could feel her heart pounding, but her mind was calm. All night she'd been preparing herself for the situation that lay ahead. Now it had arrived, and it was almost a relief. She opened the door and looked out into the corridor. There was no one in sight.

"You thinking we should hide?" Theo whispered.

"We're going to jump off the train." With Theo on her heels, she hurried to the rear end of the train and opened the door, stepping out onto the narrow railed platform at the back of the car. The tracks unfolded behind them, disappearing into the dawn sky as the train continued to pick up speed. Wind sucked at the sides of the platform and the wheels clanged against the rails in a quick, accelerating staccato.

"You sure about this?" Theo said into Sophia's ear, over the noise. "I'm no expert on trains, but we're going pretty fast."

"If we don't jump, they'll find us. We should do it now before they notice we've gone."

Sophia walked to the far end of the railing. Suddenly, Theo grabbed her arm. "Wait a second," he hollered. He pointed to the narrow ladder that led up from the platform to the roof of the railcar. "Maybe we can just climb up there and wait them out. They'll think we've jumped. We can watch from there and see when they leave."

Sophia hesitated. She looked down at the blur of rocky ground beside the tracks and back at the ladder. "All right," she called out. "I'll go first." Climbing deftly onto the railing, she swung around to grasp the ladder. The wind buffeted her, but she held onto the rungs and moved swiftly. When she reached the roof, she dropped onto her stomach and clung to the flat metal surface.

A moment later Theo appeared. They inched out carefully on hands and knees to the middle of the car and then lay flat, the slick metal vibrating against them. "This should do it," Theo shouted over the wind. "Now we just wait them out."

Help us escape them, please, Sophia implored the Fates.

For several minutes they lay silently, listening to the whir of the wheels against the rails. The metal roof was hard against her ribs and she palmed the surface desperately, feeling as though a sudden jolt or turn would toss her away like a crumb brushed from a sleeve.

Then she heard it, the sound she'd been dreading: the rear door of the railcar slamming shut. Someone had stepped out onto the balcony. A moment later, she heard the clang of boots. "They're on the ladder!"

Theo braced himself. "We have to run." He rose, stepped over Sophia, and put his hand out. "Come on!" She pulled herself up and tried to get her balance. Theo let go and began moving toward the next railcar.

Sophia took a few steps forward and then broke into a halting run. She turned to look over her shoulder, nearly toppling; Mortify was climbing onto the roof. *"Run!"* she shouted. "Keep running!"

Theo reached the edge and in one easy bound jumped to the next car. Though the distance between them was only a few feet, Sophia felt her knees buckle at the prospect of hanging in midair above the moving train. She looked over her shoulder again; Mortify was halfway across and he was somehow, despite the moving train, loosening the long rope of the grappling hook from his belt loop. Sophia crouched, her knees shaking, and then jumped.

Fly, Sophia, fly! A distant pair of voices reached her: the memory of her parents, holding her high above the ground. For a moment she did fly, or float, caught in midair by the wind. She looked down and saw the tracks, two long black smudges on a gray canvas, and then her feet landed on the other roof, as if the two hands that held her had let her down again gently, safely.

She ran haltingly across the whole length of the second car. The train moved under her each time she put her foot down, and every step threatened to pitch her sideways. She held her hands out rigidly, balancing herself. Mortify had jumped the gap between the first and second car, and he began closing the distance. He loosed the grappling hook and held it deftly in his right hand, readying himself to throw it.

Theo and Sophia jumped, one after another, onto the third car. The violent clang of metal striking metal sounded over the rushing of the wind. The grappling hook had struck the edge of the car and Mortify was hauling it back toward him like a fishing line. "We have to jump off," Theo shouted.

"No, wait," Sophia said. *"Look!"* A train heading in the opposite direction had stopped on its parallel tracks to allow their train to pass. In a few seconds it would be beside them.

"Perfect," Theo shouted. "Get to the first car." He took off, and Sophia ran with abandon now, her arms flailing at her sides, no longer looking to see where her feet landed. She kept her eye on the front of the train, covering three railcars, then a fourth, and then a fifth. They were almost at the front. The other train loomed, waiting.

"All right," Theo yelled. "Let's go!"

Then they were abreast of it. A burst of air shook the car. Theo quickly regained his footing; then he took a running start and jumped. Sophia glanced behind her. She had only a few seconds. She saw Mortify, a car-length away, launch the grappling hook. It seemed to hang in the air, suspended: a whirling shape that caught the light of the rising sun. The bright cluster of silver grew larger, swinging toward her, its sharp points glittering as they twirled.

Sophia yanked herself back to the present. *Don't lose track of time now!* she told herself desperately.

She ran with all her might toward the edge. She jumped. A moment later she felt hard metal slam against her face, her back, her knees; she was rolling—rolling fast, like a marble over a table top. She could find nothing to hold onto, and the edge rose up before her. Suddenly something fell across her legs, pinning her down. She opened her eyes. Her head was hanging over the edge of the railcar, but she was safe. Theo had tackled her, and his weight was holding her in place.

She scrambled up just as the train jolted into motion, heading east. The other train was already far in the distance. "Where is he?" she cried. "Did he follow us?"

"He didn't jump," Theo said, raising his voice to be heard over the mounting noise. Sophia saw with surprise that he was smiling at her with frank admiration. "That was totally reckless, but it worked."

"What?"

"Waiting until the last second so he couldn't jump after you." He pointed to the far edge of the roof. The grappling hook hung from the ladder like a snagged kite, its rope dangling.

"Right." Sophia took a deep breath. The train began to pick up speed. "We have to get off."

"Next station," Theo shouted.

They lay against the cold roof as mile after mile of flat land passed by. Sunlight yellowed the fields around them, making fog of the humid air. The metal rattled painfully against Sophia's chest, and the station seemed ages away.

Finally, the train began to slow. It rolled up alongside the platform of the station they had passed at dawn. ROUNDHILL, read the wooden sign swinging over the station door. Sophia and Theo crawled to the end of the car and made their way off the roof.

14
The Glacine Age

1891, June 23: Shadrack Missing (Day 3)

In the chaotic political wake of the Disruption, the Vindication Party emerged as more stable and lasting than most. Founded on the philosophies of Mary Wollstonecraft's A Vindication of the Rights of Women, *the party pushed aggressively—and successfully—for women's rights. Perhaps without the Disruption the Vindication Party would have met with more resistance, but in such turmoil, it laid claim to certain territories that were never again contested. Suffrage became a stepping stone, and soon women could be found in parliament, at the head of major manufactories, at the helm of universities, and in other seats of power.*

—From Shadrack Elli's History of New Occident

SHADRACK HAD SLEPT very little during his nights of captivity. Though they had given him water and a few scraps of food, he could only taste the wooden block. The damp wood, reeking of other men's fear, left a horrible aftertaste that nothing could erase. His face had not been cut by the wires, but he did not want to test his luck a second time. He had good reason to believe that in Blanca's mansion the bonnet was only one of several horrors.

They had moved him from the chapel to a small room in

a high turret. His room—a low space that must once have been used for storage—contained only a basin and a ragged length of blanket. A narrow window, no wider than a forearm, allowed a view of the circular drive near the entrance. He used it to keep track of the passing time, doing his best to shake off the chilling influences of the stone walls and the conversation with Blanca.

She had destroyed Carlton, leaving him a mindless shell. Exactly how, Shadrack did not know, but it seemed clear that she felt no compunction and would easily do the same to him. Nevertheless, he knew that under no circumstances could he help her find the *carta mayor*. Much as he grieved for Carlton, he drew his mind forcibly to the problem at hand. He *could not* allow Blanca to succeed.

The problem of how to stop her kept him awake at night. But he could not concentrate; the mansion was full of peculiar noises. At times he heard a cooing or weeping, faint and ethereal, hovering above a louder and more jarring sound: a near-constant, high-pitched creaking, like that of a pulley or a wheel. It seemed to stretch through his room like a fine, caustic web, allowing him no sleep. It settled in the air, so that even when it stopped he continued to hear it.

On the second night of his captivity, one of the Sandmen opened the door and placed a cup of water and a rind of dry bread on the floor. "Please tell me what that sound is," Shadrack said. He was sitting with his back against the stone wall, his injured leg, bruised and sore, resting on the cold floorboards.

"What sound?" the man asked.

"That sound—the creaking."

The man stood silently for a moment, as if attempting to connect Shadrack's words with a meaning. His scarred face worked slowly over the problem. Finally a dim illumination passed into his eyes. "It's the wheelbarrow."

"The wheelbarrow? For what?"

"For the sand," the man replied, as if this were self-evident.

"The sand for what?" Shadrack persisted.

"For the hourglass." The light vanished from the man's eyes, as if the very mention of the hourglass had snuffed out his thoughts. He stepped back and slammed the door before Shadrack could speak again. The creaking continued, sharp as a saw.

The third morning dawned cool and gray, and Shadrack watched, through his narrow window, what appeared to be travel preparations. The journey to the estate by unscheduled train had suggested from the start that Blanca had powerful ties to one of the railways. The presence of private railcars in the drive with a distinctive hourglass insignia confirmed it. For several hours, the Nihilismians had been loading supplies. At midmorning, two of them appeared at his door and led him from the room.

Shadrack made no effort to resist. He could hardly summon the energy to stand. At first, he thought they might take him to the railcars, but instead they wound their way deeper into the building through long stone passageways. It was Shadrack's first view of the artwork and historic treasures that filled the mansion. The paintings, tapestries, sculptures, and cultural artifacts overflowing the corridors put Boston's museums to shame. "Tintoretto," he groaned under his breath, pained both by his leg and by the brief sight of such a masterpiece hidden away from the world. Indifferent to the fabulous treasures around them, the Sandmen dragged him down several sets of stairs and finally entered a vaulted corridor that ended behind the altar of the chapel. Blanca waited in the center of the room.

"Shadrack," she said quietly, ignoring his rumpled clothing and look of plain exhaustion. "You and I are leaving soon. Our errand is more urgent than you realize, and our time is running short. But where we go depends entirely on you." She hesitated. "I know how much you disapprove of my plan at present, and I realize you need persuasion to assist me in finding the *carta mayor.*"

"I'm not sure 'disapprove' does it justice," he replied.

Blanca walked toward him, the gray silk dress she was wearing quietly rustling, and she gently touched his arm with her gloved hand. "Once I explain, I have no doubt that you will be persuaded," she went on, as if he hadn't spoken.

She pointed to a large calfskin map of the New World that lay pinned to the wooden table. Scattered over the map and making odd patterns across it were piles of sand—black, nut brown, and white. Toward the southern tip of the continent, a handful of white sand blanketed all of the unknown territory still referred to by cartologers as Tierra del Fuego. It reached upward into Late Patagonia. "Do you know what Age lies here—at the very edge of the hemisphere?"

Shadrack shook his head tiredly. "No explorer has succeeded in reaching it."

"It is another Ice Age, like the Prehistoric Snows that lie north of here."

He was suddenly alert. "How do you know this?"

"I have been there."

"How did you reach it? I know many who try and cannot succeed in traveling south of Xela."

"That is not important at the moment," she said. "Believe me; the Ice Age is there. What is important is this: the Great Disruption did not occur as you believe it did. You believe the physical earth came loose from time and then came together again, coalesced along fault lines that separated the Ages."

"More or less, yes."

"It did begin that way," she said, tracing her gloved finger along the calfskin map. "But it did not end that way. For decades the fault lines have been still. Now, once again, they are moving."

Shadrack stared at her in an undisguised mixture of astonishment and skepticism. "Explain what you mean."

"It is simply this—the borders of the Ages are shifting." She pointed to New Occident. "Perhaps you have not been far enough north before to realize that in some places the Prehistoric Snows are melting away before the advance of New Occident. Yes," she said, before he could speak. "This very site was once bound in ice. But the ice has melted, and trees have sprung up everywhere. Now the air is warmer, and there are people native to your Age. Here, the change is piecemeal and decisive. The snows disappear and new states, contemporaries of New Occident, take their place."

Shadrack gazed at the sand, trying to make sense of what he was hearing. Suddenly a set of images, like a scattering of impressions from a memory map, flashed through his mind. But the memories were not from a map; they were his own. He recalled the letter sent so many years ago by the explorer Casavetti, whom his sister and brother-in-law had set out to find: *"In this place I thought I knew so well, I have discovered a new Age."* It was this discovery of a new, hostile Age that had led to his capture, which had prompted Minna and Bronson's journey halfway across the globe.

In his mind's eye Shadrack saw Sophia poring over the two maps of the Indies, only a few days earlier. She had asked how a convent could have been replaced, in only a decade, by a wasteland. She had *seen* the evidence of a similar change. And he had been too blind to recognize the significance of her discovery. With all of his training, experience, and intuition, how had he failed to see it? After a moment of stunned silence, he spoke. "Are all the borders in flux?"

She shook her head. "Not all—but many," she said, with a note of satisfaction at Shadrack's dismay. "And they are shifting at different paces. The border changing most quickly is this one." She pointed again to Tierra del Fuego, at the southern tip of the Western Hemisphere. "The border of this Ice Age is the Southern Snows. It has been moving unevenly but consistently northward through Late Patagonia for the last year. Mile by mile, it is shifting toward the Baldlands, and every Age it touches disappears beneath the ice. I believe," Blanca continued quietly, "your niece is traveling south, is she not?"

Shadrack felt the blood rush to his temples; in sending Sophia to the safest place he could think of, he had mistakenly sent her into terrible danger. "But then," he asked slowly, "the people who are there now . . . ?"

"They will vanish," Blanca said. "Or—I should be precise. The advance of the border is rather more . . . damaging. The glaciers do not approach quietly. Everything they touch is destroyed."

"They must know of it—the people will flee the advancing border," Shadrack said desperately.

"In fact, they have already been told that a powerful force is moving northward. But they believe it to be a weirwind—a destructive weather system and nothing more."

Shadrack stared at her a moment, trying to comprehend. "You planted this belief *yourself*?"

Blanca shrugged. "I could not have the entire mass of humanity that inhabits the Baldlands rushing north like a torrent of scurrying ants. Princess Justa Canuto, whom I know well, is a typical monarch: she wants most what is best for her, not what is best for her kingdom. It was a simple matter to persuade her that Nochtland would survive the weirwind by staying put. Besides, it will make no difference whether they run or not."

"How quickly are the Southern Snows moving?" Shadrack demanded.

"They began slowly, but the rate seems to be exponential.

What began as an imperceptible shift, inch by inch, is now mile by mile."

"There must still be some way," he insisted. "Some way to stop it. What is causing it?"

"I believe we are causing it."

Shadrack stared at her. "How?"

"The cause is unknown. You, with your spirit of empiricism, will doubtlessly dispute my theory, which is more speculative. I have come to the conclusion that we have caused it by failing to live according to a single time. Do you know how many forms of time-keeping currently exist in the world? More than two thousand. The world can no longer hold such disparate Ages. Time is quite literally being torn apart before our eyes." She paused, seemingly weighing the effect of her words. "I knew you would be persuaded. Now you understand: unless we move quickly, the entire world will be engulfed by the Southern Snows."

"Move quickly where?"

Blanca gestured at the map in frustration. "I do not know, Shadrack. This is what you must tell me. We have to reach the *carta mayor* before it, too, is encased in ice. Then you, the only living cartologer who can write water maps, must revise it. You must restore the world as it was before the Disruption."

"But there is *no such thing* as a world before the Disruption! You are plagued by the same delusions as your Nihilismians. There can be no restoration of a lost past. Assuming there were a *carta mayor,* and assuming we found it, and assuming I could revise it in time, how would I determine the proper age of the globe? We do not know when the Disruption occurred. In our Age? Four hundred years after it? To what Age would I restore the world?"

When Blanca spoke, Shadrack could hear her smiling. "To mine."

"That is pure hubris," he replied impatiently. "We cannot know that our Age—"

"To *mine*. Not yours."

"To yours? What do you mean?"

"We are not from the same Age, you and I," she said. "What your Age is to man's prehistoric past, my Age is to yours." She paused. "Imagine an Age where peace holds sway over every corner of the globe; where there is perfect comprehension of the natural world and its science; where humankind has reached the apex of its endeavors. This is where I come from. You have not heard of it, Shadrack. It is called the Glacine Age."

Shadrack listened to the fervor in her voice with astonishment. "Forgive me if I fail to be impressed. If the Disruption has taught us anything, it has taught us that no Age is perfect or inviolable."

Blanca planted her gloved fingertips in the sand. "I don't believe you understand, Shadrack—the Glacine Age is superior to all other Ages in every way." She shook her head, and when she spoke her voice was pained. "Do you have any idea of the *mistakes* that humankind has made over the Ages? The terrible acts of destruction, the missed opportunities, the inane cruelties—the Glacine Age is entirely beyond them. Imagine a world without those horrors. In the Glacine Age, all of the world's terrible mistakes lie in the past. They will vanish like specks of sand in the sea. It will be as if they never existed." She paused and gave a little sigh of pleasure. "You will revise the water map, Shadrack, just as you would a paper map: erasing it carefully, line by line, to redraw a completely new map. You and I will draw the Glacine Age, whole and intact, so that it covers the world."

Shadrack shook his head. "This is madness."

"Is it?" Blanca asked softly. "You are a scientist—you know that time passes and the earth's surface changes. All the Ages pass away. Do you not wish for the arrival of an Age in which there is knowledge, and ease of life, and peace? You are simply afraid of losing the world that is familiar to you."

"Your arrogance is astounding," Shadrack said with disgust. "I have never seen such blind faith."

Blanca shook her veiled head. "It is you who are arrogant," she replied quietly. "Think of the cost of preserving the primitive Ages you cling to. To satisfy such sentiment, you are willing to put up with petty tyrants, never-ending wars, widespread ignorance. You, who value scholarship so highly, should welcome an end to these dark Ages, where every piece of hoarded knowledge is false."

"Without our 'false knowledge' and our 'mistakes,' your Age would never have come about," Shadrack said sharply. "Every future Age owes a debt to its past Ages."

"But the *consequences* of those falsehoods," Blanca said. "Your blindness is more destructive than you realize."

"Surely you overestimate me. In your vision, I am only an irritating speck of sand from the past."

"That may be true. But you, in particular, are a speck of sand that matters."

He laughed bitterly. "If this is meant to win me to your cause, it isn't working."

Blanca looked at the map. Then she took a handful of white sand from the nearby pile and carefully poured it out, covering every landmass. All that remained was ice and ocean. "These dark Ages will not survive, regardless. The Southern Snows are moving northward, Shadrack. We can dispute everything else, but not this."

Shadrack looked hard at the veil, his heart pounding. He abhorred her entire vision, and in part he still did not believe her. But in at least one respect, he could not risk disbelieving her. If an Ice Age was truly descending on the Baldlands, and rapidly, he had to find Sophia before it reached her. He felt a momentary flash of fury at himself for sending her to Nochtland. Then he composed himself. "What do you plan to do?"

For a moment, she was silent. "I am in a difficult position. I do not know the location of the *carta mayor,* and you will not tell me."

"Because I do not know it," Shadrack said curtly.

"Nor will you tell me where Sophia is going with the Tracing Glass." When Shadrack did not answer, she shrugged. "I might make a globe of your memories to find out." She paused, waiting for him to protest. Shadrack looked down at the ground, disciplining his face into stillness. "But then I would be without your skills as a mapmaker." She moved closer to Shadrack and took one of his hands between her two gloved ones. "I need more than your memories to revise the *carta mayor.* I need your hands. When you agree to help me, I can tell you more." Shadrack stood silently. "Consider," Blanca said earnestly, pressing his hand and then releasing it, "that the Ice Age is already advancing. It has begun here, and here, and here," she said, indenting with her fingertip the sand spread across Late Patagonia. "It is no longer a matter of weeks—more likely days—before the border reaches Nochtland." She touched the capital of the Baldlands, leaving a shallow depression. "Come," she said encouragingly. "Tell me where you have sent the Tracing Glass."

Shadrack wheeled away from her, struggling to control his frustration. There were few times in his life when he had been so entrapped by his circumstances, and he did not like the feeling. Blanca seemed to know Sophia was heading south, and she would pursue the Tracing Glass whether he assisted her or not. If he assisted Blanca, the glass would almost certainly fall into her hands, and Sophia's safety would be all but irrelevant.

There was only one course he could follow. He had to escape as they traveled south and find Sophia himself. It was the only way to keep both her and the glass safe. He turned back to Blanca. "I will do everything I can to prevent you from ever seeing or touching it."

For a moment, she did not speak. "Ah. Well, I have learned *one* thing. You believe the *carta mayor* exists. Otherwise, you would not go to such lengths." Shadrack clenched his jaw, his eyes hard. "You should reconsider. It is only a matter of days before we find your niece."

"I will take my chances," Shadrack said hoarsely.

"If you agree to help me, I will be sure she is treated kindly when she's found. I have fifty men at the stops along the railway route she travels. She cannot get off or on a train without my knowing." She lifted one shoulder. "That is the advantage of owning the second largest rail company in New Occident."

Shadrack blinked. "Oh, the private train and rail line leading here weren't evidence enough for you? Yes. You may appreciate the irony of it: I took the first step toward making my fortune on the gaming tables of New York, playing with parliament time. From there it was a simple matter to buy my first tobacco plantation—tobacco is *such* a vice in New Occident." She shook her veiled head. "One plantation easily becomes ten. Ten plantations are enough to finance any amount of speculative investment. Steel, for example. And of course steel manufacturing is so useful for building rails. White Smoke Tobacco, White Anvil Steel, and the Whiteline Railroad Company. A neat symmetry, don't you think?" Her tone was triumphant.

Shadrack pressed his lips together tightly.

Blanca gave a small sigh and turned toward the Sandmen, who stood waiting. "We leave in an hour. Put all of the items from Boston in a trunk—or more than one, if need be. Don't let him near any scissors," she added.

15
Safe Harbor

1891, June 24: 8-Hour 00

Roundhill Station: This station was built in 1864 by the Whiteline Railroad Company, only half a mile to the north of See-Saw, where the final Battle of See-Saw took place in 1809.

Station sign

THE GLASS MAP was unharmed, and Sophia still had her pack, containing the atlas, all the folded maps for their route, her sketchbook, and an assortment of drawing instruments. Just as vitally, the leather purse had remained attached to her belt; without funds, her lifewatch, or her identity papers, they would not have gotten far. The compartments on the train were sold out, so she bought two bench-car tickets for New Orleans and then she and Theo sat at the edge of the platform to wait a whole slow hour for the next train heading west.

All of the nervous energy that had carried her through the evening and early morning had dissipated like air leaking from a balloon. Her chin and knees were bruised; her ribs and back ached from landing on the roof of the railcar, and all she wanted was to sleep. *Surely,* she thought, *we don't have to worry about the Sandmen appearing here.* She slipped her hands into the pockets of her skirt for the two talismans that gave her comfort: the smooth disc of the pocket watch and the spool of silver thread. Time was securely in hand, and the Fates were watching over her.

The humid morning air settled over her like a damp rag as the hour slowly dragged on. More people began appearing on the platform, their dusty boots rattling the floorboards in a wearying procession of shuffles and taps. Sophia leaned back against a trunk that someone had left unattended as Theo placidly looked out over the tracks. She closed her eyes, and it seemed to her they'd been closed only a moment when a shout jolted her awake.

Sophia looked up to see the most extraordinary woman striding toward them. Everyone standing on the platform stepped aside as they saw her coming. She was tall and extravagantly dressed in a billowing charcoal-gray silk gown trimmed with lace and a black plumed hat that covered most of her face. Strapped to her narrow waist was a leather belt with a holster and a silver revolver. Her white-gloved hands planted on her hips, she stopped before them; the scent of orange blossoms wafted toward Sophia. "Thought you could take it from under my nose, did you?" she asked with a look of hard-edged amusement. Her smile was not friendly.

Sophia looked up at the woman's face. She was beautiful;

her long, dark hair hung to her waist, and her black eyes glittered. Sophia felt a moment of panic—*Mortify is on a train speeding west, so Montaigne sent someone else!* She sprang to her feet and Theo joined her. Compared to this commanding woman, she felt very much a child. Her knees and palms were raw from having skidded across the roof of the train, and her skirt—plain striped cotton, even on the best of days—was ripped in more places than one. Her clean clothes, of course, were lost somewhere on a trunk heading west. She balled her fists and tried to wear, at the very least, a dignified expression. "It's not yours," she said, in a voice that sounded far less grand than she intended.

The woman laughed. "Is that going to be your defense? Because I don't see how you hope to explain its contents."

Sophia contemplated running, and then she looked at the revolver and thought of Shadrack. She swallowed hard and her voice trembled. "Where is my uncle?"

The beautiful woman's expression abruptly changed, turning pensive. "You've misunderstood. I'm not that kind of pirate. And the trunk would make poor ransom," she said.

"The trunk?" Sophia asked, confused.

The woman gave her a good long look, and then she laughed until her hat shook. When she was through, she gave Theo and Sophia a broad smile. "I believe I've misunderstood as well," she said. "I'm referring to that trunk by your feet. And unless I'm mistaken, you're referring to something else entirely."

"You can have the trunk," Theo told her.

"We just found it here," Sophia said at the same time.

"Well, sweetheart, my apologies. But I confess to being intrigued. Has your uncle been taken by pirates?" She seemed genuinely curious, and her voice was full of warmth.

"No," Sophia replied, before Theo could say anything.

The woman raised her eyebrows. "Secret, is it? Well, don't worry about me; I know all about secrets. I'm Calixta," she added.

"I'm Sophia. And this is Theo."

"A great pleasure to meet you. I apologize that you had to see my vicious side first, and so entirely without provocation. Let me make it up to you properly," Calixta continued, looking at something far in the distance, past Sophia. "Share my compartment, won't you?"

Sophia followed Calixta's gaze and saw a moving speck on the horizon; the train was approaching. "Oh, thank you. But we have tickets for benches in the main car."

Calixta waved a gloved hand. "Bother the main car. I have the largest compartment at the front of the train, and it has far too much room for tiny me. Porter!" she called. A moment later, two men emerged hurriedly from the station house. "Decidedly not real porters," she said in a lofty aside. "Who leaves a trunk *by itself* on a platform? But we'll pretend. And such a pitiful little station, in the middle of nowhere," she added. "Please bring my other trunks," she told the men, who jumped to obey.

The moment the train stopped, the doors flew open and the ticket collectors emerged. Calixta walked directly to the front, followed by the porters, and boarded the first car.

"Should we really sit with her?" Sophia asked in a low voice.

Theo shrugged. "Why not?"

"She's a pirate!"

"She's harmless. Just a little extravagant."

"I don't know," Sophia said, as they handed their tickets to the ticket collector.

The main car was packed. A woman with five children, three of whom were wailing at the tops of their lungs, was attempting to wrestle her brood onto a single bench. By the window, a heavyset man had rudely commandeered two benches by sitting on one and dropping the muddy boots he'd removed on another. The pungent smell of his socks was already drawing expressions of consternation from the passengers around him. Sleeping here would be impossible.

"Okay," Sophia said to Theo. "Let's find her. Don't tell her anything about the map or Shadrack, though." They walked through the noisy car and then two others before reaching the front of the train. The left-hand compartment was open, and Calixta was inside, supervising the placement of her trunks.

"There you are! Thank you very much," she said to the two porters, handing them each a coin from her purse. "Ugh!" she sighed, sitting down abruptly. Her gown ballooned around her. "I can't wait to escape this miserable swamp and get back to my ship. The air smells like dirt, everything is covered with dust, and the people! Is it me or do they never bathe?" She patted the seat beside her. "Sophia?"

Sophia closed the compartment door and sat down stiffly next to Calixta. Theo, across from them, seemed tongue-tied. "You're sailing out of New Orleans?" he managed to ask.

"Yes, finally. The *Swan* will be at the dock—my brother will have it waiting—and then we head out from there." She began unpinning her hat. "Give me a hand, won't you?" Sophia succeeded in removing the last pin, and Calixta set her hat on the shelf above the trunks. She smoothed her hair into place as she sat back down. "What a day! And it's only beginning." She started pulling off her gloves. "Aren't you hungry?" She continued removing them as she got up again. "Hello?" she called into the corridor, stepping out of the compartment for a moment. The whistle blew, and the train began rolling forward.

Sophia and Theo exchanged glances. Calixta abruptly reentered, closing the door behind her. "That's settled, then—breakfast for three. Now," she said, as the train picked up speed and the breeze whirled in through the open window, "I won't ask yet about your fascinating uncle or what you insisted *wasn't* mine, but perhaps I can ask where you are going?"

"Yes." Sophia hesitated. "Theo has to get back to the Baldlands, and I'm going to Nochtland."

"You're also sailing out of New Orleans, then?"

"We were thinking of riding down to Nochtland from the border," Theo put in.

"Oh, you don't want to do that. Takes ages, and you get your horses stolen every other day. You should sail down out of New Orleans to Veracruz. Only a suggestion, of course, but if I were you, I wouldn't want to stay on land a moment longer." Calixta rolled her eyes.

"Why were you here?" Sophia asked, with what she hoped sounded like polite interest.

"Oh, I only came to negotiate a new contract with a merchant. Last chance, with the borders closing and all that. I tried to send my brother Burr, seeing as I *am* the captain, after all, and he is only quartermaster, but he says that I negotiate better. And, well," she sighed, "my brother is a darling, but it is also true that he rarely seems to land the lucrative contracts I do." She trilled with laughter. "Nor does he land the proposals! Had I known my trip would result in three highly ridiculous marriage propositions, I would have refused, contracts be damned. One was a banker who insisted on agreeing vehemently with everything I said. Charming, but not so much with his mouth full of food." She wrinkled her nose delicately. "Under the mistaken impression that he would benefit financially from marrying me, no doubt. Then a lawyer who has quietly married and buried no fewer than *three* wives already; rather suspicious, no? And, lastly, the merchant's son, who almost certainly proposed only to enrage his father. How well he succeeded! Men may irritate women entirely by accident, but I believe they infuriate one another wholly by design." Calixta laughed merrily, fanning herself with her gloves. "Truly," she said, with a hint of pride, "I am always far more trouble than I'm worth."

Sophia couldn't help it; she found herself smiling. "I wouldn't say that. We really appreciate your inviting us to sit with you." She knew it sounded very stiff and serious.

Calixta smiled at her. "Not at all, sweetheart. My pleasure."

A knock at the door interrupted their conversation, and Calixta called, "Come in."

A waiter from the dining car rolled a cart into the

compartment. "Three plates of eggs, ma'am."

"And they actually smell like eggs. Thank you," Calixta said, reaching into her purse for a coin.

After the waiter had left, they ate breakfast, and soon Sophia realized that the warm food and the dull hum of the train were making her drowsy. "Why don't you sleep in the bunk?" Calixta suggested.

"I should stay awake," Sophia murmured.

"Nonsense. You need to sleep. Theo and I will keep watch."

Sophia nodded, not bothering to ask what they would keep watch for. She climbed up to the bunk, put her pack next to her pillow, and put her head down, falling into dreamless sleep.

—12-hour 05—

THE TRIP FROM the town near the Georgia border to New Orleans took several hours, and Sophia slept most of the way. She woke gradually to Calixta's low laughter, the sound helping to dispel her lingering sense of worry. *Truly,* Sophia thought, *the Fates have been kind to place such a good-humored benefactress in our path.*

The pirate's mood was infectious. Usually it was Theo who charmed people, but in Calixta he had clearly met his match. He had dropped the cocky self-assurance and was readily answering her questions. "I grew up with a bunch of kids. No parents around. The bigger kids took care of me, and then I took care of the smaller ones. We all raised each other, you know?"

"How sweet," Calixta said. "Regular band of pirates."

Theo laughed. "Pretty much."

Sophia rolled over onto her back and quietly checked her watch. It was twelve and five—well past midday. If she had read the schedule correctly, they would be arriving in New Orleans soon.

"Was it an orphanage, then?" Calixta asked.

"That's right," Theo said. "Run by nuns. They pretty much left us on our own, though."

Sophia put her watch away, suddenly alert. *Theo's lying,* she thought, with a strange sense of tightening in her stomach.

"Were you very young when your parents left you there?"

"Not so much." Theo's voice was light; he didn't sound like he was lying. "They were traders. I was six when our house was crushed by a weirwind; killed them both. I made it, just barely."

"What a sad story," Calixta said, with feeling. "Is that how your hand was injured? When you were six?"

"Yup. The nuns took me in after that. All the kids called me 'Lucky Theo,' because our house was a pile of rubble, but I'd survived."

"No doubt it was the nuns who made you such a little angel," she said slyly. "Risking your life to help the girl you love. It's charming. I suppose you'd go anywhere for her."

Theo gave an awkward laugh. "Sophia and I just met."

"Oh, you can't deceive me, Lucky Theo," Calixta said sweetly. *I don't want to hear this,* Sophia thought, the tightness in her stomach giving way to a dull heaviness. "You may have just met," Calixta went on, "but here you are, rescuing her uncle."

"Nah," Theo scoffed. "I'm not rescuing anybody. I don't do that." The heaviness seemed to move through Sophia's whole body until she felt immobile. *Or maybe he's not lying. Maybe he was lying to me. He just says whatever people want to hear. And everyone believes him.* She felt flooded with shame and her face grew hot. *I told myself that I shouldn't trust him, but I did anyway. What an idiot I am.*

"Oh!" Calixta said with faint surprise. "Here I was, under the impression that you and Sophia were riding into the Baldlands to rescue her uncle. It certainly sounded that way."

Sophia knew that she should sit up and put a stop to the conversation, but she couldn't bring herself to move.

"You've got it all wrong," Theo went on. "Sophia's uncle ran off a few days ago with an actress from Nochtland. He even left her a note saying the beautiful actress had stolen his heart and he would never return. Obviously," he put in expertly, "Sophia mistook you for a beautiful actress."

Calixta chuckled, acknowledging the compliment. "Is that what happened? Well, that makes it all clear."

"If you ask me," Theo continued, unstoppable now that his story had taken shape, "it's a cruel thing to do. Abandon your niece, who has no one else in the world, for an actress?" Sophia's face was so warm that it seemed to burn, and the heavy weight in her stomach had begun to ache. "But that's the kind of man he is." He sighed. "Of course this whole journey to Nochtland is hopeless. Sophia's not going to find him, and if she does, he'll just tell her to go home. I'm not sticking around to see *that*," he grimly concluded. Sophia felt her eyes fill with tears—from the truth and the lie both—and she brushed them away angrily as the train began to slow.

"Well, better wake the poor girl. We're finally getting to New Orleans."

Theo's head appeared at the edge of the bunk. "I'm awake," Sophia said, her voice choked.

He smiled innocently. "Get up, then. We're here."

The train began pulling into the station and Calixta opened the door to the compartment to call for a porter. As Sophia climbed down, her pack on one shoulder, the man came into the compartment and began carrying out Calixta's trunks.

"I'm taking a coach to the dock," the pirate said, putting on her hat. "And, if you like, I'll take you to the depot where you can negotiate for horses. If that's really what you want to do."

Theo was about to follow her out, but Sophia grasped his arm. "I heard everything you said about Shadrack."

He grinned. "Pretty good, right?"

"Pretty good?" Sophia exclaimed, tears again filling her eyes despite her effort to control them. "How could you say that about Shadrack? *An actress?"* To her dismay, Theo laughed. "It's not funny!"

"Come on, lighten up. You're taking this way too seriously."

Sophia felt her cheeks once again turning bright red. "I don't see anything wrong with being serious. This *is* serious! I heard what you said about not sticking around. I never asked you to stick around. You can leave whenever you want. I'll go by myself."

"Hey," Theo said, taking her arm. "Calm down—it was just a story I told her. You said not to tell her about Shadrack. I thought it was a pretty good way to distract her."

"Were you lying? About all of it?"

"Of course I was lying—that's what you said to do."

"I didn't tell you to *lie*. I just said not to tell her anything. How am I supposed to know when you're telling the truth?"

"Sophia, what I told her didn't mean anything. Trust me."

She gave a short laugh and looked away. "Right. *Trust you*." She realized that new passengers were boarding. "We have to go," she said tersely, turning on her heel to leave. Theo shook his head, then followed her.

Sophia stalked off the train and saw Calixta at the far end of the platform, directing the porters as they tied her trunks to the top of a coach. As Sophia started to walk toward her, she heard a sudden shout. She wheeled around and saw them instantly: three—no, four—men with identically scarred faces running along the platform. For a moment she stood frozen. Then she gripped her pack and burst into a run, her feet pounding against the wooden floorboards.

Theo soon reached and then passed her. It took Calixta, whose trunks were now securely tied to the roof of the coach, only a moment to grasp the situation. With one easy motion she threw open the door and drew her revolver. "Get in!" she shouted. Theo dove in first and Sophia scrambled after him. Calixta put her foot on the step of the open coach and grabbed the luggage rack with her free hand. "*Drive!*" she cried.

The horses sprang into motion and they jerked forward as Calixta leaned gracefully out and fired a single shot at the platform. Sophia watched as the men changed direction and scrambled toward the line of coaches; the horses were rearing in confusion, panicked by the pistol shot. Calixta ducked into the coach and closed the door. "Help me with my hat again, darling, would you?" she asked.

Sophia put her pack aside and tried, with trembling fingers, to pull the pins from Calixta's hat while the coach jolted madly along the road. "They're out," she finally said, tucking them into the hat ribbon.

Calixta shook out her hair and leaned through the window. "Driver," she called. "Triple the fare if you get us safely to the end of the dock. The ship with the red and white sails." She pulled her head back in. "They'll have gotten into a coach by now."

The streets of New Orleans rushed past. The driver had taken them along the edge of the city, but there was still a fair amount of traffic, and the shouts of people dodging the racing coach could be heard clearly. Sophia glimpsed a fruit stand toppling unceremoniously to the ground as the horses sped by, and a number of yapping dogs set upon them in pursuit.

"Only another minute," Calixta said, peeking out through the window. "When we get there, leave the coach at once and find the ship with red and white sails." They nodded. "And watch my hat," she told Sophia. "Don't look so grim, sweetheart." She smiled. "I'm an excellent shot."

The coach jolted and then jumped as it suddenly reached the dock. "Get out of the way," the driver shouted. The horses swerved around an upturned cart and a pile of crates collapsed behind it.

Suddenly a loud crack exploded at the rear of the coach, just between Sophia's head and Calixta's shoulder. "That's them,"

Calixta said. "Keep your heads down." She leaned out the window and fired two careful shots. Then they came to a clattering halt. Calixta threw the door open. "Come on then," she called. "The red and white sails. Tell Burr to come himself, because I'm certainly not leaving my trunks behind." She stood with her feet planted firmly apart and her eye on their pursuers.

Sophia stumbled out carrying Calixta's hat and looked anxiously for the sails. Where were they? Where was Theo, for that matter? He had vanished. There were crates everywhere, sailors, a horse with a gleaming black saddle pulling agitatedly on his reins, and two barking dogs with long red tongues. Was Theo hiding somewhere? Sophia crouched behind a pile of wooden crates and glanced down: sawdust and half of a dead fish. For some reason, the air smelled of rum: as if it had *rained* rum. She looked up; where was the ship with red and white sails? The sails were *all* red and white—and blue, and green, and yellow.

Then she saw a number of deckhands running toward Calixta; they had to be coming from her ship. A shot and then another rang out behind her, and she peeked out from behind the crates to see the pirate standing calmly, defending the coach with precise shots while the deckhands slid the trunks off the roof. Sophia stood and prepared to run after them.

But as she turned, she saw Theo some distance away, gesturing urgently to her with one hand; he held a pistol in the other and was walking backward, firing steadily, while a heavyset man beside him carried one of the trunks. *Theo could shoot?*

Then, suddenly, Calixta was no longer by the coach. In fact,

Sophia realized with horror, the dock was nearly deserted. And there the pirate stood, on the deck of a ship with red and white sails. The ship had been anchored only a stone's throw away, its sails tightly furled. Now they were catching the wind, fluttering like ribbons. Theo stood beside Calixta on the deck, pointing. He was pointing at Sophia, who was separated from the ship by a line of Sandmen.

I lost track of time! Sophia realized, aghast. Worse still, she noticed with agitation, she didn't have her pack. She still held Calixta's hat, but the precious pack was nowhere to be seen. *I must have left it in the carriage,* she thought frantically. The Sandmen fired toward the ship; they had not yet seen her. With the hat balanced on her head, Sophia began crawling on hands and knees back toward the coach. Theo, Calixta, and two other pirates were still exchanging volleys with the Sandmen, one of whom was readying his grappling hook.

To Sophia's relief and surprise, she saw one of the pirates wearing her pack securely on his shoulders. *Calixta must have found it. Now if I can only get to the ship.* She could see the gangway. Five quick dashes would take her to it.

She stood up to run, burst forward, and collided with a tall, slim man wearing a hat even wider than Calixta's. He held a revolver in one hand and a long sword in the other. With the tip of the revolver he pushed his hat back, revealing a handsome, bearded face and a wide grin. He looked Sophia over appraisingly. "When my sister said to keep her hat safe," he said, "you really took her at her word."

"I—I'm sorry," Sophia stammered.

"Wisest thing you could have done," he said cheerfully. He tucked the sword into its sheath, took Sophia's hand, and led her, running, to the gangway of the ship with red and white sails. As they ran, the Sandmen sighted them and immediately changed course. Sophia heard footsteps pounding on the wooden dock, then a spattering of sharp cracks as something splintered. There was silence and then shouts from all sides. A grappling hook bit into the wooden board just beside her foot. Sophia found herself stumbling across the gangplank and onto the deck.

She turned, breathlessly, as the ship pulled away. The dock was abandoned apart from four strange figures: the Sandmen, mired in a thick, black syrup that had trapped them like flies in honey. Sophia squinted, not comprehending. Then a wave of violent dizziness washed over her. She reached for the deck rail and found it had vanished. She sank to her knees. Then her cheek lay against the polished wooden deck, and the whole world had tipped on its side.

16
Seasick

1891, June 24: 16-Hour 46

If the lands of the New World remain largely unexplored, the seas remain even more so. Philosophers of New Occident have considered the question: if a patch of ocean belonged to the thirtieth century, would we ever know it while sailing through it? Pragmatically speaking, there is no proven method to determine the various ages of the oceans.

—*From Shadrack Elli's* History of the New World

After the initial dizziness that pitched her to the deck passed, Sophia propped herself up and watched with queasy awe as the ship swung into motion: Calixta's men trimmed the sails, shouting to one another across the deck until all the sails were taut with wind. The sun faded behind a passing cloud, and the smell of the ocean suddenly engulfed her. Sophia took a deep breath. When she could speak, she tried to apologize for having risked their departure by losing track of time, but no one seemed to think she had done anything wrong. "You'll want to thank this lad here for spotting you," Burr had said, throwing his arm around Theo with a grin, "as I've thanked him for being such a fine shot. Molasses, eh? You must have hit four barrels. Those are some sticky scoundrels you left behind on the dock. Natural-born pirate, you are." Theo beamed, seeming almost bashful in the face of Burr's compliments.

Furthermore, any inconvenience Sophia might have caused apparently paled alongside the tragedy suffered by one of Calixta's trunks, which arrived on deck with two bullet holes. She vented her fury on the pirate who had carried it and on her brother for failing to carry it himself. Burr strode across the deck as they left the harbor, calling out casual instructions and shaking off the abuse that Calixta hurled at him.

"Would it make you feel better to put a few bullet holes in Peaches?" Burr asked. "Do, by all means." He cheerfully gestured toward the unfortunate Peaches, an older man who was tugging on his frilled cuffs with a woeful expression.

"I *should*," Calixta roared. "Do you know how difficult it is to find petticoats of the right length?"

Peaches shook his head disconsolately. "I'm sorry, Captain Morris."

"Rather than telling us all about your petticoats, dearest," Burr said, "perhaps you should check the damage."

Calixta glared for a moment longer and then opened the trunk. She inspected the clothing in silence with Peaches standing warily in attendance, and finally she looked up with a mollified expression. "Well, it seems my powder-box stopped the bullets. Peaches," she said icily, "you owe me a new box of face powder."

"Certainly, Captain; the moment we arrive in port," he replied, greatly relieved. Calixta went off to her cabin after her trunks. As the pirates moved about with easy laughter and efficiency, Sophia held her head and tried to control the waves of nausea that swept over her.

The pirates were not in the least as she had imagined them. They seemed more like wealthy vacationers, with their extravagant clothing and their nonchalant air. All of them spoke with the precise, almost quaint locution of the Indies. Even the lowliest deckhand seemed to Sophia more like a fancy footman than a sea-toughened bandit.

Theo was already a favorite after his display of marksmanship, and he had been pulled away into conversation with the deckhands at once. "Hey, you all right?" he asked now. Sophia, knowing it was petty but too angry to care, took refuge in her seasickness and would not speak to him. Finally he shrugged and drifted off.

She was rather more inclined to count on the pirates than Theo, since Calixta had saved her pack and Burr had saved *her*; though it would have been simple enough to leave her stranded on the dock. *I'll have to ask the pirates for help getting to Nochtland,* Sophia decided, trying to quell the anxiety that only worsened her dizziness. She could only hope that in Nochtland she would find Veressa and that then, somehow, they would rescue Shadrack before something terrible happened to him.

Even after hours of sailing, the violent seasickness would not recede. She resigned herself to sitting inertly, watching the horizon and battling nausea. As evening fell, they reached a spot of calm weather and the air grew pleasantly cool. Calixta called to her from across the deck. "Sweetheart, dinner in my cabin."

"I'm going to stay here," Sophia replied. "I feel worse inside. I'm not hungry anyway."

"Poor thing. All right, feel better."

Calixta withdrew, and Sophia made an effort to rise so that she could get a better look at the sunset. Overhead, the stars were beginning to appear and the sky curved in one continuous descent from purple to blue to pink. Sophia stared hard at the pink edge of the sky and momentarily felt her nausea subside. A moment later she heard footsteps and turned to see someone walking across the deck toward her.

"They sent me up to keep you company, dear." Sophia looked curiously at the old woman who stood beside her. She was no taller than Sophia herself and almost as thin. Though she held herself straight and spoke in a clear voice, she looked older than anyone Sophia had ever seen. Her white hair was braided and pinned up on her head in a long coil, and she wore a neatly pressed lilac dress with innumerable pleats in the skirt and sleeves. "I'm Grandmother Pearl," she said, laying her wrinkled hand on Sophia's. "Even though I'm nobody's grandmother." She smiled, holding Sophia's hand in both her own. "And you, they tell me, are seasick, poor child."

"Yes," Sophia said. She realized suddenly, from the gentle pressure of Grandmother Pearl's fingers and the way she held her head, that the old woman was blind. "It won't go away."

"Ah," Grandmother Pearl said, smiling. Her small, white teeth shone—not unlike pearls themselves. "I know why. I can feel it here in your palm."

Sophia blinked. "You can?"

"Of course, love. It's plain to anyone who takes your hand. You're not bound to time. Of course, the way you've heard it explained probably makes it sound rather worse. No internal clock, is that what they say? No sense of time?"

Sophia felt herself blushing in the growing darkness. "Yes. It's true that I have—I always lose track of time. It's not something I'm proud of," she mumbled.

"It's nothing to be ashamed of, love," Grandmother Pearl said, still smiling. "It's a rare gift to be unbound from time. Think of it—you are free to drift, free to float, like a ship with no anchor weighing it down."

Sophia glanced down at the wrinkled hands around her own. "But sometimes you want an anchor."

The old woman led her over to the chairs on the deck. "And you have one. Don't you carry a watch around with you? Don't people always remind you of the hour? Aren't you surrounded by clocks, ticking away, telling you the time? Aren't we all?"

"I guess that is true."

"So what do you need an internal clock for? Trust me, love. You're better off. In my ninety-three years I've met only three others not bound to time, and they were all exceptional people."

Sophia absorbed this doubtfully. "But why does that make me seasick?" she asked as they sat.

"Why, because we're sailing through a soup of all the different Ages. When the Ages came apart, the waters were in one place. Now different Ages mix in the sea, so that every cup contains more than a dozen."

None of Shadrack's explorer friends had ever mentioned this. Sophia held her face up to the briny air, as if testing the truth of it. "Is that possible?"

"I've lived on ships for most of my life, and I've seen mysteries that can only be explained in that way."

"Like what kind of mysteries?"

"Strange cities built on the water's surface that appear one moment and disappear the next. Selkies and mermen building pockets of sea to contain a single Age. Mostly, I've seen peculiar things underwater—fragments, you might say—that seem like broken pieces of many Ages, lost in the currents."

"So you once had your sight?" Sophia asked, fascinated.

"Yes, I did—although, if you ask me, my sight was somewhat like that anchor we were talking about. Just as you are better off without your sense of time, I am better off without my sense of sight. I know it sounds strange to say it, but it was only when I lost my sight that I began understanding the world around me."

"What do you mean?"

"Well, take your palm, for instance. In my youth I might have taken your hand in just the same way, but I would have been looking at your eyes and your smile to get a good sense of who you were, and I wouldn't even have paid attention to your hand. After I lost my sight, I noticed things I would never have noticed before, distracted as I was by seeing."

"I think I understand what you mean," Sophia said. She was suddenly conscious of how much she was relying on Grandmother Pearl's appearance in order to get a sense of who she was: her hair, her neat dress, the deep wrinkles around her eyes. "So I have to think about what I notice, since I don't notice time."

"That's right, love," her companion said approvingly. "What else is there that no one else is seeing because they're looking at the time? You're not distracted by time, so you're bound to notice something everyone else doesn't." She paused, letting Sophia consider this. "It may take you a while to discover it, mind!" she added, with a laugh.

Sophia smiled. "You're right." She looked at Grandmother Pearl's wrinkled hands. "If you're ninety-three, that means you lived through the Great Disruption."

"I did, although I don't remember it. I was only a baby then. Though I learned of it from my mother. In the United Indies, where everyone's livelihood depended on constant travel to either side of the Atlantic, the shock was extreme. The old European ports vanished. The colonies in the Americas transformed. And the Baldlands plunged into warfare and chaos and confusion. Imagine hundreds of thousands of people all waking to find the world around them scrambled—all of them solitary exiles from worlds that no longer existed. It seemed the entire continent had gone mad. My mother always spoke of it as a dream—a deep, long dream that left the world changed forever. Then again, my mother was a dream-reader, and she knew better than most that the boundary between waking and dreaming is an uncertain one."

"Was your mother a"—Sophia hesitated—"pirate, as well?"

"Ah, she was, but piracy was a different thing in those days. Dangerous, underpaid work. Not like now. My mother was raised on ships and never owned a pair of shoes in her life, poor thing. She made her fortune divining the weather and reading dreams. Her life was a hard one. But now—this is the great age of piracy."

Sophia thought, hearing Shadrack's voice, that in truth it was the great age of exploration. But she didn't contradict her. "Captain Morris's ship is certainly well-off," she said mildly.

"She's a good captain. We're all well treated and we have regular holidays. Burr and Calixta make a good profit—no doubt there—but they're not greedy; they share it with the rest of us. We none of us have reason to complain. Still, if you saw other ships, you'd see that this one is modest in comparison." Grandmother Pearl shook her head. "More wealth on one of those than on some of the smaller islands, I swear. The larger islands, of course, are a different story. Have you been to Havana, dear? It's awash in coins of every kind."

"I've never been to the United Indies," Sophia admitted. "I've never been to the Baldlands, either. In fact, before this trip I'd never been south of New York."

Grandmother Pearl laughed and patted her hand. "Well, all the more to look forward to. The Baldlands will take your breath away; they always do, the first time."

"That's what everyone says."

"Remember what I told you about a cup of water from the seas? Well, the Baldlands are just like that—only on land. All the different Ages, brought together in a moment."

"I can't imagine it," Sophia said, frowning slightly.

"Well, you don't see it that way, not all at once," the old

woman explained. "Perhaps just after the Great Disruption you could see the lines of where Ages collided; one street in one century, the next street in another. But now, after more than ninety years, the Ages have settled. In the Triple Eras, for example, the three eras have melded into one. You can't tell that one building is from the past and another is from the future, or that someone is wearing a mixture of clothing from three different eras, or that an animal from the ancient Age sits beside an animal from a later one. Now it seems just what it is—a single, whole Age derived from three."

Sophia leaned forward eagerly. "Tell me about the animals. I've heard it's the creatures that are the strangest."

"There are wondrous animals, it's true," Grandmother Pearl agreed "But in the Baldlands you have to be careful how you use those words—animal or creature.'"

"Oh! Why?"

"Because of the Mark of the Vine and the Mark of Iron." She paused, hearing Sophia's silence. "Have you heard of them?"

"I've read about them." Sophia recalled the passing mention in Shadrack's atlas. "But I didn't really understand them. What are they?"

Grandmother Pearl settled back in her chair. "Well, I'm not surprised. People don't like to speak of it. Particularly people from the Baldlands. But you won't understand the place unless you understand the Marks. They've always been there, at least since the Great Disruption, but the cruel way of seeing them has come about over time. Would you like to hear the story of how it all started?"

"Of course."

"It was put to verse by the poet Van Mooring, a man from Nochtland who became a sailor. Every mariner knows it." She began a slow, mournful song in a voice that spun out over the deck like a fragile thread.

"At Nochtland's gates of iron strong
The guard kept watch to block the throng
Of those who would have broken through
To see the palace so few knew.

A glimpse of peaks and shining glass
Amidst the gardens thick and vast
Was all the towering gates allowed
To passersby and city crowds

Until the stranger did appear
And with his hooded cloak drew near
Demanding to be ushered in
And claiming kinship with the king.

The guard refused; the stranger fought.
His hood fell back and as they sought
To pin him his arms and bind him tight
The stranger hurtled into flight.

His cloak fell free; his wings spread wide
And showed the stranger had not lied.

The emerald leaves with which he flew
Were Mark of Vine and proved him true.

The guard leaped up with mighty bounds
And tore the stranger to the ground.
He fell to earth with broken wings
And broken pride unknown to kings.

The Iron Mark had brought him low.
The cruelty of the Mark's harsh blows
Was paid by all the guard in kind:
The cost of being metalmind."

Her voice trailed off, yet the vivid images stayed in Sophia's mind. "What does that mean—'The cost of being metalmind?'"

Grandmother Pearl inclined her head. "Why don't you tell her, dear, about the Mark of Iron?"

Sophia looked past the old woman's chair and saw with surprise that Theo was standing on the deck in the near darkness, out of sight, but apparently not out of earshot. She realized she had briefly forgotten all about both her nausea and her anger. After a moment's hesitation, he moved closer and sat down. "The Mark of Iron," he said quietly, "may be any bone made of metal. Most often it is a person's teeth. They are sharp and pointed, and they tear."

Sophia recoiled. "They tore the man's wings with their *teeth*?"

"They were defending the gate. They were only doing what was expected of them."

Grandmother Pearl nodded. "It's true that the guards argued in their defense that they had been protecting the gate. And there was, they claimed, no way for them to know that the stranger was in fact a nephew to the king, returning to Nochtland after years on the northern frontier. The king, however, declared that the Mark of the Vine should have been proof enough."

"What happened to the king's nephew?" Sophia asked.

"His wings were shredded by the guards but over time they re-grew, like new leaves."

"But the guards were put to death," Theo added.

Grandmother Pearl turned toward him. "The guards were sentenced to death, yes, and the long enmity between the two Marks began to deepen. It had been a mere dislike before, a suspicion, but with the execution of the palace guard the gulf between them grew. The Mark of the Vine is held to be a sign of privilege and aristocracy. Among the royals, the mark often emerges as wings. For others, it might be a patch of skin, a lock of hair, a pair of fingers. The palest weed, if you're lucky enough to be born with it, is enough to make the humblest child a blessed one. Those who have the Mark are favored in the Baldlands, and those who don't have it—ordinary people like you and me—attempt to emulate it. The Mark of Iron is held to be a sign of barbarism and disgrace. Today, no one with the Mark of Iron would dare set foot in Nochtland. They've all been driven out. The royal family have come to see conspiracy in the smallest piece of metal. It has gone from being disdained to being criminal."

"Not farther north," Theo put in.

"Very true," Grandmother Pearl agreed. "The raiders in the north wear their iron teeth with pride, and they take no shame in baring them to all the world. You will even see them in Veracruz, and on the roads around the city. Still, they all avoid Nochtland. Fair to say?"

Theo gazed out toward the water. "For sure. People with the Mark of Iron have a way of ending up on the wrong side of the law, even if they've done nothing wrong."

"And some will class those with the Mark of Iron as wild men—or worse. It's not unusual to hear them called 'creatures' or 'animals' by those who are especially narrow-minded, which is why I warn you."

"But are those with the Mark of Iron really so terrible?" Sophia asked.

"Of course not," Theo scoffed. "The raiders I know are no worse than anyone else. They're just people—some good and some bad."

"So you see," Grandmother Pearl said, "it's a cruel way of thinking, that has divided people in the Baldlands over many decades."

Sophia realized that the sun had set completely. The sky was dark and filled with stars, and a slender moon hung on the horizon. "So that's what they mean when they talk about 'creatures.'"

"Well," the old woman said, "there are also what you and I would call creatures—animals from other Ages and strange beings you don't see on land or sea."

"Like the Lachrima," Theo said. Sophia rolled her eyes in the darkness.

Grandmother Pearl was silent for a moment. "Yes, like the Lachrima." She lowered her voice. "I don't hold with superstition, but there are some on board who wouldn't like to hear you say that word. It's thought that naming them brings them closer."

"Who would have thought? Pirates *are* afraid of something, after all," Theo said, grinning, the somber air that had previously taken hold of him apparently banished.

"Oh, yes! We like gunfire well enough, but apparitions and Lachrima are another matter."

"Have you ever heard one?" Theo wondered avidly.

"I have," she said somberly. "The first time was long ago, in the Baldlands, but only a few years back, when we were in Havana, I heard one haunting a ship called the *Rosaline*."

"They're not just in the Baldlands, then?" Sophia asked.

"They're most often found there, but you might hear one almost anywhere. This one had been aboard the *Rosaline* for weeks. The poor sailors were at their wits' ends. When they came ashore in Havana, they abandoned ship, and the captain couldn't convince a single soul to return. In the end, either the captain or someone else cut the ship loose, letting it drift empty with nothing but the Lachrima. If it hasn't sunk, it's out there now, sailing around the world with its lone passenger. Eventually it will no doubt fall to pieces—an empty vessel on an empty sea. The Lachrima will disappear and fade with time."

"Oh, they *disappear,*" Sophia said with sudden comprehension. She thought back to Mrs. Clay's story and the Lachrima's abrupt vanishing at the border. "How? Why?"

"Hard to say. It's for this reason that they appear to some as monsters, to others as phantoms, and to still others as only a distant sound. In Xela they appear most in the last form; people refer to the crying as *el llanto del espanto,* 'the spirit's lament.' No one knows how they disappear. They are not understood well at all, poor creatures. But my sense is that they comprehend their fate. They know that they are disappearing. And they are terrified of it. Wouldn't you be?" Grandmother Pearl pushed herself to her feet. "Well, with that I'll leave you. Have I distracted you from your seasickness?"

"Yes, thank you." Sophia said earnestly. "I forgot all about it."

"Good. Tomorrow we'll talk of happier things, no?" She rested one hand on Sophia's forehead and then let her hand float until it found Theo's forehead. "Good night, children."

"Good night, Grandmother Pearl," he said, taking her hand in his and kissing it gently.

"Ah!" she said, gripping his hand between both her own. She felt his scars almost tenderly. "That's why you gave me your left hand before, dear boy." She smiled down at him. "There's no shame in this hand, Theo. Only strength."

He gave a forced laugh, but didn't reply.

"Only strength," she repeated, patting his hand. "Good night. Sleep well."

17
A SWAN IN THE GULF

1891, June 25: 17-Hour 41

After 1850, with the expansion of the rum and sugar trade between the United Indies and New Occident, piracy in the Caribbean grew increasingly lucrative. Plantations in the Indies were faced with the prospect of either continual theft along the trade route or costly collaboration. Most opted for the latter, and as the years progressed pirates saw many of their ships transform into legitimate businesses charged with managing the trade route. There resulted a widening gulf between thieving pirates and their more prosperous cousins in the plantations' employ.

—*From Shadrack Elli's* History of the New World

CALIXTA AND BURTON Morris came from a long line of pirates. Their parents and grandparents had sailed the dangerous waters of the Caribbean when every ship, regardless of its sail, was a potential enemy. No one who met Calixta and Burr, as he was known to all, suspected at first from their easy manner the tragedy that lay in their past. In fact, it was the tragedy itself that allowed them to enjoy life so fully; they knew it could be taken away in an instant.

They had been twins, two children among seven. Their

mother had been the daughter of a pirate captain. Their father was the first mate of the infamous *Typhoon*. For years they sailed together, along with their growing family, until the captain of the *Typhoon*, in his zeal to maintain his ship's reputation, attacked an ambitious rival. The battle was long and bitter, and when it ended the ships were nothing more than burnt shells.

Calixta and Burr, less than a year old at the time, lay together in their baby basket and drifted on the charred remains all the way to shore. Grandmother Pearl was one of the *Typhoon*'s few survivors, and though the fires caused her to lose her sight, she stayed with the basket and protected the infants with all her remaining strength.

It was Grandmother Pearl who raised them, and it was she who chose the *Swan*, the ship sailed by kindly old Captain Aceituna. Though Aceituna called himself a pirate, he had grown cautious in old age, and he sailed only the safer routes. He dedicated himself to shipping the rubber tapped in the southern Baldlands to the United Indies and New Occident, where the material was used to make Goodyears, boots, and other valuable commodities. The "weeping wood" grown on the outskirts of the Triple Eras had made many people, including Aceituna, quite rich.

Of course the tragedy of their family's death hung over Calixta and Burr, but Grandmother Pearl and the others on the *Swan* made life for the two children as happy as they could. When Aceituna retired, leaving the ship in their care, Calixta and Burr vowed that the *Swan* would never become like the *Typhoon*. They did not aim for greatness; they aimed for prosperity. The *Swan* never attacked without provocation. The Morrises laughed good-naturedly when pirates from other ships mocked them as the "polite pirates." "Better polite than dead," Burr always replied. "Besides," he would sometimes add, "why look for a fight when the best fights always come to me?" Calixta kept track of the routes sailed by other pirates and mapped the *Swan*'s path to prevent unexpected confrontations.

On her second night aboard, Sophia had occasion to study the ship's nautical charts, and it gave her the opportunity she'd been waiting for. She had already decided to ask Burr and Calixta for help in reaching Nochtland. She had no choice, but even if she had been able to get there without them, she would have asked. The way that Burr had helped her on the dock in New Orleans and the fact that Calixta had saved her pack when she easily could have either left it or taken it for herself had paved the way. Grandmother Pearl's kindness convinced her further. The pirates clearly had nothing to do with the Sandmen and Montaigne, and it could only help, she decided, to tell them what had happened to Shadrack.

She sat on the deck surrounded by lanterns, poring over the charts and weather maps that Burr had brought from his cabin. He and Calixta were a few paces away, attempting to teach Theo the rudiments of sword-fighting. Grandmother Pearl sat listening to them with a smile.

"Molasses, don't stand there facing me like you're asking to be skewered," Burr counseled. "Turn your body sideways."

"It's heavy," Theo protested, pacing backward with the sword in both his hands. "I'd rather just use a revolver."

"And lazy to top it off," Burr said, advancing toward him and rolling his eyes at Calixta. "Calixta's half your size and she wields that sword you're holding like one of her hat pins."

"Half his size?" she exclaimed, whirling on her brother and disarming him with the wooden pole she held. "What do I look like to you, a fat fish?"

"Fish aren't nearly as vain as you are, dearest," Burr replied, dodging the pole and rolling across the deck to retrieve his sword. "And they don't look as charming in ruffled petticoats," he conceded, turning back to Theo. "Use your other hand," he said, "the one you apparently like to use as a dartboard."

Theo grimaced and passed the sword to his scarred hand. "I'm just saying, a revolver's a lot easier."

Burr quickly loosened a length of rope near him and Theo looked up, too late, and was trapped beneath a sprawling fishing net. "Agh!" he shouted, dropping the sword with a clatter and struggling against the knotted ropes.

"Pistol wouldn't do much for you now, would it, Molly?"

"We just bought that net last month," Calixta complained.

"He's not going to cut through it. Look at him." Burr chuckled as Theo fought to disentangle himself. "What were you saying about fat fish?"

Sophia, who had been entirely absorbed with the charts she was studying, suddenly let out a gasp. "Oh!" she exclaimed, holding up a paper map. "This is Shadrack's!"

"Who, dear?" Grandmother Pearl asked.

Sophia collected herself. "My uncle, Shadrack Elli. He made this map."

"Did he, now?" Burr said with interest. He and Calixta peered over her shoulder. "Ah, yes! Quite a map, that one. This island," he said, pointing, "is so remote that most people have never even heard of it. Only pirates ever go there. And yet this map is incredibly exact. Every stream, every rock—it's remarkable."

"Yes. It's a lovely map," Sophia agreed, gazing down at the fine lines drawn in her uncle's familiar hand.

"How does he do it? He's never been there, I'm sure."

"I don't really know," she admitted. Shadrack was an exceptional cartologer, of course, but even with all that she knew of his methods, there were many that still eluded her. "He probably talked to an explorer. That's how he makes a lot of his maps."

"But with this degree of precision?"

"He's good at that. If you describe something to him, he can make a perfect map of it."

Calixta shook her head. "But people never *know* entirely what they see. They always forget things or miss them. Are all his maps like this?"

"Well," Sophia replied, hesitating, "he really has all kinds of different maps." She paused a moment longer and then slowly reached into her pack. "In fact, this map he left me is very different. I still haven't been able to make sense of it." Sophia drew out the glass map, which she had left awake. Its etched lines shone faintly. "You see, Shadrack didn't run off with an actress. He would never do something like that," she said, giving Theo a scathing look just as he emerged from beneath the fishing net. "He was kidnapped. He left a note telling me to find a friend of his in Nochtland, and he left me this. The men in

New Orleans—the Sandmen. This is what they were after."

Burr gave her a keen look while Calixta sat down beside her.

"It's a glass map," Sophia said. "Have you ever seen one?"

Calixta and Burr shook their heads. "They won't have heard of it," Theo said. "They're common in the Baldlands, but nowhere else."

Burr raised his eyebrows. "Can we take a look?" She nodded, and the two joined her.

"Describe it for me, will you?" Grandmother Pearl whispered.

"It's a sheet of glass," Sophia said, "that in the moonlight becomes covered with writing. Most of it in other languages."

"Here it says in English *You will see it through me,*" Burr said.

"But that's just the writing," Sophia said.

"What do you mean, 'just the writing'?" he asked, without taking his eyes off the glass.

"It's a memory map." Now that she was confronted with it again, she felt reluctant to experience the memories she knew it contained. "Theo and I have read it before. I think it's the same wherever you place your finger."

"And then what happens?" Calixta asked.

"You see the memories that are in the map."

For a moment the pirates stared at Sophia in disbelief, and then Calixta leaned forward. "Me first." She eagerly placed her fingertip on the glass, and immediately her expression changed. She closed her eyes, her face still and thoughtful. When she took her finger away, she shuddered.

"Heavens, Calixta. What is it?" asked Burr.

"You try it," she said shortly.

He touched the glass surface, his expression grave as the memories flooded his mind. "I've never seen anything like it," he said slowly, when they had run their course. "What, exactly, is this map *of*?"

"We don't know," Sophia said. "My uncle left it for me. I'd never seen it before. And it's strange that it's all writing. I have no idea when or where it's from."

"I'd like to try it, dears," Grandmother Pearl said, reaching forward. "If one of you will just guide my hand."

Sophia did so, and as soon as she touched the glass, the old woman gasped. Sophia drew her hand away. "No—I want to see the whole thing," she said, and Sophia placed her finger once again on the smooth surface.

"Did your uncle ever mention such an event in another context?" Burr inquired.

Sophia shook her head. "Not that I recall."

Grandmother Pearl finished reading; her face was withdrawn, her brow furrowed.

"The thing is," Sophia said with some consternation, "I don't know that much about memory maps. I was only starting to learn about them. Shadrack said that they come from people's memories of the past. That's really all I know."

"Are you very sure, love?" asked Grandmother Pearl.

"What do you mean?" Sophia asked.

"I wonder," the old woman said. "It reminds me of something. The part in the memory when something heavy is rolled off the edge, and then everything is destroyed. It sounds so much like an old legend my mother used to tell me. Could the map be a story? Could it be something made up?"

Surprised, Sophia returned to the glass map. "I don't know. Shadrack says a map can only contain what its author knows. I suppose that could be a story, as long as it's true. It bears the mapmaker's insignia, which means whoever wrote it swore to make an accurate account. What's the legend?"

Grandmother Pearl leaned back in her chair. "It's a story I never told you, Calixta and Burton, because it's too sad and terrible. In truth, it was very foolish of my mother to tell it to me."

Burr smiled at her. "Well, now we're all grown up, Granny. Do your worst."

Her face lit up with tenderness. "You foolish boy. This story strikes terror into any heart, young or old. It's a story about the end of the world. I believe my mother told it to me because she was haunted by it herself. She called it 'the story of the boy from the buried city.'"

—18-Hour 20: Grandmother Pearl's Story—

"THE STORY GOES like this.

"In a city far away, in a time yet to come, there's a boy—an orphan. The boy is an outcast; no one wants him because of a terrible burn on one side of his face. He doesn't know where the burn came from; he only knows that it has left him marked forever, and that no one loves him because of it. He wanders the streets alone, and he is cast out of every doorway. Then, in great sadness and despair, he climbs all the way to the high temple, where, at the top of five hundred steps, the stone god that protects the city sits on a ledge. He asks the temple seer how he has come to be what he is and how he can change it. The seer stares for a long time at the bones that fall in a pattern before her, and finally she tells him this: 'You are not from here,' she says. 'You are from an underground city. That is your true home. That is why no one here loves you and you do not belong.' The boy asks her how he can get to the underground city, but the seer does not know. She too recoils from his burnt face. 'All I know is that the stone god protecting us will fall before you find it.'

"The boy is haunted by this knowledge, and he searches through the entire city for some entrance, some doorway, some tunnel to the city underground. He never finds it. Finally, in desperation, he devises a plan. He will make the stone god fall. He will destroy the city and find the passage underground in the ruins. He has been too unloved, after all. Perhaps if there were one person in the city he could think of kindly, he would be unable to do it. But there is no one he can think of in that way. He runs all the way up the five hundred steps and from there to the ledge where the stone god sits. The boy is small, but the stone gives way easily and falls. The entire temple begins to crumble around him, and as he races down the five hundred steps, the fires begin.

"The city burns for a whole week, until nothing but ash remains, and the boy picks through the rubble, searching for the entrance to the underground city. What he finds surprises him. There are entrances to the underground city everywhere—in almost every building and on every street. But before the fire they were carefully boarded up; they were sealed and covered and hidden; it seems when the city was created, everyone was intent on keeping whatever lay underground out.

"The boy follows one of the passages deep into the ground. He travels for hours. And at the end he finds the city that the seer promised him. It is a beautiful city, built underground from shimmering stone. It has vast pools of water and wide walkways. Precious metals line the roads and jewels wink at him from the doorways. There is only one difficulty. The city is empty. As the boy walks through it, he hears his own footfalls echoing through the vast, deserted caverns. He spends many days exploring the empty city, and on the fifth day he discovers, to his surprise, another person. At the very center of the underground city he finds an old—very old—man, who says he is a seer. The boy sits down wearily before him. 'I have had enough of seers,' he says. 'So I won't ask you my destiny. But tell me. Why is this city empty? Where have all the people gone, and why are you still here?'

"The old man gazes at the boy steadily, and though it pains him to answer, he speaks. 'This city was abandoned long ago. A seer told the city elders: "A boy from this underground city will destroy your entire city, and every one of you who remains in it will perish." Fearing the seer's words, the elders abandoned the city, and they moved to the surface, where they hoped to escape the prophecy. My mother was the seer, and she was the only one who remained. She was of the belief that words, once they are spoken, have a way of coming true. My mother has long since passed away, and now it is only I who live here.' The boy listens to the words of the seer, and he realizes that in his attempt to find his home he has destroyed it. He weeps until he can hardly see, and his tears make a pool, not unlike the underground pools all around him. When he stops weeping, he opens his eyes and sees his reflection in the pool made by his tears. And then, as he watches, the scars on his face begin to vanish. They fade away, and a whole, beautiful face stares back at him. Those who had known him certainly would have loved him. But no one else survives. He remains underground with the seer, living in the buried city for the rest of his days. And that is how the legend says the world ends."

They were all silent. "Your mother told you *that* as a bedtime story?" exclaimed Calixta.

Grandmother Pearl sighed. "She lived so much in the dream world, and she had a hard life. She was never very sharp on where ordinary life ended and tragedy began."

"I should say," Burr commented.

"But it's not *true*, is it?" Sophia asked anxiously. "It hasn't really happened?"

"Well that's the strange thing about time in our day and age," Grandmother Pearl said. "You never know what happened before and what happened after. I really don't know. My mother always told it as a legend."

"I don't understand why that story would be on this map, or why the map would be so important."

Grandmother Pearl nodded. "I might be wrong, after all. It just sounded similar. These memories could take place almost anywhere. There is no shortage of such destruction."

Sophia turned the map over gently to still the images, and as she did so she glimpsed something through the glass. She held it before her and peered at the deck, where one of the floorboards seemed to shine as if lit from within. "What is that?" she asked. Without the glass, the floor of the deck once again looked uniform in the dim moonlight.

Burr looked at her curiously. "What?"

Sophia raised the glass again and the floorboard stood out clearly. "There," she said, pointing. "One of the floorboards seems to have light coming out from behind it." She put the glass down. "That's strange. But only when I look at it through the glass."

"Let me see that," Burr said, with less than customary politeness. Sophia handed him the glass. "Amazing," he whispered. "Calixta, look at this."

Calixta held the glass up and caught her breath.

"What is it?" Grandmother Pearl asked anxiously.

"Seen through the glass," Burr said slowly, "one of the floorboards appears luminescent."

"Aceituna's floorboard?" Grandmother Pearl exclaimed.

"Yes. Captain Aceituna," Burr said, turning to Sophia and Theo and lowering his voice, "left us all his paper maps and charts. He also left us a map that points to his—what would you call them, Calixta?"

"Emergency funds," she said, returning the glass to Sophia with a thoughtful expression.

"Buried treasure?" Theo breathed.

"Well, not actually buried," Burr said. "But yes—treasure. Emergency funds. In case of hostile takeover, he engraved the map in cedar and placed it—face down—in the deck of the ship. It is that floorboard—the one that shines so brightly through your glass, Sophia."

18
CHOCOLATE, PAPER, COIN

1891, June 26: 2-Hour #

We accept ONLY cacao, silver, or Triple Eras bank notes. No stones, glass, or spice will be accepted. Bank notes from New Occident are accepted at a 1.6 exchange rate. To change other currencies see the money changer.

—Vendor's sign at Veracruz market

IT TOOK ONLY a few experiments to determine why the Tracing Glass illuminated Aceituna's instructions. Though she examined almost every inch of the *Swan* through it, Sophia found that only one kind of object shone: maps. The nautical charts that Burr had brought her shone like sheets of hammered gold; the map of the island drawn by Shadrack glowed as if alive with starlight; Calixta's cabin, the walls papered with maps, seemed flooded with light that shone through a dozen map-sized windows. As a final experiment, Sophia asked Burr to draw a map on a blank sheet of paper while she observed him through the glass. At first, the blank sheet, Burr, and his quill all looked quite ordinary. But the moment the faint line he had drawn became a route, the paper took on a different aspect. When he drew a small compass in the corner, the sheet fairly glowed.

Clearly the glass map, whatever else its contents, illuminated other maps. Sophia pondered the significance of her discovery while Burr, Calixta, and Theo slept in their cabins and Grandmother Pearl sat beside her on the deck, snoring lightly. In most cases, of course, the glass would be redundant: Burr's nautical charts were clearly nautical charts, and the glass did not make them any easier to read. But if one were looking for a hidden map, Sophia reflected, her mind whirring, the glass might be very useful. *What if a glass map was disguised in a window?* she thought. *Or what if in a whole library there were only three maps?* In such circumstances, the Tracing Glass would be invaluable. *So* tracing *means* finding, *not outlining,* she reflected. The multilingual instructions, which had once seemed so strange—"you will see it through me"—now made perfect sense. Anyone who could read would be told the purpose of the glass at first glance.

It brought her no closer to understanding the memories, but the discovery made her reconsider why Shadrack had entrusted the glass to her. *Maybe it's not to help find* him *but to help me find another map. A map no one can else can see, perhaps? Is Veressa supposed to help me?* Her thoughts drifted, and suddenly she sat up, electrified. She rummaged quietly through her pack and drew out her notebook. Flipping through the pages, she found the drawings she'd made after the confrontation with Montaigne.

All the different pieces of the puzzle were there: the Lachrima from Shadrack's note, the glass map, Montaigne, and the Nihilismians who traveled with him. There had seemed to be no connection, but suddenly there was, at least for some of the pieces, because she remembered what she had been unable to recall before. Back at East Ending Street, while learning to read maps, she had asked Shadrack about a map of the world, and he had told her about something called the *carta mayor*: a memory map of the entire world, which he had said was a Nihilismian myth. Could it be that the Nihilismians believed the glass map would show the *carta mayor*? *Maybe the map of the world isn't really hidden,* Sophia thought. *Maybe it's hidden in plain sight.* She held the glass up before her and gazed through it at the dark night sky. "You will see it through me," she whispered. The stars on the other side of the glass winked, fluttered, and stared like thousands of distant eyes.

—6-Hour 37: Port of Veracruz—

THE SWAN COASTED into port early the next morning. The city of Veracruz, eastern entry to the realm of Emperor Sebastian Canuto, gleamed like a white seashell. From the deck of a ship, Veracruz appeared like a jeweled promise; it belied the vast, fragmented landscape that lay beyond it. The cities—Nochtland, Veracruz, and Xela—preserved and even heightened their luster year by year, leaching all the wealth from the surrounding towns and flourishing in a state of exaggerated, heady splendor. Princess Justa, from her perch in the shining castle at the heart of the Canuto empire in Nochtland, could pretend that the entire land enjoyed such luxury. Her father, Emperor Sebastian, who had traveled north to pacify the bands of rebellious raiders, knew better. He understood that beyond the walled cities of the Triple Eras, the empire existed only as a smattering of besieged forts, impoverished towns, and miserable farms surrounded by wild, unexplored terrain. Sebastian had long since abandoned the goal of unifying his empire. He fought the northern raiders now less to subdue them and more to avoid the prospect of returning to a castle that he had come to understand ruled almost nothing. The thought of once again donning the meaningless robes, the glittering crown, the air of courtly gravity, depressed him and filled him with dread. He would leave such illusions to his daughter, to whom they were better suited.

Yet in the Triple Eras, to both visitors and inhabitants, the illusion appeared most convincing. Sophia stood on the deck of the *Swan* and looked out with trembling excitement: a cluttered dock; a sprawling town of white stone; and past the town, palm trees and sand as far as the eye could see. Gulls flew low, their cries hungry and urgent. She could see the muddled movement of a hundred ships crowding the shore. The discovery of the glass map's properties had opened an unexpected door, and she had the sense that she was about to burst through it. The whole vast world of the Baldlands lay before her, its mysteries waiting to be uncovered. She was finally arriving—after what felt to her like one long, fevered age—and one step closer to finding Veressa. Her stomach jumped and then, to her great relief, suddenly grew calm as the *Swan* eased into port.

Burr gave the crew special instructions: apart from Grandmother Pearl and Peaches, who would be staying with the ship, they were granted a week's holiday. Burr announced that he and Calixta would be accompanying some of their merchandise into Nochtland, and that he would carry parcels or messages for anyone who planned to avoid the trip inland. "We'll be sailing at eight the night we return," Burr told the crew. "And don't forget we're on the nine-hour clock here. So when I say eight, I mean eight on the Baldlands clock."

The pirates dispersed, and Burr joined Calixta, Theo, and Sophia. "It's market day. Why don't I go in to find Mazapán?" he asked his sister.

Calixta gave him a look. "I think we should just hire a coach. You're being cheap."

"Is it expensive to get to Nochtland?" Sophia asked worriedly, realizing she had no idea how far New Occident currency would take her.

Calixta waved her hand dismissively. "You and Theo are guests of ours, darling, so don't even think about spending a penny. The coach hardly costs anything anyway," she said to Burr.

"Mazapán has a cart," Burr said. "There's no sense hiring a coach when he can take us. I'll go find him, come back for the crates, and we'll be off in an hour. You stay here and collect marriage proposals, eh, dearest?" Calixta walked off in a huff. Burr settled his broad hat comfortably onto his head. "Sophia, Theo—any wish to see the market?"

"Do you think we're—is it likely we've been followed to Veracruz?" Sophia asked worriedly.

"Possible," he admitted, "but unlikely. Your admirers in New Orleans may have discovered our intended route, but they can't have gotten here before us."

They needed no further persuading. "While we are there, would I be able to post a letter to Boston?" she asked.

"Best to leave it with Peaches. He'll take it to the next *paquebot* bound for the Indies, and from there I'm sure someone will be traveling to Boston."

As they crossed the crowded dock, Sophia found it easy to keep Burr in sight because of his enormous hat, but somewhat difficult to keep up with his long stride. He easily dodged men carrying crates on their backs, a swinging load of timber, and a runaway pig that was screaming its way to shore with its owner close on its heels. The Boston waterfront seemed a quiet and orderly place in comparison to Veracruz.

The tumult of leaving, loading, unloading, and boarding was made worse by the activity just beyond the docks, a dense network of stalls, carts, and makeshift counters. The mass of people around them seemed to be carried by a tide that flushed them through like grains of sand: streaming along quickly, piling up and clogging the way, and spilling over irresistibly. Beyond them and slightly to the right, a white border of stucco buildings—the city of Veracruz—made but a feeble dam against the market's onslaught. As Burr pushed through the crowd, Sophia clutched her pack and at the same time took a firm hold of one of his coattails.

Once they had entered the market, it was difficult to see clearly, because Sophia was immediately sandwiched tightly between Burr and Theo. As they inched along, she caught glimpses of vendors selling tomatoes, oranges, lemons, cucumbers, squash, onions, and dozens of kinds of produce that she had never seen before, spread out on blankets or piled high in baskets. They passed a stall with bags of white and yellow powders that she realized were flours, and another that sold fragrant spices: cinnamon and clove and pepper filled the air. A woman with a small tent set up about her had cages full of chickens, and just past her was a man with pails full of fish. Sitting placidly beside the man, wearing an awkward collar around its slippery neck, was a toad the size of a full-grown man. Sophia's eyes widened, but all of the people around her ignored it, as if nothing could be more commonplace. The vendors hollered as they passed, some in English and some in other languages, naming their prices even as they wrapped their wares for customers and counted change.

Beyond the wave of murmurs and shouts, Sophia could hear another sound: wind chimes. At least one dangled from every stall, and many of the vendors sold the chimes that hung along their tents' edges. The air was filled with a constant melodic chiming and tinkling and ringing that reminded her of Mrs. Clay's upstairs apartment.

Burr took a quick turn to the right, and they abruptly passed through a row of fabric stalls. One vendor after another called out her prices and displayed bolts of cloth colored in brilliant red and blue and purple. An old woman whose broad smile had a few missing teeth waved a flag made of ribbons to the passersby, jangling the chime that hung above her. The stalls that followed sold feathers and jars of beads and spools of thread. Sophia took it all in with wonderment, but Burr was quickening his pace and she had to walk briskly to keep up. He turned to the left, by stalls selling soap and bottled perfumes and incense, and then suddenly the air went from soapy to sweet, and she found herself surrounded by confections. Candies of all shapes and sizes were laid out in boxes: nougat and caramel and spun sugar and meringues. Many of the stalls sold candies she had never seen, and she only knew that they must be candy by the delicious smell that filled the air.

"We're almost there," Burr hollered over his shoulder.

Sophia didn't answer—she could hardly catch her breath. Then Burr ducked into a cream-colored tent at their right. "Mazapán!" he shouted at the tall, pink-cheeked man who stood behind the cloth-covered table that served as a counter, surrounded by shelves of plates, cups, and dishes.

"Morris!" the man shouted back, his face breaking into a grin. He finished dealing with a customer, then embraced Burr. The two of them proceeded to yell at one another over the commotion, but Sophia had stopped paying attention. A woman handed her little boy a spoon that she had just purchased. With a look of delight, the boy bit off the end and walked away, following his mother, his mouth smeared with chocolate. Sophia stared at the contents of the cloth-covered table. Mazapán, she realized, was a chocolate vendor.

But his was not ordinary chocolate. Anyone who passed

by the stall would have told you that Mazapán was actually a potter. His table was stacked high with beautiful dishes: plates, bowls, cups, pitchers, forks, knives, and spoons; a cake dome, a serving platter, and a butter dish; and a long procession of coffee pots with delicate spouts. They were painted with flowers and intricate designs of every color. Sophia was awestruck. She touched a small blue cup experimentally; it felt just like a real one. She looked curiously at the man who had created it all, who was still in loud conversation with Burr; then her attention was caught by the vendor at the neighboring stall—a tiny person with a fierce expression, arguing with one of her customers. "I take cacao, silver, or paper. I don't know where you're from, but here you can't pay with pictures."

The thin man holding out a small black rectangle said something, and the woman responded fiercely. "I don't care if it's a map reader. You still can't pay with it." She snatched back the man's parcel and pointed over her shoulder. "If you want to talk maps, go see the woman who sells maps."

Sophia watched, wide-eyed. The thin man, who wore a dirty overcoat, leaned forward to ask a question. It took him a moment to get the vendor's attention; she had already moved on to another customer. When he tugged on her sleeve, the woman looked at him crossly. "Yes," she said curtly. "The one selling onions."

Turning to look behind her, Sophia caught a glimpse of a woman standing behind several baskets full of onions. Burr was still talking excitedly to Mazapán, who had begun to pack up his dishes. Theo was nowhere to be seen. She thought he'd been following as they wound through the market, but now she was not so sure. With one last glance at Burr, Sophia decided that his hat would make an easy landmark and dove into the crowd.

If it was difficult to squeeze through the market with Burr, it was even harder on her own. She was caught up and pushed along past several stalls. *It's like being on a trolley made of people,* she thought. She glimpsed a basket full of onions. *And here's my stop.* She wriggled out as hard as she could, using her elbows perhaps more fiercely than was necessary, and a moment later found herself pressed up against the baskets. Next to her, the thin man was leaning forward to talk to the vendor.

The woman shook her head as he spoke. "I'm sorry, sir. I only have onion maps. You'll find the market in Veracruz thin on maps. All of the map vendors stay in Nochtland."

The man turned away dejectedly and drifted back into the crowd. He seemed tired and haggard, as if he had been traveling for too long. *An explorer from another Age, short on funds,* Sophia thought sympathetically. She watched him go and then turned to the baskets full of onions. The one closest to her had a little paper pinned to the edge that said NOCHTLAND. Another basket said XELA, and yet another was labeled SAN ISIDRO.

"Where are you headed, dear?" the vendor asked loudly. "I've got maps to any place in the Triple Eras, many other places besides." Her dark hair, entwined around half a dozen fragrant gardenias, was pulled back in a tight bun, and she had tiny leaves and flowers painted in dark green ink across her brow.

Sophia hesitated a moment. "Nochtland," she said.

"They're right in front of you, then," the woman said cheerily. "But frankly, you don't need it if you're leaving from here. Just follow the main road. Can't miss it. It's about two days travel with good horses."

They seemed to be ordinary yellow onions with coppery skins. "How do these work?"

"What's that, dear?"

"How do these work? Are they really maps?" Sophia wished she could look at them through the glass map, but it was midday, and the crowded market was no place for something so precious.

The woman seemed unsurprised. "Not from here?"

Sophia shook her head. "I'm from Boston; from New Occident."

"Well, these are Way-Finding Onions. Guaranteed to have been planted in their location's native soil. Each layer of the onion leads you onward until you arrive at your destination."

"What do you mean, 'leads you onward'?" Sophia asked, fascinated.

"They don't necessarily take you by the quickest or easiest route, mind you," the woman said. "But they'll get you there."

Sophia reached into her purse for her money. "Do you take money from New Occident?"

"Cacao, silver, or Triple Eras paper. But I'll take New Occident paper; I can change it at a better rate."

Sophia was taking out her money when she suddenly felt a violent push from the crowd behind her. "Watch it," she said irritably. Then she felt an arm around her waist, and someone pulled her away from the stall and into the crowd. "Hey!" she said. As she clutched her money and her pack and tried to keep from falling, she looked at the person who had grabbed her and saw with astonishment that it was Theo. "You're hurting my arm," she shouted.

Theo ignored her protests. "Come on," he said, dragging her onward. He wove through the crowd, keeping his head low and holding Sophia's wrist tightly.

"Theo, what is it?" she panted, when she had the chance. "Is it Montaigne?"

For a moment, he seemed to not recognize the name. He frowned, looked over his shoulder, and led them behind a stall selling leather goods.

"Is it Montaigne?" Sophia asked again, her voice rising.

"It's not Montaigne," he said brusquely. "It's a raider I used to know."

Sophia realized that, amid the usual commotion of the market, there was an even greater commotion coming toward them. Angry shouts erupted as two people toppled against a stall, sending it tumbling. "A raider?" Sophia asked, gasping for air as they ran along an empty stretch between two of the leather shops. "Why is he chasing you?"

"I can't explain right now. Just have to get away from him."

They burst out into a quiet part of the market where all the stalls were filled with baskets. "Here," Sophia said, twisting out of Theo's grasp. She ran toward one of the vendors. The tallest baskets were large enough to hold a whole wardrobe full of clothes—or the person who wore them. "Crouch down," she said quickly.

"In that?" Theo exclaimed.

"He's coming," Sophia warned, hearing nearby shouts.

Theo stood frozen for a moment, and then he abruptly crouched down. Sophia took the nearest large basket and overturned it on top of him. It looked like just another among the many the vendor sold. "Don't move," she whispered. Then she ran to the astonished vendor and thrust out the bills she'd been holding. "Please—we'll give it back in just a moment."

The woman gave a small nod. She pocketed the money without a word and gently pushed Sophia toward the back of the stall. Saying something Sophia couldn't understand, she handed her a small, half-finished basket.

A man burst into the quiet square. He looked in each direction, taking huge, heaving breaths. His blond hair came down almost to his waist, and his beard fanned out like the arms of a jellyfish. Both were laden with silver beads and bells that rang out every time he turned his head. His worn leather boots were coated with yellow dust, and the rawhide coat he wore trailed its ragged edges on the ground. As he turned toward her, his fists clenched, Sophia saw that every single one of his teeth was made of metal. They were sharp and made a jagged line, like the tips of old knives sharpened many times. They glinted in the sunlight, as did the silver in his hair and the long knife he drew from his belt. He stood staring back at Sophia—she could not take her eyes off him—and then slowly walked toward her.

He pointed the knife at her chest. "What. Are. You. Staring. At?" he snarled, jabbing each word at her like another knife.

Sophia couldn't help herself. She wasn't afraid yet; she was only fascinated. "Your teeth," she breathed.

The man stared at her for what seemed to Sophia like an hour. Then suddenly he broke into laughter. He lifted the knife and slowly ran its edge along his teeth, making a dull clinking sound. "You like them, sugar? How about a kiss?"

Sophia shook her head slowly. She met his eyes, and the raider's teeth disappeared into a scowl. "You can skip the kiss if you tell me which way the kid went," he said.

She pointed to her left, away from the central market.

The raider smiled, and Sophia saw a quick glint of silver. A moment later he was gone.

Part of her still could not believe what she'd seen—the metallic glimmers from his hair, his teeth, his knife, and the silver clasps of his coat. The group of basket vendors had gone silent when the raider appeared in their midst. Now they began talking to each other in low voices. It seemed to Sophia that all of them were looking at her.

She put the half-finished basket down and hurried over to where Theo was hidden. "Are you all right?"

"I can't see behind me. Is he gone?" he asked in a muffled voice.

"He's gone. Come out, and we'll find Burr." She lifted the basket and Theo stood up. He glanced quickly around the square. Sophia turned to thank the vendor, and as she did so the woman handed her two straw hats. Her crown of braids, interwoven with long green grass, nodded as she patted her apron and spoke.

"What's she saying, Theo?"

He was gazing distractedly around the stalls but turned back briefly. "She's giving you those for the money you gave her."

Sophia took the hats. "Thank you. Thank you for helping us." The woman smiled, nodded, and returned to her tent. Sophia put on one of the hats and gave the other to Theo. "We'll be a little hidden with these," she said.

Theo donned the hat. "Come on—I know the way back. This way." He put his hand on her arm and found that she was trembling. He stopped abruptly. "What's wrong?"

"Nothing," Sophia said, clenching her fists. The danger had passed, but only now did she feel the waves of fear washing over her. "That raider was scary."

For a moment, his tense expression softened. He put his scarred hand in Sophia's and squeezed tightly. "You sure fooled me. You looked like you weren't scared of anything." He pulled at her gently. "Come on, let's get out of here."

19
The Bullet

1891, June 24: Shadrack Missing (Day 4)

Most firsthand accounts of the Great Disruption describe witnessing the passage of a year while time was suspended. But the prophet Amitto claims to have perceived all time past and present during his revelation, experiencing each day of twenty hours as any other. The Chronicles of the Disruption *are thereby organized into 365 days: one day for each that he purportedly lived through. The days are commonly understood as chapters. Nihilismians follow the practice of naming themselves with the first word of the chapter corresponding to the day that they joined the sect.*

—*From Shadrack Elli's* History of New Occident

Shadrack had traveled extensively by electric train, but he had never been on a train quite like the Bullet. It was, true to its name, quicker and lighter on the rails than any he had ridden. But it was also better-equipped in its interior. He had passed through a full kitchen and a well-furnished study before being forced into his improvised cell. Bound hand and foot to a chair, he sat in a small, windowless closet. The wooden slats of the closet door admitted bars of feeble light.

When the light dimmed, his internal clock told him that it was past seventeen-hour.

His thoughts were moving as quickly as the train, keeping pace as the Bullet raced south. It was obvious to him now, in retrospect, that the borders were indeed shifting. The signs had been there for years, but his supposed knowledge of the Great Disruption had prevented him from seeing their meaning. He cursed himself for his stupidity. He had violated one of his most valued principles: *Observe what you see, not what you expect to see.*

Of what use am I as a cartologer, he berated himself, *when I could not even reliably see the world around me?* Now, because of his blindness, he had placed Sophia doubly in harm's way. He had sent her fleeing the ambitions of a madwoman, into the path of destruction.

It was well past eighteen-hour when the door suddenly swung open. The Sandmen lifted the chair with their grappling hooks to carry it through the doorway and set it down facing the center of the adjoining room.

Shadrack blinked in the lamplight. He was in a study as opulently furnished as the rest of the Bullet, with broad windows, thick carpeting, and a variety of desks and chairs. The Sandmen stationed themselves at the doors.

Blanca sat in the middle of the room at a long table. On the table was a sheet of copper. Beside the table were the two trunks filled with Shadrack's mapmaking equipment, which the Sandmen had packed when they took him from East Ending Street. "I won't deceive you, Shadrack," Blanca said, in her musical voice. "While I know the route your niece is traveling, she and her companion are resourceful; they have managed to evade the men I sent to meet her."

Shadrack tried not to show his relief too plainly. Then he wondered: *A companion?*

"This makes your situation more difficult, because it means I am less patient." Her veil shook slightly. "As you know, I need two things from you: Sophia's destination and the location of the *carta mayor.* So I will give you two choices. One for each thing I need." She lifted the square sheet of copper, which glinted in the yellow lamplight. "You can draw me a map of the *carta mayor*'s location and tell me where Sophia is going." Then she drew her other hand from under the table, revealing the dreaded block of wood with its attached wires. "Or, you can wear the bonnet," she said almost kindly.

Shadrack stared at his lap, using the last of his exhausted energy to hide the panic he felt at the sight of the wooden block and wires. After a few moments he said, "We've already discussed this. You have my answer."

Blanca sat silently for a moment. Then she stood. "You make this very hard, Shadrack. I do not like having to play the bully, but you leave me with no choice." Her voice was mournful. She turned toward the younger of the two men. "Leave his hands and legs tied, Weeping. If he nods, take off the bonnet strings and call me. If he hasn't done so by twenty-hour, tighten them."

Had Shadrack imagined it, or did Blanca speak to Weeping with particular favor? The young man's face, he noticed with surprise, was unmarked. His brown hair was clipped short, and his cheeks were clean-shaven. He pressed his lips together as Blanca gave him instructions. As she left, she gently patted Weeping's arm. The door opened, and Shadrack caught a brief glimpse of the interior of the next car: a wooden floor, dim lamplight, and a wheelbarrow piled high with sand.

He did his best to keep from gagging as they placed the wooden block between his teeth. He did not resist; they would only jam the block in more forcefully if he did. The wires tightened across his cheeks and he grew still. He concentrated all of his attention on clearing his mind so that he would not choke. If he choked or gagged, his face would pull at the wires, and they would cut him. Shadrack breathed deeply through his nose until his pulse settled. The moment he felt calm, he knew that he would not be able to wear the bonnet for more than a few minutes. He looked up at the two men, both of whom were watching him.

The older man bore the familiar scars and the blank expression that was also, by now, familiar. He held the grappling hook as if it were an extension of his own hand: casually, almost thoughtlessly. The scarred Nihilismians had none of the usual fervor Shadrack had seen in the followers of Amitto. They lacked the zealous passion that Nihilismians carried like bright flames; no, the eyes of these men suggested loss, confusion, and an aimless sense of searching. But the unscarred younger man, Weeping, was different. He seemed like a *real* Nihilismian: his eyes were focused and bright with conviction. Dark green, they gazed into Shadrack's unflinchingly. Though no compassion lingered there, they seemed to suggest something else: a clarity of purpose.

Shadrack thought quickly. First he had to get the bonnet off. He would not be able to escape right away, but it might be possible to distract his guards, and that was as good a start as any. He locked eyes with Weeping and nodded. Immediately the young man loosened the wires and pulled the wooden block away. "Call her," he said to the older man.

"Wait," Shadrack said, turning in his chair. "Listen to me." The older man was already walking to the door. "June fourth," he said quickly. "*Weeping is for the cursed, who bear the face of evil. All grief is of the false world, not of the true world. Trust not the weeping, and weep not.*"

The older man stopped and turned and looked at him, as if the words touched the edges of something terribly remote that he had to strain to remember. The younger man clasped his medallion and murmured, "Truth of Amitto."

Shadrack spoke in an urgent undertone. "Truth, indeed. But she is hiding the truth from you—the truth about the very passage for which you are named. *Trust not the weeping*, Amitto says." He lowered his voice to a whisper, forcing the man to lean in. "I know you have heard the weeping, as I did, at the mansion. Can you deny it?" The man's silence answered him eloquently. "I can prove to you that this weeping, this evil," Shadrack pressed, "which she is hiding from you, is close at hand."

The older man had not moved; he stared at Shadrack, troubled, as if still trying to work out the meaning of the words that he had quoted from the *Chronicles of the Great Disruption*. Weeping, looking intently at Shadrack, deliberated. "How?" he finally asked.

"Do you know what causes the weeping—where it comes from?"

The young man hesitated. He shook his head. "No one knows. If you know, tell me."

"I cannot tell you. There is no way but to show you," Shadrack said. "If you will give me my tools, I will map the memory that will allow you to see."

"Don't give him anything," said the older man reflexively.

"Tell her I am drawing the map she requested," Shadrack insisted. "I promise you, Weeping—I will show you Amitto's truth."

Weeping looked down at him, the force of obedience and the Nihilismian fervor warring like water and fire in his green eyes. He had obligations and loyalties in this world; but nothing surpassed his commitment to Amitto's truth. The fire won. He leaned toward Shadrack and mouthed his words, so that the older Sandman standing by the door would not hear him. "Very well." Then he straightened up and spoke in a loud voice. "You will draw the map she ordered or no map at all."

Shadrack bowed his head, pretending to be cowed.

"Ashes," the young Sandman said, turning toward the older man. "You may go and tell her that he has agreed. I will oversee his drawing of the map."

20
At the Gates

1891, June 26: 10-Hour #

Welcome to Ensueño Inn. Please stable horses and anchor arboldevelas after checking in. Please do not bring your horses into the courtyard. Our floors will thank you!

Sign at the inn's entrance

Normally, Mazapán relied on hired guards for protection on the route between the Veracruz market and Nochtland, where he had his chocolate store. His wagon bore the royal seal—a leaf encircled by its stem—which attracted highway bandits. But on this trip, Calixta and Burr could offer more expert protection. Burr hired horses for Calixta, Theo, and himself. Sophia, who had never ridden, sat in the cart with Mazapán.

She had been hoping for a chance to speak with Theo. The last of her anger had faded as they walked back through the market, his scarred hand in hers, and it had given way to a compounded sense of anxiety. For one thing, they were back on land and once again easy targets for Montaigne and his men. And now they had Theo's dangerous raider to worry about as well.

She couldn't help it; staying angry with him was impossible. She wanted to know who the raider was, and why he was chasing Theo, and whether he was likely to return accompanied by more like him. It was obvious to her, now, that Theo had been telling her the truth about his past—but he had told her too little of it. What she most wanted now was to sit down and hear everything, from beginning to end. But he rode separately, sometimes ahead and sometimes behind, and apart from asking an occasional question about the route, he seemed utterly uninterested in the journey.

Instead, the story she heard was Mazapán's. He told her about his store in Nochtland and the winding street that led to it and the delicious pottery he made in the large, sun-filled kitchen. He spoke with the accent of the southern Baldlands, like Mrs. Clay. His clothes—thin leather boots, white cotton pants, and a shirt embroidered with vines—while apparently commonplace in the Baldlands, would have stood out in Boston. His sizable belly, wavy brown hair, and large mustache all seemed to shuffle back and forth when he laughed. Sophia was only half listening and kept turning around to see if anyone was following them. Only when Mazapán handed her the reins and said, "All right, concentrate now—keep them at a steady pace," did she realize that the kindly chocolate vendor was doing his best to distract her. She felt suddenly grateful and a little ashamed. "Why do they call you Mazapán?" she asked. "Is that your whole name?"

He smiled. "Actually, my name is Olaf Rud. But no one here can pronounce it. You see, my grandfather was an adventurer from the Kingdom of Denmark—a place that today lies in the far north of the Closed Empire. He was traveling here when the Disruption occurred. It became obvious afterward that he could not return; everyone he had known and loved had disappeared."

Sophia nodded, intrigued. She had read about such stranded travelers—exiles who lost their home Ages—but each case was different and uniquely interesting. "So he stayed."

"So he stayed. And with him, his unusual name, which no one can pronounce. Everyone calls me Mazapán. It is the Spanish word for marzipan, and Spanish is one of the many languages still spoken in the Triple Eras. In the past I was known for making marzipan candy"

"Why in the past? Don't you make marzipan anymore?"

His mustache drooped. "Ah, that's not such a happy story."

"I don't mind," Sophia said. "If you don't mind telling it."

Mazapán shook his head. "No, I am past minding. I'll tell you, though I am afraid it will not give you the most pleasant impression of Nochtland. Still—I am sure you will discover its charms.

"You see, I learned to make marzipan with my teacher—a master chef who could have turned his talents to anything, but decided he liked candy best. From him I also learned to make chocolate and spun sugar and meringues—all manner of confection. Well, my teacher was not young when I began learning from him, and he passed away just a year after I opened my own shop. Much of his business passed to me, and I did what I could to match his high standards. I was fortunate to attract the attentions of the court, and I began serving banquets for the royal family—in the palace of Emperor Sebastian Canuto."

Sophia was astonished. "Banquets of *candy*?"

"Oh, yes—nothing else. I suppose I could cook some beans if my life depended on it, but I have to rely on my wife for everything of substance. I am not much good at anything other than candy. The banquets were quite complete in their details, if I do say so myself. Everything on the table—the tablecloth, the plates, the food, the flowers—was made of candy. The plates were made of chocolate, like those you saw, but the food and flowers were usually made of spun sugar and marzipan. The pleasure people derived from the banquets was in how the candy was disguised. It all looked like real food, real flowers, real dishes. And it is one of humankind's simplest and most eternal pleasures to be knowingly deceived by appearances. I, too, enjoyed the banquets; I created more and more fantastic feasts with more elaborate and detailed dishes.

"Unfortunately, someone used my displays of innocent deception for a less innocent purpose. For Princess Justa's sixth birthday, the banquet was more resplendent than any I'd served the royals before. All the members of the court were there; the emperor and his wife and daughter were at the head of the table. I had made marzipan orchids for decoration, because the empress's favorite flower was the orchid. You have heard of the Mark of the Vine?"

"A little. I don't really understand it."

Mazapán shook his head. "To my mind, it is simply one more of the infinite differences that distinguish us from each other. My hair is brown; your hair is fair; Theo's is black. Simply different. In the Baldlands, there are some who take great pride in having a particular shade of hair or skin. I find it rather ridiculous. But to continue—the empress had the Mark of the Vine. Her hair was not hair like yours or mine; it consisted of orchid roots."

Sophia wrinkled her nose. "Orchid roots?"

"To you, no doubt it sounds strange. The entire court considered it the height of beauty. They were thin, white strands, the orchid roots, which she wove and bound into towering designs. Naturally, it gave her a love and affinity for the orchid flower. Her daughter Justa inherited this trait."

"She has roots on her head, too?"

"No, Justa's hair also bears the Mark, but it takes the form of a grass—long and green. I have not seen her since she was a child, but I am told it is very beautiful."

Sophia diplomatically said nothing to contradict him.

"I had created marzipan orchids particularly for the empress, and there were vases all along the table. As the banquet began, the guests sampled the food, the flowers, the utensils, and even the plates. At one point—I was watching from the side of the room, naturally, to ensure everything went smoothly—the empress took up a marzipan orchid and ate it. I knew she would; there were banquets when she ate nothing but the flowers! She had another, and another. And then—suddenly—I knew something terrible had happened. The empress's face was horrible to see. She clutched her throat and then her stomach. She crashed forward onto the table, her fabulous hair cascading onto the plates. Immediately, the entire room was on its feet. A doctor came at once, but it was too late; the empress was dead. She had been killed by a very rare poisonous orchid that someone had placed among the marzipan orchids."

Sophia gasped. "Did they accuse you?"

Mazapán shook his head. "Fortunately, no. I was questioned, of course, but they soon realized I had nothing to gain from the empress's death."

"How terrible," she said sympathetically.

"Indeed. Though they did not blame me, the emperor never wanted another such banquet, naturally enough. And I, for my part, though I knew I had not been to blame, could not help feeling some responsibility. Had I not created the marzipan orchids, no one would have been able to plant the poisonous orchids among them."

"But that's ridiculous!" Sophia exclaimed. "They just took advantage of how real the banquet looked."

"Yes." Mazapán shook his head. "But why invite such danger? I gave up the marzipan and the spun sugar and the meringue. I stayed with the chocolate dishes and utensils, because they, at least, cannot be used for ill. The worst that can come from biting into a plate or cup substituted for one of mine is a broken tooth!" He laughed.

"I suppose you're right." After a moment, she added, "Princess Justa must have been heartbroken to lose her mother."

"No doubt she was," Mazapán said, but his tone was uncertain. "As I said, I haven't seen her since her sixth birthday, but she was a strange child. She was—how to say it?—cold. I could not tell whether she was truly emotionless or simply very shy, but she seemed so devoid of the usual charm of children that I confess I never warmed to her. If what I hear is true, she has become a quiet, withdrawn woman." He paused, lost in thought for a moment. "We'll be changing horses soon," he resumed. "There's a place up the road."

The land they were passing through was flat, the vegetation cut away from the road to prevent thieves from hiding and ambushing travelers. They passed a few peddlers with wooden cases on their backs and a pair of riders.

Sophia had noticed that the wind chimes, so prevalent in the Veracruz market, also hung at regular intervals on posts at the side of the road. Their constant ringing had become familiar—almost comforting. "Are those to mark another path?" she asked now.

"Ah—no," Mazapán said, following her gaze. "Those are warning chimes. They warn travelers of a weirwind. Do you have those in the north?"

"I'm not sure."

"Weirwinds can be long or short, wide or narrow, but they are all deadly. Powerful walls of pure wind that draw you in with a force of a cyclone."

"Like tornadoes."

"Yes, very similar; like a wall of tornadoes. For weeks now, they have forecast the approach of a weirwind from the south. The chimes will announce its arrival so that people on the road and in the cities can take cover underground. Ah—here we are."

They had a quick meal at the inn, which to Sophia's relief was all but deserted. While Burr and Theo changed the horses, Sophia stood with Calixta and Mazapán by the cart, keeping an anxious watch on the empty road.

A strange shape appeared on the horizon, moving toward them at a tremendous speed. She was about to call Calixta, but then she saw what it was and her jaw dropped in disbelief.

It appeared to be a sailing tree—a slim wooden vessel twice as high as Mazapán's cart, propelled by broad green sails. Enormous leaves grew from the base of the mast and were tied at its tip, cupping the wind. The spherical wheels, woven like baskets from a light wood, were painted gold. The ship seemed to float, gliding effortlessly on its tall wheels. A girl not much older than Sophia leaned lazily over the railing at the stern.

Sophia watched, enthralled, until it was no more than a speck. "Mazapán, what was *that*?"

"Ah! You've never seen an arboldevela."

She raised her eyebrows.

"Boldevela for short. It's a vessel with living sails and a wooden hull."

"Do you have one?" she asked eagerly.

He laughed. "They're rather expensive for ordinary people. But they're not uncommon. You'll see more of them in Nochtland on the roads and in the canals."

They changed horses twice more before stopping for the night at the halfway point between Veracruz and Nochtland. Sophia had been dozing off for the last several miles, resting her head against Mazapán's arm. As the horses slowed, she opened her eyes and fumbled for her watch. It was one by the Baldlands clock and past two by the clock of New Occident.

"The innkeeper here saves a room for me," Mazapán told her. "If we're lucky, there will be another one empty. We'll be tucked away and sleeping in no time."

After stabling the horses, they made their way up the tiled walkway to the main building. The royal seal beside the door and an imposing portrait of the royal family in the foyer announced that the inn was a licensed lodging house. Mazapán lit a candle from the stack left conveniently on the foyer table and led them down the open corridor of the inn's inner courtyard. Sophia and Calixta took one of the rooms that stood open and Burr, Mazapán, and Theo took another. As she stumbled sleepily out of her clothes, Sophia realized she hadn't had a chance to speak with Theo all day. She shivered. The room felt cavernous, with its bare stucco walls and high, beamed ceilings, and the sheets were stiff from having hung to dry in the sun; but Sophia hardly noticed. She dropped into her narrow bed and fell instantly asleep.

—June 27, 3-hour: At the Inn—

SOPHIA AWOKE IN the dark, her heart pounding. The nightmare she'd been having still filled the edges of her mind like a fog. She could hear the weeping: the piercing cry of the Lachrima that in her dream grew louder and louder until it obliterated all other sound.

The inn was quiet; the delicate ringing of chimes, swinging gently in the night breeze, was all she could hear. She reached for her watch, and her fingers trembled as she opened the familiar brass disc to read the time, but the room was too dark to see it.

Sophia dressed and pulled on her pack. With a glance toward Calixta—a white shape under the sheets of the other bed—she opened the door and stepped out into the cool night air.

Padding along the tiled corridor of the inn's courtyard, Sophia felt the nightmare dissipating. Night jasmine wound up along the beams, filling the air with intoxicating sweetness. Her watch, by the light of the night sky, read just after three-hour. She walked toward the courtyard's entrance, toward the stables. The chimes hanging from the beams of the open corridors tinkled softly as she passed under them.

A rock garden with cacti and wooden benches divided the guest rooms from the stables. She stopped, surprised, at the sight of someone sitting alone in the moonlight. It was Theo. He had turned at the sound of her approach and slid over to make room on the bench. "Can't sleep either?" he asked.

Sophia shook her head. "I was having a nightmare. What about you?"

"Yeah, can't sleep."

She studied him. His scuffed boots were untied. He looked out intently into the darkness as if waiting for something to emerge from it. "Are you worried about the raider?"

"Not so much."

Sophia hesitated. She wanted to know more, but she didn't want to hear another set of lies. She took in his thoughtful expression and decided to risk it. "Why was he chasing you?"

Theo shrugged, as if to say that the story was hardly worth telling. "His name is Jude. He usually stays pretty far north—near New Orleans. Remember I told you about the girl who kind of raised me, Sue? She was about ten years older than me, and she got to be really good at raiding—one of the best. She joined Jude's gang a while back. I found out a couple years ago she'd been killed in a raid because Jude sent her in by herself and warned the people she was coming. He set a trap for her."

"That's awful," Sophia said.

"He doesn't like anyone being better than him. Smarter than him. Well, I knew it was just a matter of time before Jude wandered over to the New Occident side. In the Baldlands there's no law to speak of and the raiders do whatever they like, but in New Occident . . . New Orleans has the biggest prison I've ever seen. I just made it my business to tell the law that Jude had blown up all the railroad lines they'd been building into the Baldlands." He smiled with satisfaction. "Next I'd heard, they'd put him in prison for eighteen months."

"Was it true?"

"Sure. Raiders don't like the idea of having tracks into the Baldlands, because then there will just be more people and more towns and more law."

Sophia examined him critically for a moment. "So you didn't do anything wrong," she finally said.

"I don't care if what I did is wrong or not. I got back at him, didn't I? He got Sue killed—he deserved it."

"And you're not worried he'll follow you?"

Theo shrugged again. "Doubt he will." He winked and snapped his fingers into a pistol. "Besides, Jude's nothing compared to the guys hunting *you*."

Sophia's heart sped up again. "I hope they don't know where we are."

"Haven't seen hide nor hair of them yet."

"I think I might have figured out why they want the map, though."

Theo looked at her with interest. "Why?"

"Well, you know how I told you the Nihilismians think our world isn't real?"

"Yeah."

"Shadrack told me once that they believe in a legend about a map called the *carta mayor*: a map of great size and power that contains the whole world. The Nihilismians think it shows the true world—the world that was destroyed by the Great Disruption—not just our world. But no one knows where it is."

"And the glass you have might find it—the *carta mayor*."

"Yes. If it's something that doesn't look like a typical map"—she remembered the onions at the market—"the glass would make it visible. But I have no idea what the *carta mayor* is supposed to look like or where it is. Shadrack made it sound like it wasn't actually real."

"But these guys think it is."

"Clearly."

"You know," Theo said thoughtfully, "your uncle did go to a lot of trouble to keep them from finding it—the glass. Maybe *he* thinks the *carta mayor* is real."

"I thought about that. But the glass map could just be valuable on its own. I mean, it could be useful for all kinds of things. Not just what the Nihilismians want it for."

"That's true, I guess."

Sophia was silent for a moment. "Hopefully Veressa will know."

Theo kicked off his boots and pulled his knees up to his chest, resting his socked feet on the bench. "Have you thought about how to find her?"

"Once we get to Nochtland, I'll ask where the academy is. The one they studied at. I'm sure they keep track of everyone who went there. I think that's the first step."

"Yeah. And then she'll know where Shadrack is for sure."

She wished she could be as certain as he was. "I hope so. I really don't know." She paused. "Maybe we should have followed the Sandmen off the train when we had the chance. They could have led us to Shadrack."

"No way; we did the right thing. Look, you're doing what he said to do. Mazapán will know the academy. Calixta might even have heard about it—have you asked her?" Sophia shook her head. "Then you'll find Veressa. And she'll know what to do."

Sophia didn't answer, but sat quietly, listening to the chimes. "I like the pirates," she said eventually. "We were lucky to meet them."

Theo grinned. "Yeah. They're solid. You can count on them."

"I was lucky to meet you, too." She watched him as she said it.

Theo's smile flickered like a sputtering candle, but then his grin returned, easy and calm in the moonlight, and Sophia thought she must have imagined it. "They don't call me Lucky Theo for nothing."

—8 Hour 30: On the Road to Nochtland—

A STEADY RAIN had begun to fall, and Mazapán kept stopping to check that the flap over the cart was secure. "I'm sorry, Sophia," he said more than once. "But if the dishes are wet, I'll get an earful at home."

"It's okay," Sophia said, curling up as tightly as possible under the cart's narrow awning. She longed for the spare clothes that were in her abandoned trunk, probably stowed in a train depot somewhere along the Gulf line.

Calixta and Burr rode side by side under broad, colorful umbrellas, engrossed in conversation. Theo trailed behind the cart, seemingly unwilling even to ride with the others. When she did see him, he stared sullenly at his reins and refused to meet her eyes. *He reminds me of me,* Sophia thought, *when I'm moping.* She was baffled. When they'd parted, close to four-hour, Theo had seemed to be in good spirits.

It was some time past sixteen-hour on Sophia's watch when she saw something on the road ahead of them. At first she thought it was only a group of travelers, but as they approached she realized that it was many travelers—hundreds of travelers—all stalled on the road. They had reached the outer limits of Nochtland. She could just barely make out the high profile of the city walls through the heavy rain and the falling darkness.

"They check everyone who comes in through the gates," Mazapán explained with a sigh. "I'm afraid we'll be here for hours. I'd forgotten the eclipse festivities are taking place in a few nights. Everyone from miles around has come to see them. They occur so rarely, and the astronomers say this will be the first total lunar eclipse since the Great Disruption."

Sophia was too tired to engage him in conversation. She could see the sails of a boldevela far ahead of them in the long line. Calixta and Burr slowed their pace to ride alongside the cart, and Theo rode up briefly. "I'm going to see how long the line is," he called out. Before anyone could say anything, he had spurred his horse and taken off. Within seconds, he was swallowed up by the darkness.

"Why is he checking the line?" she asked Mazapán uneasily.

"Who knows? Long is long. We'll be here at least until nine-hour. Twenty-hour, for you," he added, with a smile. "What a relief that my day is eleven hours shorter. I won't have as long to wait."

Sophia knew he was trying to distract her. "That's not how it works," she said with a faint smile, staring into the rain. Ahead of them were a large party of traders traveling on foot. They shuffled along slowly, hunched under their cloaks. As the line inched forward, Sophia saw Theo returning. He rode up to her side of the cart, and she realized that his expression had grown even more strained. He was pale, his eyes tense with anxiety. "What is it?" she asked immediately, thinking of the raider from the market. "Did you see someone in the line?"

Theo leaned toward her. "I said I'd see you safely to Nochtland, didn't I?"

"Yes," Sophia said, even more uneasy now.

"Well, we're here," he said, his voice hard. "You kept your word, and I kept mine." He leaned in farther, pulled her face toward his, and gave her a rough, awkward kiss on the cheek. "'Bye, Sophia." He turned the horse away and galloped off in the opposite direction, back toward Veracruz.

Sophia stood up. "Theo!" she shouted. "Where are you going?" For a moment it seemed to her that he turned to look over his shoulder, and then he was gone.

"Let him go, Sophia," Mazapán called up to her. He eased her back onto the seat. "I'm sorry, child, but you're getting soaked. Take this cloak and try to keep warm." He put his arm around her. "He rode away," Mazapán shouted over the rain, by way of explanation, to Burr and Calixta, who were trying to ask what had happened. "No, he didn't say why—he just rode away," he repeated.

"Just like that," Sophia said emptily.

PART III
Entrapment

21
The Botanist

1891, June 28: 5-Hour 04

According to pages unearthed in an abandoned storeroom near the western coast, there existed at one point in time a continuous city stretching along the Pacific from the thirtieth to the fiftieth latitude. The date of the pages is unknown, and only very fragmented segments of the Pacific City, as the pages term it, remain.

—From Veressa Metl's Cultural Geography of the Baldlands

The city of Nochtland stretched for miles along the floor of a wide valley. Protected by its high walls, it was more an island than a city, not only because it was crisscrossed by waterways, but also because its inhabitants rarely ventured outside. Traders shuttled back and forth to Veracruz, scholars traveled south to the universities in Xela, and adventurers journeyed north to the wild lands on the Pacific coast. But otherwise the people of Nochtland stayed within its walls, claiming that anything and everything they could ever want lay somewhere in its web of narrow streets and vast gardens. It was a wealthy city, where cacao, bank notes, and crown-issued silver passed hands easily. It was a cosmopolitan city, because people from many different Ages had heard of its beauty and gone to live there. And it was a generous city, to those with the Mark of the Vine.

Nochtland itself seemed to bear the Mark of the Vine. The outer walls were covered with climbing milkweed, balloon vines, morning glories, and bougainvillea. From a distance, the flowering mass appeared almost a living thing: a sleeping creature sprawled out at the end of a long road.

Princess Justa Canuto of the grass-green hair would have banned metal, that despised substance, if she could, but without it the city would cease to function. So, with special dispensation, for which the citizens laboriously applied, the carefully prescribed use of metal was permitted: nuts and bolts, harness fixtures, locks and keys, buckles, iron nails. The Nochtland attorneys grew rich shepherding such applications through the courts. Of course, the royal family had no such constraints, and some people complained bitterly that while they waited two years for a permit to own a steel-wire embroidery needle, the very gates of Nochtland, imperfectly hidden by vines, encased the city in pure wrought iron.

The travelers waited all night in the rain, and when they finally reached the gates of Nochtland Sophia was fast asleep. She had stayed awake late, staring blindly into the pouring rain, hearing Theo's last words and feeling the slight pressure of his lips against her cheek, until her whole mind and body went numb. Finally she fell asleep against Mazapán's shoulder. She awoke briefly in the middle of the night to a dark sky and saw that the guards at the gate—tall shapes dressed in long, hooded capes—were inspecting Mazapán's cart. Then she drifted again into an uneasy sleep, opening her eyes only when Mazapán gently shook her shoulder. "We're here, Sophia," he said. "Wake up. You will want to see the city at dawn—there is no better time."

Sophia sat up drowsily and looked around. As she surfaced from sleep, the sense of frozen numbness persisted. Calixta and Burr rode only a few feet ahead of the cart; the gates were just behind them. The thought of Theo slipped through her mind like a tiny, silvery fish through icy water: briefly there and then gone. Lifting her head, she looked around for her first view of Nochtland. She had anticipated her arrival with such excitement, but now she felt nothing.

The rain had stopped, leaving only thin, jagged clouds that turned blue with the dawn. The cobblestone streets still shone darkly. Chimes tinkled all around, as if engaged in murmuring conversation. The cart horses plodded slowly down a long, straight road lined with trees that scattered drops of rain and filled the morning air with the scent of lemon blossoms. Behind the trees, high stone walls and even taller trees beyond them spilled out from the city's enclosed gardens. Some of the trees were so broad and full that they seemed to crowd the houses, and Sophia noticed that one of the massive trunks was encircled by a set of stairs that led upward to a gabled house set high in the branches.

She could hear water everywhere. A fountain in the wall to her right disgorged a gurgling stream from the mouth of a stone fish; spigots in the high garden walls spewed rainwater onto the cobblestones. The cart rolled over a bridge spanning a long canal; it stretched out on either side, bordered by low walls and long gardens. Sophia caught a glimpse of the innumerable red-tiled roofs of the houses along the canal as they crossed. Then the road narrowed; on either side, the stone walls were dotted with low doors and closed wooden shutters. The tree houses behind them were curtained and quiet. All Nochtland was still sleeping.

Almost all: there was a child peering out from behind a set of curtains. As their eyes met, Sophia felt a sudden pang at the sight of that surprised, rather lost-looking face. She slipped her hands into her pockets to hold her watch and the spool of thread. They calmed her: time was ticking peacefully, and the Fates had been kind. Perhaps they had taken Theo away, but they had given her Calixta and Burr and Mazapán; surely they were weaving some pattern that ensured her safe travels.

The cart turned the corner and suddenly they found themselves in a wide, tree-lined avenue. "This is the road to the palace gates," Mazapán said.

"Is your shop near here?"

"Very near—but we are not going to my shop. I will leave you with Burton and Calixta at the palace. You can rest there."

It took Sophia a moment to understand his words. "At the palace?" she asked, confused.

Mazapán smiled. "You are fortunate in your travel companions. Burton is good friends with the royal botanist, and you will enjoy the best accommodations Nochtland has to offer. Much better than my place," he said, winking. "Look—on the other side of that fence are the royal gardens."

Across from the long stone wall along the south side of the avenue was a tall, wrought-iron fence. Behind the fence was a hedge of densely planted juniper trees, and beyond that a rank of taller trees stretched to the horizon.

"It is difficult from here, but you might catch a glimpse of the palace through the trees," Mazapán said. "It is mostly made of glass, and when the sun shines upon its surface it gleams like a thousand mirrors."

Calixta and Burr, a few lengths ahead, had paused in the cobblestone road at an enormous fountain, a wide, low pool around a jet of water as tall as a palm tree. "We are almost at the gates," Mazapán said, slowing the cart to a stop.

Calixta dismounted and walked up to them. "You poor thing," she said to Sophia, "sleeping all night in those wet clothes."

Sophia heard the pity in her voice. "I'm fine," she replied lamely.

"I promise you," Burr said, leading his horse toward her, "breakfast and warm blankets are only a short walk away." He leaned into the cart. "Mazapán, my friend, we cannot thank you enough."

"It is nothing," he replied, gripping Burr's hand, as Sophia got out. "Come see me when you have finished your errand." He gave her a wink. "Come by later for some chocolate!"

"Thank you, Mazapán," she replied, making an effort to smile. "I will." She watched as the cart rounded the fountain, heading off down the long avenue toward the narrow streets of Nochtland.

"Why don't you ride the last part while I hold the reins?" Burr asked Sophia.

"All right," she agreed. He lifted her onto his horse and led it past the fountain to a row of guards who stood before a set of imposing gates. Wrought iron, they arched upward the height of five Nochtland spears laid end to end.

Like those she had seen while half-asleep at the city gates, the guards wore long, hooded capes and masks made entirely of feathers, showing nothing but their impassive eyes. Tall plumes quivered over their heads. Their bare arms, tightly bound with leather bands and painted or tattooed with dense, swirling lines, held long spears with obsidian heads. Sophia remembered Theo's costume at the circus, and she realized that Ehrlach had been attempting, in his limited way, to re-create the image of the Nochtland guards.

Despite their terrifying appearance, Burr chatted with the guards as if they were pirates on the *Swan*. "Morning, lads. Here to see the royal botanist, as always."

"Does the botanist know you are arriving?" the closest guard asked.

"He does not, on this occasion."

"We will send someone with you, then," the guard said, and one of the rank stepped forward. "Who is the girl?"

"Just a new recruit."

Calixta pushed her horse a step forward. "She takes after me," she said, smiling broadly. "Impatient."

The guard shook his head, seemingly all too familiar with the Morrises. He opened the gate without another word and waved them on.

They stepped onto a gravel drive that wound through the gardens and up to the palace, the walkways of colored pebbles describing a continuous pattern like a tapestry all along the drive. The path led them through a tunnel of tall juniper bushes, and when they emerged from the tunnel the palace gardens suddenly sprang into view.

Sophia had never seen anything so beautiful. Immediately before her lay a long reflecting pool full of water lilies. On either side of the pool were two gardenia trees dotted with white blossoms, and beside those were lemon trees planted in half-moon beds. Graveled walkways branched off in every direction through the gardens, circling around stone fountains. At each corner of the reflecting pool and along the walkways stood statues of royal ancestors who bore the Mark of the Vine: still faces cut in pale marble, their leafy wings and branching arms white against the green of the gardens.

Beyond the long reflecting pool stood the palace. It was long and rectangular and rose into multiple domes. As Mazapán had said, it was made almost entirely of glass, which glinted in the morning sun like mother-of-pearl. Two vast botanical conservatories of pale green glass flanked it. The guard led them to one side of the reflecting pool, and Sophia glanced down into its shallow green depths, seeing bright fish between the water lilies. The scent of gardenia and lemon blossoms filled the air as birds whirled out from among the branches.

They were led not to the stone steps at front of the palace, where another line of hooded guards stood watch, but to the greenhouses on the right-hand side. The guard left them at a low door in the conservatory wall and departed with their horses. As they waited, Sophia stood quietly, listening to the fountains and the quick calls of the birds.

The door of the conservatory was finally flung open and a small, thin man burst out. "Burton! Calixta!" he shouted. He threw his arms around Burr, squeezing him tightly, and attempted to do the same with Calixta without crushing her hat. The man wore strange spectacles with many lenses, which encircled each of his eyes like petals and winked in the sunlight. Turning his grotesquely magnified eyes toward Sophia, the man asked, "And who is this?"

"Martin," Burr said, "this is Sophia, from New Occident. Sophia, this is my good friend Martin, the royal botanist."

Then the wiry man removed his spectacles, and Sophia found herself confronted by a much more ordinary face: narrow, wrinkled deeply from laughter, and topped by a shock of unruly white hair. His long nose, like the gnomon of a sundial, pointed sharply outward and a little to his left. He observed Sophia with his wide brown eyes and put out his hand, bowing briefly as he clasped hers. "Delighted to meet you, Sophia," he said. "And how wonderful to see you two," he continued, turning back to Burr and Calixta. "What a surprise. But let's not stand here. Come in. Come in!"

The botanist led them quickly down the walkway. Sophia noticed that he had a slight limp, but it did not slow him down.

Between following Martin and responding to his questions, Sophia barely took in the leaning cacao plants, the mounds of ferns, and the light, fragile faces of the orchids that lined the path. The warm air was bursting with the scent of vegetation. "Did you just come through the city gates?" Martin called over his shoulder.

"We waited in the rain all night," Burr admitted.

"Poor children! The line must have been eternal, with the eclipse only three nights away. Have you slept at all, Sophia?"

"A little," she said breathlessly, trying to keep up.

"Do you like eggs?" he demanded, whirling to face her.

"Yes," Sophia replied, nearly running into him.

"Wonderful!" Martin said, continuing his race through the conservatory. "We'll have eggs and hot chocolate and mushroom bread." He muttered something that Sophia could not hear. "I'll even let you sleep an hour or two," he added, "before we get to work."

Sophia wondered what this work could possibly consist of, but she refrained from asking, and a moment later Martin opened a door at the far end of the conservatory. "The royal botanist's apartments," he said, ushering them in. "Please make yourselves at home."

22
The Soil of the Ages

1891, June 28: 6-Hour 34

Based on continuing research with samples collected from across the Baldlands, there have been no less than 3,427 discrete Ages identified within the territory. The range covered by the samples, if the method is correct, is to date no less than five million years. But this range is scattered throughout the entire region, and some areas contain fairly limited diversity. For example, the Triple Eras, as Nochtland, Veracruz, and Xela are collectively known, represent primarily three Ages, with very small samples of others.

—From Veressa Metl's "Local Soils: Implications for Cartology"

THE ROYAL BOTANIST fulfilled such an important role for the palace—and, indeed, for the entirety of the Baldlands—that the appointment came with a private residence at the rear of the palace, connected to the conservatories. Much like Shadrack, Martin had managed to fill his rooms with all the tools of his trade. A large kitchen, a laboratory, a study, a dining room with a table fit for twenty, and four bedrooms were fairly overflowing with strange scientific equipment, books on botany and zoology and geology, and, of course, hundreds of plants. Unlike Shadrack, however, Martin kept his rooms in order, and the chaos of vegetation and equipment was carefully contained on dozens of shelves and in heavy glass cabinets that crouched in the corners of every room.

After serving them the promised eggs and mushroom bread—all the while talking without pause about the cultivation of the cacao that had gone into making their hot chocolate—Martin reluctantly allowed his visitors to rest. Burr clearly knew his way around, and he disappeared with a yawn.

"The back bedroom?" Calixta asked, already leading Sophia away.

"Yes," he replied. "Sleep well!"

A broad, sun-filled bathroom with tiled floors and walls—and more than a dozen potted orchids—adjoined the bedroom. Sophia, knowing how particular Calixta was about the state of her clothes and hair, greatly appreciated her kindness in offering to bathe second.

Here, in the botanist's apartments, Sophia felt almost as safe as she had in Boston. She lay in the porcelain tub and watched the sun glitter against the tiles, the water's warmth stealing through her. She moved the soap absently over her skin and then lay still, letting her muscles relax. Finally, she stepped out of the tub and wrapped herself in a bathrobe, the cotton soft against her skin. As she tied the sash around her waist, she felt a long sigh building up in her chest; and then, suddenly, the icy numbness in her mind cracked and thawed. She hiccupped, choked, and found that she was crying.

She doubled over, weeping. "There, there," said Calixta,

putting her arms around Sophia and rubbing her back. The cries seemed to twist their way out in painful jerks. Sophia hardly knew where these heaving sobs came from. But she knew that the horror of Shadrack's disappearance had been made easier, somehow, by Theo's presence, and now he was gone. And Shadrack—

Sophia gave a sharp gasp. Shadrack might be dead, for all she knew. "That's it, sweetheart," Calixta whispered, as Sophia's tears diminished, "get it all out." After a long while, Calixta gave her a squeeze and then a reassuring smile. "Let's get your hair untangled before you go to sleep." Calixta dried her hair with a towel and then combed it out, humming quietly all the while. The gentle pull of the comb and the low wordless song made Sophia unbearably sleepy. She hardly remembered crawling into one of the high beds, which she had to reach by means of a little ladder. A cotton nightgown that was not hers but that fit her well was laid out on the bed. She drew it on over her head and fell asleep the moment she lay down.

When she awoke, she did not know where she was. Then she remembered and sat up.

Something had changed while she slept; Sophia felt better than she had in ages. The agonizing wait in the rain, Theo's desertion, the long ride from Veracruz, the unending seasickness aboard the *Swan*, the unlucky train ride through New Occident: they were all over. She felt bruised and sore, as if her body and mind had been trampled, but at least the worst was over. An unexpected wave of relief rushed through her.

Calixta had closed the wooden shutters, and sunlight leaked

in through the cracks, filling the room with a pale, amber light. She was fast asleep in the other bed. Sophia climbed down the ladder as quietly as she could and rummaged in her purse for her pocket watch. It was past ten, by New Occident time—half the day already gone.

She could not find her clothes, but someone had left a white dress embroidered with blue vines on the chair near her bed. Surprisingly, it fit; the pressed cotton smelled faintly of starch and lavender. A pair of blue slippers beside the chair were only a little large. She took her pack and slung it over her shoulder. Slipping her watch and the spool of thread into the pocket of the dress, she quietly closed the door behind her.

For a moment she stood on the cool stones of the corridor, letting the newly found sense of recovery settle through her. She could almost feel her limbs gaining strength. Then she heard Burr's unmistakable chuckle from a nearby room, and she made her way along the corridor until she found the open door of the laboratory. Martin was studying something through his spectacles and talking animatedly to Burr, who stood next to him, beaming.

"It's like nothing I've ever seen!" Martin exclaimed. "I cannot even begin to date it, though that in itself . . . Astonishing! And you say a sailor took it from an island where?"

"Good rest?" Burr asked, seeing Sophia in the doorway.

"Sophia!" Martin smiled, blinking hugely through his spectacles. "How did you sleep?"

"Very well, thank you. Calixta is still in bed."

"Let her sleep," Martin said. He pulled her to where he had

been standing at the table. "Burr tells me you are of a scientific family. You simply must see this."

"You'll have to explain a bit," Burr put in. "I haven't told Sophia anything about your work."

"I will, I will," Martin said impatiently, pulling a short footstool toward the table. "Up you go." Sophia was nonplused, but climbed the footstool nonetheless. "Look into the glass!" Martin exclaimed excitedly. "Oh!" he said, suddenly removing his spectacles. "You need these." He fastened them onto her face. Everything around her was a blur of color. "Here," Martin said, gently tipping her head down, over the desk.

Sophia found herself looking at what appeared to be fist-sized rocks with jagged, golden stripes. She gazed at them in confusion and then took off the glasses. There on the table was a jar filled with loose, sandy soil. "I don't understand," she said.

"This soil," Martin said, "was found by a sailor on a remote island—where?" he asked Burr.

"South of the Indies, close to the coast of Late Patagonia."

"And it appears to be from an Age we know nothing about. I cannot even begin to guess what Age it comes from, but I know it is an undiscovered Age just from looking at the soil!"

"How can you tell?" Sophia asked doubtfully.

"Because this soil is manmade!"

"How is that possible?"

"It isn't!" The botanist laughed with delight. "That is what is so extraordinary. It is utterly impossible, and yet it has been done. This soil comes from an Age that we know nothing about—I am guessing in the extremely distant future. *But who knows?* It might be a past Age." He raised his eyebrows and smiled.

"I really don't understand," Sophia said again.

"Come," Martin said, pulling her peremptorily off the stool. "Follow me." He limped rapidly toward the other end of the room.

Sophia followed as quickly as she could, and Burr joined them at a round table near the window. Pinned to it was a paper map full of penciled notations and numbers. "The earth," Martin said excitedly, "is probably about four and a half billion years old. That is—dated from our time. Though the Baldlands contain a vast collection of Ages, a great number of them lie in the thousand-year span to which the United Indies and New Occident also belong. You might say we are roughly in the same Age-hemisphere. But other parts of the world contain Ages that are thousands—or even millions—of Ages away from ours. My research—one small part of it," he qualified—"is to date the various Ages by dating their soil."

Sophia examined the map more closely, but the numerical notations were still unintelligible. "So all these numbers are dates?"

"It is easiest to think of them that way, yes," Martin said. "I believe my method is the most straightforward empirical way of eventually identifying every Age in our new world. Burr here collects soil samples for me—or, rather, his colleagues do—and, as you can see, we have managed to identify many Ages all across our hemisphere." Martin spoke with noticeable pride. He beamed at Burr, who gave a quick smile.

"It is very impressive," Sophia said politely. She understood the significance of Martin's research, but the map was still a mystery to her.

"But that is not all! Let's show her the green room!" he said eagerly to Burr.

"By all means."

"Let's try that new soil, shall we? Come!" He limped off toward the other end of the room, where Sophia saw a narrow, glass-paned door that she had not noticed before. It led directly into a small greenhouse—a greenhouse within the larger conservatory that they had walked through that morning. "This," Martin said grandly, indicating the mostly empty flower pots and trays, "is where the great experiments take place!"

"What experiments?" Martin's enthusiasm was contagious.

"The soil experiments, of course." He leaned in until his long nose was almost touching hers. "The *botanical* experiments!" he whispered. "What we do," he continued, straightening up and turning to a tray of odd-looking plants, "is combine different seeds and cuttings with soil from different Ages. The results are sometimes *extraordinary*." He pulled one of the nearby pots off the shelf and held it toward Sophia. "What do you think this is?" he asked.

"It looks like a strawberry," Sophia said doubtfully.

"Exactly!" Martin said. "But taste it." He picked one of the berries from the plant and handed it to her.

She stared at it skeptically for a moment and then popped it in her mouth. "It's not"—and then her mouth was flooded with an unexpected taste—"Wait, it tastes like mushrooms!"

Martin was even more delighted now. "Yes, mushroom! Remarkable, isn't it? These are what I used for the bread. I have no idea why, but strawberries taste like mushrooms when they're planted in this soil from the northern Baldlands. It is most curious." He put the strawberry plant aside. "Over here we have my newest experiments with mapping vegetation," and he gestured toward a long table with what looked like an ordinary vegetable garden. "Anise, celery, and onion, mainly."

"Oh! I saw an onion map at the market in Veracruz," Sophia said instantly. "How do they work?"

"Those were very simple to develop, really," Martin said modestly. "Plants are greatly shaped by their native soil. The soil is magnetized, like a compass, and then the vegetable or root leads back to the soil in which it was planted—like a divining rod, if you will. It works better with some plants than others." He scratched his head. "For some reason, pineapples always lead to the ocean."

He took out an empty pot. "But what I am truly looking forward to is this manmade soil that Burr found for us. The sample?" he asked.

Burr obligingly handed over a glass container, and Martin spooned a small amount of soil into a tiny pot. "Let's see," he muttered, opening a long drawer and rifling through dozens of small paper envelopes. "Petunias? Oranges? Basil? We could use a clipping. But I think I would like to try—yes. Let's use this." He held up a brown envelope. "Morning glory!" He dipped into it and plunged the few small seeds that stuck to his fingertip into the pot of soil. Then he carefully smoothed the soil over and watered it with a ceramic pitcher. "In a few days we will see what has emerged," he said, dusting his hands off happily. "And if I am right, it will be something remarkable."

"What other experiments do you do?" Sophia asked, intrigued.

Martin did not have a chance to reply, because Burr suddenly gave a shout of alarm, seized Sophia's arm, and pulled her away from the pot.

A small green tendril, lithe as a snake, was winding up out of the soil and into the air. As they watched, the green stem split in two, sprouted a delicate spade-shaped leaf, and reached farther upward. Suddenly the tiny pot exploded, and a dense web of silver roots burst out onto the counter, clinging to and spreading across it. The green shoot, dotted with leaves, had now nearly reached the low ceiling of the greenhouse. Thin shoots sprung off it like wires, spiraling into the air. Then a tight white bud appeared near one of the leaves. Another bud and then another materialized. Almost simultaneously, the white buds turned green and then faintly blue and then deep purple as they grew and elongated. And finally, in a sudden burst, the morning glory flowered like dozens of tiny parasols opening at once. But that was not the most surprising thing. What astonished the speechless observers most was the *sound* that came from the flowers. A dozen high, flutelike voices called out in some unknown tongue that was not quite speech and not quite song: a high, undulating call that Sophia was sure contained words of some kind, though she could not understand them. Martin was the first to step forward toward the plant.

"Take care, Martin!" Burr exclaimed.

"There is nothing to fear," Martin said, awestruck, reaching out toward the plant. "It is resting at the moment. How remarkable," he said, more to himself than to the others. "Its roots are made *of silver.* I wonder—yes. The stem is vegetable matter. Truly fantastic." He turned to Burr and Sophia with an expression of wonder. "This morning glory is like nothing I have ever seen. It is only half plant."

"What is the rest of it?" Burr asked tensely.

"I believe it is manmade." Martin shook his head. "Not entirely manmade, but something in between, a hybrid. It has grown like a plant, but its substance is partly metallic. I have read about such plants in an obscure history from my daughter's collection. But I believed it to be hypothetical, or fictional, or fantastical. I never imagined such plants could truly exist."

"Why is it making that sound?" Sophia asked.

Martin smiled. "I have no idea. But I will find out." He took a last look at the morning glory. "We have much to do! I will visit the library, and we will examine these flowers under a strong lens, and then perhaps we will attempt another sample." He wiped his eyes, which were damp with emotion. "What a discovery!" Then he hurried back to his laboratory, followed by Sophia and Burr, who closed the greenhouse door firmly with a grim expression.

"Perhaps we ought to consider the matter, Martin," he said, following the older man as he whirled around gathering supplies. "Must I remind you that the experiments on occasion have . . . unexpected consequences."

"Nonsense," Martin said absently.

"*Nonsense?*" Burr exclaimed. "What about the strangling creeper? What about the lying labyrinth of boxwood, which would have been the death of five royal attendants had you not killed it with poison? What about the blood-apple tree, which I hear is now the source of innumerable horror stories designed to keep children from wandering unattended in the park? Or the fanged potatoes? Or the walking elm? *Martin!*"

Martin looked up, startled. "What?"

"There is something strange about that flower. Its voice unsettles me. We have no way of knowing its true nature. We must be a little cautious. Please."

The botanist looked at the tall nine-hour clock near the courtyard door. "Almost lunchtime," he muttered to himself. "I'll ask her to look it up in the library. Morning glory. No, that wouldn't be it. Soils? Manufactured soils?" He shook his head. "There won't be a thing."

"Martin," Burr repeated gravely.

The old man beamed at him. "Since when are you so serious, Burton? This is very unlike you. We must seize the opportunity! A discovery like this occurs once in an age!"

"It is you who makes me serious. Normally I throw caution and care to the wind, but I have learned that you need minding. I must be the voice of reason to you. Consider the greater circumstances. Consider . . ." He paused. "Remember the whispering oleander," he said gently. "It too could speak."

Martin hesitated.

"The whispering oleander?" Sophia echoed quietly.

"That was a different thing altogether," Martin finally said. "It is an absurd comparison!"

Burr took a deep breath, clearly frustrated. "Martin, I am only asking you to proceed carefully. Silver roots—in this palace? You will be accused of treason."

Martin rolled his eyes with exaggerated impatience. "I tell you, Burton," he exclaimed, "there is no danger."

"What dangers are you ignoring now?" someone asked.

Sophia turned, expecting Calixta, and saw instead a slight woman with hair piled intricately atop her head. She wore a long, close-fitting garment that swept the floor; it was covered with tiny silk flowers of a deep midnight blue. A high pearl choker encircled her neck. The dress left her arms bare, and at first Sophia thought there was a long line of sequins running from the woman's wrists to her shoulders. Then, as she joined the group, Sophia realized that they were thorns: each no larger than a fingernail, they were pale green, slightly curved, and seemingly quite sharp. The woman smiled kindly at Sophia. She seemed young, but her expression was serious and thoughtful, as if borrowed from a much older face. Sophia suddenly understood what people meant when they called Sophia herself "wise beyond her years"—it was here, in the woman's face. She smiled back. The woman turned to Martin, and Sophia noticed that her jet-black hair was dotted with tiny blue flowers.

"My dear, you've arrived just at the right moment! I need

your help immediately!" he exclaimed, hurrying toward her.

"A great pleasure to see you once again," Burton said, kissing the newcomer's hand.

"Likewise, Burr," she said, smiling. "How is Calixta?"

"Dearest, we have no time for this," Martin exclaimed, seizing her hand. "You must come see the soil Burr brought me. It's most extraordinary. You simply won't believe—"

"Father," she said gently. "Won't you introduce me to your other guest?"

Martin caught himself. "Of course, of course—I'm so sorry, my dear. This is Sophia, a friend of Burr and Calixta's. Sophia," he said, turning to her with a little bow, "this is the royal librarian and court cartologer.

"My daughter, Veressa."

23
The Four Maps

1891, June 28: 11-hour 22

Lock the doors, stop your ears.
The Lachrima will sense your fear.
And if it's drawn in by your fright
You'll surely see it in the night.

—Nochtland nursery rhyme, first verse

Only when Veressa murmured, "A pleasure to meet you," did Sophia finally find her tongue.

"*You* are Veressa?" she exclaimed, the words spilling from her mouth too loudly. "The *cartologer*?"

"Yes," Veressa replied, both surprised and amused. Sophia felt dizzy. She put her hand out toward the table, and Veressa seized it. "Are you all right?"

"You—my uncle," Sophia said, attempting to collect herself. "My uncle sent me to you. I came from Boston all the way to find you. My uncle, Shadrack Elli. Do you know where he is?"

It was Veressa's turn to stare, her eyes wide. "You astonish me," she said, her voice no more than a whisper. "I have not heard that name in many years."

Sophia bit her lip as disappointment rushed through her. She had been hoping that somehow, once she found her, Veressa would know what had happened to Shadrack and have a plan for his rescue. Her hand closed around the spool of thread in her pocket. *Why would you lead me so easily to Veressa,* she asked the Fates, *if she cannot lead me to Shadrack?*

"Come," Veressa said gently. "Let's sit and talk this over." She put her hand on Sophia's shoulder and guided her gently toward the kitchen.

Martin and Burr followed them and stood uncertainly by while she and Sophia sat at the long table. "Now," she said, "tell me everything, beginning with how things were before Shadrack sent you to me."

Sophia explained as best she could, though it was difficult without being certain how much Veressa already knew about glass maps and railroad lines and any number of other things. Veressa stopped her to ask questions: once about Mrs. Clay's story about the Lachrima, and a second time about Montaigne. Otherwise, she listened attentively, pressing Sophia's hand encouragingly when the story grew confusing or difficult to tell. When Sophia was through, she sat thoughtfully for several moments. "May I see Shadrack's two messages and the map?" she finally asked.

Veressa read the notes briefly and then held the glass map to the light for a moment. She placed it on the table with a heavy sigh. "I had not thought it would happen this way," she said, "though it was bound to happen." She glanced up at her father. "I'm sorry, Papá, there are some things I have not told you that you will hear for the first time." She looked down at the table. "I had good reason for not telling you."

Martin sat down abruptly, apparently more astonished by this than by anything else that had happened all day.

Veressa touched the glass map for a moment and shuddered, as if she saw something on its surface. "I know this map," she said quietly. "Shadrack and I came across it together, many years ago. Part of me wishes we had never found it." She shook her head. "Let me tell you how it happened."

—11-Hour 31: Veressa Tells of Talisman—

"IT WAS WHEN we were students, as Mrs. Clay told you, that we knew one another. She is right that we were close." Veressa paused. "Very close. But something," she continued quickly, "came between us. What Mrs. Clay did not know was the extent of our work in cartology. She could not know the dedication—thc passion—with which we pursued it. Mapmaking with all materials—glass, clay, metal, cloth, and others besides—was naturally part of our studies. However, we learned in one of our courses that there were other materials for mapmaking that were forbidden in our school. Our teachers would not say what they were. But by and by we heard of a former teacher who had been dismissed because he persisted in experimenting with them. He was called Talisman, Talis for short—I do not know if that was his full name.

"If they had told us of Talisman's terrible experiments, we

would have been disgusted and lost all interest. But our teachers' silence only made us more curious. I can't remember which one of us came up with the idea of finding Talisman, but once the idea had taken hold neither Shadrack nor I could shake it. Piece by piece, we put together the story, and we discovered that he lived alone not far outside of Nochtland.

"We were wise enough to write to him beforehand. We told him we were students of cartology, and that we desired to learn something of his methods. To our surprise, he responded almost immediately. He said we would be most welcome, and that he would be happy to share his learning with us. In person, we found him just as kind and welcoming, if older and more tired, than we had expected—his face was that of someone who had lived through a time of great grief. His vast home was dilapidated, but he did his best to make us feel comfortable. He showed us the rooms where we would stay and the study where we would work. I remember that he spoke with us for only a few minutes before leaving to prepare dinner—he had no servants and seemed to live alone. Those were the only minutes we passed in relative peace.

"Shadrack and I made our way to the dining room, as Talisman had instructed us, and we waited for nearly an hour. There was no sign of him. After the hour had passed, we began to hear a strange sound from somewhere far away within the house. It was the sound of weeping.

"I was uneasy, but Shadrack reassured me, saying that we knew not what private grief Talisman suffered. We had only to wait, he insisted. Another hour passed, and then another.

There was no sign of Talis. The sound of weeping grew louder, and finally became so inescapable that I felt desperate to leave. But then it would subside, and I would steel myself to wait a while longer. Then, suddenly, when it was almost nine-hour, Talisman appeared in the door of the dining room. I say it was Talisman, but he was almost unrecognizable. He waved his arms furiously and shouted at us in a language we did not understand. Shadrack and I clung to one another, terrified. But we soon saw that he meant us no harm. In fact, it was almost as though he could not see us—he appeared to look right through us. He shouted at something that stood before him, railing at the empty air. Then, just as abruptly as he had arrived, he turned on his heel and left.

"Shadrack and I fled to my room. We pushed a chair against the door and sat up the entire night. We heard the sound of weeping rising and falling through the early hours, but we did not see Talisman again.

"We had already made our plans to escape as soon as it was light, but at dawn we heard a faint knocking on the door. Shadrack cautiously removed the chair. To our astonishment, Talisman stood in the hall—contrite and disheveled—begging our forgiveness. He seemed to have no memory of what had occurred, but he suspected that all was not right. It was painful to see how he attempted to apologize while being entirely unaware of what he had done. 'Did you find supper to your liking?' he asked anxiously. We answered that we had not had the chance to eat. 'I am terribly sorry,' he said, tears filling his eyes. 'I can't—I don't know how to apologize. Please, let me make it up to you with breakfast.' It would have been cruel to deny him. We followed him to the dining room, entirely perplexed by the change in circumstances, and proceeded to have an ordinary breakfast.

"After breakfast, Talisman seemed to regain some of his energy, and without being asked he turned to the topic of cartology. 'I am honored that you have shown an interest in my methods,' he said. 'And I am only too happy to share them with you. As it stands, there are no others who practice them, and I fear that when I go'—a shadow passed over his face as he said this—'there will be none to carry on.' We assured him that while we knew nothing of his methods, we were enthusiastic students and open to every manner of experiment. 'Wonderful,' he said, his face brightening. 'Has it not struck you as remarkable that the principal method for reading memory maps is human touch? How is it that the fingertips have this ability to transmit memories to the brain? In fact,' he went on, his enthusiasm growing, 'it is not only the fingertips but the entire human body which responds to the stored memories on a map. Try it—your elbow, your wrist, your nose—they are all the same. It is as if human skin were a great sponge, simply waiting to absorb memories! In fact, this is exactly the case—we *are* sponges and we *do* absorb memories.'

"I heard then for the first time the theory that has since been confirmed by other scholars. At the time, I was not certain whether or not to believe Talisman. Now I do without question. He applied his knowledge to shocking ends, but there is no doubt that his observations were true. 'The Great Disruption,'

Talis went on, 'disrupted the world in ways we are only beginning to understand. But one thing we know—there are borders, fault lines, edges to the Ages that resulted from the Great Disruption. I have always sought to understand these borders. What did they look like? What happened along them when the Disruption took place? Perhaps we will never know entirely what it was like, but we can try. I imagine a great, blinding light that sears the earth along a jagged line.' He laughed. 'But perhaps I am being fanciful. What we know beyond a shadow of a doubt is what happened to those people who were *on the fault line* when the Disruption occurred.'

"Shadrack and I looked at him in surprise. This was unexpected. 'Have you never contemplated it?' he asked, equally surprised. 'I have been obsessed with the question. And *now I know.* Those unlucky people fell into a great chasm of time. Every event that ever took place on the spot where they were standing passed through them, like blinding light passing through a prism. Can you imagine what such a thing would do to you? Can you begin to conceive the damage to the human frame, the human mind, of being plunged into infinite time?' He shook his head, awed by his own question.

"'Contrary to what you may think,' he continued, 'they did not die. Oh, no—much the opposite. They passed *beyond* time, extending their lives to unnatural length by decades, perhaps even centuries. Nevertheless, they were lost—hopelessly lost. A million memories that did not belong to them remained echoing in their brains. Consider: black is the absence of color, while white is the sum of all colors. What is the result when all of those strange memories are forced into your mind? Utter blankness, utter whiteness. Their minds were blank. And so were their faces. Just as a contented old woman wears the grooved wrinkles of every laugh, and a bitter old man wears the furrows of every frown, and an old warrior bears the scar of every battle, so their faces showed the traces of every memory of their engulfed minds. They wore the face of nothingness.'"

Sophia, absorbed as she was in Veressa's story, let out a gasp. "Of course! That is why none exist in Boston."

Veressa nodded. "At that moment I understood, and I could see that Shadrack did as well. 'The Lachrima,' he said.

"'Yes!' Talis exclaimed. 'What we call the Lachrima, who weep for the surfeit of memories, among which their own are utterly lost: the Lachrima who weep even as their long lives fade, so that before expiring they are nothing more than a sound, a lament. They are truly the lost souls of this earth.'

"I then realized the meaning of what I had heard the day before. 'Can it be,' I asked him, 'that we have heard a Lachrima here—in your home?'

"He rose from his chair. 'Follow me!' he said, hurrying from the room. 'You have heard a Lachrima who has lived with me for nearly three years!' We were stunned. 'Yes!' he said breathlessly. 'Three years!' He stopped suddenly and laid a clammy hand on my arm. 'And I have attempted *to save it.*' He rushed onward, through the twisting hallways, and we followed him, riveted and horrified. Finally, at the end of a long corridor, we reached a door that was heavily chained. Catching his breath,

Talis took a key from his pocket and unlocked the massive lock that held the chain in place. 'Quiet,' he whispered, 'it sleeps.'

"He slowly opened the door. The room was small, with high ceilings; bright light poured into the room from a barred window. Underneath the window was a narrow bed, and at first I could not identify what I saw upon it. It was a shape—a female figure only partly hidden by white sheets. There was something draped across it that I suddenly realized was the Lachrima's arm. It was entirely covered with strangely colored designs that I took for some peculiar pattern on its clothing. Then the Lachrima turned toward us, and I saw the long, pale hair that trailed across the bed and onto the floor. And the face—oh, the face. It was horribly wounded and scarred, as if it had been repeatedly cut in long lines. 'You see!' Talisman whispered, gesturing with trembling pride. 'My great cartologic invention. I have drawn the map *upon its skin.*'

"I understood then that the web of unintelligible markings that I had taken for clothing were lines of ink drawn upon the body of the Lachrima. Shadrack frowned. 'But what have you done to its face?' he asked.

"'With careful incisions,' Talisman exclaimed, 'I have twice almost found its hidden features!'

"I shuddered, taking Shadrack's arm, and a cry must have escaped my lips, for the Lachrima suddenly stirred and lifted its head. It faced us in silence, its horribly scarred countenance a mockery of a human face; and then suddenly it let out a terrible, heartrending cry. Covering its face with hands that were, like its arms, laden with inscrutable markings—it shrieked over and over, as if in agony. The shriek resolved itself into words: *'HELP ME! HELP ME!'*

"I bolted from the room, dragging Shadrack behind me, and Talis followed us hurriedly, locking the heavy door. But it did not muffle the cries of the Lachrima, and I felt that if they continued, I would lose my mind. Then I saw from Talisman's face that he was even more affected than I. He dropped to his knees, suddenly, and looked up at us. 'Apff?' he said, in the high, gurgling voice of an infant.

"'What is wrong with him?' I cried.

"'I don't know,' Shadrack replied. 'He seems to think he is a child.' The shrieking of the Lachrima continued, and I knew that I could bear it no longer. I turned and ran down the corridor, fleeing from the sound and from the frightening sight of Talisman on his hands and knees. Shadrack ran after me, and though we lost our way in the hallways more than once, we finally found our way back to the dining room and from there to the bedrooms to gather our belongings. We seized them and ran toward the stables, where we had left our hired horses. I was trembling from hand to foot, and I could barely manage the saddle. And yet, as we were readying the horses, the sound of the Lachrima faded and finally stopped. Still, I wanted nothing more than to leave as quickly as possible.

"Suddenly Talisman threw open the stable door and came unsteadily toward us. I felt an irrational fear surge through me. 'Please,' he said faintly. 'Wait—I beg you.' I would not have waited, but Shadrack hesitated, moved by pity. The old man looked beaten down and exhausted, and I understood then the constant expression of grief that he wore, even when he was not under the Lachrima's spell. He carried a wrapped bundle carefully in his arms, and as he walked toward us he shifted it to one hand and held his other out toward us appealingly. 'I beg you,' he said again, hoarsely. 'Wait.'

"'We are leaving, Talisman,' Shadrack said firmly.

"'I know, I know,' he said, crestfallen. 'I know it frightens you. It frightens me as well, but I must explain to you. *Someone* must know. The Lachrima's cries confuse my sense of time. I lose my way—I know not who I am nor where I am, nor *when* I am.'

"'Let the Lachrima go free,' Shadrack implored. 'Come away with us. We will find you a doctor in Nochtland. Your mind might still be restored with care and rest.'

"Talis shook his head. 'I cannot. It is my life's work. I aim to restore that creature's mind, even if it costs me my own.'

"'But can you not see the further damage you are doing? You are restoring nothing!'

"'I am drawing a map of its life upon its skin. Then it will remember its one, true life.'

"'I ask you once more to show it mercy and leave with us,' Shadrack said, taking the old man's arm.

"Talis pulled away and handed Shadrack the bundle. 'If you must go, take these with you. They are too valuable to be left here, where they might soon be lost with me.' He smiled feebly. 'Do not fear—they are maps like those you know. They hold the key to a great mystery, and it will not do for them to be buried with an old man.'

"Shadrack accepted them, at a loss for words, and Talis stepped back. He raised his arm as if bidding us farewell and slowly left the stables. Shadrack seemed to hesitate, debating what to do. Then he put the package in his saddlebag and mounted his horse. 'Let us leave this place,' he said to me.

"We returned to Nochtland without stopping, and we could not bring ourselves to speak of what had happened. Back at the academy, we sat listlessly at our desks, thinking only of what we had seen—of that tormented creature and how little we had done to save her. Shadrack came to my room the following day with the bundle that Talisman had given him. 'I think we should look at these together,' he said.

"Inside the carefully wrapped bundle we found four maps—glass, clay, metal, and cloth. Four maps that fit together and told a tragic story. Despite the horror we had felt during our visit, we recognized that the maps were, indeed, keys to a great mystery. After studying the maps we came to the same conclusion: they held a memory of how the Great Disruption had come to pass."

Everyone at the table gasped, and Veressa looked down at the glass map. "What we could not agree on," she continued in a subdued voice, "was what to do with the maps. The glass map, in particular, since apart from being a memory map, it was clearly also a tracing map—a lens used to identify and draw other maps. Shadrack believed we should use them for exploration, to discover where the Disruption had taken place. It was his theory that if we followed the maps we would find the *carta mayor*—the fabled water map that shows the living world.

The idea had occurred to both of us; indeed, among cartologers, it would have occurred to anyone. But I," Veressa paused, shaking her head, "I feared the maps would lead to ill. The *carta mayor* is a dangerous legend, and it has led many explorers to disappointment or death. Some say it is an ordinary water map. Some say it has much greater power: that the *carta mayor* does not only show all possible worlds—past, present, and future—but that it also offers the power to change them. A change in the map produces a change in the world. Who knows if such a thing is true, but it hardly matters; the rumor of such power is enough. People believe what they will. I worried about what would happen if the maps fell into the wrong hands."

Martin reached across the table and took his daughter's hand. "Shadrack and I could not resolve our difference of opinion," she said sadly. "And our arguments grew increasingly bitter. I think, beneath it all, we were suffering from guilt. The Lachrima had asked us for help and we had fled. Finally, by way of compromise and out of respect for my wishes, Shadrack agreed to separate the maps as a way of minimizing their potential power. The glass map was a formidable instrument, but alone it could not tell the whole story of the Disruption. I know that he has used it with the utmost wisdom, relying on its excellent quality to draw exquisite maps of his own. He has only used the tracing glass to add knowledge to the world of cartology, and he has tried to keep its existence hidden. Nevertheless, its reputation has traveled. Even here, I heard rumors of what came to be known as the 'Polyglot Tracing Glass.' It was inevitable that as its reputation grew, so would covetous explorers and cartologers seek to find it. The other three maps were mere stage scenery without the glass layer. I kept them.

"Shadrack and I parted on bad terms. He wrote to me only once, to tell me that he had returned to Talisman's home, but the man's mind was past repair. Shadrack freed the Lachrima, who fled at once, and brought Talisman to Nochtland, where he settled him in a convent hospital. From time to time I visit. He is like a child now—lost in some private world which the rest of us cannot see. But Shadrack I never heard from again—until now." She smiled wanly at Sophia. "And so, with you, the glass map returns to Nochtland."

"But where are the other three, my child?" Martin demanded. "I have never seen such maps here."

Veressa sighed. "They are in the library safe. The four maps are together in the same place once more."

24
Into the Sand

1891, June 26: Shadrack Missing (Day 6)

Arboldevela: A term to describe the arbol de vela, or sailing tree, a vehicle powered by wind and used to navigate both on land and on water. Early models were developed for the court of Leopoldo. Stored wind-power generated by the sails is used to propel the vehicle with woven wheels that convert to paddle wheels when used in water. Common in the Triple Eras and the northern periphery.

—From Veressa Metl's Glossary of Baldlandian Terms

Shadrack knew that they would soon be abandoning the train, because all morning the Sandmen had been packing Blanca's belongings. He tried to keep his mind on the task at hand. He had rapidly transferred his memories into the rectangular sheet of copper, and now the painstaking work of ordering and manifesting those memories into a map had begun. Shadrack leaned over the copper sheet with a magnifying glass, studying the pattern of oxidation he had created. His tools—a microscope, an array of small hammers and chisels, a case full of vials with colored liquids, and a brazier with cold, ashy coals—lay around him on the table. Weeping stood by, watching Shadrack's progress with studied patience. The two had hardly exchanged another word, but Weeping had somehow communicated their lie to Blanca, and she had not returned.

Shadrack estimated that the train had almost reached the border of the Baldlands. He had no notion where Blanca would go once the rails ended. His time was running short; he would have to make his attempt to flee soon.

As he scraped gently at the metal sheet, the door suddenly opened. Blanca entered, followed by four Sandmen. "We are leaving the Bullet," she announced. "Your niece has boarded a ship called the *Swan* in New Orleans, and the ship's destination is Veracruz." It sounded as if she was smiling. "So we are heading south. When we reach the border, we will board a boldevela and travel to Veracruz."

Shadrack deliberately did not acknowledge her. "I give you this information as a courtesy," Blanca added, "and so that you are assured of being soon reunited with your niece. Your map of the *carta mayor's* location should be ready just in time." Her attention turned to the copper map. "Have you completed it?"

"Not quite," Shadrack said quickly.

"Let me see it," she said.

"I would like to finish it before you read it."

Blanca reached across the table and picked up the map. "A match, Weeping."

Weeping hesitated only a moment before drawing a matchbox from his jacket pocket. He lit a match and held it before him. Blanca held the map to the flame, then set it down on the table; its entire surface swarmed with inscrutable drawings. She quickly pulled off one of her gloves and placed her fingertips on the copper surface. Shadrack was tense with anticipation.

For several seconds she stood motionless; then she pulled her hand away from the map as if burned. "This cannot be its location, because this place no longer exists. *How do you know this place?*" she whispered. "*Tell me how you know it!*" The fear and anger coursed through her words and into the room, palpable and overwhelming. Weeping winced and stumbled backward.

Shadrack felt the rush of blood in his ears as he rose abruptly from his chair. "I would ask you the same," he shot back, trying to stay calm. The sound of her voice alone was enough to make the steadiest heart skip a beat.

"*How do you know this place?*" She nearly choked on her scream.

Clearly, even Weeping had never seen Blanca in such a state. The other men stared at her in terror, paralyzed. "I have been there," Shadrack said evenly. "And so have you."

"*You lied to me,*" Blanca wailed, charging around the table. "*You deceived me.*"

"I said I would draw you a map."

She strode toward him, her fury spilling forth like flames from a burning house, and for a moment Shadrack believed she was going to throw herself upon him. She stopped, her veiled face inches from his; he expected any moment to feel the force of her exploding anger. Then suddenly she shrank visibly, as if the fire had been doused, and Shadrack heard nothing but ragged breaths. The veil shook before his face. "I see how you are, now," she said, her voice trembling. "You are cruel. Impossibly cruel to remind me of that place. How could you?"

"I did not intend to be cruel," Shadrack said. His voice was earnest but firm. "I intended to show you that I understand." He stared into the veil. "If you would but let them see the map," he added softly, "they would understand as well."

Blanca turned suddenly, electrified. "Who else knew of this?"

The Sandmen shook their heads. Weeping looked at her with fire in his eyes and said nothing.

"What did he tell you he would draw?" Blanca demanded.

"He said he would explain my name. The origin of the weeping. I wish to understand the truth," Weeping added firmly—perhaps recklessly.

She stared at him in silence. When she spoke again, her voice had changed. "You wish to understand the truth, of course," she said quietly, almost sweetly. "How foolish I was to leave you untrained so long, Weeping. You will understand the truth, certainly." She turned to Shadrack. "And *you* will understand the cost of deceiving me. You may save yourself by being indispensable, but you cannot save anyone else." She stepped quickly around the desk and motioned to the petrified men who stood pressed against the wall. "Bring them," she said brusquely, motioning at Weeping and Shadrack.

Weeping and Shadrack were each half carried, half dragged into the adjoining car. The wheelbarrow that Shadrack had heard so many times stood against the corner wall. In the middle of the car was an hourglass the size of a grown man. It rested on its side, suspended within a circular metal track. Each chamber of the hourglass was made of petal-shaped sheets of glass, soldered along the edges. One chamber was closed and filled with sand. The other chamber was empty and open, one of the petals opening outward like a delicate door. Shadrack realized immediately what was about to happen. "No," he cried, trying to shake himself free. "You will gain nothing by doing this."

"You have lost your chance to negotiate with me," Blanca said coldly. Then she addressed the Sandmen: "The bonnet and jacket."

"His memories are useless to you!"

Weeping had stopped struggling. He stood stoically, his gaze turned inward, as if contemplating a distant memory. His fingers rested lightly on the amulet around his neck. Two Sandmen forced him into a straitjacket that wound his arms around his body, lacing it tightly closed behind him. A helmet of canvas and wood was placed over his head, covering his eyes. Then they thrust the wooden block in his mouth and pulled the wires up and through the helmet.

"If you do this," Shadrack said, his voice hard, "I will not lift a finger to help you."

"I believe you will feel differently when it is your niece who wears the bonnet," said Blanca. Shadrack froze. "I am merely giving you a demonstration here. Remember, Shadrack. It is not I who made this happen—it is you. You leave me no choice."

The Sandmen pushed Weeping into the empty chamber. He lay awkwardly, face-up, his knees pulled in toward his chest.

Shadrack could see the metal wires of the bonnet straining against his skin. The Sandmen fastened the glass door. Then they rotated the hourglass upright so that Weeping lay, crushed and helpless, in the bottom chamber. The sand began to pour down upon him. Weeping struggled to breathe. His composure left him. He began kicking uselessly at the glass, battering his head against it. But he succeeded only in cutting his cheeks, and blood mixed with the sand.

"That's enough, pull him out!" Shadrack shouted. "You've made your point." He struggled to free himself, but the other Sandman pinned his arms behind his back. He watched as Weeping writhed ever more helplessly and the sand funneled on steadily, inexorably.

"You may turn it back now," Blanca finally said.

The two Sandmen rotated the hourglass once again, so that Weeping was carried high up over their heads and the sand that had engulfed him began to pour back into the other chamber. They all waited silently. Weeping no longer struggled. He lay inert.

"Take him out," Blanca said, when the chamber had emptied. She watched, arms crossed, as the Sandmen rotated the hourglass to its side, opened the chamber, and caught the buckles of the straitjacket with their grappling hooks to lift Weeping. He was limp as they lowered him on the floor, loosened the straitjacket's laces, and removed the bonnet and the wooden block. He lay with his eyes closed. Two long, bloody lines stretched from his mouth to his ears.

"How much has he lost?" Shadrack asked numbly. "Will he be like Carlton?"

The train suddenly came to a halt, and the Sandmen shifted into action. "We've reached the border," Blanca said. "Unload the trunks and the contents of the study. I need twenty minutes to convert this sand. Do not disturb me until I am through." Then she addressed Shadrack. "From Carlton I took everything. But Weeping will be like these others," she said coolly. "Unburdened of most of their memories, but still conscious men. Still remembering dimly with some part of their minds what it means to be a Nihilismian. To mistrust the reality of the world, to believe in that which is unseen, and to pursue it blindly. My Sandmen," she added, almost affectionately, as she looked down at Weeping. Then she turned and left the compartment.

25
THE ROYAL LIBRARY

1891, June 28: 13-Hour 48

Vineless: A derogatory term used particularly among the inhabitants of Nochtland to describe someone who is considered pitiful, weak, or cowardly. Part of the family of words derived from the phrase "Mark of the Vine," to designate those who are physiologically marked by botanical matter.

—From Veressa Metl's Glossary of Baldlandian Terms

SOPHIA STILL COULD not believe that she had carried something so precious in her pack for so may days: not simply a tracing glass, but a memory map of the Great Disruption! Now she was certain that Montaigne and the Nihilismians wanted to use it to find the *carta mayor,* and Veressa was inclined to agree.

Veressa had offered to show them the other maps, so they had all gone to the palace library, where she retrieved them from the safe. The tracing glass could not be used because it was still day, but even reading the other three maps together was overwhelming. Each of them took a turn with the layered maps that possibly told the story of the Great Disruption, and each came away silent, lost in the past. Sophia struggled to match the three parts she had just seen with her memories of the glass map. *How do they all fit together?* she wondered.

Veressa returned the three maps to the library safe and led them back through the palace. The floors were stone tile, covered by thick carpets of fresh petals or leaves. As they walked along a corridor strewn with fragrant pine needles, Sophia heard a light tinkling sound, like the ringing of glassy bells, and she was surprised to see Veressa hurry to the wall and kneel. Martin followed suit, lowering himself carefully on his bad leg. "Everyone kneel by the wall," Veressa whispered urgently. Calixta, Burr, and Sophia did as they were told, though it struck her that all of them—the pirates particularly—looked very odd. They were not the kind of people who bowed to anyone.

The tinkling sound grew louder, and then Sophia saw a slow procession round the corner. It was made up of women dressed in pale green silks that trailed to the floor, their skirts adorned with glass bells; orchids studded their elaborately dressed hair.

One woman wore her hair long and loose. It was bright green—the shade of an uncut meadow—and grew to her waist. Folded down across her back were what appeared to be two long eucalyptus leaves that grew from her shoulder blades. They were wings.

"Greetings, Royal Botanist," Princess Justa said, "Royal Librarian." She had the same accent as Veressa and Martin—sharp, with rolled *r*'s—but her tone was high and imperious, as if she spoke from a great height.

Veressa and Martin murmured their greetings without raising their eyes from the floor. Calixta and Burr, Sophia noticed, were staring straight ahead—neither at the floor nor at the royal entourage. Sophia could not help herself; she looked directly at the princess. Justa's gaze traveled over the small group and finally rested on Sophia, who felt a chill as the princess looked her over disdainfully from head to foot—or, rather, from head to knee. "What are *those*?" she asked icily.

Everyone in the hallway turned to stare. The princess's attendants seemed to gasp in unison, and an alarming tinkling of bells ensued as they scuttled to the opposite wall. "I'm sorry?" Sophia said, more meekly than she intended to.

"In your ears," the princess demanded.

Sophia's hand flew up to her right ear. "Oh," she said. "My earrings." She looked at Veressa anxiously and was alarmed to see her vexed expression.

"Silver, if I'm not mistaken," the princess said. She was smiling, but there was no mirth in her smile.

"Yes," Sophia admitted.

The princess looked coldly at Veressa. "We are surprised at the guests you choose to bring into the palace," she said. "If we did not know you better, we would ask you to answer for your intentions. This royal family has been relentlessly persecuted, our own mother a victim of the iron conspiracy, and we continue to survive only by the strictest vigilance. Is it your wish to expose us to danger?"

"Do not doubt my intentions, Highness. She is only a child—and a foreigner," Veressa said respectfully, without looking up. "She meant nothing by it."

A long pause ensued, while the waiting women fussed and their many bells tinkled. "We will trust your judgment in this matter," Justa said finally, "but consider this a warning. Clearly you must be reminded that the Mark of Iron are baseless creatures. The dungeons of this palace are filled with cowards who have attempted to destroy us, from without and from within. Sending a child to do their work is precisely the kind of attack they would attempt."

Veressa murmured an apology. The princess lifted her head, took a step forward, and moved on, the glassy tinkling fading as the procession disappeared around the corner.

All five of them rose to their feet. "I'm so sorry, Veressa!" Sophia cried. "I didn't think!"

"My dear, you've done nothing wrong," Martin told her.

"Of course she hasn't! It is absolutely absurd," said Veressa, as she strode down the corridor. "The level of fanaticism and intolerance that has taken hold of this royal family. Imagine objecting to a pair of silver earrings."

"Good thing we've kept our swords and revolvers hidden," Calixta said cheerfully.

Veressa and Martin stopped in their tracks. *"You didn't!"* Veressa asked in a whisper. Martin glanced in either direction, as if the walls might have overheard.

"We never leave them behind," Burr said firmly. "And they are *very* well-hidden."

"You would certainly be arrested if the guards discovered them! My father and I would be unable to intervene. Indeed, they might well arrest us as well, and we would all be joining those poor fools in the dungeons."

"I'm sorry, Veressa," Calixta put in. "But we've always brought them when we come to see you. Why should it be any different now?"

"I had no idea," Veressa said, her voice tense and quiet. "You've been running an extraordinary risk. The palace is even more guarded than usual because of the eclipse festivities in two days and the weirwind that is moving north."

The pirates exchanged glances. "We should leave," Burr said. "Our apologies for having placed you in danger."

Veressa sighed. "No, *I'm* sorry," she said regretfully. "The situation is ridiculous, and I am embarrassed on behalf of the princess—embarrassed that we make ourselves so inhospitable. Please stay at least until tomorrow. For your own sakes, I won't urge you to stay through the eclipse, but it's much too late to leave today."

Martin shook his head with exasperation. "They shouldn't have to leave at all. But I agree that it will be safer if you do," he had to admit.

Sophia silently removed her earrings as they returned to the royal botanist's apartments. Justa's suspiciousness worked through the five of them like a poison—they could not seem to agree on what to do next. They agreed that finding Shadrack was essential and discussed how to handle Montaigne and the Sandmen, but formulating a plan without any real knowledge of who and where they were proved impossible. They were stymied.

Sophia listened, but her mind kept drifting to the four maps. Something about them unsettled her, demanding her concentration like a riddle, worming this way and that, elusive and urgent. Their memories were so detailed and so real that she could have sworn they were her own—but, of course, that was how memory maps worked. As the others talked around and around in circles, Sophia tried to work out the riddle by drawing in her notebook. She found no solution.

Her thoughts continued through dinner—maize cakes and squash flower—and later, in bed, she searched Shadrack's atlas for something that would help. But the more she read, the more obscure the riddle seemed, and nothing explained why the memories from the four maps seemed so strangely familiar. She finally turned to the bedroom bookshelf for distraction and saw a volume titled *Lives of the Nochtland Royals.*

There was little about Princess Justa's early years. By contrast, the story Mazapán had told of the princess's death took up several pages—especially because he had not described the terrible consequences.

THE EMPEROR DISCOVERED, BY THE vital assistance of his advisors, that a pair of brothers with the Mark of Iron had cunningly disguised their metal and risen to positions of prestige. Elad and Olin Spore would not confess, no matter how rigorous the interrogation, but it was speculated that

> they had placed the orchids on purpose to poison the empress and then prey upon the weakened emperor. If this was their plan, they were sorely disappointed. Far from weakening, the emperor sentenced them both to death. Then he scoured the court for any others with the Mark of Iron, and he finally sought comfort in the Religion of the Cross, though he had never before been a believer. The court was reduced to only a few close advisors, and the emperor ordered greater and greater penalties for those who wore or used metal of any kind. And yet it was never known for certain who had poisoned the empress. Some months after her death, the emperor began his prolonged and noble quest to conquer the far reaches of his territory.

Sophia sighed. It was no wonder, she reflected, that Princess Justa showed such intolerance.

—19-Hour 27—

SOPHIA AWOKE LATE in the night to find the room entirely dark. She could hear Calixta breathing from the other bed, but that had not awoken her. It was her dream, she realized. She had been dreaming about the four maps. They had all returned to the library as soon as the moon had risen, and though considering the four maps together had yielded no new answers, something about them had stayed with her and worked its way into her dreams. She bolted upright and fumbled for her pack, which was lying beside her pillow; then she thrust the atlas into it and strapped it over her shoulder before scurrying down the short ladder. She stepped into her slippers and hurried out of the bedroom, quietly opening and closing the door behind her.

As she shuffled along the dark corridor she became aware of the night noises around her: crickets in the patio; the murmuring of the garden's fountains from beyond the walls; the quiet tinkling of the wind chimes, delicate and high-pitched or thrumming and deep. Sophia was surprised to see the door of Martin's workroom open and light streaming out of it. *Perhaps it is not as late as I think,* she considered, reaching for her pocket watch. It was past nineteen-hour. Curious, she peered into the laboratory.

Plants crowded the wooden work surfaces and hung from every inch of the ceiling. Glass canisters filled with soil were clustered beside tall flasks of blue water and tiny green dropper bottles. Martin was on a stool, examining something through his enormous spectacles. Sophia was astonished to see on the table what looked like a wooden leg with Martin's sock and shoe at the end of it. His left pant leg was entirely empty from the knee down. "Martin?" she asked tentatively.

He jumped in his seat. "Sophia!" he said. "How you startled me." He removed his spectacles. "What are you doing up?"

"I was having a nightmare," Sophia said, unsure herself of what the dream had contained.

"Ah well—it happens. Strange place and strange doings." He

noticed that she was staring at the leg. "Oh! You hadn't seen my prosthesis."

She shook her head, embarrassed that he had caught her staring but relieved that he seemed not to mind. "I didn't—Is it made of wood?"

Martin took up the leg and looked at it critically. "Indeed, it is made of wood. Brittle, lifeless wood, I'm afraid."

"What happened to your real leg?" Sophia asked. "Your previous leg, I mean."

He winked at her. "I lost it adventuring. Before I was old," he said, putting down the wooden leg, "and before I had a limp, and before I was a botanist—I was an explorer!"

"You were?" Sophia exclaimed, delighted.

"I was. Not a very good explorer, as it happens. In a remote region of the northern Baldlands, I discovered a valley full of strange animals."

"What kind of animals?"

"Enormous beasts—some as large as the conservatory! They were clearly from another Age. Well, I foolishly believed myself to be safe among them because I observed that they ate only plants—not flesh. But," he said, smiling ruefully, "I had failed to consider that to them I probably looked like a plant."

"What do you mean?"

Martin lifted his right pant leg. His shin was a strange color—whitish green, like the trunk of a beech tree. "You see, my legs are more tree trunk than muscle and bone."

"I had no idea!" Sophia thought of the "sequins" on Veressa's arms: living thorns, just like Martin's living trunk of a leg.

"Nor did I have any idea that I would so closely resemble a tasty sprig!" Martin laughed. "I was happily taking notes when one of the beasts suddenly reached its huge head down, toppled me over with a little nudge, and bit off my foot!"

"Oh, how horrible!" Sophia exclaimed.

"It was not picturesque," Martin admitted. "Fortunately, I was not traveling alone, and my companions helped me to safety. When I returned home, a fine sculptor created this wooden leg for me. I still have a limp," he said, "and I could no longer be an explorer. But in fact I am grateful to that giant beast. Were it not for him, I would never have discovered botany."

Sophia had to smile. "I suppose that's true."

"I hope I haven't given you more nightmares."

"No, I don't think so," she said, turning to go. "Are you going to work all night?"

"Just a little bit longer. I'll see you in the morning. Sleep well."

Fortunately, Sophia's erratic inner clock did not affect her inner compass. Although the palace was very dark and she had only been to the library once, she had no difficulty finding her way. The pine needles covering the floor muffled her footsteps entirely.

Sophia checked to make sure she was alone, then slipped quietly through the double doors into the deserted, dimly lit room.

Earlier, her attention had been so focused on the four maps that she had not even thought to look around. The high bookshelves were interrupted by six tall windows that looked out over the gardens, letting in the pale, silvery moonlight; a narrow spiral staircase led to a balcony that ran the length of the shelves. Shadows clustered in the corner of the ceiling, beyond the reach of the dim table lamps.

She crossed the carpet of fern leaves to the wooden safe where Veressa kept Talisman's maps; she had shown Sophia how it worked, the door made of intricate movable pieces, like a puzzle. Taking out the maps, she pulled up a chair and used her breath, as well as the water and matches left on the desk, to awaken the first three maps. Then she held the final map, the tracing glass, to the moonlight and rested it on top of the others.

As soon as she touched it, the memories again flooded her mind. The recollection of fleeing, full of fear, through the crowds of people was unchanged. But the other maps added a complexity that was almost transformative. The metal map, which allowed her to see the manmade structures around her, brought memories of being inside an impossibly tall pyramid. The long spiral wound its way up to the high peak. The walls around her were made of something almost transparent, like frosted glass. *No,* Sophia corrected herself: *foggy glass, because parts are entirely clear.* There were colored panes, like artwork, on the walls, but she could not see them clearly; whoever the map's memories belonged to had rushed past them, intent on escape. When she reached the top of the pyramid, she saw the heavy object that she would soon roll off the ledge: a round stone. She took the final steps to the top, heaved against the stone, and pushed. She did not see it land, but she felt its impact as the walls around her began to shudder.

The clay map allowed her to see the landscape beyond the high tower—a vast terrain marked by high peaks and what looked like tall white buildings. And the cloth map showed strange weather unlike any she'd ever seen. Lightning flashed continually beyond the walls of the pyramid, illuminating the gray sky. A constant snow fell, ticking against the foggy panes.

But this was not what Sophia wanted to see most. She waited, and then the memory came: she burst out through the doorway onto a snowy expanse and turned to watch as the entire pyramid collapsed in an explosive burst of breaking panes and clouds of snow. Then she turned away and looked into the distance, where something almost out of sight—a black speck on the snow—moved toward her. It seemed like a person. As it drew nearer, there was a dull twinkle from something the person was holding. And then the memory faded.

Sophia was certain—certain beyond a doubt—that she knew that person. There was something about the way they ran toward her. Or perhaps it was simply the feeling—the certainty in the map's memory—of knowing who they were. What was the glint in their hand? Something they were holding, surely—a mirror? A blade? A watch? It could be almost anything. She opened her eyes with a sigh, steeling herself to read the map once again.

"You really like libraries, don't you?"

Sophia was on her feet in an instant, scanning the room. "Who's there?" she whispered.

Someone moved in the shadows near the door. She heard a low chuckle, and then time came to a sudden halt as the figure stepped into the yellow light of the table lamp.

It was Theo.

26
Of Both Marks

1891, June 29: # hour

Weirwind: A weather phenomenon common in the northern Baldlands. Thought to have originated after the Great Disruption, the weirwind is the subject of numerous legends. Some maintain that the weirwinds "speak." Scientific observers have found no evidence of this; they describe solid walls formed by continuous winds of varying strengths. The strongest weirwind on record was five miles wide and covered four hundred miles in ten days.

—*Veressa Metl's* Glossary of Baldlandian Terms

Sophia stared at Theo, her heart pounding; but no matter how hard she looked at him, it was not enough. Only a day had passed, yet it seemed much longer. He still wore Shadrack's clothes—rumpled and a bit dusty—and the scuffed boots he had taken from the shoemaker in Boston. His expression was untroubled, his smile as impudent as always. "What are you doing here?" she whispered.

"Not happy to see me then?" Theo asked, sitting down comfortably in one of the chairs.

Sophia flushed. "I asked what you were doing here. And how did you get in?"

"They don't guard the whole length of the wall—mainly just around the gates."

Part of her wanted to step forward and touch him—to know that he was really back; part of her felt the surging sense of injury and uncertainty that seemed to well up whenever Theo was around. "I just don't understand," she finally said.

"I couldn't very well abandon you to those pirates, could I?" he replied with a grin.

"I wish you were one-tenth as reliable as those pirates." Her voice was dangerously unsteady.

"I'm reliable," he protested. "I'm here, aren't I?"

"But you left. Why didn't you just come in with us at the gate? Why did you have to sneak in? You could get in trouble. The people here—other than Veressa and Martin—are not friendly."

Now it was Theo's turn to stare. "You found Veressa?"

"Yes. This is her library," Sophia said, dropping her voice to a whisper once more as Theo looked around. "She's the royal librarian and court cartologer. Her father is the royal botanist. He's known Burr and Calixta for years."

Theo gave a low whistle. "Does she know where your uncle is?"

Sophia shook her head, unable to meet his eyes.

"Well, it's a good thing you found her anyhow," he said, his voice acquiring a new tone. "Are Calixta and Burr still here?"

"Didn't you see them?"

"No. I just got over the palace walls last night. I came through this thing like a greenhouse over to the side. I saw you walking along the corridor, so I followed you."

"Last night?"

Theo turned to the windows. "Look. It's nearly dawn."

Sophia scrambled for her watch. He was right; it was almost six-hour. The sense of confusion and uncertainty at seeing Theo still coursed through her, making their conversation seem odd and staged. The words she wanted to say and the questions she wanted to ask flitted, trapped and unspoken, through her mind. *What scared you off? Was it me? Something else? Were you always planning to come back? Are you going to leave again?*

"Where are you and the pirates staying?"

"Right by the greenhouse, with Veressa and her father—Martin."

"Well, you have to talk to them." His voice was unusually grave.

"Why? What's wrong?"

"That thing moving north that everyone's talking about—it's not a weirwind."

"What is it?" Sophia asked, her anxiety building.

"The raiders I met up with on the road saw thousands of birds flying north, full pace. I didn't believe them at first, but then I saw them, too. Birds don't do that with weirwinds."

"But then, what is it? What's happening?"

As Theo was about to answer, they heard the heavy tread of the palace guards patrolling the halls. He swiftly rose from his chair, keeping his eye on the door. "Tell Burr and Calixta about the birds," he whispered. "I don't have time to explain the rest, and I can't stay here. If you meet me outside the city gates in an hour, I'll tell you all everything. Bring your stuff with you so we can leave."

"*Leave?*" Sophia sprang to her feet and gathered up the four maps—forgetting that three of them were not hers to take—and shoved them hastily into her pack. "Why don't you just tell me now?"

"I'll meet you outside the gates," Theo said, eyes still on the door. The sound of footsteps was fading.

"Tell me now. Just in case."

Theo slowly turned and met her eyes. He wore a curious expression, one Sophia had never seen on his face before. She realized with astonishment that she had hurt his feelings. "You really don't trust me."

Sophia didn't know what to say, because he was right. She wanted to believe him; she partly believed him—but how could she? Everything about him was uncertain and unpredictable. It was just as likely that he would vanish again, as he had at the gates of Nochtland. "I'm sorry," she whispered. "But I never know what you're going to do."

He stared at her for several seconds and then gave a quick sigh. "Is there somewhere I can hide while you all get ready to leave?"

Sophia was caught off guard by his change of mind. "Yes," she said after a moment. "We'll be safe with Veressa and Martin."

"All right," he said, tipping his head toward the door. "Let's go, then."

They moved quickly and quietly over the fern carpet, and, after checking the corridor, into the hallway. She made sure to shut the door behind her. As they hurried back to the botanist's residence, she kept watch ahead, and he behind. Fortunately, they met no one.

As they tiptoed along the open corridor of Martin and Veressa's home, Sophia noticed that the lights were on in the kitchen. "Someone's already up," she whispered.

They found Martin preparing an elaborate breakfast at the tiled fireplace that served as both stove and oven. He looked up as Theo and Sophia walked in. "Hello! What's this?"

"Martin, this is Theo," Sophia said hurriedly. "He traveled to Nochtland with me from New Occident. And he has something urgent to tell us all about the weirwind moving north."

Theo nodded. "It's not a weirwind."

Martin took in their words. "Best wake the others, then," he said matter-of-factly, wiping his hands on his apron.

—1891, June 29: 6-Hour 33—

"THEO!" CALIXTA EXCLAIMED as she walked into the kitchen. "Where did you spring from?" Sophia, while quickly changing out of her robe, had encountered some difficulty in persuading Calixta to leave the bedroom without her usual lengthy toilette, but the pirate captain had risen to the occasion.

"I've been here all along," Theo said, raising his eyebrows and dodging the question. "Not my fault if you didn't notice."

Calixta laughingly threw her arm around him and kissed his cheek. "We're glad to have you back, even if you are such a scoundrel. You ran off without explanation and left us quite heartbroken," she scolded, glancing at Sophia.

Sophia flushed. "Where's Burr?"

Martin was putting the finishing touches on their breakfast when a sleepy-looking Burr walked in. "Ah, Molasses, I missed you. Where have you been, you imp? Why did you leave us?" He enfolded Theo in a hug.

"Pay wasn't good enough," Theo replied, hugging him back.

"I forbid you to leave us stranded again, Molly. Look at us. We've had to rely on our wits and see where it's landed us—some impoverished hole in the wall where they don't even feed us properly." He reached for one of the round, yellow cakes that Martin was pulling from the oven.

"Well, I've come to save you," Theo said, straight-faced.

"Veressa, this is Theo," Sophia said to Veressa, as she joined them.

Theo gave a slight bow. "Theodore Constantine Thackary."

Veressa extended her hand. "Do I understand correctly that you entered the palace in secret? Unimpeded?"

"Right over the wall."

"I cannot believe the guards did not see you," she said, with some alarm. "I mean, I hope they didn't. Did they?"

"I don't think so. But even if they'd seen me, I had to come. I'm here to tell you that you have to get out of the city." He had remained standing as the kitchen filled with people, and now his impatience made itself even more apparent. "*As soon as you can.*"

"Tell us what you saw, Theo," Sophia urged.

"I was taking the road north, see, the one that lies west of Nochtland. I met up with some raiders there yesterday morning—ones I know from home. They said they'd seen birds migrating north. Which made no sense, because it's not the right time for that. And the birds weren't in flocks—they were just flying, thousands of them, all kinds, together." Martin had been serving breakfast, but one by one they put down their forks and lost all interest in their food.

"A weirwind wouldn't cause the birds to migrate north like that," Veressa said slowly.

"That's right. That's what we said. And then we heard from one of the travelers on the road about the Lachrima."

"What about the Lachrima?" Sophia asked. Only Martin continued steadily eating his eggs.

"He said there's an Age, far to the south. An unknown Age, populated entirely by Lachrima." Everyone other than Martin stared at Theo. "And now they're marching north."

After a long silence interrupted only by the sound of Martin chewing, Sophia spoke. "That doesn't make sense. Veressa told us yesterday, Theo," she said, "that the Lachrima were born along the edges of the Disruption. They are made by the border itself."

"What are you getting at, Sophia?" asked Burr.

"The thing is," she said, thinking aloud, "it seemed strange that no one knew about the Lachrima in New Occident. Of course they would be in the Baldlands, if they were made along the borders and borders were *everywhere* in the Triple Eras." She paused. "But why would all these Lachrima suddenly appear?"

"I told you," Theo said. "They live in this southern Age and they've decided to march north."

"But that doesn't seem right. Everything I've heard is that the Lachrima aren't like that. They don't move around together; they're solitary—aren't they?"

"That's true," Veressa agreed.

"What if—" Sophia thought of Veressa's and Mrs. Clay's stories, Shadrack's note, the distant memory of reading maps in the hidden room of 34 East Ending. And then two images sprang into focus—the maps of the East Indies she had read on the day that Shadrack disappeared: one with the memories of a quiet convent; the other, drawn a decade later, showing nothing but a deadly stillness. "What if an Age south of here suddenly changed, and a new border appeared?" And then she said: "*That's* where the Lachrima are coming from—the new border."

Everyone except Martin looked at her in surprise.

"I see what you mean," Veressa exclaimed. "If we agree that the Lachrima are ordinary people transformed by the sudden appearance of a new border, the appearance of such a border would make itself apparent by the sudden emergence of Lachrima. Yes, that could be it."

There was silence at the table. Martin put down his knife and fork, drank the last of his coffee, and energetically cleared his throat. "Well," he said, loudly. It was the first time he had spoken since they had all gathered in the kitchen. "I believe this is where I come in." The group turned to looked at him. "Young Theo is right. We should leave the palace—and the city. And, you, my dear," he said to Sophia, "are also right." He pushed his chair back and slapped the table dramatically. "And I have a piece of proof to offer each of you." He removed two small glass containers from his pockets. They both appeared to hold soil. "I finally looked up the coordinates for the island, Burton," he said, "and I realized why it seemed odd when you first gave me the sample. This," he said, holding up the glass container in his right hand, "is a sample of remarkable manmade soil that Burr brought me yesterday. It was collected on a very small island some fifty miles off the eastern coast of Late Patagonia. This," he said, holding up the other container, "is a sample of twenty-first age soil that he brought me nearly a year ago. What I did not realize until late last night is that these samples are *taken from the same island*."

It took a moment for them to grasp the significance. "You mean the soil on the island changed," Sophia said. She knew then, without any doubt, that she was right; the maps of the Indies *had* shown two different Ages.

Veressa gasped. "Good heavens, Father—not only are there new borders, but the borders are moving!"

The table erupted with questions. "Yes," Martin said over the din, "we don't know how or why or to what effect, but the borders are indeed moving. I had thought it might be an isolated incident, but what Theo says makes it appear far more likely that the shift is a continental one, and that the change is occurring across the entire length of Late Patagonia. If the circumstances were different"—again, he raised his voice to silence the exclamations—"I would not recommend leaving

Nochtland. After all, our best resources for understanding this mystery are here, in my laboratory and," he said to Veressa, "your library. But I am afraid my second bit of proof somewhat changes the possibilities."

To Veressa's obvious confusion, her father gave her an apologetic look and covered her hand with his own. "I am sorry, my dear." Then, to everyone's complete astonishment, he began to roll up his pant legs. "You see," he said, speaking with effort as he bent over, "after my extraordinary experiment yesterday with the morning glory seeds, which Burr and Sophia were fortunate enough to witness, I found myself wondering about the potential of this curious manmade soil." He had rolled up his right pants leg to his knee, and everyone in the kitchen could clearly see the barklike texture of his uninjured leg. "Late last night I had a sudden inspiration," Martin went on, his voice somewhat muffled as began to roll up his left pants leg. "I thought to myself, if it has such immediate and surprising results with a seed, what would it do to a cutting? Or, in this case, a stump?" He straightened up, rather winded by his efforts.

From the knee down, his left leg was solid silver.

"*Father!*" Veressa exclaimed, running to him. "*What have you done?*"

"Unbelievable!" Burr said under his breath.

Sophia tentatively reached out, touching the cold silver of his shin.

"And yes," Martin said ruefully, "I'm afraid it is very real and very permanent. As Sophia and Burr observed, the morning glory threw silver roots. I was not sure whether the stump would grow as a branch or a root, and here we have the answer. It seems I now have one leg with the Mark of the Vine, and one leg with the Mark of Iron." He shook his head and stared down at them. "And I consequently doubt very much whether it is wise for me to stay in the palace."

Veressa sprang to her feet. "No—we must leave as soon as possible." Her voice was calm but quite firm. "You'll stay here and pack our things, while I tell Justa that she must evacuate the city. Then, when I return, we'll leave together."

"We shouldn't go by land," Calixta put in. "The *Swan* will be much quicker."

"I agree," Burr added. "We can sail immediately—it will take us two days to return to Veracruz. All of you are entirely welcome to come with us." He turned to look at Sophia, whose eyes were downcast. "Sophia?"

Sophia folded her hands around the straps of her pack, which at the moment felt indescribably heavy. It seemed the wrong thing to do; she had not expected to leave so soon. Her mind whirled over all that she had learned since arriving in Nochtland. These discoveries were significant, and there was something important to be done. They could not leave—not now. And yet there seemed to be no other choice. "Thank you. I'll go back to the *Swan*, too."

"Then we must prepare." Veressa began clearing the table. But as the rest of them were hurrying out into the courtyard, they heard something unexpected: a heavy knocking on the wooden door separating the botanist's house from the main castle.

27
With an Iron Fist

1891, June 29: 7-Hour 34

Palace Gardens, soil guidelines—

Western Rose garden: import ONLY from the Papal States

Center garden and fountain: native (central Baldlands)

Periphery, juniper bushes: Northern Baldlands, coastal

—Martin's notes on the gardens

"Who is it?" Veressa asked through the closed door that connected with the palace.

"The royal guard requires entry, Miss Metl," a voice replied. "An intruder was seen entering the greenhouses. We need to search your apartments." As the guard finished speaking, a chorus of barking dogs erupted.

Veressa looked at her friends and father with alarm. Martin was hurriedly rolling down his pant legs. "I've only just gotten out of bed. Can't you come back later?"

"I'm sorry. We have orders to search now. If you don't

open the door, we will have to enter forcibly through the greenhouses."

"All right, all right." Her voice was deceptively calm. "Give me just a minute to find my robe."

There was a pause, then a terse reply: "One minute."

Veressa hurried into the courtyard. "All of you—there's no time. Hide in the greenhouses and try to make your way out if you can."

"Certainly not," Burr said indignantly. "Calixta and I will present ourselves when you open the door."

"I can't allow you to put yourselves in danger. Once the dogs get near my father"—who looked away as she gave him a worried glance—"our lives will not be worth protecting."

"Don't be absurd," Calixta said, taking Sophia and Theo each by the arm. "All the more reason for us to stay. I'll hide these two, along with my sword and pistol. Burr, you'll do the same," she said firmly. Burr strode off to his room. "And we'll just make sure they don't search every room. Come with me, sweethearts." Calixta spoke calmly but quickly. "We will answer the door while the two of you wait in this bedroom." She threw her pistol and long sword into one of her open trunks and locked it. "I very much doubt they will want to search the entire place after we are done speaking with them, but if they do, I am sure you will have noticed that this window"—and she pointed—"leads to the gardens."

Sophia and Theo nodded. Calixta straightened up, instinctively reaching for her gun belt before remembering why she did not have it. For a moment, the beautiful pirate looked strangely vulnerable as she let her hand fall against her skirts. She recovered herself quickly. "Back in a moment!"

As soon as she was gone, they pressed their ears to the wood, straining to listen. First they heard Veressa's clear voice as she admitted the guards. There was conversation; Sophia heard a deep voice, but she could not tell how many guards there were. The whining and barking of dogs punctuated their speech. Then what seemed to be Martin's voice launched into a long-winded monologue followed by a brief silence, and then, unexpectedly, a shout. Sophia could not tell whom it came from. A moment later she heard the unmistakable clang of sword on stone. The dogs burst into unrestrained snarls. Sophia and Theo looked at one another in alarm. "Your reliable pirates," he whispered. "I guess on land the quartermaster ignores the captain's orders."

There was an escalating commotion, and then a shot rang out from what must have been Burr's pistol. A moment later, someone came running down the corridor. He tried the door of the bedroom and found it locked. "Open this door!" a voice shouted.

Sophia and Theo made for the window, leaping easily over the sill onto the ground below as the pounding on the door grew more urgent. For a moment they crouched in the flowerbed, looking out into the garden. Sophia clutched her pack to her chest. Behind them, the pounding had turned to battering. "I came in that way," Theo said, pointing. "In the corner behind the bushes, there's a loose bar in the fence."

Sophia noticed a long walkway bordered by bougainvillea hedges that cut diagonally through the garden. "If we go through there, they might not see us."

As they ran, Sophia glanced over her shoulder more than once, but all she could hear was the sound of running water and the chirping of birds. In the shelter of the bougainvillea, it was as if the castle didn't exist at all. Even the glass spires and the high juniper hedges along the garden wall were out of sight.

Guards shouted in a distant part of the garden, but as they reached the end of the path, the sound of rushing water grew louder. They emerged abruptly onto a lawn with a tall stone fountain; mermen and mermaids crowded around its wide bowl, and a great rush of water fell over them in wide arcs. Sophia saw through the mist of the fountain what she'd been hoping: the high juniper bushes at the southeast corner of the garden. They rounded the fountain and rushed toward the junipers. "Where's the opening?" she asked nervously.

Suddenly a shrill whistle, like the distorted cry of a bird, sounded from across the garden. Sophia and Theo turned to see a guard approaching with his spear held high, his cloak fanning out behind him, the feathered mask trembling as he ran. He glided like a bird of prey descending toward its target. Theo pushed at the hedges, searching for an opening. "Here! Here it is," he exclaimed. Taking Sophia's hand, he pulled her through into a narrow space between the bushes and the iron fence. He scrambled at the base of the fence, trying the bars in order to find the loose one. He found it and began wriggling it free.

Sophia pressed her face into the hedge and saw with horror that the guard was only a dozen paces away, his teeth bared with exertion as he closed the distance. "Theo," she said with panic in her voice, "he's coming."

"It's out!" Holding a half-length of iron nearly six feet long, he pushed Sophia through and followed her into the street. They were not a moment too soon. The guard threw himself against the fence, trying furiously but uselessly to squeeze after them, the bird of prey suddenly caught in a cage. His feathers mashed against the iron bars and he glared from behind his mask. Then he stopped struggling—and smiled.

Sophia turned with a sense of foreboding. Another guard towered over her, his spear raised high. For an eternal moment she could not move. His fierce mask had the keen aspect of a raptor, and his bare arm strained as he thrust the spear toward her and Theo with all his might.

And then something inexplicable happened.

Theo shoved out his right hand—a useless gesture of self-defense—and met the head of the spear. The obsidian blade hit his palm and stopped, the force of the blow pushing them both toward the fence. Sophia found herself pressed up against the bars behind Theo, his hand still raised. They stood there, pinned like butterflies, while the guard's eyes blinked in surprise and he continued to strain uselessly against Theo's right hand. Then Theo raised the iron bar in his left and swung, hitting the guard squarely in the ribs. The man groaned, releasing the pressure only slightly, but it was enough. His captives broke free. They ran across the avenue, dodging the spear that flew after them.

They dove into the narrow streets of Nochtland, their feet clattering on the cobblestone. Neither turned to look behind them as they jostled passersby and stumbled over the uneven paving, flying past avenues and side streets. "Here!" Theo shouted at the sight of a narrow alley.

They came to an abrupt halt. Panting heavily, almost unable to hear anything over their own breathing, they strained their ears and waited for any guards who might have followed. "They're not behind us," Theo said, gasping. They searched the alley for a place to hide. As they neared the canal, Sophia saw a stone ledge below one of the bridges. They slid down the steep embankment and crawled with relief onto the damp shelf. Backs to the wall, well hidden from the street above, they sat recovering in the shade.

"Show me your hand," Sophia demanded.

Theo, still catching his breath, placed his right hand palm-up on Sophia's knee. Sophia felt her throat constrict when she saw the raw, bleeding gash. And then, as she had guessed—too late, the moment they stood pinned to the palace walls—she saw the hard metallic glint inside the wound. The iron bones of Theo's hand had stopped the spear.

She understood now why he had tried so hard to stay out of Nochtland, and she understood what a risk he had taken by entering it. Ripping savagely at the seams, she tore off the long sleeves of her cotton shirt, dipped one of them in the canal water, and wiped the blood from the wound. With the other sleeve she bound his hand, tucking the end in over his knuckles. Theo did not complain or resist. He sat with his head against the wall of the bridge and his eyes closed. "It'll close up quickly," he said tiredly. "It always does."

Sophia sat back. She felt tears on her cheeks, and she wiped them roughly away. "I'm sorry I didn't agree to meet you outside the gates this morning," she said, swallowing hard. "I should have trusted you." She wanted to put her arms around him so he would know how sorry she was, but she couldn't bring herself to do it.

Theo smiled, his eyes still closed. "Don't be. No reason to believe a liar." Sophia could not tell if he was joking or not. She held his bandaged hand loosely in her own and sat silently, watching the sparkling water of the canal grow dark as it glided silently under the bridge.

—8-Hour 42: Under the Nochtland Bridge—

THE MORNING PASSED, the traffic overhead on the bridge growing louder. Once her immediate exhaustion passed, Sophia began to feel restless and uncomfortable on the stony ledge below. They could not leave the city without knowing what had happened to Veressa, Martin, and the pirates. Perhaps, Sophia thought, they could ride to Veracruz to enlist the help of the *Swan*'s crew, but the trip there and back would take four days. At that rate, the Lachrima might already be upon them. She checked the time; it was nearly nine by the New Occident clock.

Theo opened his eyes. "Yeah," he said. "We should get going."

"We can't leave without them. For all we know, they're being tried and sentenced for treason."

"I knew you would say that. Ordinarily, I'd argue with you. But we need them if we're going to sail out on the *Swan*. And," he added with a smile, when Sophia grimaced at his selfish logic, "I think we can actually help them."

Sophia had to smile back. "Of course we can," she said, though she sounded more confident than she felt. For a moment, she listened to the water chuckle quietly as it passed under the bridge. "Do you think Justa will evacuate the city?"

"No way. Even if Veressa gets the chance to tell her, Justa won't believe her. They'll probably think it's all part of the great conspiracy by the Mark of Iron. Think about it. Martin's got a silver leg. Burr pulled out his sword and pistol. And there's nothing to prove what I told them about the Lachrima. They're probably all sitting in a dungeon somewhere right now."

"The city will still think it's just a weirwind moving north."

"Yeah, and they'll be waiting for the wind chimes to announce it." Theo gave a derisive snort.

"So if they don't evacuate the city," Sophia thought aloud, "they will still have the eclipse party tomorrow. Martin said it lasts all night. People come from everywhere to attend it." She paused. "*All kinds* of people."

Theo eyed her thoughtfully. "I see what you're thinking. We could sneak in and they might not notice us." He nodded. "Good idea. But we'll need costumes."

"And we need somewhere to stay until then. Maybe we can

stay with Mazapán." Sophia paused. "Unless the guards think to go there."

"They will." Theo flexed the fingers of his injured hand experimentally as he stared out onto the canal. "Do you know where his store is?"

Sophia shook his head. "He described it to me, but he didn't say where it was. We can ask."

They left the safety of the bridge with reluctance, climbing the embankment onto the sunny street filled with pedestrians and horse-drawn carts and boldevelas. Keeping an eye out for guards, they walked toward the city center. Theo asked an old woman selling violets if she knew the store of the chocolate vendor known as Mazapán, and she directed them without hesitation toward a narrow alley a few blocks away. When she saw it, Sophia recognized the awnings and storefront Mazapán had described.

But they were too late. The store was surrounded by guards in long capes and fierce feathered masks. Beside her, Theo drew in his breath. "They're already here," he whispered, surprised.

"But Mazapán didn't *do* anything!"

"They must have arrested Burr and Calixta. Mazapán brought them to Nochtland. They'll have questions for him," Theo said grimly.

"Poor Mazapán." She shook her head and backed into the alley. "We'll have to go somewhere else."

28
Sailing South

1891, June 28: Shadrack Missing (Day 8)

And when it hears your beating heart,
The Lachrima will take apart
Your very peace, your every dream
With its intolerable scream.

—Nochtland nursery rhyme, second verse

THE SMALL CABIN where Shadrack had already spent one day and one night was in many respects similar to a ship's cabin. Two narrow bunk beds were wedged into the walls, across from a round porthole that looked out onto the road as the boldevela sailed along. But unlike a ship, the boldevela took its shape from the massive tree at its center. The cabins were built among the roots, and behind their walls lay the packed dirt that sustained the tree's growth. The rooms smelled of earth, and the occasional root had wormed through the walls. Shadrack could see little else, as the Nihilismians had bound him hand and foot and tossed him onto the upper bunk. At certain moments, as the boldevela met with forceful winds, it took all his strength not to roll off.

The time would have passed with crushing slowness under ordinary circumstances, but for Shadrack it was made worse by his state of mind. Escape now seemed impossible. He had hoped to gain Weeping's trust—perhaps even his assistance. Instead, he had cost Weeping his mind and lost his best possible ally. He was on his own, unable to free himself, in some corner of a ship sailing overland south at incredible speed, and utterly unable to save himself—let alone Sophia.

The Southern Snows were moving north, destroying everything in their path. He strained against the ropes in frustration. For all he knew, the snows had already reached Nochtland. The glaciers would arrive, and the city would vanish, leaving nothing but the footprint of its lakes and canals. Sophia would be gone forever. He lay still for a moment; it would only make him more useless if he assumed the worst. He had to believe there was still time, and he had to find an opportunity for escape.

They had been sailing since boarding the vessel, and Shadrack estimated that they were already well into the Baldlands. Most likely, he assumed, they would not stop until they had arrived in Veracruz. That would be his next opportunity. At whatever cost, he had to break free when they reached the coast.

Toward midday, they came to an abrupt halt. A sound like a distant storm reached him. Moments later, someone came running across the deck and the door slammed open. To his astonishment, a Sandman yanked him from the top bunk and cut his ropes in one savage movement. "Don't just stand there; we need every hand we can get, or we're all dead." Without waiting to see if his prisoner would follow, he turned and ran. After a moment's hesitation, Shadrack bolted from the cabin and hurried along the narrow corridor.

When Shadrack reached the deck, he understood at once the urgency of the situation. The boldevela had almost collided with a sinister-looking weirwind, and all of the Sandmen, their grappling hooks embedded in the hull, were straining to pull the ship back before it was sucked in and destroyed. The entire mast, including the broad green leaves that were its sails, strained toward the weirwind like a young sapling in a storm. The wind howled and groaned as if hungering for prey, drawing the ship into its destructive embrace inch by inch.

Suddenly, he realized that without the boldevela Blanca would have no way to pursue him. *This is my chance,* he thought, lunging toward the rope ladder at the ship's side. The ladder carried him only so far; he dropped the last ten feet, his legs buckling beneath him.

Rolling to his feet, he stumbled and then steadied himself. He headed west, arms pumping, running parallel to the wall of wind, trying to stay far enough away so that he was not drawn toward it, but it was like fighting the tide. He would think he had opened a good distance between himself and the weirwind, but then he would look to his left and realize that he was much closer than he'd thought. As he veered north insistently, his lungs began to feel the pinch of the dry air and exertion. He whirled and ran backward to see if the ship had been destroyed yet; it was still poised as if on the edge of a precipice, hundreds of meters away.

The terrain was dry and flat, with the occasional rocky outgrowth. He did not know how long the weirwind extended or what he would do once he reached the end of it; he only knew that he had to run. Somewhere to the south, Sophia was waiting for him.

He glanced over his shoulder and saw the boldevela, a dark smudge in the distance. Was it his imagination, or was it larger than it had been a moment before? He turned away, and with his failing strength, ran.

29
The Leafless Tree

1891, June 29: 13-Hour 51

Metalmind: a derogatory term used in the Baldlands, especially Nochtland, to describe a person whose mind is "made of metal." The only portion of the human body that can be made of metal, as far as we know, is the skeleton, therefore the term is used not literally but figuratively. To be "metalminded" is to be crass, brutish, violent, or stupid.

—*From Veressa Metl's* Glossary of Baldlandian Terms

SOPHIA AND THEO had walked for more than two Nochtland hours when Sophia spotted the condemned tree. Had they not been so weary of ducking and dodging every time they sighted a palace guard, they might not even have paused. But they were tired, and the city seemed ominously empty of places to take refuge.

The tree stood far from the palace and even the city center. At its base was a wooden sign post with a notice nailed to it: CONDEMNED. ROOT ROT. CITY ORDINANCE 437. SCHEDULED FOR DEMOLITION AUGUST 1. The tree had indeed rotted from the roots up, but the massive trunk still supported the broad, bare branches that reached out over the nearby buildings. A few of the wooden steps spiraling up the trunk hung loose; a few more were missing. The house among its high branches looked forlorn with its broken windows and missing shingles. It had clearly been abandoned for some time.

Sophia and Theo looked at one another. "Do you think it's safe?" she asked.

"If we can get up there, it's safe." Theo put his foot tentatively on the first step. "I'll go up first. As long as it still has a floor, we'll be fine."

Sophia watched anxiously as he climbed. She checked to make sure no one was watching, but fortunately they had reached a less trafficked part of the city, and the only sound came from several blocks away. She lost sight of Theo as he followed the spiraling steps on the other side of the trunk.

"Fine so far," he called down, waving encouragingly. He climbed the final steps to the tree house and then disappeared within.

Sophia stared up nervously, losing all sense of how long he had been inside. Finally Theo leaned out through one of the gaping windows. "It's great! Come on up."

Holding on to the rough trunk with both hands, Sophia carefully scaled the spiral staircase. She was too anxious to appreciate the city views unfolding below her.

"Isn't this *amazing*?" were Theo's first words as she ducked in through the doorway. At first, it was hard to see why. The room was almost empty, apart from a long wooden table and a heavily dented stove with a missing stovepipe. A pair of overturned chairs stood near the staircase to the second floor. But then she saw the windows. Each was a different size and shape, from small squares to enormous diamonds; each offered a magnificent view of Nochtland.

Sophia looked around in awe. "It's beautiful. It must have been even more beautiful before the tree rotted."

Theo raced to the spiral staircase, and she broke off her reverie to follow him. The second floor had slanted ceilings and round windows. A cracked, floor-length mirror leaned against the wall; a lumpy cotton mattress was folded up beside it. "They even left us a place to sleep!"

He kicked open the mattress and sat down on it experimentally. Sophia sank down beside him with relief. For a moment she closed her eyes, grateful for the quiet, and breathed deeply; the air was scented with musty wood. She wanted to curl up on the lumpy mattress and forget about the strange, frightening city that lay beyond the wooden walls. She imagined the house as it must have been, with the green leaves of the living tree and bright yellow curtains fluttering in the breeze and a blue desk by the round window—a perfect place for drawing.

Then, with a sigh, she opened her eyes and looked up at the slanted ceiling. "So what do we need to get into the palace?"

"Costumes. Nice ones. Fancy costumes, and something to cover our faces."

Sophia sat up slowly and opened her pack. "I still have New Occident money," she said. "We could buy some things."

"Show me how much you have." He held out his uninjured

hand for the money. "All right," he said, after counting it. "You stay here and I'll go buy us some things for costumes."

"*What?* No—I'm going with you."

He shook his head. "If we go together, we'll be more recognizable. The guards will be looking for two people. And besides, you stick out. I look like I'm from the Baldlands, but you don't." Sophia looked at him in consternation. Theo took her hand, and when he spoke again his voice was serious. "You know I'll come back."

"I know," Sophia said with frustration. "Of course I know. I just don't want to sit here waiting. What about your hand?"

"It's fine."

"You can't even carry anything with it."

"Yes, I can. Trust me. It'll be safer. And easier."

She shook her head resignedly. "All right."

He got to his feet and stuffed the money into his pocket. "I'd better get going," he said, looking out through one of the round windows. "It's late afternoon, and the stores will start closing."

"How long do you think it will take?" she asked anxiously, standing up too.

"Maybe an hour. It may get dark while I'm gone. I'll try to buy candles," he added, looking around the bare room. Sophia followed him down the spiral staircase to the first floor and then watched him scurry down the trunk of the tree. "Back soon," he called up quietly. She watched him go.

Then she righted the two chairs near the staircase, placing them on either side of the wooden table. Sitting down heavily, she rested her chin in her hand and looked out over the room.

It was not that she disbelieved Theo—not anymore. She knew he planned to return. But any number of things could happen to prevent him from making his way back to the house in the rotting tree. The guards might see him; someone might ask about his hand and find his answer unsatisfactory; the raider from the market might stumble across him again. She sat, and the sky darkened, the time stretching out interminably. What would happen if Theo did not return? The dusk would turn to night, and the whole city would fall asleep, and she would remain in the tree house, waiting. Then the sky would lighten and the day would arrive, and she would have to venture back into the heart of the city and find a way to get past the guards at Mazapán's shop. The very thought of it made her stomach sink. And if she could not get through? All of her money was gone. Even if she could leave the city unseen, she would have no way to buy food, and she would have to walk all the long way to Veracruz to seek help from the crew of the *Swan*. If by some miracle she made it, how would she get back to New Occident? It was nearly July 4; after that, with the borders' closure and the inevitable lines at each entry point, it would be much harder. What if she ended up outside New Occident's borders, stranded? *I'll never make it,* she thought. *I might as well go turn myself in at the palace.*

She checked her watch; Theo had been gone more than two hours. *This is stupid,* she realized. *I'm not making anything better by sitting here agonizing. I need something to* do.

Steeling herself, she opened her pack and took out the maps. She had left the glass map awake, and now she read the maps once, twice, and then a third time. She lingered over the strange apparition that appeared at the end of the memories: a figure holding a shining beacon in its hand as it ran toward her. Each time, it seemed to grow more familiar. *I'll read the maps again,* she thought, *And this time I'll know who it is.* But nothing changed beyond the unnerving sense of familiarity. Sighing, she put the maps aside. There was something about them . . . It was almost as if they were meant for her—that their meaning lay within her grasp. But something was still missing.

Then she opened her notebook, and in the dying light of sunset she drew aimlessly, letting her pencil wander. She found herself tracing the outlines of a familiar face: there was Theo, smiling slyly from the center of the page, almost about to wink. She realized with surprise that it was a fair resemblance. It did not quite capture him, but the likeness was recognizable—far more so than her first attempt after seeing him at the wharf. She flipped back in her sketchbook and compared the two. The haughty boy she had drawn then was entirely unlike the one she had come to know. *Ehrlach disguised him with feathers,* Sophia thought, *and I disguised him with my own idea of what I wanted him to be.*

"Is that me?"

Sophia turned with a start and saw Theo himself, his arms heavily laden, standing in the semi-darkness. "You're back!" she exclaimed, flooded with relief. "You frightened me. I didn't hear you come up."

He laughed and dropped the bundles on the table. "I didn't sneak up on you, honestly. The whole palace guard could have tramped up here and you wouldn't have heard them."

"I'm so glad you're back."

"I took a long time, I'm sorry," Theo said, and it was clear he meant it. "But look at everything I got." He rummaged through one of the packages and pulled out a bundle of white candles. He lit one, dripped wax on the wooden table, and planted the candle there.

"Did anyone see you?"

"I only saw one guard the whole time, and he didn't notice me," Theo said smugly. "I stayed out of the center—got everything in stores farther out. Look at this," he said, pulling out a sage-green cloth that glimmered as if powdered with gold.

Sophia gasped. "It's beautiful—what is it?"

"A long veil. You can just wear it over your head—I'll show you. No one will see your face. And I got you this," he went on, pulling out a pale green gown with slender straps made of vine. "It's probably a little big, so you can use this to adjust it." He showed her a small wooden box with an inlaid design and opened it to reveal a packet of bone needles, a tiny pair of scissors fashioned of obsidian and wood, and four diminutive spools of thread.

"Theo," Sophia breathed. "These things are so beautiful. Did the money I had really buy all this?"

"I kept most of the money. We need it for food, anyway."

It took her a moment to understand. "You stole these things," she finally said.

Theo looked back at her, his dark eyes serious in the feeble light of the candle. "Of course I did. I had to. Why do you think I went alone? The money wouldn't have bought us more than a couple pairs of socks. Do you want to get into the palace or not?"

"I should have known."

"Come on. I *had* to steal these things. We weren't going to get in all dirty, dressed like beggars. There was no choice."

"You could have just *said so*," she snapped. "You could have just said the money wasn't enough and you had to go alone because you were going to steal it."

"Well, I didn't *lie*," Theo replied heatedly. "I *didn't* say the money was enough, and all the reasons I gave for going alone were true. I don't lie to you."

"But if you leave out the truth, it's the same as lying!"

"It was just easier not to explain. You would have argued with me, and I needed to get these things before dark. Come on, let me show you the rest of the stuff. It's great," Theo said in a placating tone.

"All right," Sophia said tightly.

"This is for me," he said. He opened a bulky package and drew out a long black velvet cloak. "Plus some new bandages. And, as much as I hate feathers, that's pretty much all there is for masks. I got these to match, to hide my hand." He showed her a mask covered with brilliant blue plumage, and the gauntlets that would conceal the cotton gauze.

"It's all perfect," Sophia said dispiritedly. "Everything you got."

Theo sat and looked at her across the table. "Don't be mad."

"I just don't understand why you have to lie about everything."

"It's just—I don't know. It's so much easier than explaining every little thing." He turned the mask over in his hands.

"But you lie about things that aren't little. Like what happened to your parents."

"Well, yeah. I don't like being pinned down."

"Pinned down?"

"You know what I mean. If you tell someone everything, it's like putting yourself right in their hands. If you lie, you keep the options open—nobody ever has the whole picture of you."

Sophia shook her head. "So you never tell the truth?"

"No, I do. I tell you the truth."

She rolled her eyes. "Sometimes."

"I do," Theo insisted. "About the important things, I do."

"Why? What's the difference?"

He shrugged. "I don't know—with you I don't mind."

She looked at the flickering candle. "You didn't tell me why you couldn't go into Nochtland."

"I should have, I know. But you could have asked me. You can ask me anything."

"All right," Sophia said. "Tell me about your hand. How did you find out about the Mark of Iron? You told Calixta you hurt it when your house fell apart. I'm guessing that's not true."

Theo turned so that he was facing the pile of clothes on the table. "Sure, I'll tell you *the truth* about it," he said, grinning.

"But first, let's eat." He produced a loaf of bread, a bottle of milk, and a basket of figs. "I actually paid for these."

Sophia smiled. "Thanks. That makes it taste a lot better."

He lit another candle and pushed the clothing aside. Sophia had once again forgotten how much time had passed since her last meal, and the two of them fell on the bread and figs, washing it all down with milk from the glass bottle.

Theo wiped his mouth with the back of his hand as she settled in her chair. "Okay. First, you've got to understand that outside of the Triple Eras, especially in the northern Baldlands, it's no big deal to have the Mark of Iron. There are raiders who even say they've got more iron than they actually do—that's how proud of it they are. Course, that can get you into trouble. I knew a raider named Ballast who claimed every bone in his body was made of iron. Well, you can imagine there were one or two other raiders who were happy to prove him wrong." He chuckled. "Dangerous to boast about something like that.

"When I was still in Sue's gang—I couldn't have been more than five—we stopped in a town called Mercury where almost everyone had the Mark. The town doctor had a magnet as big as a window that he used to figure out who had what made of iron. He wasn't going to cut into someone—do surgery—before he knew what was iron and what wasn't."

Sophia leaned forward. "I can't believe it's so common there."

Theo nodded. "Oh, yeah. Real common. But the doctor wasn't. He was one of our customers, that's how Sue knew about him. It was one of her books that gave him the magnet idea in the first place."

"She had books?" Sophia had difficulty imagining books among raiders and gangs.

"That's mostly how she supported us. See, it's not like New Occident, where all the books are from your time or before. In the Baldlands, there's books from every year you could think of. Every 'era,' like they used to say before the Disruption. Sue was a book peddler—we'd buy books in one town, then sell them in the next, buy more, move on."

Sophia bit her lip. "There must have been wonderful books."

"Yeah, there were. That's how I learned to read. There's all kinds of things you can get from books. How do you think I learned about maps?" He raised his eyebrows. "Well, the doctor bought a book from who-knows-when that talked about iron bones and magnets. He owed Sue a favor or two. I guess she'd already noticed things about my hand—she didn't say, but maybe she'd noticed it was stronger than the other one. She paid the doctor a whole dollar to have me checked for the Mark of Iron. Just so I'd know. She took that good care of me." He played with a crust of bread. "So he did, found my hand had the Mark."

"Nothing else?"

"Nope. Just my hand. Sue lectured me then; told me I shouldn't boast about having the Mark because it would get me into trouble, and I had to be careful who knew, because in some parts people thought badly of it." Theo shook his head. "Well, it wasn't long before I was ignoring Sue's advice. I let it get to my head that I had the Mark, and I started using my hand for all kinds of stupid stunts. Though the first scar was for a good cause." He showed her the edge of his hand. "One of the kids had fallen into a crevice and I kept him from falling by pulling him up by his bootlace. Cut clean through the skin, but the iron bones held." He laughed. "After that, the reasons weren't always as good."

"So what you said to Calixta never happened?"

"Nah, course not. I told you—I never knew my parents. But I wasn't going to tell her about the Mark, was I? No way to know what she'd think of it. It's what I'm saying—best not to get pinned down by telling the truth."

"I guess I see what you mean," Sophia allowed. It was clear now that Theo didn't intend any harm with his innumerable small lies. She could see how there were sometimes occasions when it was useful, but she couldn't imagine them. And then she could. *Right now,* she realized with surprise, *we're going to lie to get into the palace. We're going to lie about who we are. And I don't care.*

Sophia found herself looking across the table at her open notebook, the drawing of Theo dressed in feathers.

As if reading her thoughts, he asked, "So you never said. Is that drawing of me?"

She blushed, grateful for the darkness in the little tree house. "It is."

"You have a good memory—that's exactly what the costume looked like."

"No, I drew it then. The day I saw you."

Theo's eyes opened wide with surprise. "You did?"

Sophia nodded. "You know when you went to my house to find Shadrack?" Now he nodded. "I wasn't home because I'd gone to the wharf. I looked for you."

Theo wore a strange expression. "What do you mean?"

"I'd seen you that once, in the cage. I went back to the circus to see if I could get you out. I know—it's stupid." Sophia laughed to hide her embarrassment. "I planned to rescue you."

For a moment he stared at her. Then a slow smile spread across his face. "Well, thanks."

"But I didn't rescue you!"

Theo, still smiling, reached across for the last piece of bread. "We should put the candles out soon," he said, "so people in the other houses don't know we're here."

30
THE ECLIPSE

1891, June 30: 16-Hour 50

Just as the variety of time-keeping methods in the Triple Eras gradually gave way to the nine-hour clock, so the variety of calendars gave way to the lunar calendar. Festivities were organized around the calendar, and today no festival is greater than that reserved for the occasional lunar or solar eclipse. These are often marked with costume balls, in which the revelers cover their faces just as the sun and moon "cover" theirs.

—*From Veressa Metl's* Cultural Geography of the Baldlands

SOPHIA AND THEO spent the following day in the tree house. They descended twice to buy food but otherwise remained high in the bare branches, gazing out through the windows at the vast city and wondering what the night would bring. Perhaps it was Theo's easy banter, or perhaps it was the sense that the time for nervousness had passed; Sophia felt a steady calm descend as the day wore on. She knew what lay ahead and she was not afraid. When dusk fell, they began donning their costumes.

Sophia had to admit, examining herself beside Theo in the cracked mirror, that they were nearly unrecognizable. The high shoes he had stolen for them added several inches to their heights. Theo's feathered mask covered his entire face, and the dark cloak made him seem bulkier than he was. His bandaged hand was concealed by the feathery gauntlet. Sophia's gown cascaded around her in a rush of rippling silk blanketed with fern leaves. Fortunately, the fronds were thick enough to conceal the bulky shape of her pack, which she wore under her gown, strapped at the back of her waist like a bustle. She had no mask, but the sage-green veil powdered with glitter was enough. Looking at herself in the mirror, she could see only the outline of her face.

"We look so old," she murmured.

"That's the idea," Theo replied, pulling the cloak around his chest. "As long as we walk right, no one will know." He turned to her. "Are you ready?"

"I think so." Sophia took a deep breath and drew herself to her now considerable height. "I'll have to put these back on when we reach the palace," she said, pulling off the high shoes. "Good-bye, tree house," she said quietly, looking around the condemned room before descending the stairs. "Thank you for keeping us safe—at least for a little while."

Half an hour later, they were approaching the palace gates. The air was filled with fluting music and the chatter of the arriving guests, and Sophia could see at once that Theo had chosen their costumes well: no one gave them a second glance. Nonetheless, Sophia felt her heart flutter at the sight of the guards. Squeezing her arm, Theo pointed to a large party of extravagantly dressed guests that was making its way noisily toward the entrance, and the two of them insinuated themselves into the group.

As they slowly moved forward, one of the women turned and looked them up and down. Sophia caught her breath, preparing herself for the shout of alarm. Then the woman leaned forward and asked, "A Lorca design?"

"Yes," Sophia said, hiding her surprise as best she could.

"I compliment you on being able to secure her services. When I tried to order *my* gown, she said she could no longer take orders!" The woman gestured down at her pea-green tunic, which looked a bit wrinkled.

Sophia struggled to think of a fitting reply. "One does have to order very early," she said, in what she hoped was a lofty tone.

The woman nodded sagely. "Quite right. I will do so next time." She turned to follow her companions, but by that time the leader of the party had spoken to the guard and all of them—including Sophia and Theo—had been waved through the gates.

Sophia let out a sharp sigh of relief. "That was easy, wasn't it?" Theo said smugly.

As they entered the garden, she caught her breath. It had been transformed by a thousand lanterns that hung from every tree and above every fountain. The water in the lily pond shimmered, reflecting the lights. Clusters of people drifted in and out among the hedges and walkways, some of them carrying long poles with bright lanterns shaped like moons. For a moment, she forgot any danger and lost herself in the floating music and winking lights of the eclipse festival.

Theo moved single-mindedly toward the lily pond, leading Sophia by the elbow as she turned to look at the frail paper boats gliding across it. "I'll show you the way I got in last time," he murmured.

Sophia did not reply, consumed as she was by the sights and sounds. A little boy dressed like a bird, complete with feathery wings, fluttered past them laughing; a taller girl pursuing him held her skirt in bunched fistfuls so that she could run. Sophia watched, a smile stealing over her face, and suddenly her smile froze. She seized Theo's arm.

"What?" he asked in surprise. "The guards won't recognize us . . ." The words died in his throat as he saw the man standing only a few feet away, contentedly eating a tall piece of cake.

It was Montaigne. He had not noticed the young man with a feathered mask and the veiled lady. He took another bite of cake and then drifted away from the side of the lily pool and wandered into the gardens.

"I can't believe he followed you all the way here," Theo whispered.

"He must have followed the *Swan*, which means he knows about Calixta and Burr. If we stay with him we might find out where they are," Sophia said under her breath, pulling Theo onward.

They kept their eyes on Montaigne's retreating back and stayed well behind, following him as he made his slow way through the garden, stopping occasionally to take a bite of cake or dip his fingers in one of the fountains. He skirted a broad wooden dance floor, empty save for sawdust, that stood awaiting the dancers who later would whirl upon it under the darkened moon. Then he rounded a corner onto a lawn bordered by lemon trees, where a trio of musicians was performing. He sauntered up to the audience from behind and sat in one of the empty chairs.

Sophia and Theo watched through the screen of the lemon trees. Princess Justa sat with a dozen attendants, but the rest of the audience were strangers. Veressa and Martin were nowhere to be seen. Sophia moved forward to get a clear view of Montaigne—and then she stopped in her tracks. Beside him was a small woman, her long, fair hair pulled back, a delicate veil covering her face. Seated next to her, half-obscured and slumped over, as if sunk in melancholy, was Shadrack.

In that moment, Sophia understood what a precious gift it was to have no sense of time. What for ordinary people would have seemed like a fragment of a second seemed like hours to her. During that time out of time, she had all the time in the world to think. Montaigne had followed her, and he had brought Shadrack with him. Perhaps he had traveled with Shadrack from the start: all the way along the Western Line, to New Orleans, to Veracruz, to Nochtland. Sophia imagined that journey and all the routes it might have taken, all the difficulties Shadrack might have faced. It didn't matter how he had gotten to Nochtland; he was here now, and so was she. And with still more time to deliberate, Sophia thought of how she might draw him away.

She found herself back in the Nochtland gardens, her plan complete. "He's here!" she whispered urgently. "That's Shadrack."

"I see him," Theo said slowly. "What do you want to do?"

"We need a distraction. The dance floor. And the lanterns."

Theo understood at once. "You get to Shadrack. I'll find you." He broke cover and moved toward the empty dance floor. Sophia stayed behind, her eyes fastened on her uncle.

The fluting music rose up over the audience and through the trees, and the laughter of the revelers tinkled like glass chimes. Sophia marked time by when one song ended and another began. As the trio commenced a third piece, another sound suddenly cut through the air: a shout of alarm. Another echoed it, and a moment later frightened shrieks pierced the music and brought it to a halt. "Fire!" someone cried. "The dance floor is on fire!" The audience rose in confusion. The flames spread, and she could see the worried faces of the audience. A loud crack burst out behind her as the floorboards were engulfed, and suddenly everyone panicked. Princess Justa's attendants seized her arms and hurried her away. The other guests rushed across the lawn, toppling chairs and bumping into one another.

"Water, get water!" Sophia heard the sharp sizzle of water against burning wood. She kept her eyes trained on Shadrack. He had remained behind while the others around him fled in panic. Even the shouts and the light and the heat of the fire did not seem to affect him.

As soon as the clearing was abandoned, Sophia stepped forward. Shadrack was sitting motionlessly at the end of the aisle. She could not see his face, but he seemed to be simply staring at the trees in front of him. *What's wrong with him? Why doesn't he move?* Sophia was suddenly terrified. What had happened to Shadrack that he did not even flee at the sight of fire?

Her heart was pounding as she hurried toward him. She placed her hand gently on his slumped shoulder. "Shadrack?" she said, her voice trembling. Hearing his name, Shadrack looked up at her abruptly, and his eyes stared blankly, uncomprehendingly, at her veiled face. Sophia lifted her veil with shaking fingers. "It's me, Shadrack. Sophia." She bent down and threw her arms around him.

"Is it really you, Soph?" Shadrack asked hoarsely, his arms moving slowly to embrace her.

"We have to get out of here before they notice us," she said desperately, pulling back even though she didn't want to. "Are you all right? Can you get up?"

He gazed at her face as if waking from a long sleep. "I thought you were lost. When we arrived, they said you were killed trying to escape the palace grounds."

"Oh, Shadrack," she cried. "No—no, we escaped." She put her arms around him again and Shadrack squeezed until she felt that her ribs would break. Over his shoulder, she saw the guards still trying to douse the flames. Theo was hurrying toward them, his feathered mask still in place.

"I can't believe you're here. You're alive," Shadrack said with a deep sigh.

"I can't believe *you're* here, Shadrack," she said, pulling away. "Shadrack, this is Theo," she said, as he joined them. "We never imagined—we came back for Veressa and the others. Do you know what happened to them—where they are?"

Shadrack had overcome his shock, and after assessing the commotion around the fire, he rose hurriedly. "Come," he said, taking Sophia's hand. "I haven't seen her, but I know where she is." They ran toward the palace, passing the smoldering remains of the dance floor. The palace guards and guests who had extinguished the fire with water from the fountains were coughing from the acrid smoke. No one noticed their escape.

The front entrance, they could see even from a distance, was lined with guards. The doors of the conservatory were firmly shut. But they tested Martin and Veressa's windows and found to their relief that the one Sophia and Theo had escaped through was unlocked.

For a moment they paused in the dark bedroom, listening for any sounds of pursuit in the garden or the house. There were none. Sophia kicked off the high shoes and then they left, stealing along the corridor toward the door that connected with the main palace. "They're going to notice by now that you're gone," Sophia whispered, as Shadrack pulled open the door.

"I know," he said tersely. "We have to hurry." He seemed to have a map of the palace in his head and turned without hesitation at each corner. They whirled through the empty corridors strewn with eucalyptus leaves, the sharp smell rising as they ran, until they reached a flight of wide stone stairs leading downward. "The servants' floor," Shadrack said, panting. "The entrance to the dungeons should be here."

The corridors here were narrower, and their hurried footsteps echoed on the bare stone floor. Yet these hallways were also blessedly empty; the festivities required every free hand. The bedrooms, narrow and spare as monastic cells, were all deserted. They turned a corner and suddenly found themselves at a dead end. Shadrack stopped short. "No, it's not here," he said to himself. "It must be . . ." he trailed off. "Wherever the guard are housed."

After hesitating for a moment, Shadrack turned back the way they'd come, back past the stairs in the opposite direction. Soon they were racing through the long, cavernous rooms that housed the royal guard. These, too, were empty, though littered with equipment and weapons, and at the far end of the largest room was an arched, torch-lit entryway and a descending staircase.

"That's it," he said, glancing behind them. The shadowed stairs seemed to go down forever. At the bottom, they found themselves in a dark, dank passage whose stone walls were covered—unexpectedly—with pale vines growing in twists and turns and dense spirals. As she hurried along, Sophia ran her hand over the cool leaves.

Suddenly, the corridor opened out onto a vast, high chamber with a domed ceiling. The walls were covered by the same pale creepers. Fires in deep clay pots dotted the stone floor, and in the center of the room was what appeared to be an empty pool. As they walked toward it, breathing heavily with exertion, Sophia realized that it was actually a pit. She ran to the edge and peered in.

The pit was more than twenty feet deep, its walls covered with sharp, irregular shards of glass. At the bottom, huddled around a small fire, sat the four luckless prisoners: Veressa, Martin, Calixta, and Burr. "It's me, Sophia," she called down, her voice echoing throughout the chamber.

At the sight of her, the four sprang to their feet. "Sophia!" Veressa cried. "You must leave here!"

Shadrack and Theo reached the edge of the pit. "We're not leaving without you," Shadrack said. "There's a ladder. We'll lower it and you can climb out."

"Where are the guard?" Burr demanded. "How did you get past them?"

"They're outside," Sophia said. "Everyone is watching the eclipse."

Shadrack and Theo lowered the wooden ladder into the pit and held the top of it securely while Burr held the bottom and, one by one, the other three made their way up. Martin went first, climbing slowly because of his silver leg, and when he had emerged safely, he embraced Sophia. "My dear, I'm not sure it was wise of you to come here."

"We had to, Martin," she said, leaning against him.

Calixta reached the top of the ladder, and then Veressa emerged. Burr followed them, leaping out over the last rung. "Right. Now how do we get out of here, Veressa?" he asked.

She was on the verge of answering when there was a sudden sound. Turning as one, they saw Montaigne's companion, the veiled woman, standing in the doorway, surrounded by more than a dozen of the Nochtland guard. She strode toward them, more of the guard pouring out of the corridor behind her, ominous as gathering vultures. They held their spears aloft, directed at the small group that stood by the open pit.

"Princess Justa was right after all," the woman said, her sweet, sad voice filling the cavernous chamber. Her delicate veil fluttered as she spoke. "She assured me you would return for your friends. I thought you would have more sense," she said softly, walking directly toward Sophia. "For once, I'm glad to have been proven wrong."

Shadrack put his arm across Sophia. "Leave her, Blanca," he said hoarsely.

Blanca shook her head and began to remove her gloves. "This is the moment we were always heading toward, Shadrack. You simply chose not to believe it." She extended her bare hand toward Sophia. "I'll have the bag you are carrying, please." Sophia did not move. "You may not care for your own safety, but surely there are some here whom you would not like to see at the end of a spear?"

Sophia turned reluctantly to retrieve her pack from under her gown, and after an awkward struggle it was free. She handed it to Blanca. Their hands touched for a moment; Sophia felt the pressure of the woman's cold fingers. "Thank you," Blanca said. Without wasting a moment, she opened the pack and removed the four maps. She ran her trembling fingers over them lovingly and then held the glass map up like a trophy, gazing at it. Sophia stared at the cavern wall through the treasure that she had just lost. "You must understand, Sophia," Blanca said softly, "that they belong with me. For three years I shared a home with them—they were almost mine. I might have read them a thousand times, except that I could not."

With an easy motion she lifted her veil, and in the flickering firelight Sophia saw that the woman's face had no features, only skin that was deathly pale. The skin was deeply scarred, as if a dozen knives had carved through it: as if a patient hand had cut across it, again and again.

PART IV
Discovery

31
The Lined Palm

1891, July 1: 2-Hour 05

The dungeons are from an another period, likely the earliest of the Triple Eras. Soil sampling from the underground vaults of the imperial palace in Nochtland suggests that the extensive subterranean architecture dates to several hundred years before the topsoil upon which the palace is built. In other words, the visible structure of the palace, which has been in place since the Great Disruption, belongs to a different age than do its foundations.

—From Veressa Metl's "Local Soils: Implications for Cartology"

YEARS BEFORE BLANCA knew of the glaciers' advance, she had sought to enrich her railway company by extending the track south through New Occident's Indian Territories and all the way to Nochtland. Princess Justa, unsurprisingly, looked favorably upon the investor who promised to connect the isolated capital with the wealthy cities to the north. Over time, Blanca had proven herself to be more than a match for the insular monarch, easily securing a monopoly on the railroad route and then persuading her that a mere weirwind was moving north.

But it was no weirwind that sped toward Nochtland under

the shadowed light of the eclipsed moon. What had begun as an imperceptible movement far away in Tierra del Fuego had accelerated day by day into a rapid, erratic progress that left little time for flight. The glaciers had passed Xela and were making their way north, obliterating everything that lay in their path.

A jagged border divided the vast plains and mountains of the Baldlands from the gleaming Southern Snows. Where the two Ages met, a brilliant light, wild and unpredictable as a lightning storm, pierced the night air. All who saw it fled in terror, and only a few who glimpsed the distant flashes on the horizon understood what they meant: to see the lights was to have already waited too long.

Justa's prisoners had been returned to the glass-shard pit in the depths of the Nochtland palace; Sophia, Theo, and Shadrack had been forced to join them. Blanca had again fooled the princess, this time with a story about an elaborate conspiracy by the Mark of Iron, hatched in the Indies and executed with the assistance of palace insiders. Justa's suspicious mind accepted the tale without hesitation, and she placed the captives entirely in Blanca's power.

At first, amidst reunions and urgent conversation, the prisoners hardly noticed the walls around them. Shadrack described his capture, Blanca's ambitions for the *carta mayor,* the long voyage south, and his thwarted attempt to escape. Sophia told him everything that had happened since she had discovered him missing in Boston. And Veressa related how Martin's silver leg had been detected when one of the guards' dogs had sniffed it out; Burr had impulsively drawn his pistol, and they had been thrown into the dungeons immediately. But once Theo had repeated the rumors of the Lachrima moving north, and once Shadrack had explained that their advance doubtlessly resulted from the Southern Snows' rapidly encroaching border, a shocked silence overtook them. Nothing, it seemed, would stop the Ice Age from inexorably erasing everything in its path, creating and then driving a multitude of Lachrima before it.

Only Sophia was not downcast. She leaned against Shadrack's shoulder while he spoke with Veressa, indifferent to the packed dirt floor and the somber half-darkness. The elation that came with being reunited with her uncle, Theo, and the others buoyed her, and their resigned faces only filled her with determination. She could not believe that they had traveled so far merely to be engulfed by glaciers. *The Fates have left us with enough,* she thought, clutching her watch and the spool of thread in her pocket, *and we have to make the most of it.* Her mind raced ahead to the danger that awaited. She could not imagine the advent of the Southern Snows, but the image of countless Lachrima fleeing the site of their erasures was vivid. She shivered. Seeing Blanca's mutilated face had been horrible enough.

"Tell me again why her face is like that," she said to Shadrack, who had paused in his conversation.

"You mean why it's scarred?" She nodded. "You remember Veressa's story of our visit to Talisman's house, all those years ago? As I said, I realized as soon as I saw her that Blanca was the Lachrima he kept imprisoned there."

"Yes. But *why* did he cut her face?"

Shadrack shook his head. "The man had been driven mad. He believed he could somehow cut through her skin to find her face underneath."

"The poor wretches," Veressa murmured. "Both of them."

As she spoke, a trio of guards appeared at the edge of the pit and began lowering the wooden ladder. The prisoners looked up expectantly. "Only the girl is to come up," said one of the guards. The other two held their spears aloft, as if to enforce his command. "The girl named Sophia."

"She's not going without me," Shadrack called up.

"Only the girl."

"I'll be fine, Shadrack," Sophia said. "We don't have a choice anyway."

"Send her up," the guard called again.

"She's right, Shadrack." Veressa took his hand and pulled him aside. "Let her go."

Sophia began carefully climbing the wooden rungs, eyes fixed on her hands, not daring to look at the sharp glass shards inches away. When she reached the top, the guards swung her up by the arms. She caught a brief glimpse over her shoulder of the forlorn group clustered at the bottom of the pit, and the sight brought a knot to her throat.

The guards walked her back through the cavernous room and then the deserted servants' quarters. Emerging onto a vast stone courtyard, Sophia felt her eyes drawn upward to the peculiar light in the sky. The mottled face of the pale moon was almost hidden, as if by a dark veil. Sophia was surprised to hear music and laughter in the distance—the festivities for the eclipse, which seemed as if it had occurred days earlier.

The feeling of unreality continued when they entered a set of apartments at the rear of the palace, overlooking the gardens. The airy opulence took Sophia's breath away. Carpeted with pale yellow petals, the main room was lit by tall glass candle-lamps that cast a flickering patchwork of golden light and dark shadows. Clusters of white flowers draped over the furniture emitted a heavy, sweet smell, and strings of clear glass bells hung in the open windows. Their quiet tinkling reminded Sophia of Mrs. Clay.

But it was not Mrs. Clay who awaited her. Blanca stood by one of the windows, her veil once again covering her face. "Leave her with me," she curtly told the guards. "You may wait outside." The guards left Sophia near a pair of brocaded chairs.

Blanca settled herself in one of the chairs and motioned Sophia into the other. Faint music through the closed windows could not distract Sophia from the image of the scarred face she had seen in the dungeon; she stared at the veil, unable to think of anything but what lay beneath.

Then in one fluid motion Blanca lifted it. Sophia was once again shaken by the gruesome face, where the scars were so numerous they made a mass of muddled flesh. "That's right," Blanca said softly. "Count them. Count them, and imagine the pain they cost me, and then imagine how little now it costs me to pain others. You should know that, before you decide to resist my will with a child's conception of right and wrong." She said these words sweetly, as if promising Sophia something wonderful. "What have you known of pain? Nothing."

The pain that Blanca described was genuine—that was clear—and she had indeed suffered more than Sophia could ever know. As she forced herself to look at the scars, Sophia felt her terror ebb, replaced by a wave of sympathy for the creature who sat before her, first robbed of her precious memories and then burdened with unspeakable new ones.

"You're right," Sophia said, willing herself to look directly at where Blanca's eyes should have been. "I haven't known pain like you have. I hope I never will."

"Your uncle has told you, then, how I earned my scars?"

She nodded, transfixed by the lines that rumpled and shifted across Blanca's face as she spoke. "How is it that you can see and talk?" Sophia blurted out.

Blanca's face went still as ice and Sophia's heart jumped. She had not meant for the question to burst forth. But she could not help it: along with sympathy, she felt curiosity.

Then, to her surprise, Blanca laughed. "I have never met a child like you. I see you truly do not frighten easily. There is no doubt you are your uncle's niece." She shook her head. "To answer your question," Blanca said, her voice direct, absent its former enveloping sweetness, "no one knows how it is that the Lachrima can see and speak and smell despite our lost features."

Sophia considered this for a moment. "I have never met another Lachrima, but I didn't think they spoke and . . . behaved the way you do."

"They usually do not. But you see, I am different." She paused. "I will explain how, since I respect your sense of inquiry. I have known many who felt horror at my face, but few with a desire to understand." The Lachrima shifted in her chair, so that her face was partly hidden in shadow. "A few days ago, when I read the map your uncle drew of that place—that hell where I suffered for three years—I could not fathom how he knew of it." Her voice dropped. "I had no wish to be reminded of it. But then I remembered his face. It was your uncle who came, in the end, and who opened the door to my freedom."

Sophia felt her heart swell with pride.

"But your uncle does not know everything that happened to me there. Do you see this?" She held out her ungloved hand. A clear gray line was inked across the palm, tracing the long wrinkle that curved toward her wrist.

"What is it?"

"The cartologer made my ruined face even worse. He drew thousands of maps across my skin in vain. But, whether he knew it or not, he drew one true line, and this was it. When he made this line, only weeks before I was freed, I remembered everything from my past life. It came upon me instantly, and as I traced my own palm with the fingers of my other hand, it was as though I was reading my own history."

"Everything?"

"All the memories that I had the day they were lost." Blanca sighed. "I remembered my home—my Age." Sophia could hear a smile in her voice as she continued. "The wondrous Glacine Age. I remembered being only a few years older than you are now when the Great Disruption occurred. The beautiful and terrible Disruption, which felt like falling into a deep pit of endless light." Blanca stood and walked to the window. She looked out into the gardens with the glass bells tinkling quietly above her. "It was the day I turned twenty. I had gone to our Hall of Remembrances to spend my birthday among its beautiful maps." She saw Sophia's enquiring look. "It was a great chamber, with maps recounting the city's history. The Glacine Age has many such edifices." Blanca paused. "You have seen one, as a matter of fact."

Sophia blinked in surprise. "I have?"

"The four maps," she replied quietly. "The memories in the four maps took place in such a hall."

Sophia recalled the long climb up a spiraling stairwell, the many people around her, and the building's slow collapse. "But does that mean the Disruption occurred in your Age?"

"I do not know," Blanca said so softly that Sophia almost could not hear her. "I do not know. I am still attempting—" Her voice suddenly broke with frustration. "I am still attempting to understand the maps. What I do know," she went on more firmly, turning back toward Sophia, "is that the *carta mayor* will explain everything."

She crossed the room to open a low cabinet and returned holding something which she handed to Sophia: her pack. "I believe there are other things besides the maps of value to you here." Sophia took it in silence and held it closely to her chest. "I cannot stop the glaciers. But I have appealed to your uncle to do what he can—not only for my Age, but for all the Ages: for the world. Now I make that appeal to you, as well. You are the only one who can persuade him." Blanca's voice, musical and mournful, filled Sophia with a sudden sense of longing for all the things she would never see once the Southern Snows had encased the world in ice. She would never see the distant Ages she yearned to explore; she would never see Boston again, or the house on East Ending Street; and she would never, she thought desperately, see the parents she hoped were still somewhere far away, waiting to be found. "This New World is ending," Blanca went on, as if reading Sophia's thoughts. "But we can still determine what takes its place. If your uncle helps me to find and rewrite the *carta mayor*, we can ensure that the world emerging from the destruction is a whole world—a *good* world. Now that I have read the four maps, I am more convinced than ever. He is our only hope."

"Shadrack will not do it," Sophia said matter-of-factly, without hostility. "Even if he could. He said so."

The tinkling of the glass bells mingled with the distant laughter and music that drifted up from the gardens. "Perhaps your uncle has not told you," Blanca finally said, "how complete the *carta mayor* is. The map shows everything that has happened and everything that will happen. Do you know what that means?"

Sophia gazed at the scars on Blanca's face, a slight spark of an idea forming in her mind. "I think so."

"It means that if Shadrack read the map, he could tell you anything you might want to know. *Anything.* All your curiosities about the past, satisfied. The *carta mayor* would allow you to know, once and for all, what happened to Bronson and Minna Tims so many years ago."

Sophia felt a sharp sting at the edge of her eyes.

"Yes, I know of their disappearance," Blanca said gently. "I know many things about you, Sophia: I know of your illustrious family past; I know that you and Shadrack are inseparable; I know that you have no sense of time. Carlton Hopish's memories of you are fond ones." She paused. "I cannot give you your parents back," she continued, her voice heavy with sadness, "but with the *carta mayor* I can tell you for certain what became of them."

Sophia stared down at her lap and struggled to hold back her tears. *To know for certain what became of them,* she thought numbly.

As if sensing her confusion, Blanca leaned forward. "Think what that would mean." Then she gracefully stood and walked slowly to one of the wardrobes that stood against the wall. "Have you ever seen a water map?"

"No," Sophia said dully. "I was only starting to learn about maps."

"It may interest you to see one," Blanca said, returning with a white bowl and a tall glass flask. "They are rare. They require skill and a patience few possess. They are made of condensation. Drop by drop, the mapmaker encapsulate the meanings of the map in vaporized water, then gathers those vapors to make a whole. This one was made in a cave far north in the Prehistoric Snows. The mapmaker, who was also an explorer, recounted his journey there." Placing the bowl on the table that stood between them, she uncorked the flask and poured out its contents. To Sophia it looked like an ordinary bowl of water, except for the fact that it was unnaturally still.

Blanca returned to the wardrobe and came back with the glass map, which she held over the bowl. "Do you see how it changes the appearance of the water?"

Sophia beheld what looked like a bowl full of shimmering light. She nodded.

Putting the glass aside, Blanca held a small white stone over the bowl of water, which looked ordinary once more. "Now watch the surface." The stone fell from her fingers into the bowl. The ripples that formed in the water took on extraordinary shapes, rising like hills, dipping into shallow valleys, and curling into unlikely spirals high above the rim. Fine lines of color wove through the water, giving the shapes texture and depth.

Sophia gasped despite herself and leaned in to see more. "How do you read it?"

"It requires years of study. I am barely able to understand them. Your uncle," she added, "is the only person I know who can both read and write water maps. Both are difficult, but it can be done. The Tracing Glass before you makes it easier; it is one of the most powerful instruments in the world, and with it your uncle could certainly revise the water map you see before you."

Sophia could not take her eyes from the color-laced terrain. "It is beautiful," she whispered.

"Imagine a map like this one, but as wide as a lake and with the mysteries of the world written upon it," Blanca murmured. "Wouldn't you wish to see it? Wouldn't you wish to gaze upon the living world on the water's surface? To ask it your questions and hear its secrets?" She gently lowered the Tracing Glass and sat down. Before her lay an ordinary bowl of water with a small stone at the bottom.

Sophia sat back with a sigh. She listened to the laughter from the garden and let her eyes drift from the water map to Blanca's face. The sense of sadness she had felt, imagining the Ages that would be lost beneath the glaciers, changed as suddenly and swiftly as the surface of the water. What had been lying still within her suddenly rose up, taking definite shape. She saw the course she had to follow clearly, as if it were drawn on a map. She stood up. "Give me a chance to talk alone with Shadrack," Sophia told Blanca. "I will convince him."

32
Flash Flood

1891, July 1: 2-Hour 21

Tell me whether you hear the Lachrima,
That voice of Ages lost.
It has wept beside me once before
When I had no sense of its cost.
I traveled a lifetime seeking to flee
the grief it placed within me.
Now I hear it still, but its voice has changed
And I hear it only dimly.

—*"The Lachrima's Lament," Verse 1*

Even those who lay far beyond the glaciers' reach had begun to see signs of their advance: inscrutable signs, never seen since the Great Disruption, of an Age disintegrating at the edges. Howling storms seized the islands of the United Indies; colossal waves crashed upon their shores; weirwinds several miles long rambled like exiled ghosts along the deserts of the northern Baldlands; as far north as New Akan, the streets and farms were paralyzed by the unprecedented arrival of a snowstorm.

And the changes were not only above ground; below the visible surface of the earth and all across the central Baldlands, the groundwater rose, pushed by a mighty force that transformed the very rocks and soil.

Theo was the first to notice, soon after Sophia was taken away, when the feathered mask he had tossed into a corner of the pit suddenly floated toward him. With a shout he was on his feet.

Burr rushed over. "What? What is it?"

"There's water seeping in—fast." Theo pointed at the growing pool in the corner.

"How fast?" Veressa asked quietly.

Martin put his ear to the dirt floor for several seconds. Then he stood, his face smudged and his eyes wide. "We should call the guards."

Calixta began shouting at once, and Burr added his voice to hers, hollering up to the distant edge of the pit. After a moment, Theo joined them, putting two fingers in his mouth to emit a piercing whistle.

"How fast is it rising?" Shadrack asked, his voice tight.

"I predict that it will arrive like an underground tidal wave," Martin said. "Probably it will be over in minutes. The water will recede again, but not before it has flooded the pit."

"Will the shards come loose?" Veressa asked anxiously, looking at the studded walls.

"The soil is only a few inches thick. It depends on whether the shards are lodged in the soil or in the rock beneath it."

"You mean the shards might—"

"Burst out from the wall in a torrent of water," Martin said grimly. "Yes."

Suddenly the wall nearest to them grumbled, and with a brief clatter a knot of soil and stones and glass shards was spat out onto the ground. The flood rushed into the pit after it, and within seconds they were ankle-deep in cold water. For a moment they all stopped shouting and stared, aghast, at the rising water around them. Then Calixta took a deep breath and released a high-pitched scream that the others echoed, redoubling their efforts to alert the guards.

Martin observed the wall with trepidation. "Better this way. Releases the pressure. Might prevent a greater breach. This is good," he said over the shouting, trying to make himself heard.

No guard had yet appeared, and the water had reached their knees. Shadrack noticed with alarm that some of the smaller glass shards had come loose from the walls and were swirling—harmlessly, as yet—through the rising water. He began to feel his throat growing hoarse.

"How can they not hear us?" Veressa asked, exasperated, her voice cracking.

"What if I wear the gauntlets to cover my hands," Theo said raggedly "and climb up on the shards?"

Burr turned to him. "I already thought about that. I doubt you'd get cut, with your boots and the gauntlets. But the problem is the glass—no single piece is thick enough to hold your weight. You would fall before climbing three feet."

"What if you get on Shadrack's shoulders and I get on yours? And then I jump out?"

"It won't work," Shadrack said. "Think about it—by my estimate that would put your head just at the edge of the pit. Even if we can pull off an extraordinary balancing act, how would you get to the edge without crushing yourself against the shards?"

"Stop planning and shout, will you?" snapped Calixta. "Once the water is high enough—and that will be soon, since it's already at my waist—then we'll stick to the center and float to the top. Shark circle."

"You're right," Burr said at once. Seeing Theo's confusion, he explained: "Something we learned once after a nasty shark ate our rowboat. We make a circle, arms linked, tread water."

"That's our best chance," Shadrack agreed. They all resumed shouting at the top of their lungs, but he knew the water would rise over their heads before anyone arrived.

Minutes later, Veressa, Calixta and Theo were forced to start treading water. "Okay, shark circle now," Burr said, pulling them in. "Right arm over, left arm under." He put his right arm under Martin's shoulder and his left arm over Veressa's. "Ow. Except for Veressa. Those thorns are very pretty but dashed sharp." He tucked his left arm under Veressa. With Calixta, Theo, and Shadrack they formed a tight circle. "If we start drifting toward a wall, Calixta and I will kick us in the other direction."

Martin and then Burr and finally Shadrack, who was tallest, began treading water. There was no more shouting. The pirates managed without difficulty, but the others, who had not spent years on the sea, were soon out of breath and weary.

"Cheer up, crew," Burr said with a grin. "Could be much

worse. There aren't actually any sharks. And soon we'll be out of this damn pit."

"Thanks to the water," Calixta said, grinning back. "Couldn't have planned a better escape if we'd tried."

The others smiled weakly. Minutes passed. Shadrack kept his eye on the wall and estimated the shortening distance to the pit's edge. The water had risen halfway up the wall when Martin suddenly dropped his head. "I can't kick any longer—this metal leg," he gasped. "It's like carrying an anchor."

"All right then," Burr said easily. "Shadrack and I have got you—take a rest. Bend your other knee and rest the metal leg on it."

Martin did so and sighed with relief. "I'm sorry," he managed.

Silently, the others went on treading water. "Won't you sing us something, Calixta?" Burr asked. "It would help us pass the time."

"If you'd done half as much shouting as I'd done," Calixta retorted, "you wouldn't have the breath to ask."

As Shadrack felt his legs growing numb from the cold water and the repetitive kicking, he realized that they were only a few feet from the top of the pit. He raised his eyes. "They're here," he panted.

The three men were looking down into the pit with astonishment.

"Don't just stand there," Veressa said wearily. "Get us out."

"I never thought I'd be so glad to see the Nochtland guard," croaked Theo.

33
The Nighting Vine

1891, July 1: 3-Hour 12

The wails of pain and the gasping cries
Left me speechless, mindless, dumb.
After so many years of hearing her song
I grew hardened and strong and numb.
The sound I feared and the grief I fled
eclipsed my life's whole meaning.
And now I want only to hear it again
To recall when I yet had feeling.

—"The Lachrima's Lament," Verse 2

When the guards led Sophia back to the dungeon, she found to her surprise that the prisoners were no longer in the pit. They sat huddled around one of the clay-pot fires that dotted the floor. The men withdrew without a word, locking the heavy door. Only when Shadrack put his arms around her did Sophia realize that they were all soaking wet. Veressa and Martin sat shivering with cold. Theo stood near the fire trying to dry his cape. Calixta was wretchedly shaking out her hair.

"Are you all right?" Shadrack asked her anxiously.

"What happened?" she asked in reply.

"The pit we were in flooded. It was a long time before the guards heard us calling," Shadrack said ruefully. "But that doesn't matter. Are *you* all right? What did she want?"

Sophia seemed hardly to hear him. "So now they've left you here? We're alone?"

"Did you see Blanca?" he pressed. "What did she ask of you?"

"She wanted me to persuade you," she said, not looking at him but scanning the enormous chamber, "to change the *carta mayor.*"

"Sophia," Shadrack said, taking her by the shoulders, "what is it? Your mind is elsewhere—what are you looking for?"

"The entryway. When we first came in earlier, I saw it—there was an opening on the other side of the room. If they left us here—"

"It is not an exit," Veressa said wearily. "It leads to the labyrinth—a maze of ruined passages. They only left us here because they know we would never go in. Father and I have been in the entrance to take soil samples. No one has gone beyond that point since the last court cartologer"—and here she paused— "vanished attempting to map it."

"I knew it!" Sophia cried, to everyone's surprise. She ran to the nearest wall, where the pale vines that grew in the corridor and lined the dungeon were faintly luminous in the firelight. "It's here, Shadrack!" she burst out, unable to contain her excitement. "I saw it through the glass map when Blanca held it up. Before—when she first took it from my pack."

Shadrack shook his head uncomprehendingly. "What is here, Soph? What do you mean?"

"I saw them through the Tracing Glass," she said impatiently. "These vines—they're not just vines—they're a *map*."

At this, the wet prisoners still sitting by the fire rose and joined her at the wall. Shadrack examined the vines with amazement. "Are you sure?" he said slowly.

"I'm sure. Martin," she asked, "do you know what kind of plant this is?"

He shook his head. "It has a popular name—Nighting Vine—but I have never been able to identify its origins. The vine is exceedingly rare and only grows underground."

Veressa, standing beside Shadrack, examined the pale leaves critically. "It has no inscription, no legend of any kind. It may be the beginnings of a map, not yet full grown."

"I'm inclined to agree," Shadrack said. "Or, if it is a map, then it is beyond my ability to read." He let the vine drop and shook his head regretfully. "I would have no idea how to—"

"But it is not on the *leaves*," Sophia cut in. "It is the *whole plant*. Look! Do you see how here there is one vine growing out of the floor, and against the far wall there is another? There, by the doorway, is a third. And all of them are identical!"

"Identical how?" Veressa asked, as she compared the three.

"The pattern of how they grow on the wall—the vines spread out in the exact same way, with the same twists and turns. Like a map," Sophia triumphantly finished.

As she spoke, her listeners stood transfixed. The pale

creeper, so delicate in appearance and yet so hardy in its growth against the dank stone, fanned out across the wall in hundreds of thin tendrils. The pattern was dense, making it hardly possible to determine whether they were truly similar, and yet if one followed a single route along the vine it became evident that the plants were, in fact, identical. "How on earth did you notice?" Veressa exclaimed, running her hand admiringly across the wall. "They are incredibly complex."

Shadrack laughed with astonished delight. "It's your artist's eye, Soph," he cried, taking her by the shoulders. "Your artist's eye!" She smiled as he released her. And Theo, winking, caught Sophia's eye and snapped his fingers into a little handgun of approval.

"And you think this is a map to the labyrinth?" Veressa asked, deferring to Sophia.

"Couldn't it be? I don't know how or why, but I think the maps to the labyrinth grow from the labyrinth itself."

"Marvelous—just marvelous," Martin whispered, lovingly tracing his finger along the winding vine.

"But where is the exit?" Veressa continued. "The vine leads to nothing but itself."

"I can't be sure," Sophia admitted, "but look—look at these," she said, pointing to three white flowers with fragile petals. "They grow away from the wall—upward. Don't you think these might be three ways out of the labyrinth?"

The others regarded the nighting vine in silence. "It's impossible to know for certain," Shadrack said pensively, running a hand through his hair.

Sophia hurriedly retrieved her notebook. "If we can draw it," she said, "then we'll have a map to the labyrinth."

"It will be a great risk."

"Assuredly," Veressa agreed, "but I see no better option. We have no other means of escape, and I doubt we have much time—perhaps a day."

"It is far more satisfying an option than waiting here," Burr put in, and Calixta nodded.

Shadrack took a deep breath. "Then we must hurry."

—4-Hour 02: Drawing the Nighting Vine—

ALMOST AN HOUR later, Sophia, Veressa, and Shadrack were still drawing the nighting vine, each creating a copy in the hope that having duplicates would correct any discrepancies. Sophia's eyes ached from concentrating in the poor firelight as she penciled in the last few lines and began checking the map. "You know," she said softly to Theo, "you'd be pleased. I lied to Blanca. It was easy."

Theo lay on his stomach and he turned to face her. "What did I tell you?" He smiled. "Comes in handy, doesn't it?"

"I told her I'd try to persuade Shadrack to help her."

He shook his head in mock dismay. "Next you'll be lying to me. I'll have to watch out from now on."

Sophia laughed. She had checked her map twice; Veressa and Shadrack were still working. Setting her paper down on her pack, she closed her eyes and rested her head on her knees. She was dressed once again in her own clothes and her comfortable boots, having changed while Calixta held up her cloak like a screen. Theo had followed suit. They were the only two in dry clothes.

"Hey," Theo said, holding up his bandaged hand. "Do you still have that sewing box? This is falling off."

"I did keep it," Sophia said, opening her eyes, "but it's not here anymore." She had found their clothing, spare bandages, Shadrack's atlas, her pencils, and her notebook when she opened the pack Blanca had returned to her. But the sewing box was gone. "And it was so beautiful, too." There was nothing she could use. Then something occurred to her, and she reached into her pocket for the spool of silver thread that Mrs. Clay had given her.

"Perfect," Theo said when he saw it, holding out his hand.

As Sophia wound the silver thread over the bandage to hold it in place, her thoughts traveled elsewhere. There was no way of knowing whether she might see Mrs. Clay again, just as there was no way of Mrs. Clay's knowing, when she gave Sophia the silver thread, that it would someday serve such an unlikely purpose. *Is this what I was meant to use it for?* she asked the Fates. No one knew what the Fates had planned; the future was truly inscrutable. As she tied the thread securely around Theo's wrist, the thought gave her an unexpected surge of hope. *Nothing is set in stone. The glaciers aren't here yet.*

Shadrack and Veressa had finished, and as they hastily compared their maps, Burr made two torches from pieces of his torn shirt affixed to foot-long shards of glass from the pit. "We must hurry," Martin said anxiously, "before the guards return."

"We *are* hurrying, Father." Veressa looked at Sophia's drawing of the nighting vine. "But we can't afford to get lost; we must be certain of the maps before we set out."

Burr handed a torch to Calixta. "This is the best we can do. We may burn through every scrap of our clothing before we make our way out."

"Burn your own clothes," Calixta muttered. "You're certainly not burning mine."

—4-Hour 17: Entering the Labyrinth—

As a group they passed, with faintly echoing footsteps, across the floor of the underground chamber. The fires flickered ominously, and smoke spiraled upward toward the blackened ceiling. When they reached the dark entryway at the far end, the cold air of the labyrinth reached out for them. They stood silently for a moment. "May we soon see daylight," Veressa said, taking a deep breath.

She walked in front with her map, illuminated by Calixta's torch, followed by Theo, Martin, and Sophia; Shadrack and Burr, with map and torch, brought up the rear. The muddy floor led to a long, straight passageway cut directly into the stone. It was clear that it had not been used in some time. Martin had to walk carefully to avoid slipping, and after a few steps he placed his hand on Theo's shoulder to steady himself.

They reached a set of steps that led deeper underground. "Here is the first turn," Veressa said as they reached the base of the steps, "you agree with me that we go left, Shadrack? Sophia?"

They had traced the simplest route through the labyrinth,

and if Sophia's theory was correct, then they had only to follow it to find their way out. The tunnel Veressa led them into was much narrower than the first, and the heavy stones on either side were cold to the touch. An atmosphere of chilled humidity replaced the smoky air of the prison cavern.

"This one is so much smaller," Sophia said to Martin

"It's what makes the tunnels so confusing," he replied with effort. "The few soil samples I did take confirmed that they were made in many different Ages. There are various networks, some of which were deliberately integrated by human hands, others of which appear to connect entirely by chance. So, you see, it is a maze across many Ages."

"How many?"

"No one knows. Maybe four, maybe four hundred. I myself have never been past the entryway."

Step after step, tunnel after tunnel, they wormed their way through the dark labyrinth. It was almost as if they were walking in place—so much so that Sophia found time slipping away from her. She began counting her paces in order to keep track, and as she did, she felt mounting disbelief at how far the maze extended. As she reached two hundred and seventy paces, the air suddenly grew warmer, and someone at the front of the line exclaimed in surprise. "What have you found?" asked Shadrack.

"A crypt of some kind," Veressa replied, waiting for the others to join her.

They had reached a low room whose stone floor was covered with indecipherable chiseled writing. The niches in the walls looked like shelves, and as Burr and Calixta held their torches aloft, Sophia saw bundles of crumbling cloth. "Burr!" Calixta exclaimed. A heavy sword lay over one of the bundles. She took it up at once and made an experimental pass. "Heavy, but perfectly effective. Thank you, friend," Calixta murmured to the cloth bundle. Sophia gripped the silver thread in her pocket, thanking the Fates.

"There must be more." Burr held his torch up to the other niches.

As they searched the crypt, Sophia heard a faint sound, like the distant rumble of footsteps. "Did anyone hear that?"

"Might be left over from the flash flood," Martin said. "There will be a fair amount of readjustment going on underground." At that moment, Burr found another sword. He eagerly claimed it, and they left the low chamber.

Beyond the crypt was a circular room with five arched entryways. Veressa checked her drawing and followed the second tunnel on the right into a narrow passage with rotting wooden floorboards. Sophia recommenced counting her steps as she watched Martin's shoes before her. At the one hundred mark, she noticed the botanist furtively take his hand from his pocket and drop something.

"What are you doing, Martin?" Sophia asked quietly.

"Just a little experiment, dear." She could not see his face but she imagined him winking at her. "I have seeds in my pockets."

She was contemplating with some trepidation what kind of experiment Martin intended to perform when there was a sudden exclamation from Veressa. They had reached a dead end.

"We've taken a wrong turn somewhere," Veressa said worriedly, peering at her map. Shadrack huddled with her and they compared routes. "I thought we were here." She pointed at her paper. "Sophia?"

Sophia joined them, holding her map up to the torchlight. "We must have turned off this way by mistake," Shadrack said, tracing downward.

"Let's turn back, then." Veressa's voice was tense with frustration. "You may as well go in front for a while."

"Very well," he agreed, taking up the map.

They retraced their steps along two passageways, and Shadrack led them through a low tunnel whose floor curved like the inside of a pipe. Sophia counted her paces as they traveled deeper and deeper into the labyrinth. The air around them was surprisingly varied—dry and warm in some places, cold and damp in others—but the darkness remained absolute. The nighting vine grew in fitful bursts along the labyrinth walls. Climbing stubbornly over broken stones and through narrow openings, the pale vine's map grew stunted and distorted.

All conversation slowly died away, and they trudged on in silence. Their footsteps and weary breathing transformed as they walked, amplifying in the high caverns and shrinking down to muffled rasps in the narrow corridors. The tunnels seemed to wind onward interminably, and still the labyrinth led them deeper. They paused several times so that Shadrack could consult the map, and as they stopped a fifth time, Sophia heard the sound again. "Does anyone hear that?" she asked. "It—it sounds like people running."

"I hear it, too," Veressa replied from behind her. "But it's not people. It's running water."

Sophia shook her head, unconvinced, but said nothing. The stone walls narrowed almost to the width of Burr's shoulders, and then, to her surprise, a break in the wall transformed the passageway. The pockmarked stone wall gave way to smooth bricks of greenish-gray, and the air felt less stale. "This is a different Age altogether," Martin muttered, without taking his hand from Theo's shoulder. They walked along the corridor for nearly two hundred paces, winding right repeatedly as the tunnels forked.

The sound Sophia had heard was replaced by the unmistakable sound of running water. *Veressa must be right,* Sophia thought. *I was only hearing the water.*

"Watch your step!" Shadrack called back. Sophia watched as each person before her dropped out of sight, and she realized, as Theo crouched abruptly, that they were passing through an opening in the floor. Martin eased himself into the hole and Sophia followed. Calixta handed her torch through and then jumped down. Sophia looked around, taking in the strange walls. Cut from smooth, white stone tinged with green, they had shallow depressions with curious adornments—statues calcified and stained from their long entombment. Shadrack, already leading the way along the corridor, climbed a short flight of steps through a curved archway and disappeared.

Sophia heard exclamations from those at the front of the line, and she waited impatiently. The air around them changed yet again, becoming warm and humid with a heavy, earthy smell. Then Martin stumbled out of the way ahead of her, and she found herself in a vast chamber as large as the palace dungeon. But the room had obviously never been a dungeon. As Burr walked tentatively forward with his torch, pieces of it came into view. The curved walls, where the nighting vine grew unencumbered, climbed two or three stories high. Pale statues of standing figures—men and women with long, obscured faces—stood in the walls' niches and at intervals along a staircase that crossed the room at a diagonal. A rush of clear water ran down the steps, vanishing into a dark tunnel.

Sophia looked around her in amazement. There could be no doubt. The room was not a room at all—it was an underground garden. Only the nighting vine survived, but stone walkways and pale urns across the dirt floor outlined where other plants had once grown. Martin, standing next to her, bent down to take a pinch of soil between his fingertips. His voice was hushed and full of wonder. "I believe we are in the ruins of a lost Age!"

34
A Lost Age

1891, July 1: #-Hour

Certain architectural remains are particularly difficult to date, since even in their corresponding Age they are considered ruins. For example, the ruins of an earthquake might survive for five hundred years, just as in some Ages cherished monuments and dwellings survive for hundreds of years. Thus the ruins—abandoned, partially disintegrated, and entirely uninhabited—seem to belong to an earlier Age while in fact belonging to a later one.

—From Veressa Metl's Cultural Geography of the Baldlands

WHILE THE OTHERS fanned out, taking in the sculptures and the cascade of water, Sophia crouched next to Martin. "What is a lost Age?" she asked.

"Lost," Martin said, pushing himself to his feet, "in the sense that these are the ruins of a civilization that declined *within its own Age.*"

"What do you mean?"

"You see," he said, moving excitedly over to the staircase, all exhaustion suddenly forgotten, "when the Great Disruption occurred, these ruins appeared. That means they were *already* ruins. I would guess that this underground garden had already been abandoned and quietly disintegrating for"—he paused, rubbing the pale marble— "perhaps six hundred years."

"Six hundred years," Sophia breathed. She looked up at the staircase and realized in astonishment that Theo, knee-deep in rushing water, was climbing it. "Theo?"

He turned to wave. He was more than twenty feet above her, near the arched entryway through which the water descended. "This is really warm," he called down. "And there's something up here."

Slowly, the others assembled near the staircase and looked upward. "It's incredibly warm," Veressa agreed, testing the water. "There might be a hot spring below the caves."

Theo climbed the last few steps. "I can't see," he called, his voice faint over the rushing water, "but it looks like there's a big cavern."

"Onward," Burr said eagerly, mounting the stairs.

Shadrack frowned thoughtfully, scrutinizing his map. "That must be it. We came in through the only entryway that doesn't have running water. According to this, we turn. Veressa? Sophia?"

Sophia nodded, reading her own map by Calixta's torch. "I think so."

"Let's try it," Veressa agreed.

One by one, they mounted the staircase. The warm water immediately seeped through Sophia's thin boots, and more than once she almost lost her footing. She was glad to see that Shadrack was helping Martin.

The others had reached the archway and were standing just

beyond it on the embankment. With the torches held high, Sophia realized that the stream of water emerged from a shallow aqueduct cut into the stone. They all turned toward the vast cavern that they could feel but not yet see. The murmur of water came from deep within the darkness, echoing quietly. Holding the torches higher only made the ground below dim. They could see nothing but the entryway to the subterranean garden behind them and a short portion of the aqueduct.

In the moment that the group stood there, pondering the depth of the dark cavern, Martin reached into his pocket and tossed a seed onto the stony floor.

"What was that?" Veressa asked apprehensively.

"Nothing," Martin replied. "Just a seed."

As he spoke, a strange rustling, distinct from the murmur of water, sounded in the darkness. After a moment's hesitation, Burr held his torch high and stepped forward. And then he stopped, aghast. A pale tendril had burst out from the loose soil. Burr bent forward as if to swipe at the vine with his arm.

"Wait!" Martin exclaimed. "Leave it!" They watched in silence as the vine spiraled into the air, turning into a slender sapling before their eyes. "I've been dropping seeds," he explained quickly, without taking his eyes off the growing plant, "in the hopes that this would happen."

The sapling thickened, throwing branches in every direction. Its metallic roots punctured the cavern floor, anchoring the little tree firmly. Then the branches began to grow shoots that unfurled into pale, silvery leaves. As the trunk sprouted upward, the leaves stretched far beyond the faint light of the torches. And then, to everyone's astonishment, the leaves themselves emitted a bright, silvery light that shone like the moon into the dark recesses of the cavern.

The pale glow of the tree cast just enough light to see that the space before them stretched farther than they could have imagined. A great underground city stood before them. The slim waterway through which they had emerged led directly toward it, passing under a metal archway that seemed to mark the city's entrance. Apart from the aqueduct, the city was perfectly still. High towers and gables shadowed one another in the silvery light like the stones and monuments of a crowded cemetery.

They stood in awed silence, gazing at the ruins. Finally Shadrack spoke. "Is there any mention of this place that you know of?" he asked Veressa.

"None. I have neither read nor heard anything about it."

"Then we are the first to explore it." Shadrack's voice was tight with excitement.

Martin hobbled forward, passing his hand lightly over the trunk of the silver tree. "What genius they must have had. That is why the roots are metallic. To reach through stone—or *ice*."

"Father?" Veressa said, going after him.

Martin reached into his pocket and dropped something else onto the ground. "Lovely," he said, smiling, his face illuminated on one side by the pale light of the tree and on the other side by the yellow light of Burr's torch. "An avenue of brilliant maples, leading to the city gates."

As he spoke, the seed that had fluttered to the ground

cracked open and plunged its thin roots into the earth. A slender stem burst upward, throwing its pale limbs into the air like smoke from a doused fire. The trunk thickened, the branches stretched upward, and the fragile limbs were suddenly filled with tiny buds that in a single, sweeping movement opened into delicate leaves. They were shaped like maple leaves, but they shone with an unearthly luminescence. Martin stood staring up at it, and then he pressed his hand reverently against the trunk. "Beautiful," he whispered.

"Father, be careful," Veressa said, taking his arm. "We don't know what these seeds do."

"It's not the *seeds*, my dear," Martin said, turning to face her. "It is the ground—the earth. The earth of *this Age*. And to think—this has been here all along."

"Then you know this Age?"

"Yes and no," Martin said slowly. "It is the same Age as the one Burr found—where he got the soil that gave me a silver leg." He bent down with effort and took a pinch of dirt between his fingertips. "Amazing. It isn't a hot spring. It is the *soil* that warms the water. The earth has heating properties." The others bent down and pressed their hands to the ground. Sophia gasped in surprise. The dirt felt as warm as if it had been baking in the sun for hours. "Look here," Martin exclaimed, pointing into the aqueduct. "The soil at the base of the aqueduct glows red—like fire, like molten rock."

Veressa turned back to Shadrack. "Where do you think we are? How close are we to finding the way out?"

"We have traveled about three miles from the Nochtland

palace," he said. "Three miles southeast. Would you agree, Sophia?"

Sophia nodded distractedly. "Three miles," she said, gazing out at the deserted city. She could see, even from a distance and in the pale light cast by the trees, that the buildings were encrusted with centuries of mineral growth: rough, sparkling surfaces like rock salt covered the walls and roofs and the tall posts that must have once been lamps. *How long has it been,* she wondered, *since someone set foot here?* The thrill of discovery, the longing for exploration that she had heard in her uncle's voice, flitted briefly through her. *Maybe Grandmother Pearl's story was real,* she thought. *Maybe the boy who destroyed the city will be here.*

Veressa bent over the map, frowning as she drew her finger along the winding underground route. "Traveling southeast three miles. Where would we be above ground? There is no road here. This is . . ." she trailed off. Then her eyes widened. "This is Lake Cececpan. We are almost beneath it. The lake must be"—she lifted her head to look across the cavern—"almost directly above us." They raised their eyes collectively to the ceiling, as if expecting to see the lake there, hanging overhead.

"Lake Cececpan," Shadrack repeated. "Could it be—"

"It is a great coincidence, if nothing else," Veressa cut in, putting the map down. "But the location of the *carta mayor* does not matter," she said firmly. "We are looking for the exit, and I believe the exit will be just beside the lake. If Sophia's idea about the flowers is correct, the passage will be somewhere here."

"I agree. It must lie somewhere in the city."

"In the city?" Veressa echoed doubtfully. "Surely it is more likely to be in the cavern wall?"

Sophia drew herself away from the alluring view of the city. "Yes, I think so, too—it would be in the wall."

"The passage may go down before it goes up," Shadrack insisted, walking forward. Logic and experience suggested that Veressa and Sophia were right, but the abandoned city posed too great a temptation. It lay there untouched, quiet and full of mystery, waiting to be explored.

"Searching the city for an entrance will take so long," Veressa objected. "The rest of us can walk the perimeter of the cavern to save time."

Shadrack hesitated. "Very well—we can keep sight of each other with the torches."

"And the trees!" Martin added. "I can drop seeds, and those will illuminate the way."

"Fine," Shadrack agreed. "Theo and Sophia can come with me. Burr, Calixta—you go with Veressa and Martin along the perimeter."

"Take some seeds, Sophia," Martin said, handing her a small fistful from another pocket.

As the pirates and the Metls withdrew, Sophia walked alongside Theo and Shadrack, dropping seeds. The towering trees blossomed behind them, and she saw another line rise up along the cavern's edge. Soon even the darkest corners were faintly illuminated by the silvery light, and Sophia looked up with awe at the high, domed ceiling. She squinted, seeing a dark patch high on the wall. "Look," she said to Shadrack. "Doesn't that look like a hole or a doorway?"

"It may be," he said absently, glancing upward only briefly. "If it is, Veressa will find it."

Sophia noticed a shadowy line zigzagging away from the dark spot. "Those might even be stairs leading up to it."

They had reached the entrance, and Shadrack paused for a moment, resting his hand against the greenish archway. The gates, like the rest of the city, were encrusted with mineral deposits that made them glitter in the silver light. The lacy trelliswork of the arch overhead had broken in places, disintegrated by the salty air and the chalky limestone. "Quite ancient," Shadrack remarked. "And not from this Age. We are in the presence of something I had never thought to see," he said. "The ruins of a future Age. Remarkable. This opportunity may never come again," he said, drawing Theo and Sophia toward the gates. "We are a fortunate few. Even if we never emerge from this place, we have been privileged to see it."

"But we *will* emerge from it?" Sophia asked anxiously.

Shadrack seemed not to hear her. "Come—let's search the city."

It was impossible to know what the buildings had originally looked like, for they were utterly transformed. High towers, connected to one other by bridges, created a second network of passageways above the streets. Many of the doorways had calcified, their doors sealed shut forever. Others stood open like sad, drooping eyes, their empty rooms staring out blindly. The ground beneath their feet was hard, but the seeds Sophia dropped threw roots nonetheless, breaking through the rock and sprouting quickly into silvery vines that climbed up the limestone walls and burst into brilliant bloom, releasing a sweet scent. There was no sign of human life; the buildings were empty of even the sparest furniture. The most visible mark left by the people who had inhabited the city were the sculptures that stood in front of almost every building. Cut from pale green stone, like those in the subterranean garden, they were deformed beyond recognition by the calcite. Had they not appeared unmistakably shaped by human hands, it would almost have seemed possible that the entire city was nothing more than a fantastic sculpture built by the earth itself.

They had seen nothing in the city to suggest a passageway or stairway leading aboveground. Sophia had lost sight of the others circling the perimeter, though she thought she could hear them over the constant sound of running water. Their voices drifted suddenly toward her; low and distorted by the echo in the chamber, they sounded like different voices altogether. She paused for a moment, straining anxiously to hear, and then the strange voices faded and the bubbling water that wound its way through the city in pale, shallow gutters drowned them out. She shook her head to clear it and walked on.

She was on the verge of reminding Shadrack about the staircase cut high in the wall when something else caught her attention. She stopped in her tracks. There was something odd in the air, she realized: a smell—no, a temperature change. It was suddenly almost freezing.

Theo and Shadrack had stopped as well, and they turned to

look at one another. "Is it colder in here?" Theo asked. His own words answered him as his breath turned white.

Sophia knew what was coming, but she did not feel afraid, only shocked. They were too late; the change had come. The glaciers were moving overhead. A sudden rumbling sound, like the roar of a storm, exploded all around them. The ground began to shake, as if quivering under the weight of some unbearably heavy mass, and the buildings around them shuddered. Then the walls of earth groaned in agony, and Sophia felt certain that they would burst, crumbling to pieces before her eyes. Suddenly, as quickly as it had begun, the groaning stopped and the city grew still. Sophia looked around her, stunned. *Is that it?* she thought. *Why are we still here?* She had dropped to the ground and she stayed there, crouching warily. The dirt beneath her fingers was still reassuringly warm. She looked at Shadrack and Theo, who wore similar expressions of confusion.

Then she heard another sound—one that was entirely unexpected: the crack of a pistol. *The pirates don't have their pistols,* Sophia thought, bewildered. Suddenly a sharp report echoed just over her head, and a chunk of calcified rock crashed to the ground beside her. She turned, hardly believing her eyes: crouched low by one of the towers was a Sandman, pointing his revolver directly toward her. Three other men standing beside him took aim.

35
Below the Lake

1891, July 1: #-Hour

In some parts of the Triple Eras, there is a great devotion to the Chronicles of the Great Disruption. *In Xela, believers celebrate the "enday of the world," a day that will spell the end of the human world. Followers of the* Chronicles *claim that the Great Disruption was the first of many, and that the Final Disruption will result in an end of all days.*

—From Veressa Metl's Cultural Geography of the Baldlands

Far above them, up past hundreds of feet of rock, the glaciers were encasing Lake Cececpan. Ice had surrounded the lake, sending the few families who lived on its banks fleeing northwest toward Nochtland. The waves of refugees from farther south had already rushed past the city, convinced that even the high stone walls would offer no safety. Though the Southern Snows were still out of sight of the city, no one could now deny their inexorable advance. A line of boldevelas streamed out through the northern gates, trailed by even longer lines of people who traveled on foot or in wagons. The exodus northward had begun.

But the glaciers had not yet reached Nochtland, and for the moment they had halted at the banks of Lake Cececpan. Though the lake was no longer visible, it was still there. It appeared to have been swallowed by a large chunk of ice shaped like a perfect pyramid. The ice struggled to gain purchase against the patches of hot soil that protected the lake and portions of the tunnels below it. The vast city below ground remained buffered from the frigid air, but beyond it, where the tunnels and caverns were cut from ordinary earth, the water had frozen solid, marbling the rocks with veins of ice. The freezing water loosened rocks, causing innumerable tremors and crumbling the walls of the underground warren. As the rocks settled, the shaking stopped and cold air filled the tunnels.

Down in the underground city, Sophia ran as fast as she could, her damp boots sticking to the dirt. She and Theo followed Shadrack as he raced through the city, away from the Sandmen's pistols and the falling rocks caused by their bullets. Sophia tried to call to him, but she was so out of breath that she could hardly find her voice. They had reached a narrow avenue, and while Shadrack slowed to find the easiest way out, Sophia managed to say, "Shadrack, up there." She pointed, feeling sure that she could see the staircase and the opening high in the cavern wall. As she did so, a bullet hit the tower near her and a chunk of white limestone splintered over her head.

"Go on, then," Shadrack replied urgently. "Hurry."

Sophia took off. Her breath came more and more painfully. She turned a corner, slipping on the loose soil, and sped over a broad archway that led to the aqueduct. *This has to be it*, she thought, running beside the aqueduct, following it under two slender bridges.

Abruptly she found herself at a gate identical to the one at the city's entrance, only a few feet from the far wall of the cavern. And she had been right—the stairs were there: cut into the stone, they zigzagged upward precipitously toward the opening in the wall. "This is it," she cried, turning to the others.

There was no one behind her.

She stood, stock still, staring in disbelief at the pale buildings. She could hear shots and the thundering of footsteps, but she could not tell whether they were near or far. She was about to dive back into the city in search of Shadrack and Theo, but then the rocks above her head splintered with a loud crack, showering her with dust.

One of the men had seen her. He came from beside a building a good distance away, advancing steadily. While he held the revolver with his right hand, he loosened the long rope of the grappling hook with his left. Sophia had only two choices: she could run along the perimeter or she could climb the stairs. For what seemed like an eternity to her, she stood, full of doubt, as the man came toward her. Then she whirled and began to climb as fast as she could.

The steps were only three feet wide, and there was no railing. She kept her eyes forward and did not look down. *He won't climb*, Sophia thought desperately, *he'll shoot rather than climb*. As she heard the wall splinter behind her, she knew that she had guessed correctly. *I have to make sure the others see me.* Without stopping, she reached into the pocket of her skirt and dropped a seed—she did not wait to see if it sprouted. Her legs were beginning to feel weak and she could tell, from the trembling sensation in her knees, that she was slowing down. The stair beneath her bottom foot suddenly gave way, and she looked down in horror to see it crumbling beneath the prongs of the Sandman's grappling hook. *Keep going, keep going!* she told herself fiercely, gritting her teeth and pushing forward. She passed another turn and dropped another seed. There was another turn, another twenty steps, another seed, another turn. . . . *How much longer?* she thought, not daring to look up or down. She counted, ticking off twenty steps and a turn and then another twenty steps. And then, at the top of the next flight, there it was: a narrow entrance in the stone.

She ran the last twenty steps and ducked into the dark entryway. Stopping to catch her breath, she looked out into the immense, domed cavern. The sight made her dizzy. The city seemed small, like a cluster of spun-sugar houses. She could still hear the occasional burst of gunfire. The Sandman was nowhere to be seen. The seeds she dropped had burst into brilliant bloom, climbing up the limestone wall and casting a piercing white light into the chamber. *If they look up they'll know where I went,* Sophia thought, her breath painful in her chest. *They can't possibly miss it. I can wait here until they notice.*

She looked out over the city desperately and suddenly saw a pale glimmer from among the buildings—a brief silver flash.

It was not a torch or a sword blade; it reminded her of something. *Light reflected on a mirror, moonlight on a windowpane, something else—what is it?* There was the flash again, and she realized that it was Theo's hand, wrapped in the silver thread. She took a deep breath. "Theo!"

A chunk of rock burst from the wall beside her leg. The Sandman was still several flights below, and the angle of the stairs did not permit him a clear shot. But he would keep climbing, and sooner or later he would reach the doorway.

Sophia turned away in anguish; she would have to keep going. It was impossible to see inside the tunnel. She dropped a seed and waited impatiently as the vine climbed the tunnel wall, springing to life with a hundred blossoms. The air smelled like honeysuckle; the flowers shone like tiny stars, and as they bloomed Sophia saw the wide tunnel that curved upward along a set of wide, stone stairs. "*More* stairs?" she cried in despair.

She kept her strength by walking at a measured pace, and whenever the faint light of the last vine grew dim, she dropped another seed so that the sweet-smelling flowers would light her way. Soon the sound of shots faded, and she could hear nothing but her own steps and rasping breath. Although there were no footsteps behind her, she did not allow herself to believe that she had outrun her pursuer.

The climb felt interminable. Her feet in the wet boots moved woodenly. She knew that she had to keep climbing, but she felt a sense of despair at having left the others. *They will see the vines,* she said firmly. *They will see the vines and know where I went.* She tried to keep track of time by counting her steps. *One step per second. One seed every fifty steps.*

When she reached five hundred steps, her legs began to shake. At eight hundred steps, she was certain she could not go on. But if she stopped, surely she would lose track of time. If she rested for what felt to her like a moment, an entire hour might pass and the man behind her would catch up. *I have to,* she thought desperately. *Just for a few seconds.* Her legs seemed to stop moving of their own accord. Leaning against the wall in the dark, she closed her eyes. Her knees were shaking so hard she could not even stand. With an involuntary sob, Sophia sank to a crouch and rested her head on her bent knees. She counted carefully: *one, two, three, four, five, six . . .*

The seconds passed. Sophia counted. She realized, as the numbers grew larger, that what was happening to her was the thing she had always feared the most: being alone, in a place where time passed invisibly, where she might close her eyes and suddenly wake up to find that days, months, years had passed. *This is what I'm afraid of. This is what I'm always afraid of.* But the thought brought her no terror. It seemed, rather, to bring a kind of clarity. *What really keeps me here, in the present? Nothing. I could open my eyes and be in the future. Instead of memories of a whole life, I'd have . . .* She opened her eyes and stared into the darkness. She had forgotten to count. The silence around her was absolute. Several thoughts flashed suddenly in Sophia's mind at once; her eyes widened.

She had a vivid recollection of standing on the deck of the *Swan*. Grandmother Pearl's voice came to her in the darkness, clear and sweet: *"What else is there, that no one else is seeing because they're looking at the time?"*

"Not bound to time," Sophia whispered aloud in the darkness. "Future, past, present—it makes no difference to me. I can see them for what they are." She rose unsteadily to her feet. The sight of Theo's hand, bound in silver thread, glinting in the underground chamber, filled her mind like a light. *It's Theo,* she realized, *it's Theo who runs toward me when the tower collapses.* She remembered the first time she had read the glass map, aboard the *Seaboard Limited,* sitting across from Theo in the moonlight. Then she had read it again, and again, and each time that same figure—more well-known, more painfully dear—had appeared at the end. The memories had seemed so vivid, so familiar, so real.

"I can see them for what they are," Sophia murmured.

No longer counting, no longer having any need, she rose and climbed. Her legs seemed to spring forward without effort, despite her exhaustion and the darkness.

She reached into her pocket for another seed. Then she noticed with surprise that it was unnecessary. She could see the steps beneath her feet. A pale light spread toward her from the top of the stairs. Without pausing to look up, she climbed onward. Suddenly a cold rush of air hit her brow and she lifted her head. There was an opening only a few steps above her. Sophia took the final step. Numbly, she dropped the seed pinched between her fingers.

She found herself at the edge of a frozen lake, inside a high pyramid with glassy walls. Beyond their frosted surfaces, snow fell silently while flashes of lightning lit up the gray sky in the distance. It was just as she had seen so many times before on the surface of the four maps. *We all thought the memories on the maps came from the past,* she thought, *but they were from the future. They are my memories. My memories of destroying this place.*

36
A Map of the World

1891, July #: #-Hour

Cartographites: The tools of the trade belonging to a cartologer. In portions of the known world where cartologers are believed to possess the skill of divination, cartographites are considered instruments of great power. The belief has some basis in fact, as the cartologer's tools are frequently found objects from the other Ages.

—*From Veressa Metl's* Glossary of Baldlandian Terms

A LONG, SPIRALING balcony circled the walls of the pyramid, leaving the frozen lake in the center untouched. Its surface, a clear slab marbled with white rime, could not entirely conceal the remarkable waters below. Sophia did not need the Tracing Glass to know that the lake was a map—the largest map she had ever seen. The *carta mayor.*

From the banks of the lake, she could see faint spurts of color swirling like tiny fish trapped below the ice. Lost for a moment in time, she considered how the memories she was about to create had found their way onto the four maps. Her mind folded hours of deliberation into a brief, illuminating second.

I had forgotten, Sophia thought, *what a map really is: a guide for the path one must follow. The glass map does not contain memories. It contains directions. It has been telling me all along what I alone must do.*

She stepped forward to look more closely at the *carta mayor* and knelt to press her palm against the frozen surface. The cold burned and rushed to her brain. She stayed there for a long time, her mind lost to the gentle movements that beckoned from beneath. As she took her hand away, she felt entirely calm. The ice had cooled her lungs and her aching legs. Her mind was refreshed. Taking a deep, cleansing breath, she turned toward the curving balcony and again prepared herself to climb.

I will climb to the top, she thought steadily, *and from there push the stone that will bring the tower down. That is what the maps say I must do.* But then something unexpected happened. Stepping onto the balcony, she placed her hand against the wall to steady herself, and a sudden rush of memories flooded her mind. She pulled away and looked at the wall more closely. The glass squares, slippery and slightly damp, were alive with finely graven images. As she glanced upward, she understood that every block in the pyramid was a carefully placed map: a map with memories of the Southern Snows.

She could not resist the temptation to walk slowly, tracing her finger across the smooth surfaces, letting the memories fill her mind.

She remembered dark days without sunlight and long

seasons of bitter cold that seemed to chill her to the bone. She recalled seeking shelter in snowy caves and struggling to find warmth in the weak flames of a fire fed with animal bones. But then the memories changed, and she began to understand how the people had carved their lives out of the ice. The world of their Age was a vast, frozen expanse. Glaciers stretched across the earth, interrupted only by the freezing waters of the sea. There was no soil, no plant life, and hardly any sunlight. The inhabitants cut their homes out of the glaciers and ate from the ocean. For hundreds and hundreds of years, they survived with nothing more.

And then, Sophia recalled, one among them received a map. There were no memories of where it came from. Painted on sealskin, the map showed a route through the heart of the glaciers to caves deep underground. Caves that were warm and dry—and dark. They built their homes in the underground chambers, hollowing out larger and larger spaces for the growing subterranean cities. They never entirely abandoned the aboveground world of ice, but over time they traveled less frequently back and forth.

Sophia paused at the map that brought her the memories of the first experiments with soil. As she walked on, her fingers passing lightly over the glass, she was overwhelmed by the discoveries that had taken place. She did not understand them, but she could see the laborious task of finding rare soils and the even more arduous tasks of transforming, transmuting, and finally inventing soils.

She was almost a third of the way up the pyramid. She

walked slowly, unaware of the empty stairway; crowds of people filled her vision as the memories flashed before her.

The discoveries in soil led to the growth of new plants—those that grew on small patches of underground soil, without sunlight, and those that grew on soil scattered across the ice. As the soils were adjusted, the roots grew more sophisticated, incorporating metals from the soil that permitted them to break through and acquire nourishment from even the most inhospitable rock and ice. The plants were bred to every purpose: to illuminate the underground caverns, to provide food where no ordinary crops would grow, to fill the labyrinthine tunnels with voices that would guide the way.

As the people grew in their accomplishments, they also grew bolder, and some migrated to the aboveground world of ice. The miraculous soil of their age meant that no climate was too harsh; they had no limits. They built wonderful cities upon the glaciers, filling the continents, making those ancient days of insurmountable cold seem a distant nightmare. And they became explorers. In their intrepid expansion across the globe, they learned to create memory maps. Cartology in the glacial Age reached the pinnacle of its achievements.

Sophia stopped. She took her hand from the wall and her mind away from the memories that had absorbed it. Something had interrupted them, but she was not sure what. Had she heard a sound from within the pyramid? No—not a sound; something else. She brought her face close to the clear wall and looked through at the world beyond. The strange storm of snow and lightning continued, but from her high vantage point she saw for the first time that the pyramid was surrounded by an entire city. Almost invisible against the glacier, the white buildings stretched out along broad avenues. She saw, too, the sight that had distracted her from the maps: there were people here and there walking far below.

She could not tell, from such a height, who they were. She did not know if Shadrack and Theo might be among them, having found their way out of the tunnels, or if the people of the Southern Snows were walking along the icy streets, unconscious of the fact that someone from another Age was scaling their pyramid, intent on destroying it.

Sophia felt a spasm of unease and continued walking purposefully up the shallow steps. She knew that she had lost track of time. The skies were the same color, but the strange electrical storm taking place over the glacier made it unclear whether it was dawn, daytime, or dusk. For all she knew, hours might have passed.

From time to time, as she scaled the steps, she tried to catch glimpses of the people she had seen before. But the higher she climbed, the more difficult it was. They had become small specks, moving imperceptibly across the ice. As she reached the top of the pyramid, the streaks of lightning grew brighter and fiercer. Above her, a rounded balcony jutted out from the wall directly below the pyramid's peak.

From the balcony, Sophia could see beyond the walls in every direction. To the south, the craggy face of the glacier stretched to the horizon. To the north were the deserted plains of the Baldlands and the gray contours of Nochtland. The city seemed pitifully small from such a distance: no more than a rocky bump in the glacier's path.

At the center of the balcony was a stone sphere almost as tall as she was, and balanced on it was a miniature reproduction of the pyramid itself, cut in glass. Her eyes traveled down the length of the wall, over the thousands of maps that spiraled toward the base of the pyramid. They recounted a long, continuous history of the Age. *Surely,* Sophia thought, *the map on the pedestal is the last—the last memories stored for the creation of the pyramid.*

Before approaching it, she walked to the edge of the balcony. The sight made her dizzy. She stepped back to steady herself and then leaned cautiously forward once again. The frozen lake was visible in its entirety. The map of the world lay below her, created by some unknown hand with some unknown instrument, trapped below the ice. It was not still. A restless light appeared to move across it, altering the colors and patterns below the surface. Sophia was mesmerized, uncomprehending. What vision of the world did it reflect? What possibilities of past and future did it capture in its frozen depths?

She pulled herself away from the balcony railing with a sense of piercing sadness. *How can I destroy all this?* she thought. There was no doubt in her mind that the memories from the four maps were meant to be hers, but she could not bring herself to do the thing that would make those memories real. Below that frozen surface lay a world of knowledge, visions, truths. She imagined the slender current of water that carried the story of how her parents had left New Occident, never to be seen again. It lay somewhere there below the ice, containing all the secrets of her parents' lives. Sophia was overwhelmed with such a sense of longing to know—to finally *know*—that she sank against the railing.

As she leaned forward, she heard an unexpected sound—a footfall. Someone had followed her. Someone had climbed all the way up through the pyramid without being seen and was about to step onto the balcony beside her. Sophia steeled herself against the Sandman with the pistol who had pursued her in the underground cavern. She did not feel afraid; her stomach hardened as if preparing for a sudden blow.

But it was not the man with the revolver. As the person who had followed her came into view, Sophia drew back inadvertently. The veil was gone and the scarred face was pale against the unbound hair, which was tousled and tangled and wet with snow.

Blanca had found her.

37
THE END OF DAYS

1891, July #: #-Hour

Enday: the term used by followers of the Chronicles of the Great Disruption *to designate the day when a given Age comes to a close. The term is ambiguous, as it remains unclear whether it used merely to designate the conclusion of a calendar Age or rather to mark the destruction of one Age giving way to another.*

—*From Veressa Metl's* Glossary of Baldlandian Terms

SOPHIA STOOD GUARDEDLY before the pedestal, watching Blanca as she stepped onto the balcony. For a moment, neither of them spoke. Blanca appeared hardly to notice her. She walked past Sophia to the railing and watched the lake.

"I did not realize until after you had left," Blanca said, "that the maps describe this moment—here, now." She turned, and Sophia saw her scarred face. "Not the Great Disruption itself—merely its distant echo." She laughed quietly, bitterly. "But you—you understood. You are a better cartologer than I am, after all. Perhaps because you have no sense of time, your mind floats free," she mused. "You see things for what they are, regardless of when they are."

Sophia did not say anything. Blanca's dress and cloak were torn, her hands scratched. The Lachrima appeared to have been through some battle with the elements or, worse, with other people, and Sophia wondered fearfully about the state of those people. "What happened to you?" she finally asked.

Blanca continued as if she had not heard. "When I realized how I had misread the maps, I rushed to the dungeons, only to find that you were already gone. The Nochtland guard told me that you had left through the tunnels, and I understood at once. Did you guess it, or did you read the truth in the maps on these walls?"

"Guess what?"

"That these advancing Southern Snows and my home, the Glacine Age, are one and the same."

Sophia shook her head. "I didn't know what the four maps meant either. I didn't know anything until I got here and read these maps. The glass maps in the walls." She paused. "And then I knew they were about this place, and that I had to destroy it." Sophia dropped her head. "I'm here, but I can't bring myself to do it."

Blanca turned with a sigh and again looked out over the frozen lake. "Poor child. You truly have no sense of time. Do you know how long you have spent here, from the moment you left the caverns?"

Sophia felt a flutter of anxiety in her stomach. "No."

"More than nine hours by the clock of the Baldlands. Twenty-five hours by the clock of New Occident. Two days have dawned."

Sophia gasped.

"You would probably linger on here until the end of time, were you left to your own devices," Blanca said wistfully.

"More than an entire day," Sophia whispered, her voice choked. "I thought perhaps an hour—or two."

"While you have been contemplating the maps of the Great Hall," Blanca said, facing Sophia once again, "I have lost my chance to save the Glacine Age. The glaciers have advanced quickly. They have already covered the *carta mayor*. We are too late."

"I don't understand. You wanted the Glacine Age to cover the earth. Why didn't you just wait for the glaciers to follow their own course? Why even bother to find the *carta mayor*?"

"You have not yet gone beyond the hall," Blanca said, with a weary wave of her hand. "You have not seen the Glacine Age as it exists now." Her sigh seemed to carry years of exhaustion. "From the moment I learned who I was—from the moment your uncle freed me—it was my goal to return to my Age. I finally found my way to Tierra del Fuego, where I discovered a portion of the Glacine Age, whole and intact. Do you have any idea—can you imagine—the joy I felt at the chance to walk once again in my own Age? To be *home*? I had so longed to hear my own language. To hear my name—" She uttered a sound that seemed unlike speech, but that suggested by its intonation a vivid lightness: glad and bright and somehow young. "You must know what I mean. You have hardly been gone from New Occident, and yet I am sure you long to return there."

Sophia knew it was not the same, but recalling her home on East Ending Street, she had some sense of what Blanca felt. "I think so."

"Well then," Blanca said, her voice catching, "imagine what it would be like to return to Boston, your beloved city, and find it deserted—in ruins. Not a living soul anywhere. Only the remains of the lives that once filled it."

Sophia could not help but glance through the pyramid's wall at the ice city below. "The Age was deserted?"

Blanca gave a bitter laugh. "Entirely deserted. The whole of the Glacine Age was an empty shell—a lifeless husk. Its people were long since dead. Its cities were falling into ruin. All that remained was ice and stone. The world I remembered was gone—*is* gone."

"But I don't understand." Sophia moved back to stand against the wall. "Isn't *this* the Age you belong to? An Age with living people in it?"

"No one, it seems, can return to the world of their own past." Blanca moved to stand beside her. "It is, indeed, my Age. But I was twenty at the time of the Disruption, and by the time I returned, more than eighty years had passed. The Glacine Age as I knew it was destroyed. The ice triumphed. Every living thing perished. Nothing but the glaciers survive."

"But I saw people walking below," Sophia protested.

"You saw the Lachrima," Blanca said dully. "The Lachrima

born of this new border. There are hundreds of them. Those are the only cursed creatures who will inhabit this Age now.

"Comprehending the full destruction of my Age, I gave it up for lost. But then I heard the Nihilismian myth, and I believed there could be truth in it; I felt hope again. If I could find the *carta mayor,* I would be able to rewrite history, avert the destruction; I would be able to make the Glacine Age whole, living once more." Blanca stared out at the frozen expanse beyond the walls. "While searching for the *carta mayor,* I learned that the Age was advancing northward. Like an expanding tomb, the glaciers were overtaking the earth, and *my* Age—the wondrous Age I knew and loved—would never exist." She put her hand against the pyramid wall. "I was too late. I am too late."

Sophia gazed out over the empty city, stunned. She looked south across the vast white expanse, imagining the thousands of miles of deserted ice, the frozen cities slowly crumbling, the underground warrens disintegrating. The glaciers were reclaiming everything in their path. Sophia glanced up at Blanca's scarred face, and she was sure that she could see grief in her featureless expression. *What could possibly be worse,* she thought, *than losing not only one's family, one's friends, one's home, but one's entire living world?* Sophia extended her hand tentatively and placed it in Blanca's. "I'm sorry," she whispered.

Blanca pressed Sophia's hand. As they watched, the storm overhead drew north, passing over the pyramid and following the advancing glaciers. Blanca turned her back, releasing Sophia's hand. "The storm is moving quickly," she said, more to herself than to Sophia. "There isn't much time." Reaching into her cloak, she pulled out the four maps and handed them to Sophia, who held them for a moment, surprised, before stowing them in her pack. Then Blanca drew from her neck the silk scarf that had once been her veil and dropped it over the pyramid that stood on the round stone. "Take this map," she said. "It will hold some of the answers you seek."

Sophia took the wrapped pyramid-map in her arms. "What are you going to do?"

"We must disperse the waters of the *carta mayor.*"

"But why?"

"I know it is difficult to accept without explanation, child, but the glaciers will stop their advance if we take the *carta mayor* out of its path. The map must be prevented from joining with the glacier."

"I don't understand," Sophia said desperately.

"It is a living map of the world. As its contents freeze, so does the earth freeze. Do you understand?" Sophia nodded hesitantly. "Then understand that, if we can ensure that the waters of the map travel into the warm soil below ground, the glaciers will halt." She paused. "You know what we must do—you have seen it." Blanca's voice was gentle, reassuring "We will roll this stone into the lake. When the stone falls, it will rupture the lake bed, and the waters will channel into the underground tunnels. Unreadable, yes. But safe."

"But the hall will collapse! All the maps—and the waters below. Shadrack will never read them. I'll never find out . . ."

Blanca looked at her in silence, her scars furrowing with pity. "I know, child, I know. I know what a loss it will be. But you must understand: the *carta mayor* below us is freezing as we speak. The living map of the world will turn into a solid block of ice. It is too late for me to rewrite the history of my Age, and it is too late for you to read the history of yours. If we preserve the map, you will not read it, but perhaps someone else, in the future, may. The waters could be pooled together, made to figure the world once more. Would you stand in the way of such a possibility?"

It seemed to Sophia that all the loss she had felt over the years had swelled, drop by drop, into a vast pool as wide as the lake. Now she hung suspended over it. She would fall into it and drown, she knew, and there was no choice but to plunge in. "No," she whispered.

"I knew you would say so," Blanca replied gently. "Then help me bring it down." And she threw herself against the stone. Her face contorted horribly as she pushed with all her might, but the sphere remained immobile. Sophia stood, paralyzed with indecision, then she put her pack and the map down and moved to help her. The moment she added her own weight, the stone gave way and began rolling. "Hurry!" Blanca cried. "Step back!" She heaved with all her strength, so that the sphere rolled more and more quickly and finally reached the edge of the balcony where it burst through, shattering the railing, meeting a long silence as it fell toward the frozen lake below.

Time slowed, and the stone hung in midair. It was as if Sophia stood before a window, through which she could see the disappearance of all the truths she would never learn—the mysteries that would remain mysteries. And then, to her surprise, she saw a face. It was her own: the sad, forlorn child who had waited by the dusty window of her imagination. The child did not seem frightened by the prospect of seeing the glass shattered; on the contrary, she seemed relieved—even glad. After all, the window had never given her the vision she so wanted; it had only kept her closed in, away from the world.

And then time sped up. A violent crash pierced the air as the stone broke the surface of the ice. The walls began to shake. Then a sudden explosion, dulled by the water, struck the pyramid with full force. The lake bed had ruptured.

She cried out inadvertently.

"You must leave," Blanca said. "Hurry!"

Sophia scooped up her pack quickly, stowing the pyramid map of the Southern Snows alongside the others. "Aren't you coming?"

Blanca stood limply at the center of the balcony, which had begun to tremble as the nearby wall supporting it shuddered over the breaking ice. "I have no reason to," she said. "Go."

"Please, come with me."

"Where would I go? I am an outcast. Many times over. I do not belong among men, because of my face. I do not belong among Lachrima, because of my memories. I do not belong to any living Age, because the world I was part of has ended. I have no place; I belong nowhere; I am nothing."

Sophia felt tears streaming down her face, and she reached out again for Blanca's hand. But perhaps the sight of those tears had reminded Blanca of the truth behind her own words, for a terrible cry escaped her lips: a wail, a scream that was heartbreaking beyond measure. She fell to her knees, covering her face with her hands, and her cry poured out into the air, echoing off the breaking walls and filling the hall with the sound of unspeakable grief.

Sophia could not bear it. "Good-bye," she whispered. She ran toward the stairs to begin the long descent. The walls were collapsing around her, and she dared not stop to look at the breaking ice below. With her hand against the wall, she ran onward. And suddenly, when she touched the wall, the vision from the four maps burst into view before her. As her fingertips brushed the glass, the graven images seemed to contain more than memories; Sophia felt the throng of people around her, speaking to her urgently from within the maps. They sent their vanished makers out into the world for the last time.

As Sophia ran she heard Blanca's cry reverberating through the hall, and she realized with astonishment that she, too, was weeping out loud, a ragged cry of anguish pulled from her throat. Her feet fell clumsily, and suddenly the stairs buckled. The top of the pyramid had collapsed, plummeting into the draining lake bed. The snowstorm raged within the hall. "Not yet, not yet!" Sophia cried, running faster. She lost her footing and slid, the stairs knocking painfully against her legs and back, but she clutched her pack and stopped herself with her feet. Whimpering aloud, she ran on.

She realized, as she rounded the last turn and saw the wall above her folding inward like a collapsing sheet of paper, that she did not know how to find her way out. She had emerged through the tunnels, and she had seen no opening above ground. Her hand still gliding against the wall, she tried to take comfort from the people around her. They were mere memories, but they had a life of their own. Were they not speaking to her? Were they not pointing urgently to a place in the pyramid wall? Sophia heard, suddenly, a pair of voices that seemed to emerge from the confusion: a man and a woman who called out to her with confidence and tender encouragement, *Fly, Sophia, fly!* She looked ahead and saw, with astonishment, a triangular entryway that stood intact. It was nothing but a slit in the wall. It was the way out.

But it lay several steps away. As she reached the base of the stairs, Sophia realized with horror that the floor had disintegrated. She was standing on a floating piece of ice. Stepping as quickly as she dared, she hurried across and jumped onto another piece that drifted before the entryway. She was almost there. Only a few more steps. She tipped across the ice, and as she breached the doorway with a sudden lurch the floating slab broke into pieces, leaving nothing but icy water in its wake.

Sophia ran onto the snow and looked across the wide, frozen terrain. Then a sound burst out from behind her: the sound of a thousand maps breaking at once. She turned and watched the hall collapse. The mighty walls shattered: sheets of glass crashed against one another, fragmenting into pieces. Puffs of snow and ice burst upward as the walls crumbled. It was a pile of rubble: broken maps over an empty lakebed, its waters infusing the warm soil below. And somewhere deep within lay Blanca. The air was still.

Then, with a sense of dread and expectation, Sophia turned

slowly away from the ruined hall. Would she see it? Would he be there? She squinted as she looked northward. There were no storm clouds in the direction of Nochtland. The sun shone brightly over the ice. And there, far across the glacier—

Sophia's heart hammered. There was a sudden glimmer on the white surface: a reflection of something tiny but bright—like an early star in a pale sky.

38
A Fair Wind, a Fair Hand

1891, July 2: 10-Hour #

Lachrima: From the Latin word for "tear." Related to the vernacular, lágrima. In the Baldlands and elsewhere the term is used to describe the faceless beings that are more often heard than seen. The sound of their weeping is legendary, and it is said that to hear the cry of the Lachrima is to know the fullest extent of human grief.

—*From Veressa Metl's* Glossary of Baldlandian Terms

As the Hall of Remembrances fell, the glaring light that had lined the glacier's edge faded, and the slow encroachment ceased. The ice stood motionlessly on the plains outside Nochtland, and a new change began. The bright sun began to melt the glacier, releasing a shallow current, as if a block of ice were melting on a tabletop. At first, the change was imperceptible, but as the sun continued to shine on the ice, it became impossible to ignore. The waters rose over the plains in a quiet flood.

Some, at least, were well prepared. Near the high ice-cliff that formed the edge of the glacier, a magnificent boldevela with bright green sails wheeled through the water at breakneck speed. It skirted the edge of the glacier, driving onward through the water on its high wheels until the depth of the water raised the ship. The ship sailed on, its wheels propelling it through the water and the cold wind billowing through the sails. Standing at the tiller shouting orders was the polite pirate, Burton Morris. "I said a *ROPE,* not *soap,*" Burr hollered to Peaches, who was running toward him holding a bucket and a brush.

The pirates of the *Swan* had, for once, succeeded in living up to their name. Traveling inland upon news of the strange weather-front moving north, they had commandeered the most magnificent boldevela they could find on the road from Veracruz and sailed it all the way to Nochtland. There they had found the entire city in disarray. It was perhaps something more than luck that drove Grandmother Pearl to insist on a southeasterly route directly toward the ominous glaciers. In the rocky hills southeast of the city near Lake Cececpan, they had come to an abrupt halt as she held her head alertly, listening.

"But how can you hear anything over this storm?" Peaches had protested.

"Hush, Peaches," she had said. "Is there a cave nearby?" she asked, turning inquiringly toward him.

So they had sailed straight toward the dark opening of the cave that they had sighted in the hills, arriving just in time to see Burr, Calixta, and four other dirty spelunkers emerging from the tunnels. Now they were all sailing with the wind, and they raced as fast as they could toward the pyramid collapsing in a burst of white snow.

SOPHIA RAN TOWARD the faint flash of silver that moved across the ice toward her. Her boots seemed to grasp at the snow and cling to it until her feet were two massive snowballs. But she thought the figure was getting larger. She stopped to kick snow from her boots. Her breath came painfully as she leaned forward and kept running.

And then, after what seemed like hours, she saw him clearly: Theo, waving his hand bandaged with silver thread. *I see what you planned now, Fates,* Sophia thought as she gasped for breath. *I can see how carefully you devised this.* They collided, Theo laughing as he wrapped his arms around her and Sophia stumbling in her snow-covered boots. "You brought it down!" he shouted.

Sophia shook her head, leaving great white puffs of breath in the air. "I didn't."

"What do you mean you didn't? Look! The whole thing's come down."

She turned and saw the snow settling over the ruins of the great hall. "Blanca—she and I, we destroyed it."

"Blanca?" Theo squinted. "Where is she?"

Sophia shook her head. "She did not—" She held the straps of the pack tightly and turned away from the collapsed pyramid. "She is gone."

Theo's eye lingered over the ruins, but then he turned away, to his left. "Let's get off this ice—I'm freezing." He looked back and grinned. "The pirates got hold of a ship!"

They ran at an easy pace to the craggy edge of the ice that formed the border of the Glacine Age, squinting against the glaring sunlight. "What about the others?" Sophia asked, out of breath but too anxious not to ask.

"They're all on the ship."

"How did you get out of the tunnels?"

"Shadrack. It's like he had the whole map in his head. He ran around until we lost the Sandmen. Calixta and Burr fought them off and nabbed a couple pistols. Still, it took us hours to find a way out."

Sophia felt a rush of relief. Shadrack was safe.

They slowed as they reached the incline at the edge of the glacier. Stumbling over the sharp outgrowths of ice, they began climbing steadily toward the ridge. They both slipped more than once; the rough surface was growing slick in the fierce sunlight. Sophia's hands grew numb as she seized the ice and hauled herself up. Theo went on ahead of her, and a moment later he gave a shout of exultation. "We're at the top! Look," he said, pointing. "Everything is melting."

Below her lay a scene she could never have imagined and would never forget. The city of Nochtland was still little more than a gray lump in the distance. All around it, like a scattering of black sand on a pale stone, were thousands and thousands of people. Sophia would not have known they were people had the crowds not extended all the way from the city to the edges of the rising waters. Fleeing the glacier's advance, they were running or riding or trudging northward. Some traveled in wagons, others in boldevelas. Some had clearly attempted to bring as many of their belongings as they could. Others walked with nothing at all. The rising waters had already pushed the refugees farther north, and at the edge of the ice pieces of clothing, a broken boldevela wheel, and other debris floated loosely.

Theo waved, and the sunlight glinted off the silver thread that held his bandage in place. "There they are." He pointed in the direction of Nochtland, at a tall boldevela that was streaming toward them through the debris.

As the ship approached, Sophia saw Burr perched on the mast. It slowed and he waved. "Aye, there, castaways!" he shouted and threw something toward them, paying out the rope. "Make sure it's well secured."

A four-pronged hook caught in the ice, and Theo pounded it down with his foot. As he did so, Sophia tightened the pack across her chest. "You first," he said.

Sophia edged down onto the rope with some difficulty, but once she had her ankles hooked around it, she was able to slide down toward the ship's mast. Burr grabbed her by the waist and swung her onto a foothold among the clipped branches of the mast. "Can you climb down yourself?" he asked. She nodded, but before descending she looked up to watch Theo. He swung onto the rope and nimbly shimmied down. Sophia began descending farther to make room, just as if she were climbing down the trunk of a tree, and a moment later she looked up to see Burr hauling Theo to safety. With both of them securely perched on the mast, Burr cut the rope. "We're off!" he shouted.

As soon as her boots hit the deck, Sophia was surrounded.

Veressa threw her arms around her. "We were so worried about you!"

Sophia smiled, but her eyes searched for the one person she had not yet seen. "Where's Shadrack?"

"I'll take you to him, sweetheart," Calixta said, leading Sophia by the hand. "He's just resting below deck."

"We're relieved you're back, Sophia," Martin said, giving her shoulder a quick squeeze.

The luxurious boldevela had a spiral staircase that descended into a long corridor; the vine-covered walls were studded with pale flowers. Sophia followed Calixta into a large bedroom. The portholes cast a sunny light on the bedding, and buttercups grew in the cracks between the floorboards. Grandmother Pearl sat in an embroidered armchair beside the bed where Shadrack, lying back on the pillows, propped himself up as they entered. "Sophia!" he cried.

"Shadrack!" In an instant she was by his side. "Are you all right?" She pulled back at once and looked down at him critically. Why was he here?

He smiled and tucked Sophia's hair behind her ears so that he could see her face. "Are *you* all right?"

"I'm fine. You won't believe everything that happened."

He laughed. “Perfect. You can sit next to Grandmother Pearl and tell me all about it, because I'll be here a while longer.” He drew the covers back, revealing his bandaged right leg.

“What *happened?*”

“Afraid one of those pesky bullets caught me while we were underground. I'm beginning to understand why people in Nochtland dislike metal so much.”

“How bad is it?” Sophia asked, looking at his bandaged leg.

“Not bad.” He drew up the blankets. “Grandmother Pearl, I have learned, is a wonderful medic in addition to being a diviner, a storyteller, a weather reader, and who knows what else.”

The old woman smiled. “He has strong bones and a strong heart. Now that you're here, he has everything he needs to get better.”

Sophia put her arm around her and squeezed gratefully. “I'm so glad *you're* here,” she said.

“It's wonderful to hear your voice again, dear,” the old woman replied. “You've been busy, haven't you? You need some food and water in you. And some rest.”

“I believe Sophia has stopped the glaciers all on her own, Grandmother,” Calixta put in.

“No, I didn't.”

“Whether it was all your own doing or not,” Grandmother Pearl said, hugging her, “the cold air has dropped and the ice is falling back. We're on a fair wind again—can't you feel it?”

Sophia went to the open porthole. Leaning out, she saw the cold waters below, the city of Nochtland ahead, and the blue skies above. She could hear the sails of the boldevela, leaves flapping in the wind, and the voices of Burr and the other pirates on deck. But she also heard a sound in the distance that made her heart race: a constant murmur, like the high-pitched whine of a thousand sirens.

Sophia drew her head back into the cabin. "It does seem a fair wind. But—that sound. What is it?"

"It's the Lachrima, my dear. I'm afraid there are many more in the world today than there were before."

39
The Empty City

1891, July 2: 12-Hour 31

Lunabviate: to conceal one's thoughts or feelings by presenting a blank face. From luna, or moon. The common perception that the moon has a blank face is applied to those who present a bright or pleasant expression but hide their sentiments.

—*From Veressa Metl's* Glossary of Baldlandian Terms

THE GLACIER RETREATED to the edges of Lake Cececpan and then stopped, planting its frozen feet into the earth below and turning a cold shoulder to the sun overhead. The Glacine Age would draw back no farther. And as the glaciers cemented their hold, their hard surfaces shining starkly only three miles from Nochtland, the borders of the Ages were redrawn.

The vast, depopulated Glacine Age stretched from the southern edges of Nochtland to the very tip of the continent. Late Patagonia had disappeared. Much of the southern Baldlands had vanished as well. Where the Ages met, three different cities lay abandoned, their streets emptied by desertion and disaster. Below ground, the mineral city remained silently calcifying, its high towers shining in the light cast by the botanist's trees. Above the ice, in the northernmost city of the Glacine Age, the empty buildings surrounded the ruins of the great pyramid like silent mourners. And in Nochtland a strange hush had fallen upon the once busy streets.

Thousands upon thousands had departed, fleeing the glacier's advance. In the weeks that followed, they walked and rode on until rumors began to reach them that the great change had concluded. Some, hearing this, stopped where they stood; they put down their packs, unhitched their horses, and rested. A short respite became a longer one, until many simply began to rebuild their lives on the very spot where they had stopped. New towns sprang up in a long, meandering line stretching northward.

But others could not believe that the glacier had truly halted its advance, and they walked on, heading farther and farther north until they found themselves in the Northern Baldlands. There, among strange people who had never even heard of the glaciers, they threw down their belongings with relief and tried to forget the catastrophe that had driven them from their now-vanished homes.

Still others had lost more than their homes. It was in the Lachrima's nature to seek solitude, and so it appeared at first that the thousands of Lachrima to emerge from the Glacine Age had disappeared as soon as they had come to light. But they had not disappeared. Many people who had once lived in Xela, or the high cities of Late Patagonia, now wandered the new terrain as faceless creatures; dreading human contact, they haunted the edges of every town on the route from the Baldlands to New Occident.

As the boldevela neared Nochtland, there were some on board who were thinking of the Lachrima's fate. Sophia, after dutifully eating and drinking what Grandmother Pearl had put before her, listened to the dull, distant wailing and thought about Blanca. Shadrack was found, Nochtland was safe, and New Occident lay waiting for them; and yet, unaccountably, she felt an uneasy grief. Blanca's cry might have saved her, driving her from the pyramid in time—but that cry had also found its way into her heart. She had no wish to look at the map that had been the sole piece of the pyramid to survive. Handing it over to Shadrack, she sat at the foot of his bed holding the silk scarf that had once been Blanca's veil. As she twisted the thin fabric between her fingers, she thought about the scars that it had served to conceal. Sophia realized that the more she had seen of the Lachrima's scars, the less they had terrified her. They moved as Blanca spoke; they reflected her thoughts and emotions just as clearly as a mouth, nose, and eyes. There was even something beautiful about the way those scars had conveyed the cold, dignified determination that lay behind them.

"Sophia," Shadrack said now. "You need to get some sleep."

"I'm not sleepy. I'll just stay here with you."

"Why don't you go ask Peaches which room to use, and just

try putting your head down. If you like, send Veressa to keep me company—she'll want to see this."

It was easier to agree. Sophia found the Metls looking out over the side of the boldevela at the icy water below. "Veressa," she said. "Shadrack wants to show you the map—the one I brought from the pyramid."

Veressa eyed her thoughtfully. "Had enough of maps for one day?"

"Yes. I think so."

"Very sensible." The cartologer rested her hand briefly on Sophia's shoulder. "I'll go down and see him."

As she left, Martin called, "Look at this, Sophia." She joined him and saw that the wheels of the boldevela were once again visible. The waters had grown shallow. The ship shuddered as the wheels made ground, and Burr shouted orders to the pirates adjusting the sails.

"We're almost at the Nochtland gates," Sophia said with surprise, looking up with at the high walls.

"Yes, almost there," Martin said.

"Why are we going back?" She looked warily at the unguarded gates, which stood ominously ajar. "What about you and Theo?"

"We'll be fine. The last thing anyone cares about now is a few iron bones."

"Burr wants to go back to look for Mazapán," Theo himself said, joining them. "Everyone says he's probably gone, but Burr says no."

The boldevela rolled through the open gates, and everyone

aboard fell silent. Nochtland was deserted. The fountains and canals still ran with water, and the crowded gardens still leaned out into the sunlight, but there were no people to be seen. "Everyone's gone," Sophia said.

"Oh, I'm sure they'll return," Martin replied, "once they realize the waters are receding."

As she looked over the desolate city, she found it hard to believe.

"Look, there's someone!" Theo said, pointing to a woman who watched them from a window.

The woman waved. "Has the storm passed?"

"Yes!" Martin shouted, waving back. "It's safe now." He turned to Sophia. "You see—not everyone is gone."

The boldevela moved slowly through the streets until it reached the broad avenue at the city center and rumbled to a stop just outside the palace. To Sophia's astonishment, the palace gates too stood open. There was not a guard in sight. "We're home!" Martin exclaimed.

While Burr and Theo went in search of Mazapán, Calixta accompanied Martin and Veressa to the palace. Sophia was aware of the pirates resting and talking to one another on the deck, but her mind was miles away, watching Blanca's face contort as she pushed the heavy stone over the edge of the balcony. The memories were as vivid as they would have been on a map.

"Sophia?"

She started. Grandmother Pearl had joined her.

"How are you doing, my dear?"

"It's strange," she replied slowly.

"What is?"

"I can't seem to get any of it out of my mind."

"You have seen and heard terrible things," the old woman replied. "And they are not easy to forget. Nor should they be. Be patient with yourself."

"We might have all become Lachrima. We could all be wandering now, lost—somewhere out there." She waved vaguely at the city around her.

"That was not our fate. Your fate," Pearl said quietly. "Yours is a different story."

Sophia reflected for a moment. "Yes. A different story. The one you told me—about the boy with the scarred face and the underground city—it's as if I saw the story happening. It wasn't exactly the same. But it was still very true."

"Ah—yes," Grandmother Pearl replied. "That is almost always the way with stories. True to their very core, even when the events and the people in them are different."

Sophia looked down at her tattered, salt-encrusted boots. "The underground city was a city from another Age. The boy with the scar on his face was a woman. The city was a hall full of maps. It all happened as the story said it would, only a little differently." She hesitated. "At least, almost all of it. I don't think the scars were erased the way they were in the story. But even with that difference, both stories are just as sad."

Grandmother Pearl linked her arm through Sophia's.

"Perhaps you're right. But you never know. There may yet be a time when you see the scars fade away."

—13-Hour 40: At the Nochtland Palace—

VERESSA AND MARTIN returned to the boldevela some time later with Calixta, and they reported that the palace was entirely abandoned. Soon afterward, Theo and Burr arrived victoriously with Mazapán, his wife Olina, and large wooden crates full of food and chocolate dishes. In the dying light of the afternoon, they prepared a banquet on the ship's deck.

Burr and Peaches carried Shadrack up the spiral staircase, and every manner of gilded chair from the cabins was brought topside. It was a night for celebration. The meal was delicious, the chocolate tableware was superb—both as serving dishes and dessert—and there was more than enough for everyone. Peaches discovered a harp that someone had left behind in the Nochtland gardens, and for several hours the sweet, lulling sound of ballads filled the air.

When they all finally went to bed, even Sophia had forgotten some of her troubling memories. Most of the pirates returned with Martin and Veressa to the palace, where they promptly took command of the royal suites. Theo and Sophia stayed with Shadrack on the boldevela. She fell asleep almost at once.

But she awoke in the middle of the night in a cold sweat, panicked by a nightmare that she could not remember. She sat up, stretched her sore legs, and looked out the porthole at the pale moonlight. Her heart took a little while to stop racing.

When it did, she quietly climbed out of her blankets.

The deck of the boldevela was still littered with remnants of the feast. Sophia stepped over the plates and cups and walked to the edge, resting her arms on the polished railing.

The moon hung over the Nochtland palace and its gardens, pale and ponderous, like the wondering face of a clock with no hands. There was the faint rushing of water from the fountains in the palace gardens.

A footstep on the deck made her turn. Theo came up and leaned his elbows on the railing beside her. "Bad dreams?"

"I can't even remember what about."

"Maybe this'll help," he said, handing her a chocolate spoon.

Sophia had to smile. She bit off a piece of the spoon and let it dissolve on her tongue. "Do you hear that?" she asked.

Theo cocked his head. "You mean the fountains?"

"No—something else. It's farther away," she hesitated. "Someone crying?"

If she had not known him better, Sophia would have said Theo looked almost worried. "I don't hear anything," he said softly.

"There must still be Lachrima in this city. Who knows how many."

"You'll hear them less once you leave."

Sophia was silent for a moment. "I suppose everyone will go different ways now," she said, taking another bite of chocolate.

"Veressa and Martin said they'll stay as long as Justa doesn't return."

"Do you think she will?"

Theo shrugged. "I doubt she'll want to—with the ice just miles from the gates."

Sophia considered the blank face of the moon. "What about you?" she asked. "Are you going to stay, too?"

"Nah. Sure, the palace is nice, but who wants to sit around all day and look at flowers? I want to be out doing things, seeing new places."

Sophia's mind turned to the pirates and how quickly Theo had taken to life aboard the *Swan*. "I'm sure Calixta and Burr would be happy if you sailed with them."

"I don't know," Theo said doubtfully. "What I'd really like is to get into exploring." He paused. "Do you think if I could get papers into New Occident, Shadrack could maybe get me started?"

Sophia felt an inexplicable wave of elation wash over her, cutting through the sadness like a current. Suddenly negotiating for entrance into New Occident, contending with the July 4 border closure, and awaiting parliament's decision at the end of August seemed trivial. "I'm sure he could," she said. "Shadrack can get you papers, because he got them for Mrs. Clay, didn't he? And there's no one better to talk to about exploring," she went on happily. "Maybe you could go with Miles when he's back. If it weren't for school, I'd go with you."

Theo smiled. "Well, maybe we could be summertime explorers."

Sophia laughed.

Then he reached his bandaged hand out toward her. "You've got chocolate all over your chin," he said, wiping her chin with his thumb. His hand rested briefly on her face and then slipped easily across her shoulders. Sophia leaned comfortably against him and looked up, finding the dark sky suddenly bright. The blank face of the moon looked down wistfully on the pair and tried to lean in just a little closer.

—1891, July 6: Leaving Nochtland—

THE GREAT MYSTERY of how and why the Glacine Age had suddenly manifested would trouble cartologers in New Occident, the Baldlands, and the United Indies for many years to come. It lay beyond their knowledge. Martin posited, and the others agreed, that being in the underground city had saved them. They were already in an outlying pocket of the Glacine Age when the rest of it arrived; the border that would otherwise have transformed them into Lachrima had left them untouched. But no one understood how the Age had shifted its borders or why draining the *carta mayor* had halted the glacier's progress.

The map that Sophia had brought with her from the pyramid seemed to hold more questions than answers. It described a strange history that began with distant tragedies—rumors of plague and illness traveling across the continent, spreading fear and then panic. The animals of the Glacine Age fell as they grazed. The birds swooped to earth to seize a worm or seed and were struck down, dead. And the people, too, fell, as the cities and towns gradually emptied. It was as though the entire Age had succumbed to an unseen poison. The mapmakers could offer no explanations: they could only record the gradual disintegration of their Age. The memories of the map faded away with the last inhabitants of what had once been a great city, and then they ended.

After a long talk with Shadrack, which lingered considerably on the question of the four maps and the surprise of locating the *carta mayor,* Veressa determined that it was best for her and Martin to remain in the Baldlands. There had been no sign of Justa's return to Nochtland, and it was rumored that she was traveling north in the attempt to rejoin her long-absent father. Besides, it would have been futile to try to persuade Martin to leave the city. He longed to study the soil of the Glacine Age—the soil that now lay only three miles from his doorstep.

Sophia entrusted the pyramid-map and the riddle it contained to Veressa, as well as the three maps that she had kept hidden for so long. The glass map would return to Boston.

They lingered a few days more in Nochtland, but then it was clear they had to depart—to go home. "These books are for you, Sophia," Veressa said, as they stood outside the palace greenhouses for the last time. "A few of mine about the Baldlands that you might like and one by someone else that I've never been able to figure out. Maybe you can."

Sophia juggled the pile of books and noted the one on top with a curious title: *Guide to Lost, Missing, and Elsewhere.* "Thank you," she said.

"It's a lovely old book of maps. Maybe you'll understand it better than I do, since you're the best at cartologic riddles." She hugged Sophia.

"Come back as soon as you can," Martin said, embracing her

as well. "There's plenty to explore in those caves. And I shall need a mapmaker."

"You have Veressa, don't you?" she teased.

Martin scoffed. "I shall need more than one."

The pirated boldevela carried them to Veracruz, where they boarded the faithful *Swan* and set sail for New Orleans. The journey was not a pleasant one; Sophia was still troubled by her memories of Blanca, and though they had left Nochtland and Veracruz far behind, she continued to hear a distant murmur that often made her sit up straight and fall silent. She felt as seasick aboard the *Swan* as she had before. And, worse, she knew that when they reached New Orleans she would have to say good-bye to the pirates as well. Theo wisely left her quietly brooding to herself. Only Shadrack and Grandmother Pearl, the one with grand plans for future exploration and the other with gentle words of reassurance, dared come near her.

"Well, Soph," Shadrack said, as they sat side by side on the deck, "it will be good to be home so we can get back to planning. Things will be different, of course, but I believe in a good way. I'm glad Theo is staying, and not just because he knows the west better than I do; he has nerve, that boy. We'll have to get papers for him, but I can manage. In the meantime," he said, sitting up so abruptly that he winced, "you'll be diving back into your cartological studies. There's so much still to learn! Though now some of it *you* will have to teach *me*," he added with a smile. "Won't you?"

Sophia leaned her head against his shoulder. "Yes, I guess so."

"You *guess* so? You were at the forefront of a great discovery, Soph!"

But for some reason, she could not summon up the enthusiasm she knew she ought to feel. All she felt was nausea.

When they reached New Orleans, they took leave of the pirates, who were entirely cheerful and not at all concerned about when they would meet next. "I'm sure we'll see you before the month is out!" Burr proclaimed happily, pumping Sophia's hand.

"Without a doubt!" Calixta agreed. "They may not let us past the harbor, but they can't do without the rum we deliver."

"So sad and so true," her brother added.

"I'm afraid they're right, dear," Grandmother Pearl said, laughing, as she enfolded Sophia in her arms.

"Good-bye," Sophia said, pressing her face against the soft, wrinkled cheek. "Even if it is soon, it will feel like ages to me."

"Then make it short, dear," the old woman replied. "Make of the time what you want."

Epilogue: To Each Her Own Age

1891, December 18: 12-Hour 40

When you lose a marble, a favorite book, or a key, where does it go? It does not go nowhere. It goes elsewhere. Some things (and people) go elsewhere and soon return. Others go elsewhere and appear to want to stay. In those cases, the only solution for the very determined is to find them: to go elsewhere and bring them back.

—*From* Guide to Lost, Missing, and Elsewhere, *author unknown*

It was winter in Boston, and the school term was coming to an end. Sophia thought, as she watched the snow piling up on her walk home, that the trolleys might be stopped the next day if the snow continued to fall. If the trolleys were stopped they would cancel school, and if they canceled school she would have the whole day free.

She made her way down East Ending Street and turned to walk backward so that she could see her footsteps disappearing. The air was gray and faintly warmer, as it always was during a snowfall. She had a sudden urge to run as she neared 34 East Ending, and she skipped through the snow the rest of the way, her satchel banging against her side and her hair streaming away from her face. She bounded up the steps of the house and threw open the door. Placing her satchel on the floor, she sat down to unlace her boots.

"Close the door, my dear!" Mrs. Clay said, walking into the entryway and doing it for her.

"It's not even cold out!" Sophia exclaimed, looking up.

"It's cold enough for me." She smiled and removed Sophia's knitted hat, which was wet with snow, shook it out, and hung it on the coat rack. "Do you want any milk or coffee? I'm just making some."

"I'll have coffee, thanks," Sophia replied, following her into the kitchen in her socks.

After Mrs. Clay had put the coffee to brew, she took two bowls from the cupboard. "Why don't you lean out the window and get some snow from the spruce?"

Sophia seized the bowls with delight. "You want some, too?"

"No, dear, but I'm sure Theo does."

Sophia opened the window, leaned out, and scooped snow from the spruce tree into first one bowl, then the other. Then Mrs. Clay poured maple syrup over the white snow in thick, even spirals. She tucked a spoon into each bowl. "Your uncle is downstairs with Miles. Arguing, from what I hear."

Sophia rolled her eyes. "About the election again?"

New Occident was on the verge of electing a new Prime Minister, and the candidates had been the subject of many a heated debate at 34 East Ending Street. The Wharton Amendment, which would have closed the borders for citizens at the end of

August, had been soundly defeated. The travelers at East Ending would have more time to plan their expedition. Shadrack hoped the defeat of Wharton's extreme agenda augured the success of a more moderate candidate, while Miles, ever pessimistic, observed that New Occident was becoming all too accustomed to the absence of foreigners and would slide further into intolerance.

"This time," the housekeeper said, "over a letter from Veressa that a traveler from Veracruz brought."

"Veressa! What does she say?"

"There's a letter for you, as well," Mrs. Clay said by way of an answer, reaching into the pocket of her apron.

Sophia had expected a letter from Dorothy, but the handwriting was entirely unfamiliar. "Strange," she said, sipping the coffee as she tucked the letter into her own pocket. "Did Veressa send any more maps of the glacier?"

"I couldn't say. The conversation was heated enough to drive me all the way upstairs. I only came down for a moment to make coffee."

Sophia took her mug in one hand and her bowl in the other and walked carefully out of the kitchen. "Thank you, Mrs. Clay."

"Be a dear—when you go down, tell Theo to come get his snow."

Walking as fast as she could without spilling, Sophia passed through Shadrack's study to the bookcase that led to the map room. As she descended she heard pieces of the heated argument taking place downstairs.

"I *tell* you," Shadrack said, "snow is *not* the same there. It is qualitatively different. The water is different. The water is different because the soil is different. It just *is*."

"And how am I supposed to believe you without ever having seen it?" Miles shouted back. "You didn't bother to bring back a sample. Am I supposed to go on faith?"

"And how, I beg you to tell me, would I have brought back a *sample of SNOW*? I'll remind you that it was July, and even the train rails were in danger of melting."

"I think," a much younger voice said with a light laugh, "this is one problem we won't solve by talking it over in the cellar."

Sophia reached the bottom of the stairs. "Did Veressa send any new maps?" she demanded. The map room, which Shadrack had put back in order upon their return, had been restored to its former glory. The shelves were loaded with books, the cabinets had been fitted with new glass, and maps were once again scattered on every surface. The only remaining sign of the destruction was the long scar across the leather surface of the table. Shadrack and Miles stood across from one another, leaning on it; Theo was in the armchair by the wall, his legs tossed over the side. His eyes widened at the sight of the bowl Sophia was holding. "Mrs. Clay made you some," Sophia said, holding her bowl firmly. Theo jumped to his feet and raced up the stairs. "Hello, Miles."

"Good to see you, Sophia." The warmth of the house and the exertion of the argument had made his cheeks pink.

"Mrs. Clay says you got a letter from Veressa," Sophia said to Shadrack.

"I did." He turned away from the table and flung himself into an armchair. "And Miles refuses to believe any portion of it."

"That's *not* what I said," Miles growled.

"Have they mapped more of the glacier?" Sophia asked again.

"For the most part," Shadrack sighed, "she wrote with news of the new mapmaking academy. They enrolled nearly a hundred students at the start of the year."

"A hundred!" Sophia repeated.

"They have the run of the palace. Best use it's ever been put to, I imagine. They have not mapped more of the glacier, although they have made short expeditions—collecting expeditions. Martin continues to work on the theory that their manmade soil became too toxic for the Glacine Age to survive. He has tested the water of the glacier repeatedly and been unable to pinpoint the source of its toxicity, which is *why* Miles here rejects the theory out of hand. I pointed out," Shadrack said, rising from his chair, "that just because Martin cannot prove *how* it is toxic does not mean it *isn't*."

Miles rolled his eyes. "For Fates' sake, man, aren't you willing to entertain the possibility that the soil of the Glacine Age *was* toxic but no longer is? That's all I'm proposing. It's merely one possibility among several."

Sophia shook her head as Shadrack launched into his reply. Theo returned, eating contentedly from his bowl of snow, and she joined him as he dropped back into his armchair. "I guess they have to think about the academy now," she said ruefully. "But Veressa promised she'd make more maps of the glacier."

"Who sent you a letter?" Theo asked curiously, seeing the edge of the envelope in Sophia's pocket.

"I don't know." She pulled it out and examined the unfamiliar writing. "I'll let you know when I've read it. I'm going upstairs to watch the snow."

Theo reached his scarred hand out quickly to Sophia's. "How many inches?"

Sophia replied with a shy smile, pressing her fingers against his palm. "There's at least four already. Maybe eight by tomorrow."

"Everyone will be on the street. We should go outside."

"Let's—come get me." She grinned. "I'll lose track of time."

Her friend winked at her. "No doubt."

In her room, she put the bowl of watery snow and the half-filled cup of coffee on her desk and sat down. After she opened the drawer, retrieving the letter opener from its place beside Blanca's silk scarf, she stopped to look out the window at the icicles hanging from the eaves. Her hand slipped into her pocket, and she closed her fingers around the spool of silver thread that still accompanied her everywhere: the gift from Mrs. Clay and the Fates that had led her across the ice in another Age.

The air beyond her window seemed almost to shimmer, and though she had not lit the lamps, her room was filled with gray light. She sighed contentedly. There was nothing more beautiful than the perfect quiet that came with a snowfall. She sat for a moment longer, listening to the silence encasing her, a small smile on her face.

Then she turned back to her desk. The letter was bulky and had no return address. Inside was a badly tattered envelope that had only her name on it and the word "Boston." Someone from the post office had written "*Please forward*" along the side. Sophia cut open the second envelope and found within it yet another one. Yellowed with age, it bore her full name and address in a wide, ornate hand that made her heart skip a beat. The envelope was not sealed. She reached inside and drew out a single piece of paper that had clearly lain untouched for many years.

The letter was short:

March 15, 1881

Dearest Sophia,

Your mother and I have thought of you every moment of every day during this journey. Now, as we near what may be the end of it, the thought of you is foremost in our minds. This letter will take ages to reach you, and if we are fortunate, we will reach you before my written words ever do. But if this letter arrives and we do not, you should know that we are following the lost signs into Ausentinia. Do not think of pursuing us, dearest; Shadrack will know what to do. It is a road of great peril. We had no wish to travel into Ausentinia. It traveled to us.

All my love,
Your father, Bronson

Acknowledgments

I AM GRATEFUL to the late Sheila Meyer for her early support, many years ago, as I made fumbled attempts to write for young readers. Her encouragement stayed with me as I followed other pursuits; I will always remember her kindness as I took those first uncertain steps.

I wish to thank Dorian Karchmar not only for finding such a wonderful home for this book but also for taking on a very different kind of project than expected and for working with me through so many versions. My thanks to Matt Hudson as well for offering detailed comments on more than one of those versions.

The wonderful home at Viking would not exist without Sharyn November, who has been tireless in her passionate, thoughtful, and really quite humbling support for this book. I have been buoyed since the pages first reached her by her unflagging enthusiasm. I appreciate the meticulous reading from Janet Pascal, the inspired contributions of Jim Hoover and Eileen Savage, and the wonderfully Shadrackian cartographical creations of Dave A. Stevenson.

I am grateful to the many friends who read versions of this book as it was taking shape. Among them, Benny, Naomi, and

Adam gave much-needed advice on an early version of Part I. Lisa and Richie also kindly read and responded to an early draft. I especially wish to thank Sean, Moneeka, Paul, Alejandra, and Heather for offering enthusiasm, detailed comments, fact-checking, and excellent ideas that have made the world of the Great Disruption more coherent and fun. I am grateful to Pablo for the frequent input—as helpful as it is humorous. Thanks to my mother, for her unshakable faith in Sophia, and to my father, for delving so earnestly (and repeatedly) into the workings of this world. One of the great pleasures of inventing it has been discussing it with all of you. Thanks to my brother for his unquestioning belief in this project at every stage. Finally, I wish to thank A.F. for taking every part of this story—metaphysics, mechanics, characters, author—to heart.

S. E. Grove is a historian and world traveler. This is her first novel.

For more information, visit:

www.TheGlassSentence.com

www.segrovebooks.com